Praise for *Golden Prey*

"Sandford is among the finer writers in the genre. In *Golden Prey*, Davenport is now a U.S. Marshal scrambling across the South and Southwest, as unfamiliar with the customs as he is with the terrain. The jarring ride gets hair-raising [and] the whole trip comes to a brakes-to-the-floor screeching stop with one sly little twisting slide that will leave you grinning."

—*The Post and Courier* (Charleston, SC)

"Sandford's trademark blend of rough humor and deadly action keeps the pages turning until the smile-inducing wrap-up, which reveals the fates of a number of his quirky, memorable characters." —*Publishers Weekly*

"With *Golden Prey*, Sandford successfully breathes new life into his most famous series, creating a page-turning thriller that will grab your attention and hold on until the very end. Taking Lucas Davenport away from his long-time job and dropping him in new territory was a brilliant move. . . . As readers follow Davenport in his pursuit, Sandford uses quick pacing and sharp dialogue to keep the plot moving. Multiple twists and turns are thrown in for good measure, all leading up to a Sandford-esque ending." —*The Real Book Spy*

"Sandford's power of storytelling shines through the pages. *Golden Prey* will definitely entertain any thriller fan." —*Mystery Tribune*

TITLES BY JOHN SANDFORD

Rules of Prey

Shadow Prey

Eyes of Prey

Silent Prey

Winter Prey

Night Prey

Mind Prey

Sudden Prey

Secret Prey

Certain Prey

Easy Prey

Chosen Prey

Mortal Prey

Naked Prey

Hidden Prey

Broken Prey

Invisible Prey

Phantom Prey

Wicked Prey

Storm Prey

Buried Prey

Stolen Prey

Silken Prey

Field of Prey

Gathering Prey

Extreme Prey

Golden Prey

KIDD NOVELS

The Fool's Run

The Empress File

The Devil's Code

The Hanged Man's Song

VIRGIL FLOWERS NOVELS

Dark of the Moon

Heat Lightning

Rough Country

Bad Blood

Shock Wave

Mad River

Storm Front

Deadline

Escape Clause

Deep Freeze

STAND-ALONE NOVELS

Saturn Run

The Night Crew

Dead Watch

BY JOHN SANDFORD AND MICHELE COOK

Uncaged

Outrage

Rampage

GOLDEN PREY

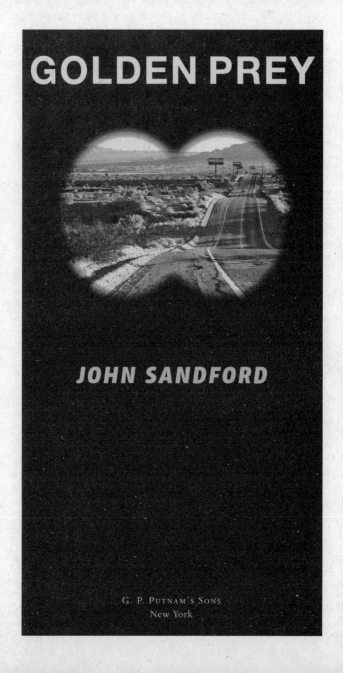

JOHN SANDFORD

G. P. Putnam's Sons
New York

PUTNAM

G. P. PUTNAM'S SONS
Publishers Since 1838
An imprint of Penguin Random House LLC
375 Hudson Street
New York, New York 10014

The Library of Congress has catalogued the G. P. Putnam's Sons hardcover edition as follows:

Names: Sandford, John, [date] author.
Title: Golden prey / John Sandford.
Description: New York : G. P. Putnam's Sons, [2017] | Series: Prey ; 27 |
Identifiers: LCCN 2017004690 (print) | LCCN 2017011952 (ebook) |
ISBN 9780399184581 (EPub) | ISBN 9780399184574 (hardcover) |
ISBN 9780735215788 (international)
Subjects: LCSH: Davenport, Lucas (Fictitious character)—Fiction. |
Murder—Investigation—Fiction. | BISAC: FICTION / Crime. | FICTION /
Suspense. | FICTION / Mystery & Detective / General. | GSAFD: Suspense
fiction. | Mystery fiction.
Classification: LCC PS3569.A516 (ebook) | LCC PS3569.A516 G65 2017
(print) |
DDC 813/.54—dc23
LC record available at https://lccn.loc.gov/2017004690

First G. P. Putnam's Sons hardcover edition / April 2017
First G. P. Putnam's Sons international edition / April 2017
First G. P. Putnam's Sons premium edition / April 2018
G. P. Putnam's Sons premium edition ISBN: 9781101988848

Printed in the United States of America
1   3   5   7   9   10   8   6   4   2

GOLDEN PREY

1

GARVIN POOLE slipped out of bed, got his lighter off the fireplace mantel, and walked in his underwear through the dark house to the kitchen, where he took a joint out of a sugar jar, then continued to the garden door.

He opened it as quietly as he could, but it chimed once, not an alarm so much as a notification. He stepped out onto the patio and continued along the flagstone walk to his work shed.

Poole was an inch shy of six feet, with the broad shoulders and big hands of a high school wrestler, which he'd never been, and now, a hint of a hard beer gut. He still had thick reddish-brown hair over blue eyes and used a beard trimmer for the three-day look. Women liked him: he couldn't go to Whole Foods without picking up a conversation.

The flagstones underfoot were cool but dry; not much rain this year. The moon was up high and bright over the garden wall, and he could hear, faintly, from well off in the distance, the stuttering midnight sound of Rihanna singing "Work." He opened the shed door, turned on the light, sat down in the office chair, fired up the joint, and looked at the guitar he was building.

He'd been sitting there for a half minute or so when Dora Box said, "Gar?" She stepped through the open door, buck naked, the way she slept. "Whatcha doin'?"

He said, "Come on, sit down." She sat in a wooden chair and didn't cross her legs and he took a long look and then said, "I'm going back to work. One time."

"Oh, boy." Now she crossed her legs. Box had a hard time getting through the day without being rubbed or squeezed, but business was business.

"It might have been a mistake, coming here," he said, waving the joint at the workshop. "I've been thinking about it a lot, for the last month or so. I like it, but we should have left the country. Gotten out completely."

"There's no other place you like that we could go," Box said. "Costa Rica was supposed to be the best, but you thought it sucked. Snakes. Oh, God, snakes. Anyway, you don't even like most of the *States*, Gar. Where'd we go that we'd like?"

He shook his head. "I don't know. Someplace crookeder than here."

"You know a place crookeder than Dallas?"

"Sure. There are places in this world where you can pay the cops to kill people for you," he said. His voice squeaked as he simultaneously tried to talk and to hold the smoke in his lungs. "Where you can do anything you want."

"You wouldn't want to live in those places. What brought this on?"

Poole took a drag on the joint and said, "I put ten years of money into gold, and now I go around trying to cash the gold out and there aren't enough places to do that, not inside a day's drive. Every time I cash a coin, the guys are giving me looks, you know? I've been back too many times. They *know* what I'm doing, that I'm cashing out hot money. They don't say anything, but they *know*."

"We could drive somewhere else," Box suggested. "Oklahoma City, Houston . . ."

"Basically the same problem. People looking at you, remembering you," Poole said.

Silence for a while, then Box said, "I thought the gold was smart."

"I did, too, back at the start. The cops were tearing up everything south of Kentucky, looking for me, and gold seemed . . . flexible. Good anywhere. Maybe I was thinking about it too much."

They'd had variations of the talk before. Gold coins were anonymous, portable, no serial numbers. He could get small bills for gold, it kept its value over time, and it was salable almost anywhere. He hadn't seen the problem with being looked at and remembered.

"I didn't see that coming, cashing out month after month. We need ten thousand a month to keep our heads above water, that's nine or ten coins a month right now," he said. "If we were in the right country, we could cash it all out at once, set up a phony company. Pretend we earned the money, give ourselves salaries, pay taxes, and maybe someday come back to the States under different names."

"Sounds sketchy," she said, and, "Gimme a hit." He passed the joint, and she took a hit, held it, breathed out, bit off another one, passed it back, uncrossed her legs, and unconsciously trailed her fingers across her pussy. The soft smell of marijuana went well with the fleshy damp odor of the nighttime garden. "If you're thinking about moving us out of the country, then why are you thinking about taking a job?"

"Because I really *don't* want to leave here. The job's an alternative," Poole said.

"Tell me."

"Sturgill called. He sees an opportunity."

"How much?"

"Can't tell from a distance, but he thinks at least Two or Three. Maybe more. Maybe a lot more." He orally capitalized the numbers. "Two" meant two million. "Three" meant three million.

Box shook her head. "That much, it's gotta be risky."

"Sturg says it's pretty soft."

"Sturg . . . Sturg always knows what he's talking about," Box conceded. "When would you do it?"

"Either one week, or a month and a week. The money's there one day a month," Poole said.

"Where?"

"Biloxi."

"Mmm. I like Biloxi. Like that jambalaya. Pass the joint." He passed it over and she bit off some smoke, played it through her nose. She handed the joint back and rubbed her arms: goose bumps in the cool night.

"The thing is, we'd get cash. All cash. We could spend it without anybody looking *at* us or looking *for* us," Poole said. "Stay here, figure out a way to move the gold. We get a couple mil out of Biloxi, we could take eight or ten years to liquidate the gold and when that's done, we got a lifetime."

"I don't like you going back to work, but it's better'n moving to Russia, or some weird foreign shit like that," Box said. She stood up and stretched: she had the body for it, too, long, lanky, lightly freckled, a dishwater blonde with small pink nipples and only a wispy trace of pubic hair. "I'm going back to bed. Don't stay up too late."

*   *   *

POOLE BOUGHT high-quality guitar parts, assembled them, then began meticulously carving and staining the surfaces, creating comic-book-like custom scenes. He'd learned woodworking at what Tennessee called, with a straight face, a Youth Development Center. Prison for kids, was what it was.

When Box was gone, he sat looking at his latest work, a bass-fishing comic being done for a pro fisherman who was also a guitar collector. It needed another two weeks; he'd have to put it aside, for now. He reached across the shed and picked up a twenty-year-old Les Paul, touched the power switch on an amp with his big toe, pulled some quiet blues out of the guitar. He liked the music, liked the woodwork, liked the smell of the lacquer. If he'd made a business of it, he figured he'd make almost half as much as an elementary school teacher.

He went to Biloxi.

BILOXI, MISSISSIPPI, and the smell of the sea.

Sturgill Darling was sitting at a round corner table in the oyster bar, a block off the Gulf of Mexico, amid the steam and sour stinks of both raw and cooking seafood. He looked like a slow, lazy hick, and stupid, too, with his farm-work forearms, bowl-cut brown hair, and worn, loose-cut jeans. He wore a floppy plaid shirt and yellow work boots, and sprawled back in the chair, knees locked and feet straight out in front of him, grinning at the passing crowd with teeth as yellow as his boots. A dumbass, for sure; an ignorant peckerwood. A mistake that any number of people had made to their lasting regret.

Poole took the chair beside him, held up a finger to a barmaid, and pointed at Darling's glass and said, "Give me one of those."

When she'd gone, Darling asked, "What do you think?"

Poole was wearing sunglasses over a gray-flecked-red week-old beard, and under a long-billed fishing hat, the better to defeat surveillance cameras. He'd spent most of the day scouting the scene of the would-be job. "We can do it, if it's no more guys than you say. How in the hell did you find this?"

"I knew the blow was coming in through Galveston but I couldn't see any money going out. They're bringing in anything up to five hundred kilos at a time, that's, let's see, about eleven hundred pounds, off big game fishing boats that meet with these boats from Honduras. Anyway, I found a guy in Houston who could sell me an ounce, and then I watched. Watched him, watched the guy he got his product from, and watched the guy he got *his* product from, and by the time I got to the end of the line, I was watching guys who could sell you a hundred kilos if you had the cash. Then I watched them backwards, watched the wholesalers paying the money guys— the money guys never touch the dope—and watched the money guys move it to the pickup guys, who travel up and down the coast from Charleston around to Galveston, with Biloxi in the middle. Watched it come down here, to the bank."

Poole thought about that, admitted to himself that Darling had a talent that he, Poole, barely understood, the ability to uncover the footprints that could lead to a treasure; but Poole also understood that he had a talent that Darling didn't: the will to act. Darling could uncover all the dope banks he wished, but he'd never go into a robbery as the leader, the designated shooter. That took somebody like Poole.

"How do they move the dope?" Poole asked.

"RV. Couple of middle-aged lesbo chicks, got some prison tats on them. They look . . . competent. They got double-load tires on the truck, I believe there might be some armor on it. These girls got a look about them—I believe they're carrying some artillery."

"Huh." That's the way Poole would have done it; he even liked the lesbo touch. Cops were usually too sexist and too lazy to pay much attention to a couple of chicks. And some of those goddamn dykes could take your face apart with their teeth.

"But we don't want the dope, even if we could take it," Darling said. "We got no way to get rid of it. Not that much of it. And the dope handlers never see the cash, except at the lowest levels."

"Just askin'. Five hundred kilos, what's that . . ." He closed his eyes for a few seconds, then said, "Twelve million, more or less, if it's not stepped on too hard. What about the money?"

"They take no chances with the money. They move it in increments. There are four bankers who travel around, meet the collectors who get the cash from the top-end retailers. The bankers and everybody else move in rental cars, I doubt they ever have as much as a quarter million in any one pickup. Then it comes together, down here, once a month. The people here bundle it and send it out on the last Sunday of the month," Darling said. "Regular as a railroad. Put it on a charter boat, drop it with a Honduran boat out in the Gulf. Whole operation is run by the Arce brothers, Hector and Simon, out of Puerto Cortés."

"Honduras?"

"Yes. The brothers aren't real big, not like the Mexican cartels, but they're smart and mean. Keep their heads down and their mouths shut, nothing flashy about them. Pay off the Honduran cops and army, everybody's cool."

Poole thought about that, in the silent, smiling, calculating way that Southerners had, and finally said, "Well. Looks like you found the honeypot, all right."

"Probably." Darling gave Poole his lazy look. "You sure you're up for this? It's been a while."

"Yup. I am."

"There'll be one outside, three inside, they all got guns," Darling said. "I've watched them for three months, always the same."

"We gunned up?" Poole asked.

"Yeah. Got your favorites, bought out of Chicago brand-new, Glock 23s suppressed, loaded up with 180s. I did the reloads myself so they'll be going out subsonic to kill some of the noise. I thought maybe . . . Sam Brooks if you think we need another gun."

"Don't need him and I don't like him," Poole said. "I'll need a day to work with the guns. You got a place I can do that?"

"Knew you'd ask," Darling said. "I got a place so far out in the woods that the fuckin' owls get lost."

The barmaid brought Poole's beer and he thanked her and they waited until she moved away, then Poole said, "Shoot the next couple days, move Sunday night?"

"Sounds good. About the cut? What do you think?"

Poole grinned and tapped the beer, swallowed, and said, "I won't argue with you."

"I'm thinking, sixty-forty, since I did all the setup," Darling said. "Took me nine months. I started working on it way last winter."

"Fair enough."

"Hot damn," Darling said, with his yellow grin. "The Dixie Hicks are back in action. What's left of them, anyway."

Poole laughed and kicked back and said, "You remember that time with Ronnie outside of Charleston . . ."

The Dixie Hicks had all kinds of war stories, some funny, some sad. In most of them, even the funny ones, somebody wound up dead. Like Ronnie, three Georgia state troopers hot on his ass, riding a stolen 2009,

556-horse Cadillac CTS-V down a rocky gulch in the Georgia Piedmont, rolling over and over and over until the car looked like a shiny sausage, thirty thousand dollars in bank money exploded all over the interior, along with Ronnie's brains.

Good old Ronnie. Too bad he killed himself.

POOLE AND DARLING drove north into the trees on the following day and Poole went to work with the guns. He'd laid off for a while, but killing is like riding a bicycle: once you got it, you got it.

Darling had gotten inside the counting house one dark night when the bankers weren't there, and said they counted at a table about thirty-two feet from the door in the outer wall—he'd checked it with a tape measure. At thirty-two feet, or any shorter distance, Poole wouldn't have to worry about where to shoot: he'd hold dead-on and pull the trigger. They set up some human-shaped paper targets out in the woods, stapled to pine trees, and Poole worked at it, getting back in the rhythm. From the first shots, he was accurate enough, but he had to work on speed.

He did that, and he knew how to do it: slow at first, feeling the weapons, feeling the rounds going out, feeling the recoil. Then a little quicker and a little quicker, Darling looking at a stopwatch.

Darling was almost scholarly about it: "You're at less than half a second," he said, holding a stopwatch. "You know better than me, but it looks like you're still trying to be *too* fast. You over-aim, then you've got to correct."

Poole nodded: "I can feel that."

He would shoot a box of .40s, the same stuff he'd use for the real thing, and then take a break, walk around, shake out his hands. At the end of the day, he could get off four accurate, killing shots in a little more than a fifth of a second. Good enough.

IN 2005, Hurricane Katrina went through Biloxi like an H-bomb, a thirty-foot storm surge taking out a good part of the town. North of the main harbor was mostly bare ground that once had houses. Here and there a building remained, but not in its original state; and there weren't a lot of people around.

Grace Baptist Church once had a fieldstone foundation up over head height, with a white clapboard structure above that, dating back to the 1890s. The frame structure, if it hadn't been atomized, was probably somewhere up in the Kentucky woods, having ridden away on Katrina's winds like Dorothy's house in *The Wizard of Oz*.

The bottom of the church, the shoulder-high fieldstone foundation, remained in place, its original floor, now covered with tar paper, serving as the roof. The church, foundation and floor only, had been sold to a man who collected antique cars and needed a place to store them. When the Honduras cartel was looking for a place to put their bank, they made the car collector an offer he didn't even think of refusing. Not that he was frightened: he was simply greedy and the offer was that good.

The spot had two great benefits: there were never any cops around, because there was nothing to steal, vandalize, or hang out at, and you could walk down to your boat in five minutes.

SUNDAY NIGHT was outgoing only, with four men doing the work. For most of the evening, two of the four men would be posted at opposite corners of the former church, seated between carefully placed Limelight hydrangeas. They both were carrying guns; at least two each, Darling thought, probably high-capacity semiautos with suppressors, and were linked with radio headsets.

Late in the evening, Darling said, one would go inside with the other two, while one remained outside, seated behind a bush by a door in the old church's basement.

He thought the three were probably packing the money, after the first two had counted and bundled it. Around midnight, the outside guard would go inside, and a few minutes later they'd all walk out of the building, carrying at least one and often two suitcases each. The walk down to the waterfront took five minutes. There, they'd get on a fishing boat. Two or three minutes later, they'd be off the boat and strolling through the quiet Sunday night back to the old church building.

Three of them would wait there while the fourth man went out to a black Lincoln Navigator that they'd parked behind a building a few hundred yards away. He'd pick up the other three, and they'd drive over to the Hampton Inn, where they'd stay overnight before dispersing to wherever they lived.

The boat with the money would ease out of the marina in the early morning hours and disappear over the southern horizon. Darling had considered the possibility of robbing the boat, but thought the money might be inside a safe, or otherwise hard to get at; taking it could get complicated and they didn't have the time or the organization for that.

AT TEN O'CLOCK Sunday night, Poole and Darling slipped out of an abandoned FEMA trailer where they'd spent most of the afternoon and evening, eating Subway sandwiches and drinking Smartwater and pissing in the no-longer-connected toilet at the other end of the trailer.

They were both dressed in dark clothes, but nothing unusual or too tactical—black Levi's jeans and long-sleeved navy polo shirts. They were wearing ski masks, which weren't often seen in Biloxi, the town being woefully short on ski slopes, and light blue surgeon's gloves.

Poole carried two pistols, Darling carried one, all suppressed, Nines for Darling, Forties for Poole. The guns, with the custom suppressors, were fourteen inches long in their hands. They were shooting wet, having sprayed water down the suppressors before screwing them back on the gun barrels, in the two minutes or so before they left the trailer. The suppressors would be even quieter wet than dry.

ONLY ONE GUARD remained outside. He was sitting behind a haggard pink rosebush adjacent to the door. They came in from the blind side of the foundation, Darling trailing as Poole led the way.

At the corner, twenty feet from the access door, Poole peeked. Because of the rosebush, he couldn't see the guard; but neither could the guard see him. Moving with glacial slowness, he duckwalked down along the wall. Ten feet out, he could smell the other man, a smoker, but still not see him. When he was three feet out, Poole rose carefully to his feet, back against the stone wall, looked down.

The guard never knew what hit him: Poole reached over the rosebush and shot him in the head, a golf-clap *pop* from the gun.

Darling came up, quiet as Poole had been. Didn't even glance at the dead man. Three more men inside. They needed instant control; couldn't abide with chaos, with some crazy gunfight. Needed to get on top of the other three immediately.

Darling took the door: he breathed, "Ready?"

The door would not be locked. They'd seen the guards go in and out without knocking or using keys. Poole got square to it, a gun in each hand.

"Now," Poole whispered.

Darling reached one gloved hand out to the doorknob, turned it, pushed. It squeaked and then Poole was inside, both guns up. He could see the three men thirty feet away, sitting side by side at a table. They all looked up, maybe expecting to see their outside man, but all they saw was a stranger in black who said not a single word but simply opened fire.

Darling was backup: Poole did the killing. Darling kicked the door shut as Poole shot each of the three men once, in a grand total of a half second, two shots from his right hand, one from his left, a little slower than he'd been on the paper targets. A half second was almost fast enough but not quite. One of the men grabbed a Nine from the counting table and got off a single wild shot.

The bullet pinched the underside of Poole's left arm, but the man who fired it was already dead by the time Poole realized he'd been shot. He was striding toward the counting table when a young girl, maybe six years old, bolted toward the back of the building from where she'd been sitting on the floor with a golden-haired Barbie doll. She knew she wouldn't make it, though, stopped, turned, and said, "You killed Grandpa."

"Sorry, kid," Poole said, and shot her in the head.

Darling, coming up from behind, said, the shock riding through his voice, "Fuckin' A, Gar, did you have to do that?"

"Yeah, I did. She was old enough to raise the cops," Poole said. He felt nothing for the kid, but needed to mollify Darling. "If we tied her up, she might starve to death before somebody found her. This was the best."

Darling stared at the Raggedy Ann body of the kid,

wrapped in a white dress now spattered with blood that looked like red flowers woven into the pale fabric. "Fuckin' A. We coulda called somebody . . ."

"Wake up, man! It's done! Get the fuckin' suitcases," Poole said. "We gotta move! Motherfucker got lucky and hit me."

"Oh, Jesus. Bad?"

"No, but I've got to look. Get the suitcases going."

POOLE COULDN'T PUSH the shirtsleeve up high enough to see the wound, so he pulled the polo shirt over his head. He found an inch-long groove on the underside of his arm; it was bleeding, but the bullet hadn't actually penetrated. A flesh wound, as they said on the old TV Westerns.

Darling was shoveling loose cash from the tabletop into a suitcase, stopping every few seconds to peer at the dead girl, as though hoping she'd show a sign of life. He brought himself back, glanced at Poole, and asked again, "How bad?"

"Not bad. Need to rip up a shirt or something. Not much more than a Band-Aid job."

"We got a bunch of shirts, laying on the floor. Rip one up," Darling said.

Poole ripped a piece off the girl's skirt, figuring that probably had the least body contact with its former owner, and was less likely to carry an infection: Poole thought of things like that, even under stress. He made a neat tie bandage out of it; it was really all he needed. He pulled his shirt back over his head, and together he and Darling checked the take. Poole had nothing more to say except, "Holy shit."

"You got that right, brother," Darling said. "Way more than I thought. Heavy, though. Can you carry?"

"Hell, yes. It hurts, but it's not bad."

He was wrong about carrying the money. The suitcases must have weighed forty or fifty pounds each, about like a deep-cycle bass boat battery, and there were six of them, instead of the three or four they'd expected. He could carry one with each hand, but not run with them; the one on his shot arm dragged him down, the grazing shot now burning like fire. Darling, carrying four suitcases, one in each hand and one bundled under each armpit, hurried ahead and kept hissing back, "C'mon, c'mon."

The stolen truck was two hundred yards away. Darling loaded his suitcases and ran back to Poole, grabbed the suitcase on Poole's bad side, and together they made it back to the truck.

They drove slowly—they were professionals—out of Biloxi. They left the stolen truck at a rest area on I-10, transferring the cases to Darling's long-bed Chevy. Darling had put a false floor in the camper and they emptied the cash through the concealed hatch, closed the hatch, and threw the suitcases on top of it.

Heading west again, they stripped off the surgeon's gloves and threw them out the windows as small rubber balls. The ski masks went after them, one at a time, miles apart. Twenty miles farther along, Darling took an exit that curled down a side road to a bridge.

They threw the guns off the bridge into the narrow dark river and headed back to the interstate. Farther up the way, they left the five suitcases sitting side by side on a sidewalk in Slidell, Louisiana, with a sign on top that said "Free."

A little more than an hour after killing the four men and the girl, they were out of Slidell, still moving west.

"What the fuck's wrong with you?" Poole asked, looking over at Darling, who was hunched over the steering wheel, his mouth in a fixed grimace.

"I raised some girls. I can't get that little girl out of my head," Darling said.

"C'mon, man. What difference does the age make? She's just another witness."

"I know, I know. Just . . . skizzed me out, man. I . . . keep seeing her. I'll be okay."

Poole peered at him for a minute, then said, "Think about it this way—it's done. Can't be undone. It's history."

THEY STOPPED at a twenty-four-hour Walmart Supercenter in Baton Rouge, off to one side of the parking lot, between two other pickups, climbed into the back of the truck, and dug the money out from under the false floor. Most of it was in hundreds, well used and a little greasy, bundled into bricks of ten thousand dollars each. There was also a pile of loose money that Darling had scraped off the counting table.

They counted out a few bundles, agreed that they were ten thousand dollars each, despite varying in size depending on the value of the individual bills in each bundle. They counted the bundles. There were seven hundred and eighty of them. "Seven million, eight hundred thousand," Darling breathed. "Man, those greasers are gonna be pissed when they hear about this."

"Fuck 'em," Poole said, and he laughed aloud.

Darling sat back on the truck floor and said, "Tell you what, man. Forget the sixty-forty. I never thought we'd get this much. Let's cut it fifty-fifty and I'll keep the loose change. Can't be more than a couple hundred thousand there."

"You are a fine and honorable man," Poole said. "Let's do it."

He held up a fist and Darling bumped it and they split up the money.

BOX WAS at a Baton Rouge Marriott. When the counting was done and the money repacked in two canvas duffel bags, Poole called her. "All done," he said.

"I been up for three hours, nervouser than a nun at a penguin shoot," she said. "Where you at?"

"Right where we're supposed to be," Poole said.

"You do good?" she asked.

"Better'n that," Poole said.

"Ten minutes," she said.

She was twelve minutes. Darling went on his way, and five hours later, Poole and Box had cut I-20 west of Shreveport and rolled across the Texas border on the way back home to Dallas, listening to Paul Thorn singing "Bull Mountain Bridge" on the Sirius satellite radio.

A ton of money in the back.

Money, Poole thought, that would last his entire life.

2

THREE LOCALS were sitting on the wide wooden porch, on a green park bench, to the right of the bar's front door. An overhead fluorescent light buzzed like a dentist's drill but didn't seem to bother them much. All three of them wore trucker hats and were drinking beer from plastic cups.

They stopped to watch when Lucas Davenport rolled his black Mercedes SUV across the gravel parking lot and into a vacant slot between a new Ford F-150 and a battered yellow Cadillac sedan old enough to have fins.

Lucas got out of the truck, clicked "Lock" on the Benz's key fob, and took in the bar.

In any other place, Cooter's would have been a dive. Out here it wasn't, because it was the *only* bar in Aux Vases, the place where everybody went, from the janitors to the bankers. Built like an old Mississippi River Delta–style house, it featured a wide front porch with an overhanging roof, warped, unpainted plank walls, and neon beer signs in the windows. A million white thumbnail-sized moths were beating themselves to death around the light over the heads of the three men, but they didn't seem to notice.

In a movie, you'd expect an outbreak of rednecks. Crackers. Peckerwoods, with ropes and ax handles.

Located two hundred yards from one of the rare exits off I-55, with a twenty-foot-wide red-and-white sign that blinked "Cooter's," then *"Drink,"* the bar also attracted anyone who might be running along the interstate between St. Louis and Memphis who might get shaky after two hours without alcohol.

Lucas crunched across the gravel parking lot, climbed the porch steps, and nodded at the three men. He didn't have to get close to smell the spilt beer. One of the three checked out Lucas's suit, tie, and black Lucchese lizard-skin cowboy boots, and said, "Evenin', sir," slurring his words enough that Lucas thought the men might not be out on the bench voluntarily.

Lucas said, "Evenin', boys."

"Nice ride you got there," the middle one said.

"Thank you. Want to buy it?"

The three all chuckled. They couldn't afford one of the fuckin' tires, much less the rest of the truck, but the offer gave them the warm glow of economic equality. Lucas nodded again, said, "Take 'er easy," went inside, chose the least sticky-looking stool toward the end of the bar, and sat down.

The bartender, a thin man with a gold eyetooth and a black string tie, came over and asked, "What do you need?"

"Make me a decent margarita?" Lucas loosened his necktie.

"I can do that, though some folks think the indecent

ones are even better," the bartender said. When Lucas didn't crack back, he said, "One decent margarita coming up."

The bartender had started to step away when Lucas asked, "How do you pronounce the name of this place?"

The bartender's face took on the look that people get when they're asked a really, *really* stupid question. "Cooter's?"

Lucas laughed. "No, no—the town. Aux Vases." He pronounced it *Ox Vasies*.

"Oh. Jeez, you had me goin' there for a minute," the bartender said. "It's, uh, French, and it's Oh-Va."

"Oh-Va. Always wondered, whenever I saw the sign," Lucas said.

"Yup. Oh-Va." He looked at Lucas a little more closely and saw a big, blue-eyed guy, whose dark hair was threaded with gray at the temples.

The bartender guessed that he might be in his late forties or early fifties. His nose had been broken at one time or another and a thin white scar ran down his forehead across his eyebrow; another scar, a round one, sat just above the loosened knot of his necktie. And the suit—the suit he was wearing was undoubtedly the most expensive suit to come through the door in the last ten years.

He went off to find some tequila.

Lucas looked around the place. Fifteen booths, twelve bar stools, a couple of game machines in the back, plank floors that creaked when somebody walked across them, and the vagrant smell of Rum Crooks and deep-fried fish sticks. He was the only man in the place *with* a necktie and *without* a hat.

LUCAS SAT ALONE, buying four margaritas over the span of forty-five minutes, and making two trips to the men's room, or what he hoped was the men's room. The only identifying signs were a picture of a cat on one restroom door, and a rooster on the other.

He was halfway through the fourth margarita when Shirley McDonald eased up on a stool two down. Lucas looked her over, smiled, and nodded. She was a skinny young blonde. *Very* young. Black eyebrows, too much eye shadow, crystalline green eyes, Crayola-red lipstick not quite inside the lines. She looked fragile, easily broken; might already have been busted a couple of times. She wore a white blouse that verged on transparent, no obvious bra straps, jeans torn at the thigh and knee, and sandals. Not a debutante. She asked, "How y'all doin'?"

"I'm doing fine," Lucas said. "For a man this far from the comforts of home."

"You got a cigarette?" she asked.

"I don't smoke," Lucas said.

"Damnit, I'll have to smoke one of my own." She grinned at him and fished a turquoise pack of American Spirits out of her purse. One of her big front teeth wasn't quite straight, but the irregularity made her even more attractive, which she certainly knew. "The goddamn things are so expensive now, I can only afford about a pack a week."

"Buy you a drink, though," Lucas said.

"I was waitin' to hear that," she said. She lifted a finger to the bartender and said, "Eddie . . ."

"Yeah, I know—expensive and sweet."

"You are such a *sugar bear*," she said. She knocked a cigarette out of the pack, tapped the end on the bar to pack in the tobacco, and asked Lucas, "What's your story, big guy?"

"I'm just a guy," Lucas said.

"A married guy," she said, as she fired up the cigarette. He was wearing a ring.

"Yeah, somewhat."

"Only somewhat?"

"You know how that goes . . ." Lucas said.

The bartender came over, put down a tall dark drink that smelled of sugar, and handed her a toothpick on which he'd speared three maraschino cherries. She sucked off two of them, then she took a sip of the drink and Lucas asked, "What the heck *is* that?"

"Jim Beam Single Barrel," the bartender said, "and Coca-Cola. We call it an Oh-Va Libre."

Lucas winced, turned back to McDonald, and asked, "What's your name?"

"Triste," she said, sucking off the third cherry. "It's French . . . like Oh-Va."

The whole cherry-sucking thing was both hilarious and the tiniest bit erotic, but it would have taken a mean bastard to laugh at her. Lucas didn't. The girl, he thought, was probably younger than his daughter Letty, now in her second year at Stanford.

ANYWAY, one thing led to another, and Lucas never did make it to Memphis. At midnight, after a few more margaritas and three more trips to the rooster room, he and McDonald wound up at the Motel 6 on the other side of I-55. Lucas hadn't more than gotten the room door shut when the girl popped the belt on her jeans and stripped them off, with her sandals, then pulled the blouse off. Lucas was still wearing his suit coat, though he'd stuffed his tie in his coat pocket.

"What do you think?" Triste asked, fists on her hips. She had pale cone-shaped breasts, tipped with the same pink color as a Barbie doll butt. They stood straight out, and wobbled when she spoke.

"How old are you, anyway?" Lucas asked.

"Fifteen," she said.

Then she snatched up her jeans and started screaming her head off.

Three seconds later, as she huddled in the corner with her jeans held to her breasts, the cops came through the door. With a key, Lucas noticed; no point in kicking down a perfectly good motel-room door.

THE FIRST COP through the door was a tall, rangy blond guy with muscles in his face. He looked angry with the world and willing to do something about it, preferably with a gun. He had a flattop haircut with well-waxed front edges; and he had a big blued automatic in his right hand. He pointed it at Lucas's head and shouted, "On the wall, asshole. On the wall."

Lucas thought, *Oh shit*, because if the guy screwed up, Lucas could wind up dead. He turned, hands over his head, facing the wall, and the cop yelled, "Hands on the wall, ass-wipe. Push your feet back. Push your feet back, weight on your hands."

Lucas said, "I didn't know—"

"Shut the fuck up!"

The second cop through the door was shorter than the first, roly-poly, with a reddish mustache and sparse red hair. He looked like a woodchuck, or maybe a beaver, Lucas thought. Both cops were wearing chest cameras. The woodchuck asked Triste, "You all right, girl?"

Triste, speaking to the cameras, said, "He said we were gonna watch a movie. He tried to force me . . ."

"Put your clothes back on then," the short cop said.

Lucas was leaning on the wall with both hands, but turned his head toward the girl and saw her grin at the cop. The blond cop had put his gun back in his holster, patted Lucas's hips and around his beltline and down his legs, then said, "Hands behind your back. You been try-ing to fuck this little high school girl, huh? Well, tonight's your unlucky night."

"I'm telling you, she was drinking and smoking in the bar—"

The cop jerked him around and popped him in the gut with a lazy right fist. Not too hard, but hard enough to bend Lucas over. "Shut up. You talk when I tell you to."

Lucas eased back up. "I'm tellin' ya—"

Boom—another shot in the gut, harder this time. "You deaf? I said, you talk when I tell you."

"Don't hit me again," Lucas said. "Don't hit me again."

The blond cop sneered and said, "I oughta smack the shit outa you."

The woodchuck muttered, "Mind the cameras, Todd."

"I don't think no jury's gonna give me a hard time for spanking a goddamn dirtbag who comes to town and tries to hump a tenth grader. That oughta be good for fifteen years, in my humble opinion."

"I did not—" *Boom*—another shot in the gut; this was getting old.

The woodchuck said to the girl, "You're gonna have to ride with me over to the sheriff's, girl. We'll need a statement from you."

"He pulled my pants off . . ." she wailed, with all the sincerity of a cup of lemon-flavored Jell-O.

THE DEPUTY put Lucas in a holding cell, hands still pinned behind his back. "Don't go anywhere," he said before slamming the steel door.

Lucas sat on the concrete bench and waited. The cell smelled like beer vomit and Clorox. His wife had ordered him to try yoga after he'd quit his job with Minnesota's Bureau of Criminal Apprehension, as a stress reliever.

That hadn't worked worth a damn, but he'd been given a calming mantra by the yoga instructor and he tried it out now: "Mind like moon . . . Mind like moon . . ."

After a while, it made him laugh.

He couldn't see his watch, but he thought a half hour had passed before he heard people outside the door. He knew the routine: they were letting him stew and worry about consequences. He heard somebody tapping the keypad lock, the door popped open, and another tall blond cop looked in at him. This one was twenty-five years older than the first cop, but there was a family resemblance, including the tense facial muscles and the well-waxed flattop. The first two cops had been wearing khaki uniforms with shoulder patches that said "Aux Vases County"; this man was wearing a sport coat and tan slacks.

"Bring him outa there, son," the man said.

The first big blond cop, Todd, came around the door and said, "Stand up, asshole."

Lucas stood, and the cop hooked him by the arm and led him out into the hallway. Then they all followed the man in the sport coat down the hall to an office, where the man sat down behind a desk. A nameplate on the desk said "Sheriff Robert 'Bob' Turner." There were a dozen pictures of him on the back wall, either receiving awards or standing with some dignitary.

The sheriff asked, "Where's Triste?"

"Waiting room with Scott," Todd said.

"Bring her in here."

TODD WENT to get her, and Lucas said, "Sheriff Turner, I did not—"

"Shut the fuck up," Turner said. "In this office, you speak when you're spoken to."

Todd was back ten seconds later with the woodchuck

cop and the girl. Turner looked at Triste and asked, "What'd he do to you?"

"He said we'd get some beer and go watch HBO, and when I got in his room, he started pulling off my clothes. He almost had me naked, I was screaming, and Todd showed up just in time," she said.

The sheriff looked at Lucas and asked, "Is that right?"

Lucas shook his head. "No. It's not right."

"You're saying she's lying?" Turner asked.

"That's what I'm saying," Lucas said.

"Huh. Well, Todd, what do you have to say?"

"We were over at the Motel 6, doing a routine check, and I was walking along that walkway there and I heard Shirley . . . er, Triste . . . cry out, and the door was unlocked and I went through it and I found her naked as the day she was born and this guy here all over her."

The sheriff looked at Lucas. "That right?"

"No. She took her own clothes off and started screaming," Lucas said. "I was not all over her—I was standing by the door and she was on the other side of the room."

"You're saying Todd's lying, too."

"Yes."

Todd reached over and slapped Lucas's face. Lucas half spun away, trying to keep his balance, which was harder than he'd thought it might be with his hands pinned behind him. The slap stung but didn't do any damage. Todd was pissing him off, though.

The sheriff puffed himself up and noisily sighed, then said, "Well, looks like we got ourselves a situation." He turned to Triste. "You pretty messed up, girl?"

"Hell, yeah," she said. "Nothing like this ever happened before. I'm pretty much a virgin."

The sheriff gazed at her for a bit, then said to Scott, "Go sit her down in the waiting room again. You stay with her. Me'n Todd will interview the subject here."

When they were gone, the sheriff asked Todd, "You check his ID?"

"Not yet. I was gonna do that when you got here."

"Well, check it. Let's see who we got."

"My name's Lucas . . ." Lucas began.

"Shut up," the sheriff said.

Lucas carried a bifold alligator-hide wallet in his front pants pocket, and Todd slipped it out, opened it, and said, "No cash, nothing but credit cards and a Minnesota driver's license. 'Lucas Davenport, Mississippi River Boulevard, St. Paul.'"

"Well, let's see what we got on Mr. Davenport," the sheriff said. He turned to a computer, tapped a key, which brought up a browser, went to Google, and typed in Lucas's name. There were a dozen articles and a hundred mentions or so, some with photographs. The sheriff read for a while, clicking through the articles, and then said to Todd, "Says here Mr. Davenport is a wealthy patron of the arts in Minneapolis and St. Paul, made his money in software. Don't say a thing about his fuckin' underage girls. Is that all true, Mr. Davenport?"

Lucas nodded. "I guess." An FBI computer specialist had done some editing of Lucas's history beforehand.

"You 'guess'? Huh. You don't know for sure?" Turner asked.

Lucas said, "Yeah, that's me."

"You so rich you don't even carry cash? You just wave that black Amex card at people?"

"I . . ."

"You know what?" Todd asked. He reached out and patted Lucas on the chest. "Here we go."

He fished a second leather wallet out of Lucas's breast pocket, opened it, and said, "Whoa, Daddy. He *is* rich." He pulled out a wad of hundreds, spread it like a hand of cards. "There must be . . . five grand here."

"That's evidence," the sheriff said. "Give it here."

Todd handed him the money and the sheriff put it in his jacket pocket, peered at Lucas for a few more seconds, then said to Todd, "Take those cuffs off him." When the cuffs were off, the sheriff said, "Sit down, Mr. Davenport. I need to explain to you some realities of the world."

THE REALITIES, the sheriff said, were that both the deputies had been wearing body cameras, which he called Obama-cams, and they clearly caught Lucas and Triste in the motel room. Triste, he said, had probably been ruined by the night's sexual experience, or, if not ruined, at least psychologically damaged. Long-term psychiatric care would be needed to fix that, and long-term psychiatric care wasn't cheap.

"I got enough to send you off to the state prison for, oh, five to ten years, but that's not gonna do Triste any good, is it? She's still ruint," the sheriff said. "I'm saying, between you and me, it might be better to cut our own little deal. I understand how you could have been misled, and everybody likes a little young puss now and then. But that's neither here nor there—she's still fifteen. You pay for her care—if those newspaper stories are right, you won't even miss the money—and we forget the whole thing. Or, you can do the five-to-ten."

Lucas didn't say anything for ten seconds, fifteen seconds, then he blurted, "You motherfuckers. You used that girl to set me up. That's what's going on here. She doesn't need that money. I bet you got her doing this three times a week . . ."

The sheriff said, "Todd? A little help?"

Todd swung harder this time, caught Lucas across the cheek with an open hand, knocked him off the chair. Lucas crawled in a circle on his hands and knees, could taste blood this time, and said, "C'mon, don't hit me, don't hit me again."

"Couldn't help myself," the sheriff said. "Accusing me of some kind of public corruption. I don't take those kind of insults. Now get back up on that chair."

Lucas got back up on the chair, feeling the blood surging through his cheeks where he'd been hit—he'd have a hand-sized bruise in the morning—and the sheriff asked, "What's it gonna be? You want to pay or you want to go to court? I gotta tell you the truth, we don't much care for Yankees down here."

Lucas dragged his hand across his mouth, tasting the salty/metallic dash of blood. "What're we talking about? How much?"

The sheriff considered for a moment and then said, "Given what the crime is, and given the fact that you're a rich man . . . twenty-five thousand. That sound about right?"

"Jesus, I don't have that much around. I don't have my checkbook with me . . ."

"What we do is this. You give me that American Express card and we'll fill out, right here, a bond statement, bailing you outa jail. We bail you out for two thousand dollars. Then you go back home and you send us a check. If you don't send us a check, we'll schedule you for trial and get in touch with the St. Paul police about extraditing your ass. If the check comes in, well, then it was a bad night in Oh-Va, but you won't be hearing from us again."

"I send you a check for twenty thousand? You already got five in cash."

"And the watch," Todd said. "That's a Rolex, I always wanted one of them. Give it here."

"Not the watch. My wife gave it to me, it's engraved on the back."

"The watch," Todd insisted. The sheriff leaned back,

amused. "Give it here," Todd said, "or, I swear to God, I'll slap the shit out of you."

"You gotta take the price of the watch off the rest, I'll get a new one . . ." Lucas said. He unfastened the watch and handed it to Todd, who admired it for a few seconds, then put it in his pocket.

"No, no. The full price is thirty-two thousand, plus the watch," the sheriff said, leaning back into the conversation. "You put two thousand on that Amex and send us twenty-five and we'll keep all of it."

"How much does Triste get? I hope she gets something from you sonsofbitches."

The sheriff smiled. "Triste does all right. Better than working at McDonald's, getting all that smoke and grease up in your hair." He leaned forward across his desk, fingers knitted together. "You look like a sophisticated man, Mr. Davenport. If you ever talk about this whole thing, the big headline's gonna say 'Mr. Davenport Fucks Fifteen-Year-Old' and the little headline is gonna say 'Claims public corruption.' Which headline do you think people will give a shit about? Which headline do you think your wife will give a shit about when Triste gets up on the witness stand and everybody gets a look at those titties?"

Lucas said, "All right. You've got the five grand in your pocket, I'll charge two more on the Amex, but I only send you twenty more. That's all."

"You trying to bargain with me?" the sheriff asked with the same shark-toothed smile. "Because you're not in much of a position . . ."

THE OFFICE DOOR opened and the deputy who'd led Triste away stepped back inside the room. His face was shiny with sweat, and maybe regret, and the sheriff broke off to say, "What . . . ?"

The deputy looked back over his shoulder, and then a dark gray semiautomatic pistol extended past his ear, pointed at Todd's head, and the deputy lurched farther into the office, and a man in a blue suit with a wide gray mustache pushed inside and said, "Todd, I don't want to have to tell you twice, but if you move a hand toward your gun, I'll blow your brains all over Daddy's office."

The sheriff pushed back from his desk, a stricken look on his face. He'd already figured it out, but he asked anyway: "Who're you? Who the fuck are you?"

"Deputy U.S. Marshal James Duffy, Eastern District of Missouri. You are both under arrest. Got a looong list of charges, we'll read them to you when we get up to St. Louis. Harry? You want to get in here, put some handcuffs on these gentlemen?"

Another man in a suit edged past the gun, which was still pointed at Todd's head. The second man, Harry, spoke directly to Lucas. "Turner really wasn't dumb enough to put the money in his pocket, was he?"

"Yes, he was, and Todd put the watch in his pocket," Lucas said. "I'd like to get the goddamn wire off me. My back is itching like fire."

"You all right other than that?" Duffy asked.

"Yeah. Todd smacked me a few times but never touched the wire pack. I was mostly worried that somebody would see me flushing those margarita sponges down the toilet in the rooster room."

The second marshal cuffed Todd's hands behind his back and said to the sheriff, "On your feet, Mr. Turner."

"That's *Sheriff* Turner . . ."

"Not anymore," the marshal said.

Todd began to cry, his wide shoulders shaking under the deputy's uniform, then he looked at Lucas and said, "You asshole."

"That'd be Marshal Asshole, to you, Todd," Lucas said.

*   *   *

THE ST. LOUIS MARSHALS arrested six people—the sheriff, four deputies, and Shirley McDonald. They'd be back, later, to get a state judge.

After they put the cuffs on her, Shirley had started talking about being extorted by the Turners, and still hadn't stopped when they pushed her into a federal car and sent her north. "Them fuckin' Turners made me do it. Todd and Scott made me suck them off, too. Ask them about that. I'm only fifteen . . ."

It all made an interesting recording, and since the marshals read her rights to her a half dozen times, and she talked anyway, it would all hold up in court.

Before he got in the car, Lucas took a breath test, which showed a 0.01 BAC—about what a man would get if he rinsed his mouth with whiskey a half hour before he took the test. Which Lucas had done. That level implied no impairment whatever, in case a defense attorney should ask.

THE STING at Cooter's had begun when a widower federal judge had run into the same trap. Turner and his son had decided he might be more useful in his capacity as a judge than in his potential to pay his way out, and made a deal: the judge agreed to give them three verdicts, any three that could conceivably be seen as reasonable, and nobody would talk about young girls in motels. Three verdicts in the right corporate cases could be worth a million dollars . . .

But they'd misjudged the judge. As soon as he got back to St. Louis, he'd contacted the U.S. attorney and made a statement about the entrapment and blackmail. He'd ad-mitted to having been alone in a room with a girl whose age he didn't know. He thought she might be nineteen or twenty, he said, but he made no other excuses.

Two days later, the St. Louis Marshals office was checking around for a rich-looking marshal with a decent backstory. They found Lucas.

THE FIVE arrested men rode north in a federal van, with two deputy marshals to drive and watch over them. Duffy, the chief deputy for the Eastern District of Missouri, rode with Lucas, in the comfort of the big Benz.

"One day ought to do it on the paperwork, but we'll need you back for depositions and so on," Duffy said. "We appreciate you coming down. Our own people are too well-known, couldn't take the chance that Turner might recognize them. Anyway, don't none of us got that slick veneer you actual rich guys got."

"It's only a veneer," Lucas said. "Underneath, I'm just another really, really good-looking yet humble working cop."

Duffy snorted and asked, "How's your caseload?"

"I'm still looking." Duffy knew about Lucas's circumstances: a freelance deputy marshal, slipped into the Marshals Service through nothing but pure, unalloyed political influence, wielded by Michaela Bowden, the Democratic nominee for President of the United States. Lucas had kept Bowden from being blown up at the Iowa State Fair the year before.

He'd been a marshal for three months, and had gone through brief training at Arlington, Virginia, across the Potomac from Washington, D.C., most of which hadn't applied to him because of his special status. On the other hand, he really did have to know about the paperwork, which was ample.

"There's some interesting stuff out there, but not

really to my taste," Lucas told Duffy. "I'm looking for something hard. Something unusual. Something I can work at and would do some serious good."

Duffy said, "Huh." He looked out the window at the countryside, damp, green, shrouded in darkness. A moment later he asked, "You ever hear of a guy named Garvin Poole?"

"Don't think so," Lucas said.

"No? Then let me tell you about him."

"Poole? Marvin?"

"Garvin. Gar's a good ol' Tennessee boy . . . maybe killed ten or fifteen innocent people, including at least one six-year-old girl, just last week, and a Mississippi cop, sometime back, and God only knows how many guilty people," Duffy said. "He's smart, he's likable, he's good-lookin'. He once played in a pretty fair country band, and he's got no conscience. None at all. He's got friends who'd kill you for the price of a moon pie. Some people think he's dead, but he's not. He's out there hiding and laughing at us. Yes, he is."

3

MARGARET TRANE nearly ran over Lucas as she trotted out of the federal building, a solidly built cop in a hurry. She grabbed his jacket lapels and said, "Jesus, Davenport," at the same instant Lucas grabbed her shoulders and kept her upright and said, "Easy, Maggie."

They backed away from each other and she said, "Hey. Been a while. Was that girl down in Missouri as young as they say?"

"She was young, she says fifteen," Lucas said. "Sort of horrifying, if you know what I mean."

"I do," Trane said. She smiled up at him—they'd always had good chemistry, even when Lucas was Minneapolis's top violent-crimes investigator and she was stuck in precinct investigations. They'd both moved on, Trane to Minneapolis Homicide, Lucas to Minnesota's Bureau of Criminal Apprehension and then to the U.S. Marshals

Service. "I hear things have been a little tense up in the marshals' office."

"Ah, you know. It'll work out, eventually," Lucas said.

"You got Bowden behind you and she's gonna be President. That oughta help."

"I try not to lean on that too hard," Lucas said. "But . . . yeah."

"If you want to talk to some real cops, stop by Homicide. Happy to have you."

They chatted for another minute, spouses and kids, then Trane said she had to run, she had a conference call on a guy who was being bad in both Minneapolis and Denver. She jogged away and Lucas went on into the federal building.

Talking to Trane had cheered him up. Because of the way he'd been appointed to the Marshals Service, he wasn't the most popular guy in the place. He'd been dropped in from the top, a deputy U.S. marshal who sat in the Minneapolis office but worked independently and took no orders from anyone in Minneapolis, although he occasionally took recommendations and requests for help. His most direct contact was with a service bureaucrat in Washington named Russell Forte. He and Forte had met only briefly, and had gone to lunch, and Lucas had gotten the impression that Forte was the best kind of apparatchik: efficient, connected, more interested in results than in methods or style.

So far, they'd gotten along.

LUCAS HAD an office on the fourth floor of the sorta-modern-looking Minneapolis federal building, down the hall from the U.S. marshal for the District of Minnesota and the other deputy marshals. The arrangement was complicated and one source of bad feelings on the part of a few deputies.

The Marshals Service had a politically appointed U.S. marshal at the top of each of the ninety-four federal judicial districts. They were appointed much as federal judges were—nominated by the President, usually at the recommendation of a U.S. senator, and confirmed by the Senate. Below them were the civil service deputies, including a chief deputy, and below him, supervisory deputies, and below that, the regular deputy marshals.

Lucas stood outside that normal bureaucratic pecking order; and some in the Minneapolis office thought he might be a spy. For whom, he had no idea, but that was the rumor.

IN ADDITION, there was Lucas's private office, which had been, until recently, a windowless storage room. Still, it was private. The resentment was further exacerbated by the fact that he didn't have to put up with the bureaucratic rigors of the other deputies, the bad hours, crappy assignments. He didn't serve warrants, he didn't transfer prisoners.

On top of it all, he was personally rich and arrived at work in either a Mercedes-Benz SUV or a Porsche 911. A federal judge with whom he was friendly had suggested a modest American car would be more discreet, until he was better known inside the service.

Lucas said, "Fuck 'em if they can't take a joke."

The judge had said, "It ain't them who's getting fucked, m'boy."

THE UNEASINESS wasn't confined to the other deputies: Lucas had wanted a good badge after leaving the BCA and had grabbed the first one offered. He really didn't mind the temporary isolation—he thought that would break down in time—but he'd surprised himself with the feeling that he was seriously adrift.

From his first day as a Minneapolis cop, he'd worked to understand his environment. He'd eventually understood Minneapolis–St. Paul and its population of bad people. If someone told him that an unknown X had murdered a known Y, he'd usually know a Z that he could talk to, to begin figuring out what had happened.

That wasn't always true, but it was true often enough to give him a clearance rate that nobody in the department could touch.

When he'd moved to the Bureau of Criminal Apprehension, a statewide organization, he'd struggled toward the same kind of comprehensive understanding, but this time, of the entire state of Minnesota. He'd never gotten as comfortable with the state as he had with the metro area, but he'd worked at it. As part of that, he'd developed a database of shady individuals with whom he'd pounded out private understandings. He'd call, they'd talk; if they got in trouble themselves, Lucas would have a chat with a judge, as long as the trouble was minor.

With the help of other agents, he'd eventually put together a roster of snitches with at least a couple of names in every single Minnesota county, and for larger cities, like Duluth or Rochester, he had an entire roll call. Included in the database were several dozen cops who formed a web of personal relationships tight enough that Lucas could get help anywhere in the state, at any time.

Even in his new job as a deputy marshal, he was taking calls from BCA agents who wanted into his database: "Who do you have in Alexandria who might know about the *chicle* coming across from Canada?"

Didn't work that way with the Marshals Service. His jurisdiction was the United States of America, including the various territories. There was no possibility of comprehending it, in any real way: he'd fallen into a morass. He could call for help from the FBI, the DEA, the Border Patrol, all the alphabet agencies enforcing the nation's laws, but he didn't know the individuals. He couldn't count on them—they were just voices on the far end of a cell phone call, and would get around to helping him as their own schedules permitted. He didn't know the bad guys at all, or who were the baddest.

He was, as his wife, Weather, had said, out there on his lonesome.

And he didn't understand the "out there."

HAL ODER, the marshal for the district, resented Lucas's independent status. Lucas took no orders or assignments from Oder, and, to Oder, had looked like a job threat. That hadn't eased, even though Lucas made it clear that he had no interest at all in Oder's job.

"I hate the shit you have to put up with," Lucas told the other man. "I wouldn't do it. I'd quit first. All I want to do is hunt. The bureaucratic bullshit is the reason I quit the BCA."

"Just hunt."

"That's right."

"If you screw up, it'll make this office look bad," Oder had said.

"I might screw up, but if I do, I'll make it clear that it has nothing to do with you or your office, that my people are in Washington, not in Minnesota," Lucas had said.

"Who's your contact in Washington?"

"Russell Forte," Lucas said.

"Don't know him," Oder said. "Are you sure he'll be happy to take the responsibility if you mess up?"

"Well, he *is* a bureaucrat. You'd know more than me about the likelihood of his taking the blame."

Oder had been tapping on a legal pad with a mechanical pencil. He thought about Lucas's comment, then said, "Look, Lucas, I know what happened when you quit the BCA, and I'm up-to-date with what happened down in Iowa. You saved Mrs. Bowden's life and you got a badge because of it. The way it looks, she's going to be President, and I don't want to fight with a friend of Bowden. But I feel like I'm stuck in the middle. I don't want to get blamed for things I don't do. But when you fuck up, and you will, it's inevitable with the job, I'll get blamed. I hate that."

"I won't be a problem," Lucas promised. "You'll hardly ever see me around the place."

ODER HAD seemed to accept that, but, in the way of bureaucrats, he let it be known that Davenport was not really *one of us*.

In an effort to further smooth things over, Lucas had offered to help out in unusual situations. The Minnesota Marshals office was perpetually short-handed, and that was how he'd wound up as a rich-guy decoy in Missouri.

Lucas and another deputy had also run down an embezzler who'd skipped his date in Minneapolis federal court in favor of a new name and a new home in Idaho, and had recovered a chunk of the embezzled cash from an Idaho safe-deposit box, which had made everyone look good.

He'd helped locate, with his Minnesota database, a redneck who didn't like federal wildlife laws and had decided to eliminate wolves and eagles in his personal hunting grounds. The guy'd been busted by the Fish and Wildlife Service, but had forfeited a $2,500 bond rather than show up for trial in federal court.

He'd told acquaintances that the feds would take him

when they "pried my cold dead hands" off his black rifle, and had suggested that he was polishing up a special bullet for the U.S. attorney. Lucas and two other deputies had hauled his ass out of a bar in Grand Marais, blubbering about his rights.

They were good arrests . . . but not what Lucas had been looking for.

Still, he'd been useful enough that he and Carl Meadows, the chief deputy, had begun taking an occasional lunch together.

THE DAY AFTER he returned from St. Louis, a bright and cool autumn Monday in Minneapolis, he and Meadows walked over to the food trucks on Second Avenue and bought brats and Lucas told the other man about the Missouri sting.

"That's all good," Meadows said, when Lucas finished, "but have you found anything to dig into? You've been sitting on your ass for a while."

"I know, but I might be onto something now," Lucas said. "Have you ever heard of a guy named Garvin Poole?"

Meadows frowned and looked down at his brat, as though it might hold an answer. "The name rings a bell, back a while, but I can't place it. Maybe a Southerner? He was on our Top Fifteen list for a while?"

"Yeah. Everything I know came out of a conversation with Jim Duffy down in St. Louis, and what I fished out of the online records this morning. Poole was an old-style holdup man down in the Southeast—Georgia, South Carolina, Alabama, Mississippi, North Florida. Came out of Tennessee originally, but didn't operate much there, at least not after he did four years in a Tennessee prison. He dropped out of sight five years ago. He was tentatively identified in an armored car robbery in Chattanooga, and nothing after that. Lot of his pals have been busted and questioned, but they all agree that he's gone. Nobody knows where. Lot of people thought he was dead. Then, ten days ago, a dope counting house down in Biloxi was knocked over. The robbers killed five people, including a six-year-old girl."

"Yeah, jeez, I heard about that. That's ugly," Meadows said.

"One of the victims apparently got off a shot before he was killed," Lucas said. "The crime scene people found a few drops of blood, ran it through the DNA database, and got a hit—they think it was Poole."

"Think? DNA's supposed to be for sure," Meadows said.

"Not this time," Lucas said. "The DNA match came from the armored car robbery in Chattanooga. The truck had internal cameras that the robbers couldn't get at. The video showed one of the robbers banging his forearm against a door frame when he was climbing out of the truck with a bag of cash. They got some skin off the frame, ran the DNA. They didn't get a hit, but believe it was Poole on the basis of height and body type and the robbery technique. They couldn't see his face, and he was wearing gloves, so there's no fingerprints, no definitive ID. Both drivers were shot to death with .40 caliber handguns, as were the five people killed in Biloxi. Poole favors .40 caliber Glocks."

"Same as we carry."

"Yeah. Well, you, anyway." Lucas carried his own .45, which was against regulations, but nobody had tried to argue with him about that.

"Any federal warrants on him?" Meadows asked.

"Old ones, but still good. Nine years ago, he and a guy named Charles Trevino robbed a mail truck out of St. Petersburg," Lucas said. "The truck was carrying a bunch of registered mail packages after a stamp-collectors convention. Trevino was busted a year later when he tried to unload some of the stamps. He said Poole was the other guy, and there was a third guy, whom he didn't know, who did the research and the setup. The U.S. attorney filed an indictment on Poole and a warrant was issued, but he hasn't been picked up since then."

"Sounds like a smart guy who works with other smart guys, if they spotted a particular mail truck full of old stamps," Meadows said.

"Apparently he *is* a smart guy, besides being a cold-blooded killer," Lucas said. "That's one of the reasons he interests me. That and the little girl."

"You've got a daughter, right?" Meadows asked.

"Three of them," Lucas said. "One's going to college, one's about to go, and I've got a five-year-old. A son, too."

"Huh. Here's a change of direction," Meadows said. "You hear that Sandy Park got hit by a bicyclist?"

Sandra Park was another deputy marshal. Lucas had nodded to her in the hallway.

"What? A bicycle?"

"Yeah. Jerk on one of those fat-tire mountain bikes, rolling down a hill, blew through a stop sign. Sandy was out jogging and got T-boned. Anyway, she's not hurt bad, but one ankle and one knee are messed up. She's going to be off them for a couple of weeks. She's good with computers. If you need some backup, she knows all the law enforcement systems inside and out. I can tell her to give your questions a priority . . . if you need that," Meadows said.

"Thanks," Lucas said. "I'll talk to her this afternoon."

"I'll tell her you're coming around."

*   *   *

LUCAS TALKED to Park, and found himself smoothing more ruffled feathers. Park was *not* being asked to do secretarial-type work because she was a woman, she was being asked to do it because Lucas didn't know how, she had expertise that he didn't, and she was working while injured, and because *blah blah blah*.

Feathers smoothed, Lucas asked her to dredge up everything she could find in the federal systems on Poole. Park said she would, and would have a brick of paper and a flash drive by the next day.

THAT NIGHT, Lucas told Weather about Poole.

"He's an old-fashioned kind of crook. Guns and hold-ups, armored cars and banks or anywhere else that has cash—he likes cash. He held up the box office at a country music show one time. Doesn't have a problem with killing people. Doesn't do anything high-tech."

He told her about the little girl killed in Biloxi, and she shook her head. "Brutal."

"Yeah." They both glanced toward their daughter Gabrielle, who was sitting on a corner chair going through a beginning-reader book with a fierce concentration, paying no attention to her parents.

"You could be going out of town for a while," Weather said. They were sitting on the front room couch, her head on his shoulder. Weather was a short woman, a plastic surgeon. Pretty, with cool eyes and a nose she thought over-large but Lucas thought was striking.

"I could be—no longer than I have to be, but it could be a couple of weeks. I don't think a month. I'll probably drive, instead of flying," Lucas said. He got up and wandered around the living room, looking at books, putting them down, thinking about it.

"Not your part of the country," she said. "That Southern thing is different."

"I know."

"You think this could really interest you?" she asked.

"If a guy is bad enough . . . he'll interest me. Poole is bad, and nobody's been able to lay hands on him."

"A challenge," she said.

"Yeah."

Weather said, "I don't like the idea of you going away too often, but it's better than having you sitting around, brooding. You're getting to be a pain in the ass."

Lucas nodded: "I get that way when I'm not doing what I'm supposed to be doing."

"Hunting."

"Yes."

LUCAS CALLED Russell Forte the next morning to tell him what he was planning to do. Forte worked at the U.S. Marshals Service headquarters in Virginia, across the Potomac from Washington, D.C.

"I remember Poole," Forte said. "He was on our Top Fifteen list for a long time. We let him drift off because we had nothing to work with. If you find him, that'd be a major feather in your cap. All of our caps. Do *not* try to take him alone. He's a killer. The first sniff you get, call me and we'll get you a team from the Special Operations Group."

"I will do that," Lucas said.

Later, at the federal building, he found Park standing over a hot printer, putting what looked like a ream of paper between hard covers. "There's more," she said. "This is the good stuff, so far. I was reading through it while I dug it out, and I'll tell you, Lucas, Poole started out as a mean kid, and he stayed that way. His father worked off and on for the state of Tennessee, different low-level jobs, but he was also a small-time crook. Got busted for scalping tickets, once for selling driver's licenses out of the DMV where he worked, but he was acquitted on that and got his job back. Was arrested a couple of times for selling stolen merchandise, but never convicted. His sister supposedly boosted a truckload of racing tires one time, but the charges were dropped, doesn't say why. Garvin stepped up from that, but he didn't come from the best of families."

"His folks still alive?" Lucas asked.

"Don't know, but I suppose so—Poole's only forty-two, if he's not dead himself," Park said. "I could find out."

"Do that, and print it all," Lucas said. "If there's anything on the parents and any brothers and sisters, I'll want it. Files on any associates, girlfriends, everything."

Park patted the Xerox machine: "I'll do it, as long as this machine doesn't break down."

WHEN PARK finished, she handed Lucas a couple of reams of paper that must have weighed ten pounds. Lucas took it home and settled into his den to read.

First up were crime scene photos out of Biloxi. Lucas had seen thousands of crime scene photos over his career, and these were nothing like the worst. All five victims had been shot in the head, and had died instantly. One of them, the little girl, looked like a plastic doll, lying spread-eagled on a concrete floor, faceup, a hole in her forehead like a third eye. She was wearing a white dress with lace, full at the knees. Lucas had seen a lot of pictures of dead kids: he glanced at the photo, and then went on to the next.

And yet . . .

He kept coming back to it. The little girl had been connected by DNA to one of the other counting-house victims, a much older man—the DNA analysts said she was his granddaughter. The grandfather may have been a dope-selling asshole, but the girl wasn't. In the photo she was lying flat on her back, her eyes half-open. They still shone with the innocence of the very young, and with the surprise of how their lives had ended so early.

The dress had something to do with it, too. It reminded Lucas of the dresses worn by Catholic schoolmates, little girls going off to First Communion. Crime scene techs had found a smear of blood on the dress, where somebody—had to be one of the killers—had ripped off a piece, probably to use as a bandage.

The girl on the floor began to work on him. He made a call to Biloxi, found that nobody had claimed any of the bodies. "We don't really expect anybody to show up and say, 'Yeah, I'm with all those dope guys, we want to give them a nice church funeral.'"

Now Lucas began to feel something of a personal hook: get the guy who'd killed this little girl. He hadn't had to, but he'd done it anyway. Why? Maybe simple efficiency, maybe she'd seen the killer's face and would be able to identify him, maybe because the shooter or shooters just liked killing people.

Pissed him off, in a technical cop way. At the same time, despite the growing spark of anger, Lucas thought, *Good shooting.* The killer, whether it was Poole or not, was a pro—efficient, well schooled, remorseless.

LUCAS PUT the photos aside, all but the one of the girl. He kicked back at his desk, looked at that for a final minute or two, then flicked it onto the pile of other photos.

Neither the photos nor the investigation reports told him much, possibly because there wasn't much to tell, other than what he could see for himself.

The Mississippi Bureau of Investigation had handled much of the work, and had done it professionally enough. When Lucas had finished reading through the reports, he called the MBI agent who'd signed off on them. It took a few minutes to get through the MBI phone system, then Elroy Martin picked up the phone and said, "This is Martin."

Lucas identified himself and said, "I'm looking into this because of his federal fugitive status. I've got all your reports, unless there's something new since yesterday."

"There isn't," Martin said.

"So what do you think?"

"If you can find Poole, the DNA will take him down. I'm positive of that. But finding him is the problem. People have been chasing him for years. Good people. Guys who knew what they were doing."

"Your notes say you don't think he did the Biloxi thing on his own."

"That's right. We don't know how many were on the job, but I don't believe it would be less than two or three. The five dead were killed with two different guns, both .40 caliber. All the slugs and brass came out of the same batch, and all were reloads. It seems possible that two shooters would share a batch of ammo, but, you know . . ."

"Probably not."

"Yeah. Probably not. Whoever did this had to spot that drug counting house—that's what it was—and we don't think it was Poole. We think it was probably somebody who knew about the counting house from a drug connection, maybe because he lives around there, in Biloxi," Martin said. "It's possible that it was a professional spotter, a planner. A setup guy. We know he used a setup guy in the stamp robbery. We don't think Poole would touch anything where he lives, because he'd know that we'd be all over it. We think he was brought in as the shooter. We don't have any idea of who the spotter was, though."

"Maybe somebody in the cartel who decided he wanted a bigger piece of the action and decided to take it?"

"We talked about that, but then, why bring in Poole? That Biloxi drug stuff comes through a Honduras cartel, a real professional operation," Martin said. "If you're in that cartel, you'd know plenty of guys with guns, but you wouldn't know Poole. Poole's not a drug guy, he's a Dixie Hicks guy. A holdup man. Completely different set of bad guys. They really don't intersect."

"Huh. If we could find the spotter, that'd be a big step," Lucas said.

"Yeah, it would, but we haven't come up with anything yet," Martin said. "We'd do anything we could to get our hands on Poole. We think he killed one of our guys a few years ago."

"I saw that."

They talked for a few more minutes, but Lucas got the impression that Mississippi was running out of possibilities. He thanked Martin and went back to the paper on his desk.

Poole first ran into the law when he was eleven years old, after a schoolyard fight. Unlike most schoolyard fights, this wasn't two punches with the loser swearing to *get* the other guy. Poole knocked the loser down, then kicked him in the face and ribs and back, until a teacher dragged him off. The loser went to the hospital in an ambulance.

There were no more fights until high school. Then, there was only one, with the same result: the loser went to the hospital. A witness told a juvenile court that Poole had "gone psycho." Poole, who'd been a running back on the junior high and then sophomore football teams, was kicked out of school.

A few weeks later, he held up a dry cleaner's with a toy pistol. The dry cleaner had a lot of cash and no protection at all: Poole hadn't gone after a place that might be ready for him, like a liquor store or a convenience store.

The holdup also demonstrated his youthful inexperience. Although he'd picked on a store well north of his home in a Nashville suburb, he hadn't known about video cameras, and two cameras were mounted on a Dunkin' Donuts store in the same shopping center and picked up Poole's face.

He looked very young and the cops took photos around to the high schools and arrested Poole the same day as he'd done the robbery, with most of the money still in his pocket. He was sent to the Mountain View Youth Development Center, where he spent nine months working the woodshop and talking to other teenage felons about the best way to proceed with a life of crime.

Three years after his release, he was arrested again after he and two other men cut though a roof into the box office of a country music venue and robbed it. They got away with a hundred and ten thousand dollars, but one of the men, Boyd Harper, had an angry girlfriend named Rhetta Ann Joyce, who ratted out Harper to the cops.

She did that after learning Harper had spent thirty thousand dollars, virtually his entire cut of the country music money, on cocaine and hookers, and she hadn't been invited. She had, however, contracted a fiery case of gonorrhea, passed on from one of the hookers and not, as Harper tried to tell her, from a toilet seat.

Harper, in turn, ratted out Poole and an accomplice named Dave Adelstein in return for a shorter sentence.

Poole and Adelstein did four years at West Tennessee State Prison. Harper got only a year and a day, at Southeastern Tennessee Regional Correctional Facility, where he studied culinary arts. He'd served only four months when a person unknown stuck the sharpened butt of a dinner fork into his heart. Poole and Adelstein couldn't have done that themselves, but Tennessee state cops believed that they paid for the killing through a contractual arrangement between Tennessee prison gangs.

They also believed that Poole and/or Adelstein might have had something to do with the demise of Rhetta Ann Joyce, who either jumped or was thrown off the New River Railroad Bridge a month after the two men were released from prison. They believed she was thrown because of the rope around her neck.

The rope might possibly have shown some intention to commit suicide, except that suicides rarely use mountain climbing ropes a hundred and ten feet long. Joyce's neck hit the bottom of the noose so hard that her head popped off. The head wasn't found until two weeks after the body, a half mile farther down the New River Gorge, washed up on a sandbar.

Lucas, looking at the riverbank crime scene photo of Joyce's head, muttered, "That's not nice."

POOLE HAD not been arrested again, but was widely understood by state and federal law enforcement officials to have been a prime mover of the Dixie Hicks, a loose confederation of holdup men working the lower tier of Confederate states.

He was also believed by the Mississippi Bureau of Investigation to have murdered a highway patrolman named Richard Wayne Coones, shot one night on lonely Highway 21 between Bogue Chitto and Shuqualak, Mississippi. The cops got his name from Al Jim Hudson, who said in a deathbed confession that he was in the car when Poole shot Coones. Hudson died shortly thereafter of internal injuries he had suffered while resisting arrest.

FBI intelligence agents learned from a source unnamed in Lucas's papers that Poole had eventually accumulated over a million dollars in gold—maybe well over a million—on which he intended to retire to Mexico or Belize. Neither the Mexican nor the Belize cops ever got a sniff of him, not that they admitted to, anyway. Lucas knew nothing about Belize cops, but he'd met a high-level Mexican police-intelligence officer and had been impressed. If the Mexicans didn't know about Poole, he probably wasn't in Mexico.

Then rumors began to circulate that Poole had been murdered by a Dixie Hicks rival named Ralph (Booger) Baca. According to the source, Baca threw Poole's body into the Four Holes Swamp in South Carolina, from which it was never recovered. A few months after he allegedly murdered Poole, Baca died in a freak accident when he turned the key on his Harley-Davidson and the Fat Bob extra-capacity tanks inexplicably exploded in his face, turning Baca into a human torch. He lingered, but not long.

Poole had not been seen or heard of again, until the killings in Biloxi. If, in fact, that was Poole at all.

Whether or not it was, Lucas thought, people died around Poole, both his friends and his enemies, including one little girl who had the bad luck to have a dope dealer as a grandfather. But if the DNA and video-camera connection was correct, Poole wasn't dead. Not yet.

IN READING through Poole's history, Lucas found several notes by a retired MBI investigator named Rory Pratt. Lucas got a number from the MBI and called him.

"Tracked him all over the South," Pratt said in a deep Mississippi accent. "We didn't always know who or what we were chasing, but we weren't gonna quit after Dick Coones got shot down. That was as cold-blooded a killing as you're likely to find. We looked at everything, but it was like chasing a shadow. We'd hear rumors that he'd been involved in a robbery at such-and-such a place and we'd be there the next day. Never really got hold of anything solid. We talked to guys who were actually involved in some of these holdups and they always denied knowing Poole—but being of that element, they knew what had happened to people who *had* talked about Poole."

"You get any feel for whether he was actually involved in any of the robberies you checked?" Lucas asked. "Lot of people think he's dead."

"He's not dead. I guarantee that. Not unless someone snuck up behind him and shot him and buried the body in the dark of the moon, and never told anyone. Another thing is, he's got a girlfriend named Pandora Box . . ."

"I read that, but I thought it was a joke," Lucas said.

"No joke. I mean, I guess it was a joke by her daddy, but that's where the joke ended," Pratt said. "There's a story that Poole once caught up with a guy from the Bandidos who stiffed him on a money deal. One thing led to another and Box cut the Bandido's head off with a carving knife, for no reason except that she could. No proof of that, no witnesses we know of, but that's the story. Anyway, Box disappeared at the same time as Poole, but two years ago she went to an uncle's funeral up in Tennessee. We didn't find out until a week later, people around there keep their mouths shut. If Box and Poole disappeared at the same time, and she's still alive, and even looking prosperous . . . you see where I'm going here."

"Did anyone check the airlines, see where she was coming in from? Or going back to?"

"They did. She didn't fly in or out. She came to the funeral in a taxi and left the same way. We think she probably drove from wherever they're hiding and then caught a cab so nobody would see her car. The uncle's funeral was four days after he died, so she could have driven from anywhere in the lower forty-eight."

"Gotcha. Listen, if you'd have time, put together an e-mail on what you and your partner did—not every little thing, but in general, and what you think," Lucas said. "Mostly what you think. Any hints or suggestions about how I might do this."

"I got one hint right now: if they get on top of you, you gotta shoot your way through, Marshal. Surrendering or negotiating will get you killed," Pratt said. "Even get your head cut off. That boy is a gol-darned cottonmouth pit viper and so's his girlfriend."

BACK IN THE PAPER, Lucas made up a list of known associates, and in particular people who actually seemed to be friends of Poole. He included Poole's parents and sister. Dora Box apparently had no living relatives. When he was finished, he had twenty-two names. He e-mailed the list to Sandy Park, the deputy marshal who'd done the computer research, and asked for reports on those people.

That done, he called the Tennessee Bureau of Investigation and talked to the head of the Criminal Investigation Division.

"I wanted to tell you that I'm coming through and let you know what I'm doing," Lucas said.

The agent, Justin Adams, knew Poole's name and some of the details from the Biloxi murders. "You think you've found him, give me a call and we'll be there. You want somebody to go around with you?"

"Maybe later," Lucas said. "First thing up, I'm going to be talking to his parents and sister and that kind of thing—I don't expect too much. If I get into something, though, I'll let you know."

SANDY PARK got back late in the afternoon, with the results on the list of people who were friends or accomplices of Poole. Of the twenty-two on the list, nine were dead—some because they'd simply gotten cancer or had gotten old, like Box's parents, while three had died violently: two shot during robberies, one in a motorcycle accident. Dora Box's sister had committed suicide after a long run on heroin. Of those still alive, eight were in prison, mostly serving life terms as career criminals. One was on death row in Alabama.

Of the other five, Lucas got addresses for three. Nothing was known about the location of the other two.

An e-mail came in from Pratt, the retired MBI investigator, with a few details that hadn't been in the formal paperwork. Poole knew how to create different "looks" for himself—he'd dyed his hair at one time or another, had been both clean-shaven and bearded, sometimes lounged in jeans and boots and workingmen's T-shirts, and sometimes appeared in expensive suits and ties. Sometimes he had white sidewalls, sometimes hair on his shoulders.

"One thing is always the same," Pratt said. "He always shoots first."

LUCAS SPENT two days with his son, Sam, at his Wisconsin cabin, cleaning it up and getting ready to shut it down for winter. Sam was eight, skipping school and loving it; they went fishing for an hour or two in the morning and Sam caught his first musky, a thirty-incher. Lucas was more excited than the kid was—not only was it a musky, but the kid was being imprinted with a certain kind of lifestyle, the love of a quiet lake in the early morning. Lucas showed him how to support the musky in the water, take the hook out with a pair of pliers, then release the fish back into the deep.

As they were washing the fish stink off their hands in the lake water, Sam said, "That's the best thing I've ever done in my whole life."

At night, they watched a little satellite TV and Lucas continued working through the Poole file. Done at the cabin, they drove back to the Cities, and Lucas told Weather he was leaving the following Sunday for Nashville—he wanted a full week to begin with, with all the government law enforcement offices open for business.

"How long will you be gone?" she asked. "Best estimate?"

"I'll leave Sunday evening, make a short day of it, get to Nashville the next day. I should know in the first week or two if there's any chance of locating him. If I get a sniff of him . . . could be two or three weeks."

"Why do you think you can find Poole when nobody else can?" she asked. They were in the kitchen, loading up the dishwasher. Sam was out in the garage, and they could hear him knocking a Wiffle ball around with a cut-down hockey stick.

"If he's alive, he can be found," Lucas said. "There'll be people who know where he is, or at least how to get in touch with him. If he was the shooter in Biloxi, at least one guy knows where to find him, the guy who spotted the counting house. If I can squeeze between that guy and Poole . . . I'll get him."

She closed the dishwasher, pushed the programming

buttons, then leaned back against it and said, "Don't be too confident. It could get you killed."

"I'll be as careful as I know how. The guy's a cold-blooded killer." Lucas smiled at her, the wolverine smile. "The best kind."

"God help you, Lucas," she said.

4

LUIS SOTO was a bad man and liked being a bad man. The badness rolled off him like a malaria sweat, a mean little rat-bastard who could walk into a bar and order a shot of Reposado Gold and everybody in the bar would figure him for a gun and a razor and an eagerness to use them.

He'd been born in Miami, and not a good part of Miami, of Cuban immigrant parents, and started his career in crime as a driver and muscle for a loan shark. He'd also burned a few buildings down for people who needed their buildings burned down, had laundered money through the Florida Indian casinos for his various bosses, had provided protection for a smuggling operation that brought Iranian turquoise in from the Bahamas. He'd spent some time robbing tourists on Miami Beach; and he'd been caught a few times, because he wasn't the brightest.

He'd been described by a Miami detective as "our all-purpose asshole."

His life had changed when he got in an argument in a parking lot of a chili bar in San Cristobal, Florida, and had cut the best part of the nose off a Jepsen County, Florida, sheriff's deputy after the deputy called him "a nigger of the spic persuasion."

The deputy had been in civilian clothing and Soto hadn't known he was a cop, but that wouldn't have stopped him anyway. He would have known that he was probably causing himself more trouble than the cutting was worth: but a man had his pride, and so he cut the deputy.

He was right about the trouble. He was carefully and thoroughly beaten for thirty consecutive nights in the Jepsen County jail and hadn't been able to walk quite straight or fuck anything at all since performing that traumatic nose job. The jailers also spent some time jerking him around on the end of a dog collar, leaving him with a rough, high-pitched voice that sounded like a crow scratching on a tin roof.

When Soto got back to Miami from Jepsen County he couldn't run or lift anything too heavy, and had finally taken up killing people for a living. He got anything between fifteen hundred and ten thousand dollars per murder, whatever the traffic would bear. His primo client was a Honduras drug cartel, his specific employer a man he knew only as "the Boss," with a capital "B."

The Boss would provide a succinct explanation of why the designated murderee needed to be dead and where he was, and Soto would set up the kill and carry it out. Most of the murders weren't exactly masterworks of subterfuge: Soto would pull up to the victim's front door, knock, and when the guy answered, fill him full of nine-millimeter jacketed hollow-points; the pistol, of course, was silenced. Not silent, but quiet enough in those neighborhoods disinclined to ask about loud, sharp noises. A day or two later, ten thousand dollars would show up in Soto's Panama City bank account—the Panama City in the country of Panama.

A few of the kills were more complicated and also paid better. Those were the punishment murders. Soto would track the miscreant, and at an opportune moment, kidnap him, or, occasionally, her. He didn't do the punishment himself: that was done by his partner.

BAD AS SOTO WAS, he was nothing like the nightmare of Charlene Kort.

Kort didn't live her life, she suffered it. She suffered it right from the beginning. Born to a long line of white trash and being fat and greasy, she had a bad time in school from her elementary years right through two years of high school. She made it all worse with a meth habit that started in seventh grade, when her parents began cooking it.

She'd once gotten dressed up to apply for a job, and asked her tweaker father how she looked. He'd said, "Like you caught on fire and somebody stomped you out with golf shoes." He really thought he was being funny.

With twenty-eight years of unrelieved poverty and bitterness following her like an incurable disease, she'd found her calling when she murdered an assistant manager at the Dollar Store where she was working the overnight shift as a stock girl.

The assistant manager, whose name was Dan Bird, delighted in giving her a hard time: she didn't work fast, she didn't work smart, she wasn't even clean enough for the Dollar Store: "When did you last wash your hair, anyway, dirt girl? Even if you don't respect yourself, you gotta respect the store, you hear me?"

Bird had gotten drunk and had done a late-night surprise drop-in to make sure that she was hard at work. He was running his mouth on that subject as Kort was unpacking an iron.

"You gotta work fast and you gotta work smart. You don't do either one, do you, dirt girl? You wanna know why? You're dumb trailer trash, white trash, trash. That's why . . ."

He got a step too close and she clocked him with the iron, knocking him on his drunken ass. Knowing the job was all over for her anyway, she hit him several more times with the edge of the iron, until his skull started to get mushy, and took intense, absolutely sexual pleasure as she watched him shake and tremble and groan and bleed.

After a while, having thought about how much fun this was, she walked over to the hardware section and got a pair of wire cutters, a drywall saw, a hammer, and a contractor's trash bag. She stuffed him in the bag, dragged him out to his own car, drove him down to a nearby river landing, where she sometimes went to smoke her meth, and tore him apart with her tools.

When he was dead, which took a while, his body went in the river. His car was parked behind an Adult Pleasures Outlet, and Kort walked back to the Dollar Store to clean up the bloody mess on the floor and to await the arrival of the cops.

The cops finally had come, she'd heard, but nobody talked to her, and eventually no more was said about the disappearance of Dan Bird. She'd gotten away with murder, without even trying.

Given her contacts in the world of backwoods meth feuds, her newfound skills and murderous enthusiasm were definitely marketable. Nobody knew exactly what she'd done, but the word had gotten around that Charlene Kort was the meanest bitch in North Florida, which would put her high on the list for meanest bitch world-wide.

Kort moved on from hammers and drywall—though the extra-large side-cutters still had a place in her tool bag—when she discovered the wonderful world of electricity, and all those battery-powered Japanese saws and drills and nail-drivers. Her redneck employers called her "the queen of home-improvement tools."

Then one day, two years after she killed Dan Bird, her employers hooked her up with Soto, who had contacts sideways across the Gulf of Mexico, where all the money was. Soto killed people, which was a valuable skill, but combined with Kort's interest in the pain of other people, they made an even more valuable team.

That, despite the fact that they'd hated each other at first sight, the gimpy Cuban and the overweight white-trash girl. Soto didn't like Kort any more than anyone else had, and Kort sensed that from the first moment she got in his car.

ON THIS OCCASION, they met in Panama City, the one in North Florida, at Alegra's Fine Pizza and Pasta, a place with checkered-plastic tablecloths, plastic baskets of supermarket rolls, and frozen pizza and pasta lightly heated in microwave ovens; they got a booth with a view of the building across the alley.

"It's complicated," Soto told Kort. "This is punishment, but we also gotta get some information. We can't cut them up and leave."

"What's the deal?" Kort asked. Soto's head bobbed and turned constantly, checking the environment, maybe looking for strange guns. He reminded Kort of a bobble-head doll with a mean streak.

"Somebody robbed the Boss's bank," Soto said. "He

wants the money back, and he wants the robbers punished. If we get the money back, we get a quarter million each. If we don't get the money back, but punish these guys, we get twenty grand each."

"So it's mostly about the money."

"Always is," Soto said.

"I'd like a quarter mil," Kort said. She thought about it, and asked, "What if we can't find him and we get nothing back?"

"Then we get nothing. But they pick up all the expenses."

"They know who robbed them?" Kort asked, as she sucked down a Mexican Coca-Cola.

"The College-Sounding Guy says it's probably a man named Garvin Poole. He's a holdup man and killer. The cops have been looking for him for ten years," Soto said. "Problem is, nobody knows where Poole's at. They do know he's probably got his girlfriend with him. Her name is Dora Box."

"How are we gonna find them?" Kort asked. "We're not the cops."

"The College-Sounding Guy is going to help out. He's in all the cop files. The thing is, Poole can't be found, but his relatives are out there like sittin' ducks. That's where you come in."

Kort nodded and said, "Okay. Gonna have to think about it. Maybe read up some."

"Read up? What's to read up about?" He didn't quite sneer at the idea.

"On the other jobs, the Boss just wanted somebody hurt bad, so the word would get around. We didn't care *when* the sucker died. If we need to get some information out of somebody, I'm gonna have to be more careful. Stretch it out."

"Makes you kinda hot, doesn't it? Thinking about it?" Soto said. "You ever been laid?"

"Fuck you," Kort said. She sucked the last of the Coke out of the bottle, pulled the straw out and crumpled it in her fist, pushed it back in the bottle. She didn't know why she did that, but always had. "When do we get the names?"

"Anytime now. The College-Sounding Guy says he has to do some research. Shouldn't take long. Go rent a car, I'll let you know. Oughta be ready to roll tonight."

THE COLLEGE-SOUNDING GUY was a computer hacker also employed by the Boss, and who had valuable entrée to almost any police files, and lots of other files as well. He'd gotten a half dozen fake IDs for both Kort and Soto, and credit cards that actually worked for two months. The amounts they paid for his services were fairly small—a few hundred to a couple of thousand dollars each time, which made Kort think that he might have a lot of accounts.

They had a phone number for him and nothing else. Kort imagined him sitting in his mother's basement, lots of shadows around, surrounded by Orange Crush bottles and sacks of Cheetos. In real life, when they called, he was usually listening to soft-rock music, like Genesis, or somebody.

When they called the Boss, on the other hand, there was no sound but the Boss's baritone voice, and a very faint electronic twittering.

Kort didn't mind talking to the College-Sounding Guy, because he had a workaday voice and casual attitude: pay me the money and I'll get you the information. The Boss, on the other hand, was remote and disembodied, and extremely courteous, and for that reason mysterious and threatening.

*   *   *

KORT AND SOTO left the restaurant separately, Soto going first. They'd rent cars for the job, although the cars they rented wouldn't be used on the job—they'd rent a different set of cars for that. Lots of cars meant lots of ways out, if the shit hit the fan.

Kort got hers at the airport, drove to her apartment, forty minutes away, threw everything out of the refrigerator but some bottles of water, took the garbage around back to a dumpster. That done, she watched a couple of hours of television and was getting into a *Friends* rerun when Soto called.

"We're going to Tennessee. I'll see you there tomorrow night, in Nashville. About an eight-hour drive. You get a car?"

"Yes."

"The College-Sounding Guy made reservations for you at the Best Western at the Nashville airport, under the Sally Thomas name."

"I'll call you when I get in," Kort said.

She rang off and went to her computer: time to do a little research. Soto had been right about one thing: thinking about the job *did* get her a little hot.

5

LUCAS LEFT ST. PAUL after dinner on Sunday, driving into the rising moon. As a night owl, he didn't mind driving past midnight, as long as he had a motel reservation. He took that one short day, plus most of Monday, to get to Nashville, watching the autumn leaves turn from yellow and red in Minnesota and Wisconsin, back to a dusty green by the time he crossed the Tennessee border.

He'd never been to Nashville. The name to him mostly meant shitkicker music, whining violins and frog-plunk banjos, and if anything, he was a rocker. The country music he *did* like mostly came from a line that might be drawn from Bakersfield, California, to Tulsa, Oklahoma, to Jacksonville, Florida, and south of that. In other words, not the Grand Ole Opry or anything involving the Appalachians or moonshine or whatever happens when you cross the Harlan County line.

A few minutes before six o'clock, he pulled into a La

Quinta Inn off I-24, twenty miles south of Nashville, checked in, took a leak, washed his face, changed into a suit, tie, and black oxfords—a high-end cop look—and then drove northeast into the town of La Vergne, where he cruised past the home of Poole's parents.

Kevin and Margery Poole lived in a beige two-story house with vinyl siding, few windows, a single-car garage, and a burned-out lawn. The sun had hit the horizon in the west and the evening was coming on, but no lights were showing in the house. There was a car parked in the driveway, not quite straight, as if it had been left in a hurry, or the driver was a little drunk.

Lucas parked in the street and went to the door and rang the bell. No answer.

He didn't want to linger, maybe warn somebody off, so he went back to his truck. As he started it up, he noticed a heavyset woman standing behind a screen door in the house across the street. Her arms were crossed in a defensive pose: either the self-appointed neighborhood watch or somebody to rat him out to the Pooles.

He drove back to the La Quinta, thinking about food. A couple of Tennessee Highway Patrol cars were parked at the motel entrance, the two troopers talking to a bearded man who stood outside an aged Ford pickup. The pickup had a camper back and a bumper sticker on the driver's side that said "Vegetarian" over a green marijuana leaf, and on the passenger side, another sticker that said "Can't we just all get abong?" The bearded man had a battered guitar case at his feet, but was not Willie Nelson.

Lucas nodded at the cops as he went by and one of the troopers called after him, "Excuse me, sir," and Lucas turned and the two troopers were looking at him, their hands on their Glocks. The taller of the two asked, "Are you carrying a gun?"

Lucas's .45 had printed through the jacket. He said, "Yes. I'm a U.S. marshal. I have an ID in my pocket on the right side of my jacket."

The cops nodded and Lucas pulled open his jacket with the fingertips of his right hand, extracted his badge case with his left hand, and dropped it open. The shorter trooper looked at it and said, "Good enough for me," and then, "Minnesota?"

"Yeah. I'm down here looking for a guy," Lucas said.

The tall trooper hooked a thumb at the guitar player and said, "It wouldn't be Rory Harris, would it?"

"Nope. He's your problem."

The bearded man said, "I know my rights."

The tall trooper said, "And it's your right to get stopped every two miles and asked if you got weed in your truck. You oughta lose the stickers. I'm not telling you that's the law, I'm just saying, make it easy on yourself."

"Don't have that problem down in Alabama . . ."

The trooper looked up at the sky, around the parking lot, peered at Lucas, lifted an arm and sniffed at his armpit, then said, "You know, I'd swear this was Tennessee."

Harris didn't see the comedy in that and didn't smile. The short trooper told him, "Get lost."

Harris got lost, tooling away in the stink of badly burned gasoline, his marijuana stickers intact. The tall trooper said, "Dumbass," and asked Lucas, who'd stepped away, "Who're you looking for?"

"A guy's been on the run the last ten years or so. Garvin Poole?"

Both troopers shook their heads. "What'd he do?" one of them asked.

"Everything," Lucas said. "Including killing a little girl and a Mississippi state trooper."

"Okay, that's bad," said the short guy. "You think he's close by?"

"Some of his family are, but Poole himself? I got no idea. I suspect he isn't," Lucas said. "I'm just starting on him."

"I know this area pretty good, I been out here eight years. I'll look him up and if I have any ideas, I'll give you a buzz," the short guy said.

Lucas and the troopers talked for a few more minutes—the tall one was curious about how to get to be a marshal, and Lucas told him, "Fill out an application—there's a whole thing about it online."

The trooper said he'd do that and Lucas asked if there might be a decent rib joint around, and they pointed him to a roadside barbeque barn a few miles away. Lucas traded cards with them before they left, then went to eat.

AT EIGHT O'CLOCK, the barbeque ribs sitting uneasily in his stomach, he was back at the Poole place, still no lights, still the aging Corolla parked in the driveway. Lucas pulled in behind it, got out, walked up the sidewalk. He knocked, got no answer.

He knocked again, waited, then turned away and saw the heavyset woman across the street, behind her screen door. He went that way and as he walked up her driveway, she called, "Are you the po-lees?"

"I'm a U.S. marshal," Lucas said.

"What do you want with the Pooles?" she asked.

"I need to interview them," Lucas said. "Nothing they've done wrong, or anything. Have you seen them around?"

She stood silently for a moment, chewing on her lower lip. Then, "I tell you what, sir, I was thinking I might call the local po-lees. Margery's car been parked there all day like that and Kevin's car is in the garage, because I looked in the window and seen it. Hasn't been moved. They tell me when they go out of town, so I can keep an eye on the place—but I didn't hear a peep from them. I haven't seen anything moving over there all day, but they were there last night. I seen them and saw lights. Today, I seen nothing. I knocked, but nobody answered. I'm a little worried."

Lucas said, "Huh." He looked back at the Poole house. "No lights?"

"That's another thing. They got those fake anti-burglar lights, you know, that automatically switch on and off with timers? They always use those when they're gone, and there haven't been any lights at all."

"Okay," Lucas said. "Listen, I'll call somebody. See if there's a way to check."

"I'd appreciate that, sir," she said.

LUCAS WENT back to the Benz, started it up, and called Adams, the TBI investigator he'd spoken to on the phone. Adams was at home, babysitting for his wife, who was out with girlfriends. Lucas outlined the problem, and Adams said, "You could go into the house without a warrant, on the basis of a neighbor's legitimate statement of concern . . . but . . . jeez, I can't leave right now. I'm stuck here with the kids. I could call the office and see if we could get a couple guys down there."

Lucas remembered the two highway patrolmen and suggested that he call one of them. "One of them said he lives out here, so he's probably close by."

"That'd work," Adams said. "They're authorized to do anything we do."

Lucas found the patrolmen's cards and called the short one, whose name was Manny Dean.

"Manny? This is Davenport, the marshal you talked to earlier today."

"Oh, yeah. What's up, man?"

Lucas gave him a quick summary, and Dean said, "I can be there in fifteen minutes. Gotta put some pants on. Meet you out front."

LUCAS WENT back to the Poole house. Under the nervous eyes of the woman across the street, he rang the bell again and knocked for a while, but got no response. Dean showed up, wearing civilian clothes but driving his patrol car. He got out with a flashlight and asked, "Nothing?"

"Nothing. Let's see what we can see."

The drapes had been pulled on the front picture window, so they went around the house to the master bedroom and guest bedroom, where the drapes were open, but both bedrooms appeared to be unoccupied. There was a tiny porch on the back of the house, leading into a kitchen. Dean shone his light through the window, looked around, stepped back, frowned, went back to the window, and said, "Hey."

Lucas was on the burnt-out lawn, looking up: "See something?"

"C'mere. Right over there by the archway going to the front . . . is that a leg?" Dean asked. "There's no body or anything, but . . . is that a leg going across there? Could be a rolled-up piece of carpet, I guess, but it kinda looks like a leg."

Lucas looked, then turned and said, "You got a tire iron in your car?"

"Yeah, and a crowbar."

"I think it's a leg. We may be too late, but we gotta go in."

*   *   *

THEY WENT through the front door. Dean cracked it with the crowbar and Lucas pushed the door open with a knuckle and the smell of death hit them. Lucas turned and said, "Don't touch *anything*."

The house was dark and Lucas shone Dean's flashlight across the living room: a man was lying on the floor, his head propped up against an eighties stereo cabinet, a short-barreled revolver lying on the floor a yard or so from his right hand. There was a bullet hole in his forehead. Scanning across the room, Lucas spotlighted a woman's body, which had been cut into pieces, fingers, thumbs, both feet, one hand . . . at which point she must have died from shock, before the torturers could get the other hand. They'd quit there, leaving her on a blood-soaked shag carpet.

Dean said, "That's not something you see on a routine basis."

Lucas glanced at him: "If you're gonna barf, do it outside."

Dean said, "I got a hundred automobile accidents a year. Blood doesn't bother me none, not anymore."

"Okay. Let's get the local cops over here and the TBI," Lucas said. "Back out—you get the locals, I'll call my guy at the TBI."

More cops began arriving within five minutes of the call. First the local cops, then the sheriff's deputies, and finally, a TBI investigator named Lawrence Post.

Post looked over the scene, asked the La Vergne cops to set up a perimeter, and got a crime scene crew moving. He took Lucas aside and asked, "What's going on?"

Lucas filled him in on Garvin Poole, and added, "I think the cartel wants its money back."

"If that's Miz Poole in there, she must've told them everything she knew."

"Maybe. I've got more bad news—Gar Poole has a sister who lives not too far from here, near a place called Beech Grove. She and her husband run a salvage yard . . . I got the details in my briefcase."

"We better get some people over there."

"It's not too far," Lucas said. "I want to walk through here when you've finished processing it, but I'm going to run down there now. That'll be faster than calling in somebody who doesn't know what's going on."

Dean had drifted up during the conversation and said, "I'm coming with you. I've got nothing to do here and I got lights and a siren."

"Let's go," Lucas said. He got his briefcase from the car and pulled out the paper on Poole's sister, Natalie Parker, and read the relevant bits to Dean.

"Hey, I know them. Hardworking, but not entirely on the right side of the law," Dean said. "They've been known to chop a car, now and then. How do you want to do this?"

LUCAS GOT his iPad from his truck and called up a satellite image of the Parker salvage yard. The yard covered several acres, with three buildings facing the road. The structure farthest down the road, Dean said, was the Parker residence. There were two buildings at the front of the yard—a small office building and a much larger Quonset hut. Dean thought the Quonset hut was a workshop, though he'd never been inside. "I've seen welding torches when I've gone by."

Lucas touched the iPad screen: "We'll park here by this creek, go in on foot."

"You think the drug guys could be there?"

"Don't know. The Pooles haven't been dead all that long—probably killed this morning, or maybe late last night, just on the basis of my nose. Whoever killed them probably isn't far away. I wouldn't want to guess wrong about them being at the Parkers' place."

Dean's eyes drifted back to the Poole house: "Got it."

6

LUCAS AND DEAN made it to the Parker salvage yard in twenty-five minutes, Dean leading with lights but no siren. Off the interstate, they threaded through a maze of rural blacktopped roads, almost like city alleys with trees tight on both sides, with Dean finally coasting to the shoulder. Lucas parked behind him; he could see lights a few hundred yards away, filtering through the roadside brush.

They got out into the night, eased their car doors shut, locked them. Lucas had a miniature LED flashlight in one hand and his non-regulation .45 in the other. They scuffled two hundred yards down the middle of the beat-up blacktop road; there was no traffic at all. The darkness was thick around them; they couldn't see their own feet but Lucas didn't want to use the flash. They could smell water weeds from a roadside creek, and cut grass and oil from the yard; mosquitoes whined past their ears as they walked.

At the salvage yard, they walked down the drive into a little more light, checked the office, which appeared to be empty. There were lights in the Quonset, and Lucas said, "Stay behind me, but don't shoot me in the back."

"That'd be embarrassing as hell," Dean whispered. He was nervous, his heavy revolver pointed straight up. " 'Course, you *are* a Yankee, I probably wouldn't actually get fired."

"Shhh . . ."

They walked around the office and back to the Quonset. An overhead pole light cast an orange sodium vapor glow, giving the leaves from a nearby cottonwood a weird flickering black glow.

As they approached the Quonset, Lucas held a finger up to Dean's face, stopping him, and he stepped sideways to a small square window and looked in. A woman and two men were working around what look like a new Corvette, under bright lights, pulling apart the front end.

He watched for a moment, as the three were apparently arguing about how to dismantle the front fender. Lucas cricked a finger at Dean, who stepped up and looked in for a second or two, then stepped back, whispering to himself. He caught Lucas's jacket sleeve and tugged him away.

"Back to the car," he whispered. Lucas followed him around the office building again and then Dean started jogging back toward their cars. When they got there, Dean pointed at the passenger side, got in the patrol car, and Lucas got in beside him. Dean was on his radio; he'd memorized the tag on the Corvette and asked that it be checked. His dispatcher came back a moment later and said, "It's on the list, Manny. Belongs to a dentist, got taken out of his parking lot between three and four o'clock this afternoon. The engine alone is worth five grand. You got it?"

"Yeah, and there's a lot more going on, too. We could use some help down here. Call the sheriff's office and tell them to meet us at the Confederate Cemetery."

Off the radio, Dean said to Lucas, "The drug guys haven't found them yet—if that's what's going on. But they're chopping that Corvette. That could give us some weight when it comes to getting Natalie to talk about her brother."

"When you're right, you're right," Lucas said.

THEY DID U-TURNS on the road and Dean led the way to the edge of the town, where he pulled to the shoulder. Lucas turned in behind him and they both got out.

Dean said, "I'm starting to like this detecting shit. Tell the truth, I'm surprised that the drug guys haven't found them. They're supposed to be, like, you know, all-seeing."

"They're not. They're a bunch of jumped-up gang guys, half of them can't even read," Lucas said. "They're not the FBI. They don't have the computer backup, the crime files. That's why they had to cut up Mrs. Poole."

"Then how'd they get onto the Pooles in the first place?"

"The Mississippi cops think Poole was involved in that robbery," Lucas said. "I heard about it from a marshal in St. Louis and we didn't have anything to do with the investigation. I suspect the drug guys may have some contacts who told them about it."

"You mean . . . among cops?"

"Yeah. Among cops," Lucas said.

"Well, that sucks," Dean said.

"It does."

Dean thought about it for a moment, then said, "I can't believe Miz Poole didn't tell them about Natalie."

"That's the problem with torture—people lie, and there's no way to tell when they're doing it," Lucas said.

"If she loved her daughter . . . and she had to know that they were going to kill her, no matter what she said. They'd already killed her husband."

"Tell me how you know that."

"He had a hideout gun in the house, probably right there in the living room," Lucas said. "He grabbed it and they had to shoot him. Otherwise, they'd have taken him apart like they did his wife. He got lucky, I guess."

"Not the kind of luck you hope for," Dean said.

"No, it's not."

A SHERIFF'S CAR pulled off the main road, did a U-turn, and pulled up next to Lucas and Dean. The deputy inside the car dropped the passenger-side window and asked, "You here for the goat fuck?"

Five minutes later another deputy and another highway patrolman had shown up, and the whole group was bent over Lucas's iPad, which was sitting on the hood of one of the patrol cars. "Manny and I have been down there, so we'll lead, and we'll try to get around behind that Quonset hut," Lucas said, tapping the screen. "There's gonna be a door back there. We'll pick up anyone trying to run."

"Think we got enough guys?" one of the deputies asked.

The patrolman said, "As long as they don't got a machine gun."

"In case of that, we ought to let the marshal lead," the first deputy drawled. "I've volunteered to hang back so I can call for help, if needed."

TEN MINUTES LATER they were all parked on the side of the road, where Lucas and Dean had parked on the first approach. Lucas and Dean led off, while the rest of the cops waited in their cars. Nothing had changed at the salvage yard: no lights in the office, voices from the Quonset hut. Lucas and Dean went down the right side of the building; there were no windows on the side and Lucas risked using his LED light. As they walked over truck-rutted ground, a dog started to bark inside.

Lucas muttered, "Big dog."

Dean got on his radio and said, "Y'all better come. There's a big dog down here . . ." As he said it, another dog started barking from the junkyard. "Make that two big dogs . . ."

"On the way . . ."

They were behind the Quonset, where a narrow windowless door was set in the back wall. They positioned themselves on either side of the door as headlights flooded the road and then the first of the cop cars swung into the yard, continuing on until the car's bumper was nearly at the Quonset's front door.

Lucas and Dean couldn't see that, but they could hear it, the doors popping open and slamming, and they could hear a woman shouting inside and the big dog began barking hysterically, which set off the other big dog, which was apparently behind a fence. A few seconds later, a thin freckled man burst through the back door.

Lucas hit him in the eyes with the flash and simultaneously stuck out a foot. The man tripped and fell facedown in the dirt, and Dean slammed the door and said, "Don't you dare get up, Jimmy."

The freckled man rolled onto his back, Lucas's light still in his eyes, and said, "Is that you, Manny?"

"Yeah, it is. You steal that Blingray, Jimmy? Probably did, you dummy. Gonna make that dentist cry a river if you already cut it up. C'mon, roll over on your stomach, let me see those wrists, you know what we're doing here."

Lucas said, "You're acquainted."

Dean said, "Oh, yeah. Jimmy here spent more time in the county jail than most of the jailers."

"It ain't like I enjoy it," Jimmy grumbled. He rolled over on his stomach and lifted his wrists so Dean could cuff him.

Lucas pulled open the back door and he and Dean marched Jimmy into the Quonset, where the troopers and deputies were looking at Ralph and Natalie Parker, who were sitting on an old church pew. A gray-muzzled German shepherd sat unleashed between them, and Natalie Parker was stroking his head with one hand and holding a toddler with the other.

Ralph Parker, a stocky, red-faced man with a pompadour, had been handcuffed, but Natalie hadn't been. The toddler, who was looking solemnly at all the cops, was teary but not quite crying. The place smelled of welding torches and engine oil.

One of the deputies crooked a finger at Lucas and they went off to a corner and the deputy asked, "What do you want to do?"

"As I see it, if this car was stolen, you gotta take Parker in. And this Jimmy guy probably stole it. You could take Natalie in or leave her with the kid. Leaving her with the kid is probably the best idea, even if she knew her old man was running a chop shop, because somebody's got to take care of the boy, and he looks like he's pretty well taken care of."

"That's my idea," the deputy said. "I thought you might want to talk to her about her brother, while she doesn't know what we're thinking about doing with her. Maybe you could tell her about the Pooles."

Lucas grimaced. "Oh, boy. Okay. Let's walk her over to the office, talk to her there."

*   *   *

THEY DID THAT. Ralph Parker called to his wife, as they separated them, "Don't say nothing, Nat. Wait till we get Comfort over here."

Comfort, the deputy said, as they left the Quonset, was a lawyer, but not a very good one.

IN THE OFFICE, Lucas and the deputy put Natalie in the single office swivel chair, still holding on to the toddler, who now was as silent as a cat, and pulled two other wooden chairs around to face her. Lucas said, "Natalie, the cops back there have read you your rights, so you know you don't have to talk to us. But you need to . . ."

She put her hands over the toddler's ears: "Fuck that," she said.

Lucas tried to take it easy: "You don't have all the information you need, and that information is really bad. Really, really bad."

Natalie Parker was a lean, auburn-haired woman, pretty without makeup, wearing jeans and a plaid cotton shirt. She looked uncertainly at Lucas's face, then said, "What happened? Did something happen?"

Lucas said, "We think your brother Gar and some other people robbed a drug counting house and killed five people. This was last week . . ."

"I don't have anything to do . . ."

Lucas held up a finger to silence her, and continued. ". . . The drug people have come looking for their money. That's what we think. They started with your parents."

Parker went pale: "They didn't hurt them?"

"I'm afraid they did," Lucas said.

"Did they kill them?"

"Yes. We found them an hour ago," Lucas said. "That's why we came down here. We were afraid your mom might have given up your location."

Parker squeezed the toddler tight, said, "That god-damn Gar. He had to go and rob some drug guys, didn't he? He just had to go and do it." She put her face into the kid's neck and she started to cry, and then the kid started to cry, and he looked at Lucas and the deputy with open fear. Lucas and the deputy sat for a moment, saying nothing, and then the deputy said, "Why don't you hand me that boy, there? I'll hold him for you."

The deputy took the kid, who struggled a bit before settling down, the deputy patting him on the back, and Natalie said, "I gotta tell Ralph. Let me talk to Ralph."

"I'll see if they're still here," Lucas said.

RALPH PARKER was still in the Quonset and Lucas got Dean to bring Parker out and uncuff him, and Lucas told him what had happened and Parker wrapped up his wife and held her for a while, but told Lucas, "We don't none of us know where Gar is. If we did, and we told you, he'd come here and kill us. That ain't no foolin'. He'd cut our throats in one New York minute."

LUCAS AND THE DEPUTY took Natalie back to the office, sat her down again, the deputy still holding the kid. Lucas said, "I'm a U.S. marshal and I'm looking for your brother. If you cooperate, Gar will never know. If the local DA decides to charge you in this car thing, I will speak privately to the judge in your case and tell him that you cooperated in something a lot more important than a car theft. I think that could keep you out of jail and with your boy. Furthermore, given what we know now, I think we might save the lives of some of your friends."

"How is that?"

"We don't know how much money Gar stole, but it

was probably a lot. Maybe millions of dollars," Lucas said. "These drug killers are not going to stop looking for him, not until they've done everything they can to get it back and punish the robbers. They've got to do that as a warning to anyone else who might try to rip them off. They figure the same way I do—somebody around here, one of Gar's relatives or old friends, will know how to get in touch with him. Once they get that connection, they can find him."

Natalie Parker's face hardened; she didn't have any love left for her brother: "I'll tell you the same thing that Ralph did," she said. "If Gar found out I talked to you, he'd cut my throat. You know his girlfriend cut off a man's head one time? And that was just over a few dollars owed."

"I heard that, about Dora," Lucas said. "I have no interest in you, Natalie. I don't have much interest in Ralph, either, but he's in the hands of the local law, now. I think we might arrange things so that you can stay with your boy and not have to go to jail tonight. I'm going to need your help to get that done, though."

Sullen, still breaking down from time to time, she reached out and took her son back on her lap, cupped her hands over the boy's ears, and said, "You lawmen can be real fuckin' assholes, you know that?"

"Wasn't us who killed your parents," the deputy said. "Wasn't us who was out there cutting some honest man's stolen car into pieces."

"Yeah, well, fuck you, anyway," she said. She took her hands away from the boy's ears and said to Lucas, "I'll tell you what I know, but it ain't much."

"I CAN'T TELL YOU where Gar is," Natalie said. "My folks had cops coming around a couple times a year, asking that, like we'd know. Garvin left home when he was sixteen and we haven't seen much of him since and not at all for the last five years, ever since they said he did that thing in Chattanooga—not like they ever proved anything."

Although she hadn't seen Gar Poole for five or six years, she had seen Dora Box, two years earlier at Box's uncle's funeral.

"I was kinda spooked, because we knew that she was probably still with Garvin and we knew the police were looking for her, too. She didn't stay long—didn't come to the church, just come out to the cemetery and threw some dirt on the coffin, cried a bit, and went on her way. Her mom and pop passed away earlier, so she's the last of that line."

She explained that Box's parents and her uncle had once lived in adjacent houses, not far down the street from her parents, which was how Box and Poole first connected in high school, and how the Pooles got to know them. Box's mother had died of breast cancer ten years earlier and her father had sold the house and rented an apartment in Nashville, and died a few years later of debilitation related to alcohol and drug abuse. She'd gone to those funerals, too.

"Who would have called Dora Box to tell her that her uncle died?" Lucas asked.

"That's a puzzle," Natalie said. "Dora don't have any relatives left, to speak of. There were about ten or twelve people at the funeral—I guess it would have been one of them. Her uncle wasn't a famous man, though somebody paid for an obituary in the local shopper newspaper, 'cause I saw it there. Could have been somebody who saw the notice."

Lucas made a note: find out who was at the funeral and who paid for the obituary.

"What about Gar? He must have a few friends . . ."

She was shaking her head. "Not around here. He used to fight in school, didn't have anybody real close. There was a guy named Jim Jacobs who came over a couple of times—he was in my class, so he was two years younger than Gar, but they both liked cars. I don't know where he lives anymore. Gar knew some bad people that he met in reform school, but he didn't bring them around. Then when he got caught robbing that music place . . . that's where he was gone from us. We didn't know either of those guys he was caught with. Never heard of them. He'd moved away from us. We were stick-in-the-muds. He wanted fast women, fast cars, and all that."

"Dora was a fast woman?"

Natalie rubbed her nose, then said, "You know, I don't know how that came about. She went to school with us, too, but her and Gar never got together until, well, must have been ten years later. She was popular in school, she was the homecoming queen. Then she got married to her high school boyfriend, he was a big popular guy, too. That lasted about three or four years, then they got divorced, and she was selling retail for a while . . . never went to college, or anything—everybody thought she would."

"You knew her pretty well?"

"No . . . She lived down the street from us. I wasn't one of the popular kids, though, so we hung out with different people. We'd stop to say hello, like that, if we ran into each other after graduation. I think that homecoming queen business . . . I think she thought that she was all set up for an exciting life and it didn't turn out that way. She had to go to work in a Sherwin-Williams paint store. Gar changed that, he was all about excitement."

Gar didn't have other long-term girlfriends she knew about. He'd had that reputation for violence in high school. Not just for being tough, but maybe a little crazy. Later on, when he'd come by the house after his prison term, he sometimes had women with him, but she didn't remember any names. "It was a different woman, every time, until Dora. I think Gar kinda got off on the idea of going out with a homecoming queen. You know, everything in life is still about high school. Then again, there was some things said about Dora . . ."

"Like . . . ?"

"She did like men, but I heard she also liked women, and sometimes she'd treat Gar to a two-fer," Natalie said. "That's something Gar would like. A lot. He was always sort of a hound. Anyway, that two-fer business, that was a rumor—I never asked Gar about it, or nothing."

IN THE END, Lucas got a half dozen names that Natalie didn't think would produce anything useful, plus the name of the Baptist church where Dora Box's uncle's funeral was held.

One of the sheriff's deputies talked to the relevant local prosecutor, who agreed that Natalie Parker should be left with her son, but that she should be told she was still liable for any of her criminal activities.

Ralph Parker and Jimmy were taken to the county jail, and Lucas headed back to the motel to think about his next move and get some sleep.

7

SOTO AND KORT left the Nashville hotel at six o'clock the next morning, Soto's pistol tucked under the front seat, Kort's tool kit sitting behind the backseat, along with a clipboard with some magazine pages clipped to it. Kort could feel her heart thumping as they headed south on the interstate: the power flowing through her nerves caused her to tremble with something like desire.

Soto, on the other hand, grew quieter and colder. He said, "Remember the move—hit her, slide sideways to let me in, you slam the door."

"I got it, I got it," Kort said.

THEY'D HIT Poole's parents the night before last, and the results had been disappointing. They had gotten to the Pooles' suburban house well before nine o'clock, cruised it twice, looking for eyes, then parked in the street in front of the house.

Kort had led the way to the porch, carrying her clipboard. Unlike most clipboards, which are made from lightweight fiberboard, Kort's was handmade from quarter-inch steel plate. After a final check, Soto had leaned against the front wall of the house, while Kort said, "Here we go," and rang the doorbell.

Margery Poole came to the door a few seconds later, a frown on her face. By Nashville suburban standards, it was late for an unexpected visit.

She saw Kort with the clipboard, asked, "Yes?" and Kort lifted up the steel sheet and whacked Margery Poole in the face. Poole flew backward into a short hallway that led to the living room, where her husband was watching a ball game.

Kort stepped aside as soon as Poole went down, a move they'd choreographed, and Soto went past her with the gun up. Kort moved inside and slammed the door. Soto went to the living room, where Kevin Poole was halfway out of his easy chair, and when he saw Soto's gun, he went sideways toward a magazine shelf and stuck his hand in and before Soto could say a thing, his hand came back out with a revolver in it and Soto had no choice but to shoot him in the head.

Kort said, "What?"

"He had a gun," Soto said. "What about the missus?"

"Shit. Couldn't you have shot him in the hand or something? Be a lot better if we had two of them."

"You don't fuck around when the other guy's got a gun," Soto said. The expert talking.

What was done, was done. They dragged Margery Poole into the living room and went to work on her.

*.   *   *

CUTTING UP Margery Poole had been entertaining, but they had gotten only one name they thought might be worthwhile. That name was John Stiner, who, like Poole, was another man on the run. They didn't know where he was, but that was what the College-Sounding Guy did.

Twenty hours later, the College-Sounding Guy called Soto with a name: he didn't know where Stiner was but he'd located Stiner's sister, Marilyn Campbell, wife of a hardware store owner in Franklin, Tennessee, farther down south of Nashville.

Soto called Kort and told her they'd be starting very early the next morning.

THE CAMPBELLS lived in a faux-historic Americana white frame house, with pillars, on West Main, with a broad green yard. Kort and Soto were outside the house early enough to see Andy Campbell leave for the store. Any kids should have already left for school, which meant that Marilyn Campbell should be alone in the house.

"What do you think?" Kort asked.

"There's quite a few cars going by, so make sure you get right on top of her," Soto said. "As soon as she goes down, I'll be right behind."

"Bring my tool kit."

MARILYN CAMPBELL opened the screen door to an ungainly young woman standing on the porch with a clipboard. She said, "Can I help you?"

"I hope so. Could I speak to a Mr. Andrew Campbell?"

"Andy's not here right now . . ."

"Good," Kort said. A half second after Campbell realized the woman was wearing plastic kitchen gloves, Kort slammed the steel-plate clipboard into Campbell's face.

Campbell, stunned, blinded, her nose broken, went down on the floor, on her back, and Soto was around the corner and up the porch steps and on top of her. After Kort slammed the door, they dragged her, still stunned but screaming now, blood coming out of her mouth.

Soto slapped her hard, with an open hand, once, twice, three times, screaming, "Shut up, bitch, shut up bitch . . ." and then flipped her onto her stomach and pulled her arms around behind her, and Kort wrapped her wrists with duct tape.

Soto said to Kort, "I'll run the house." He took out his pistol and jogged through the first floor, then up the stairs to the second floor. There were four bedrooms and a home office on the second floor. The master bedroom was empty, and so were two others, one apparently a schoolgirl's room, with stuffed animals and a quickly made bed, and the other a boy's room, with soccer gear littering the floor, and the bed a mass of tangled blankets and sheets.

The last bedroom was a guest room, neat and untouched, with an empty smell about it. Soto ran back down the stairs.

Kort asked, "We clear?"

"We're clear."

Kort was straddling Campbell's back and now she grabbed the other woman's hair and slammed her face into the floor hard enough to break her nose all over again, and shouted, "Where's your brother, bitch? Where's John? We know you know . . ."

"No, no, no, no . . ." Campbell was facedown in a puddle of blood.

"Gonna cut your foot off. Gonna cut you to pieces, and start with your foot . . ."

Soto had brought a canvas tool satchel through the door with him. Now he went to it and asked Kort, "How you want to start?"

Campbell screamed again and Kort smashed her face into the floor a few more times, and said, "Give me the DeWalt and the tie-off."

Kort knelt one knee on Campbell's back and said to her, "We're gonna explain here. We need that information, where John is right now. We need a phone number, we need an address. You don't tell us, we're gonna start by cutting off your foot, and we ain't giving you another chance . . ."

As he spoke, Soto was cinching a tourniquet around Campbell's right foot. Campbell screeched, "Don't know, don't know . . ."

"All right, let's do it the hard way," Kort said, and she pressed one of Campbell's legs to the floor and began sawing off her right foot.

CAMPBELL NOW WAILED like a fire engine, a long screech that quavered but never quit, and was one reason that neither Soto nor Kort detected the fly in the ointment, which arrived in the form of eleven-year-old Douglas Campbell, who'd been lying asleep, sick and mildly feverish, in his second-floor bedroom.

When Soto and Kort came through the front door and his mother began screaming, Doug woke, disoriented by the screams; but then he recognized quickly enough what they were, that something dangerous was happening, and heard somebody running up the stairs. He rolled off the bed and lay between the bed and the wall. Somebody ran down the hallway, stopped outside the door, then went on, and finally, back down the stairs.

When he was sure the intruder was gone, Doug crept

out of the bedroom and down the hallway to a balcony over the living room, where he peeked around a banister and saw his mother facedown in a lot of blood, and a man tying a rope around her ankle.

Doug dropped to his knees, then his belly, and slipped on down the hall to his parents' bedroom, where he got the Ruger 10/22 rifle out of his father's closet. He'd shot it with some regularity since he turned six, under his father's strict eye. His father kept two extended magazines separate from the rifle, stuffed into cowboy boots at the back of the closet. They were hidden as a precaution for when the cousins came over, which they did a couple of times a week. The cousins were a rough bunch, and if they'd found a loaded rifle in the closet, they'd be shooting the place up, and maybe each other, bigger than shit.

Doug was more responsible and so knew about the magazines. He got them from the boots, punched one into place in the rifle, put the other in the back of his Jockey shorts, jacked a round into the chamber, reminded himself about the safety, clicked it off, and walked back to the balcony.

He didn't know that he should have simply opened fire. He only knew about shooting people from movies, so he poked the rifle over the banister and shouted, "STOP THAT!" and *then* he opened fire.

The genuine Ruger 10/22 extended magazine held twenty-five rounds of high-speed .22s. Kort and Soto lurched sideways when Doug screamed, and one second later, the .22 slugs were flying around them like so many bees as they scrambled for the door.

Kort made the mistake of slowing to grab the tool satchel and felt one of the slugs slap her across the butt and then they were tumbling across the porch and into the yard and *still* the bullets didn't stop. Soto pulled his holstered Sig and said, "I think it's a kid . . ."

But Kort groaned, "I been shot . . ."

"How bad?"

"Hit in the hip, in the hip . . ."

They were in the yard, thirty yards from the door, when Doug stepped onto the porch with the rifle. Soto yanked his Sig up, way too fast for accuracy, did a little calming thing he'd trained himself to do, and was drawing down on the kid's chest when a .22 slug slapped past his ear, so close he could feel the breeze. He flinched, yanked on the pistol's trigger, knew it was way off target, saw the kid drop the rifle magazine and punch in a fresh one, long as a banana, and Kort screamed and they piled into the car, with .22 bullets banging through and ricocheting off the doors, fenders, and window glass.

They sped away, straight down West Main, and the kid didn't stop shooting at them until they were a hundred yards up the road and he'd run out of ammo.

THE CAR was a rental, but there was no possibility of taking it back to Avis with all the bullet holes and dents in it. They'd rented it with fake IDs, so that wasn't a problem. Knowing that the cops would be looking for them within a few minutes, they took a snaky route across town, Kort screaming with pain: "Jesus, slow down, slow down, take it easy, you're killing me . . ."

She eventually knelt on the front seat, because she couldn't bear to sit on it. Once on I-65, they stayed in the slow lane, because the bullet-pocked doors were on the passenger side. On the highway, their car was no longer distinctive—another one of about a billion Toyotas.

They'd taken rooms at a Super 8, where they also had the second car. The motel had been chosen because it was old-fashioned, with room doors opening directly onto the parking lot, so they'd never have to walk through a lobby. Soto let Kort out and as she waddled painfully into her room, he parked the bullet-marked side of the car close enough to their second car that nobody would likely walk between them and see the bullet marks.

He glanced around—nobody paying attention to him—and then took a closer look at the side panels on the car. Three bullets had gone through the trunk and four through the back fender on the passenger side, and one through the glass in the back window. Two more had bounced off the side of the car, and one off the window glass. He couldn't believe neither he nor Kort had been hit in the car, but the kid had been shooting too low and at too much of an angle.

He collected everything from the car—water and Pepsi bottles, wrappers from a couple of Hostess cupcakes and three Slim Jims, and a *Walking Dead* comic book, anything they might have touched with bare fingers—and followed Kort into her room. She was in the bathroom, naked from the waist down, and said, as he came in, "I can't see anything—you're going to have to look at my ass."

Not an inviting prospect, but had to be done. Either that, or kill her. He thought about it. He could tell their employers that she'd been mortally wounded and he'd had to bury her body in the woods. They'd probably believe him. On the other hand, they might send another Kort-type to talk to him about it. He decided not to kill her. Not immediately, anyway. He really did hate the bitch.

"It's killing me," Kort moaned. "Help me, you fuckin' moron."

Soto pulled a washcloth off the rack in the bathroom, soaked it in the sink and squeezed out the excess water, and said, "Lay down on the bed."

She did and he used the washcloth to wipe away a lot

of blood and took a look, a memory he wouldn't cherish. "Went through one cheek, across your butt crack, and into the other cheek but not through. I think I can see it. There's a black bump below the skin." Purple blood was seeping from the three wounds.

"Where? Put your finger on it."

Soto put his finger on the bump and Kort reached back and felt the bump, kneading it, and said, "It's the bullet. You gotta get it out."

"Ah, man, how am I supposed to do that?" Soto asked.

"Knife," she said.

"I *got* a knife," he said.

BEFORE HE OPERATED, he walked out to a Walgreens drugstore and bought a bottle of alcohol, a box of extra-large medicated Band-Aids, a roll of extra-wide surgical tape, a bottle of Aleve, a tube of Neosporin, and, almost an afterthought, a pack of single-edge razor blades, which he guessed would work better than his knife. Back at the motel, Kort was still lying on the bed. Soto looked at her butt, shook his head, took one of the razor blades out of the pack, poured some alcohol over it, and said, "This is gonna hurt."

"It already hurts. Just fuckin' do it, okay, dipshit? Do it. Gimme a wet wash rag, first. Not the dirty one, a fresh one."

He handed her a wet washcloth and she rolled it into a tube shape and bit down on it. Mumbled something that sounded like, "Go ahead."

Soto, with the razor blade in his hand, looked at several approaches—straight in, from the side, a kind of scalping move . . .

Kort spit the washcloth out and demanded, "What the fuck are you doing? What the fuck?"

"Trying to figure out the best way," Soto said. "I gotta tell you, your ass ain't the prettiest sight I've ever seen. Looks like two basketballs doing a revenge fuck."

"Fuck you."

"Put the cloth back in your mouth. I'm gonna cut."

Kort lay back down and Soto bunched up a layer of fat, with the slug at the top, like an unpopped pimple, and then with the corner of the razor blade, went straight in.

Kort screamed into the cloth, but Soto squeezed up the lump of yellow butt fat and the bullet popped out. So did a lot of blood, though the wound was small. Kort stopped screaming, spit the cloth out, and asked, "You get it?"

"Yeah, I did." He sounded pleased with himself. "You can wash the holes off yourself. Don't bother with the brown one in the middle."

"Fuck you, you asshole."

"Least I got only one," Soto said, cackling at his own joke.

Kort washed all four wounds with the alcohol, weeping as she did it, at both the pain and the humiliation. When the skin had dried, she squirted on some Neosporin, put the Band-Aids on, and then a strip of surgical tape, crossing the middle of the Band-Aids.

Soto was lying on the bed, reading the *Walking Dead* comic book. When she started digging in her suitcase for a clean pair of underpants, he asked, "All done?"

"Fuck you."

"You're still bleeding a little. Try not to get it on the sheets. We don't need any questions."

"Fuck you."

WHILE SHE got dressed, Soto went back in the bathroom to wash his hands with soap. Lots of soap.

"You know that kid?" Kort asked rhetorically, from the bedroom. "If I ever see that little fucker again, I'm gonna take him apart with my side-cutters. I ain't jokin', either."

"At least you saved the DeWalt," Soto said, referring to Kort's battery-powered saw. "That's a couple hundred bucks right there."

THAT NIGHT, they drove the two cars to an Ace Hardware store, where they bought a gas can, then out to a Mapco Mart, where they filled up the gas can, then back out to the country, where they hosed down the Camry and torched it.

As they drove away, with Kort lying on her side in the backseat, she asked, "You believe in that DNA shit?"

"Yeah, maybe. But anyway, even if it works, some guy told me that fire wipes it out," he said. "Smart guy, too. We got nothing to worry about."

By that time, the rental car looked like a firefly in the rearview mirror, burning hard a mile away.

8

THE MISSISSIPPI Bureau of Investigation had e-mailed Lucas a list of people who'd gone to the funeral of Dora Box's uncle, and he spent all morning and half of the afternoon driving around the south Nashville area, knocking on doors, doing interviews, getting nowhere, on a day that turned out to be too hot for a shoulder holster, gun, and sport coat.

The newspaper obituary, as it turned out, had been placed by the funeral home as a teaser offer for funeral services, so that lead was a dead end.

Most of the people at the funeral had at least known Box, if not well. One woman told him, "I believe that somebody who knew Dora, but didn't know Jack very well, heard about Jack's death and called her, but didn't bother to come to the funeral. I told the same thing to those officers from Mississippi. Wasn't anybody there, far as I know, who was good friends with Dora. She came alone and left alone, and I can't recall anyone even talking to her, other than maybe to nod or say hello."

That jibed with what Natalie Parker had told Lucas.

He'd worked his way through most of the funeral list when Lawrence Post called from the TBI at three o'clock in the afternoon. "We've probably got something on those people who killed the Pooles," Post said.

The TBI had taken a call from a county sheriff's office about a home invasion that had taken place early that morning in Franklin. The two invaders had tortured a woman by using a hacksaw on her leg.

"Her eleven-year-old son was in the house, they didn't know about him, he was sick and home from school. When he heard his mother screaming, he got his dad's gun and opened up on them," Post said. "We're looking at hospitals for gunshot wounds, but don't have anything that sounds good yet. We don't even know if they were hit."

Lucas asked, "You got anybody down there?"

"Crime scene support, but no investigator. The local cops have done a decent job of working through the possibilities. The two perpetrators were strangers to Miz Campbell, so it's not like we have to figure out which friend or enemy did it. They were asking about Miz Campbell's brother John, who used to run with Gar Poole. I'll e-mail you everything we got on John Stiner as soon as we get off the phone."

"The drug people got a lead from somewhere," Lucas said. "Maybe Miz Poole, before she died."

"Looks like it. And something else. This kid apparently shot up the car the perpetrators were in. It was only a .22, but the car's going to look like it was in a hailstorm, according to the sheriff," Post said. "He said the kid had two twenty-five-round magazines. He fired most of one magazine inside the house, but the other one he fired in the yard and at the car. It could have a couple of dozen bullet dings on it."

"Make and model?"

"Don't know. Small, red, probably Japanese. We've got people looking for it all over the state and all the surrounding states, so I think we'll probably find it," Post said. "I just can't tell you when."

"Tell me where I can find the Campbells," Lucas said. "I'm going down there."

MARILYN CAMPBELL was at the Williamson Medical Center in Franklin, a hospital-looking place of reddish brick and glass, and Lucas found Marilyn Campbell in a private room reading a women's golf magazine. A dark-haired, dark-eyed woman in her late thirties, she had black bruises across her face, one eye was swollen half closed with corduroy blood bruises around it. Her nose was covered with an aluminum brace, and one leg was wrapped in hard plastic and elevated. Lucas followed a nurse through the door and she looked over the magazine and asked, "Who are you?"

"I'm a federal marshal," Lucas said. "I'm looking for the people who hurt you, and also for your brother John and a man named Gar Poole, who set this whole thing off."

Her husband and son had gone to get something to eat, Campbell said, and would be back soon. She'd be happy to tell him about the attack, but confessed that she was still frightened.

"I keep flashing back to it," she said. "To that woman standing on the porch. I thought she was a Mormon or a Witness or something . . . maybe the gas company, she had a clipboard."

She told Lucas about the attack, in detail, descriptions

of the man and woman who'd attacked her, how the woman had hit her with the steel clipboard, talking faster and faster as she relived it, and the nurse took her hand and said, "We're getting a little excited here, let's slow down." Campbell said to Lucas, "*We're* getting excited. The doctors and nurses here keep saying that '*we*' thing. Isn't that weird?"

"Supposed to show empathy and that we're all in this together," the nurse said. "Of course I didn't get attacked."

"It is a little weird, though," Lucas said to the nurse. "I've been hurt a few times and it's always the *we* thing."

The nurse shrugged and grinned and said, "You'll learn to live with it. Couple days from now, you'll be saying '*Our* leg still hurts.'"

Campbell turned back to Lucas. "The doctors say the flashbacks will go away," she said. "What do *you* think?"

Lucas said, "Mostly. For most people. I was once shot right under the chin, by a little girl, and I would have died if somebody hadn't cut open my windpipe with a jackknife." He touched the scar on his neck. "That happened ten years ago. Right after I got out of the hospital, I'd relive the part where I saw the pistol coming up and then feeling the bullet hit. Now, I'll have moments when something will touch off a *memory* of it, but it's not the same as reliving it. When you relive it, you get the sweats and you can feel the adrenaline pouring into your blood and your heart starts beating hard . . . When you remember it, it's a picture in your mind, like an old movie. You're not reliving it. That's where I'm at now."

"You think that's where I'll get?" Campbell asked.

"Probably," Lucas said.

"You're not sure."

"No. I won't lie to you, I've seen people who relive bad moments forever . . . but that's rare," Lucas said.

"Really rare. If you've got a good healthy family around you, you'll be okay."

"What about Doug? He might have shot somebody."

"Can't help you with that," Lucas said. His daughter Letty had shot and killed people, but that was Letty, and Letty wasn't a typical naïve, well-protected kid. "I think it pretty much depends on the kid."

Lucas took a call from Lawrence Post at the TBI: "Told you we'd find that car. They drove it out in the woods and torched it. I'm told there's nothing left to see—apparently soaked it with gasoline and set it on fire. The chances of getting even a fingerprint are down around zero. The seats were incinerated, so we can't tell if there was any blood inside, if they were hit by a gunshot."

"Well, hell. The plates still on it?"

"Yeah, it's a rental, they got it here at the airport," Post said. "We should be able to get some video, so that might help. But I'm thinking not. Not unless they were dumb enough to go in without hats and sunglasses, and with their own credit cards."

"Gotta check," Lucas said.

"We will."

CAMPBELL'S HUSBAND, Andy, and her son, Doug, came back as Lucas was talking to Post, and when Lucas rang off, Marilyn introduced them. Andy, a tall, rawboned man with hard hands, asked, "You think they'll be back?"

"I doubt it. We're hot after them—we've got good descriptions, your son here shot up the car pretty good, and they know the cops will be keeping an eye on you." Lucas turned to the kid: "That was good work, by the way. Saved your mom's life, for sure."

Andy Campbell said, "I wish I'd been there. If they come back, I'll kill them."

Lucas shook his head: "Don't even try. These guys are professionals. No matter how good you are with a gun, these guys are probably better, and not only that, they are used to doing this kind of thing. Best thing you could do is get a steel-core door on a bedroom, keep a shotgun and a cell phone in there, and if there's even a hint of these people coming, get your family in there, lock and barricade the door, and call the cops. You really don't want to shoot it out with them. Too much can go wrong."

They talked about that for a while, the realities of gunfights and home invasions, and then moved on to the question of Marilyn's brother John.

"Marilyn still thinks that John is okay, but he isn't," Andy said. "He was a wrong one right from the start. I knew him in high school. Rest of the family was fine, but not John. From what I hear about Gar Poole, they are two of a kind."

"Some cops think Gar Poole may have killed more than a dozen innocent people, and God knows how many rivals," Lucas said to Marilyn Campbell. "He's killed eight people that we know of, including a little girl, whom he shot in cold blood. We need to stop him. If John ran with him, he'll know things that I need to know. I have to get in touch with him, right now."

Andy opened his mouth to say something, but Marilyn said, "When we talk, it's always one-way with John. He calls us from public phones. I don't know how to get in touch, not from my end."

Andy said, "For God's sakes, Marilyn . . ."

"I don't," she protested. "I used to know how to call him, but that phone hasn't been good for two or three years." She turned back to Lucas and said, "John has a straight job now. He got all messed up on drugs for a while, that's why he did some bad things. But he got off the drugs, he's trying to straighten himself out. He's not like Gar Poole—he's never killed anyone. I made him tell me and I know when he's lying."

Lucas got her to give up an old cell phone number for John Stiner, but she insisted that it no longer worked.

"What about the fact that these two people even found you?" Lucas asked. "Did you know Miz Poole?"

"I never met her—but I knew of her, her family, Gar and Natalie mostly."

"So she would have known of you," Lucas said.

"Yes."

"Can you think of anybody else she could have given up?" Lucas asked.

"Well, Natalie . . ."

"She didn't do that. Anyone else?"

She couldn't think of anyone.

THEIR SON, Doug, had taken a chair in a corner and had listened to the conversation, and when Marilyn Campbell said she had no more to give, Lucas turned to him and said, "Tell me what you did this morning."

"I'm still kinda scared," he said.

"That's normal. Sounds to me like you did a heck of a job," Lucas said.

Doug Campbell told about being awakened by his mother's screams, about rolling off the bed, about getting the gun, about loading up the rifle, about going to the balcony above the living room and opening up on the man and woman who were hurting his mother, and about chasing them out of the house and down the road.

Lucas: "They never fired a gun at you?"

Doug shook his head and said, "No . . ." but then touched his lips and said, "Oh my God. They did. I never thought about it—the guy shot his gun. I think, only one time."

"At you?"

Doug frowned. "Sort of at me. Didn't hit me or anything. Might have hit the house."

He didn't know for sure if he'd hit either of the killers, but thought he might have shot the woman in the butt. "She was trying to get away and I was tracking her with the gun, but I couldn't keep up, but this one shot, she sorta . . . jumped . . . and I think I might have hit her."

Andy reached over and scrubbed his kid on the head: "I'm proud of you, Dougie."

Marilyn jumped in: "You know what? I thought of another name . . . another person, anyway, who Margery Poole might have known." She looked at her husband and asked, "What was the name of that guy that came up to John's party, the guy from down in Alabama? The farmer guy with the cowboy hat? He had a nice wife, I remember. I think her name was Janice."

Andy turned his head to one side and squinted out the window, thinking, then said, "I can't . . . was it Steve?"

Marilyn shook her head. "Not Steve, but like that . . . it was something a little unusual." They stared at each other for a moment, then Andy snapped his fingers and said, "Sturgill? Was it Sturgill? Like the country singer?"

Marilyn pointed a finger at him: "Yes. I think it was. I don't remember his last name."

Andy said to Lucas, "John told us that Sturgill and Gar were 'asshole buddies.' Those were his words. He said that Sturgill had never been arrested for anything, though. He was more of a thinker."

Lucas thought, *Ah*.

He needed to talk with Sturgill.

*   *   *

A COUPLE OF MINUTES LATER, a Franklin deputy chief showed up and introduced himself as Chuck Lamy, the head of the Criminal Investigation Division. He said to Lucas, "We oughta talk, if you got a minute."

"I'm pretty much done here," Lucas said. "Let's find a place to sit."

MARILYN CAMPBELL had told him that her leg had been stabilized by an orthopod when she came into the emergency room that morning, but that she'd be undergoing another procedure in the next day or two to repair her lower leg bone. She wouldn't be back home for several days.

Lucas said good-bye, and Lamy led him to the hospital café, where they got coffee. As they sat down, Lucas said, "Before we do anything else . . . would I talk to you or the TBI about getting a pen register on Miz Campbell's room phone?"

"We can do that, if you tell me why," Lamy said.

Lucas explained about her brother John. "I could see the way that Andy was acting that Marilyn knows how to get in touch with him. She's going to do that. I suspect she'll wait until her husband and the kid are out of the way. I don't think she'll use her cell phone, and she can't get out of bed."

"Let me make a call," Lamy said, and he went off to do it. A pen register would only give them the phone numbers called from the phone, but that was much easier to get approved than the search warrant needed for a full phone tap.

Lamy came back ten minutes later and said, "We're getting it done. Now, tell me everything. What in the hell is a federal marshal doing down here?"

Lucas outlined the situation, and Lamy said, "So you

got two sets of maniacs chasing each other around the countryside."

"That's about it," Lucas said. "In a nutshell, so to speak."

BY THE TIME Lucas and Lamy had finished talking, it was nearly six o'clock. Lamy said they'd have hospital security watching Campbell's room and they'd have a squad car make a direct check of the Campbells' house every half hour or so for the next couple of days.

Lucas got a recommendation for a motel, found it on his iPad, off I-65, wandered through a California-style outdoor shopping area, looking for food, wound up at a steakhouse, and had a decent steak. Back at the motel, he called Weather and they talked for a while, and he told her about the attack on Marilyn Campbell.

She had no trouble imagining people as bad as the attackers: she'd encountered some very bad people since marrying Lucas. Before they hung up, though, she said, "Don't forget."

"I'm careful."

"But are you enjoying yourself?"

"Hey . . ."

"I know. You wouldn't admit it, because it doesn't seem . . . normal. But you are, aren't you?"

"Maybe," Lucas said, smiling into the phone. "Progress has been a little slow so far, but it's picking up. Yeah. It's getting interesting."

THERE WAS not much in the way of football on television, so he read through his Gar Poole files, including known associates—nobody named Sturgill—and then caught a movie.

The movie was old—the Coen brothers' *Burn After Reading*. He'd seen it before, so it gave him some space to think as he watched.

One thing he thought about was the difference between his new job and his old one. He'd already realized that he was now a small fish swimming in the ocean—and now, he thought, he hadn't realized how different the various parts of the ocean might be.

He didn't know Tennessee or any of the territory worked by the Dixie Hicks. The culture was different, attitudes toward cops were different, and even the food was strange. He'd already crossed grits, collard greens, okra, and black-eyed peas off his menu possibilities, and suspected he'd find others.

There were more guns around than in Minnesota—two cold-blooded killers had been chased off their target that morning by a grade-school kid who had access to a gun and knew how to use it, and was *willing* to use it. The last time he'd looked, less than four percent of the Minnesota population was licensed for concealed carry. In Alabama, twelve percent of the population was licensed for concealed carry, a half million permits, more than twice as many as in Minnesota, with a smaller population.

He didn't know if that was good or bad: concealed-carry people actually committed fewer felonies per year than cops did . . . Still, the mid-South and South had a gun culture stronger than Minnesota's, which he'd always considered pretty tough.

If he stayed with the Marshals Service, in his current job, he might find himself working in the Pacific Northwest, New England, the desert Southwest . . . it was going to be strange. Even unnerving; part of him was looking forward to it. Part of him was already missing Weather and the kids, on his third night alone.

He went to sleep thinking about grits and especially okra. Who in God's name was the first guy to stick an okra in his mouth? Must have been a brave man, or starving to death . . .

Lamy called him at eight o'clock the next morning. "Miz Campbell made one call, to a phone we don't know. Looks like it's down in Orlando, Florida."

"Wonderful," Lucas said.

9

LUCAS GOT a late morning flight out of Nashville to Orlando on Southwest Airlines. As he was driving to the airport, he called Russell Forte, his contact in the Washington office, and gave him a full report.

"We'll look at the phone right now," Forte said. "Your tickets will be waiting for you when you get to the airport."

"Hope there's space," Lucas said.

Forte laughed: "There's always space, if you're the federal government."

And there was: Lucas checked his bag, collected his tickets, and while he was waiting in the gate at the airport, he got a call back from Forte: "We don't know that phone. Either doesn't have a GPS or the GPS is turned off. It's almost certainly a burner, and it's used only rarely, a couple times a month. We've got a list of numbers that the owner's called and we can tell you that the outgoing calls have been made from Orlando Fashion Square. He probably lives around there, and he's probably calling out from the mall in case somebody comes looking for him. Like us. Hard to spot him in a place where two thousand people are on their phones, all at once."

"Where did Campbell's call go?"

"Can't tell you precisely, but generally, through a cell tower in the same general area of Orlando. We'll e-mail you a map. We've talked to the Orlando FBI. When you get there, they'll launch a plane with a Stingray unit and when you call Stiner's phone, they should be able to spot it."

"We gotta get the FBI involved?" Lucas asked.

"If we want the Stingray. We don't have our own in Orlando. You got a problem with them?" Forte asked.

"Sometimes I prefer to be a little more informal than they are . . ."

"Huh. Well, what do you want to do?"

Lucas thought a moment, then said, "Let's go with the Stingray, but tell them I don't need any help on the ground."

"Okay. Stiner has two federal warrants on him, by the way, both for interstate flight," Forte said. "You're good there, but I got to tell you, the underlying warrants aren't worth much. One for assault in Nashville—a street fight—and another for a bus theft . . ."

"He stole a bus?"

"Yeah, in Montgomery. He used it as a getaway vehicle after his own car broke down after a burglary. They found it in Tennessee somewhere. He'd sold it to a bunch of hippies for cash. The guy seems to run across a state line every time somebody comes looking for him. Which technically makes it federal, every time."

"Does he shoot people?" Lucas asked.

"He's carried a gun, but there's no evidence that he in particular has ever shot anyone."

"Okay. I gotta go, they're calling the plane. How about this guy named Sturgill? The thinker?"

"Nothing so far, but we're working it. There's more Sturgills out there than you'd think."

"Okay," Lucas said. "If I get Stiner, I'll push him on a better name."

"Good hunting, man."

THE FLIGHT was an hour and a half of white-knuckled terror, though the crazy old lady in the adjacent seat seemed to enjoy it thoroughly, drinking coffee, gazing out the window at the landscape while never quitting her knitting, apparently unaware of the fact that they were thirty-five thousand feet up in the air in a mechanical device *over which they had no personal control*. The flight attendant, a motherly woman, stopped twice to ask Lucas if he was feeling okay, and he'd nodded, "Just fine," thinking, *for somebody about to be torn to bits in a plane crash*.

Then Lucas was on the ground in Orlando, in a Jeep Compass, the best Hertz could do on a busy day with no reservation—the Hertz agent told him it was International Food and Wine Festival at Disney World that week.

Before he left the airport, he checked his e-mail on the iPad, found a note from the FBI agent-in-charge, who said Forte had sent him an e-mail summary of what Lucas was doing. Lucas sent a note back with his phone number and told the AIC that he was on the ground and rolling. He pulled up a map of east Orlando and went that way.

The Jeep would eventually drive him crazy, he thought, as he headed north. The thing was rattling like a Brazilian maraca, tracking like an aluminum fishing boat. The steering wheel wasn't adjustable and threatened to crush Lucas's chest even without an accident.

He was sitting at a stoplight when the AIC called: "We're putting a plane in the air. Do you have a nav system in your car?"

"I've got an iPad with Google Maps."

"Good enough. Find the Orlando executive airport and get over, say, a half mile east of it and give us a call," the agent said. "We'll place the call to Stiner from here, make a pitch for a Visa card, and vector you in to wherever the phone is."

"Got it."

Lucas worked his way north, following his progress on the iPad, and when he was east of the airport, spotted a high school parking lot and pulled into the driveway. He called the feds, and the AIC took the call and said, "Sit right there. We'll try to sell him that Visa card."

As he was talking, a security guard appeared from between the cars farther down the lot, heading toward Lucas in a fast walk. Lucas said, "Hang on a second, I've got a high school security guard who's going to try to roust me."

The security guard came up and asked, "You got a problem?"

Lucas hung his ID out the window and said, "Yeah. I'm a federal marshal and I'm on a call to the FBI. I might need some directions from you, so go stand on the other side of the road. I'll wave you back over in a minute."

The guard, an older man with expansive nostril hair, said, "Oh." He hitched up his pants and said, "Okay," and walked to the other side of the driveway.

Lucas got back to the AIC and said, "Sell the Visa card."

"Doing it now."

Dead air for fifteen seconds, then the AIC said, "No answer on the phone, but we hooked up to it and we've got a close location but not exact. It's a little shopping mall not more than a mile or so from where you're at, off Goldenrod Road. Here's the address . . ."

Lucas wrote the address in a notebook and said, "I hope he's not just shopping . . ."

"Well, you said it was a burner. You think he'd be carrying it all the time?"

"Don't know. Could you keep the plane around until I get there? In case he moves."

"Sure. Call me when you get there," the AIC said.

LUCAS RANG OFF and waved the security guard over and asked, "What's the fastest way to Goldenrod Road?"

The guard rubbed his chin and then said, "Jeez, I know where it is, but I don't think you can get there from here. It's complicated."

Lucas pulled up the high school location on the iPad, and the guard traced out a route that went west, north, east, and finally south on Goldenrod to the mall.

When they'd worked it out, the guard asked, "What's going down?"

"Fugitive."

"Am I gonna see it on TV?" the guard asked.

"Hope not," Lucas said.

"I'll look for it anyway," he said. He took a step back, spread his arms, and said, "Nice ride, by the way."

Lucas said, "Beauty's in the eye of the beholder, huh?"

"What?"

TWENTY MINUTES LATER, Lucas sat across the street looking at the Lakeview Mall, a collection of what appeared to be dying small businesses. He got back on the line to the AIC and asked, "That plane still up there?"

"Yes. Let me make another call . . ."

He was back a minute later and said, "Still no answer,

but the phone's in the same location. I bet it's in a drawer or something and he uses it like an answering machine."

"All right. I'm gonna go look."

"Easy does it."

The entry drive had a permanent sign that said "Space Available," with a paint-peeling picture of a lake with a palm tree. A mostly empty parking lot fronted the mall and a driveway ran around to the back, to the stores' loading docks.

Lucas drove around to the back, to see where a runner might go, if he found Stiner, and if Stiner decided to run. Running would be tough, though: a seven-foot-high splintering board fence separated the mall from what appeared to be a junkyard, or maybe somebody's private collection of rusting shipping containers, no lake in view.

Lucas drove back to the front of the mall and parked. A third of the storefronts were vacant, and at the far end, a teenager sat on a tilted-back chair on the sidewalk outside a vacuum-cleaner store, peering at his cell phone. Lucas picked out a dusty-looking coffee shop called the Koffee Korner, which wasn't on a corner. With any luck, the barista would know everybody in the mall.

Lucas made sure the Jeep was locked, patted his pocket for the enlarged mug shot of John Stiner, and walked over to the coffee shop. Inside, he found a man behind the counter peering at a computer screen that he hastily blanked when Lucas pushed through the door. He was a middle-sized man with a poorly trimmed black beard and long black hair tied back into a ponytail with blue ribbon.

He said, "He'p you?" with the kind of accent Lucas had just left in Nashville. Lucas took the mug shot out of his pocket, looked at it, looked at the man behind the desk, mentally subtracted the beard, and realized that he was looking at John Stiner.

He said, "Yeah." He pulled out his .45 with one hand and his badge case with the other and said, "U.S. marshal, John. We need to talk."

Stiner's eyes went from the gun to the badge and he said, "Aw . . . shit."

"You got a gun on you?" Lucas asked.

"One under the counter," he said. "We don't got much to steal, so it's not much of a gun."

Lucas told him to sit back down in the office chair, wheel it to a closed window, and then sit facing the window. "If you try to mess with me, I'll beat the hell out of you and then I'll call the FBI," Lucas said. "If we can have a civilized conversation, none of that might be necessary."

Stiner wheeled his office chair to the window and Lucas went around behind the counter where somebody had epoxied a cheap plastic holster to the counter wall. A chrome, long-barreled .38 revolver had been stuck into it. The .38 was probably older than Lucas, but when he dumped the shells out onto the counter, they looked reasonably new.

He scooped the shells into his jacket pocket and said, "Now, I need to ask some questions. What happens afterwards depends on the answers."

A sandwich sign with a clock face on it, with wooden hands, under an inscription that said "Back in a mo'," was standing in a corner. Stiner gestured at it and said, "Maybe I should put my clock outside."

"Do it, but don't run, 'cause if you run, I'll chase you down and we'll talk at the federal building," Lucas said.

"I'm not running," Stiner said. Lucas went with him as he put the sandwich board on the sidewalk, then they both walked back inside and Stiner locked the door and asked, "You want a Coke or a beer? I can't honestly recommend the coffee."

"Coke is fine."

Stiner got a Coke and a bottle of Pabst Blue Ribbon from a refrigerator, twisted the top off the Pabst, and asked, "What?"

"I TAKE IT you've heard from your sister," Lucas said.

"I didn't know what to do," Stiner said. "That's the worst thing I ever heard of. They were going to cut off her feet? Jesus Christ, what's happening in the world?"

"They did a lot worse to Garvin Poole's folks. They didn't get interrupted," Lucas said. He told Stiner about the scene at the Poole house, and Stiner stared at him over the PBR, sweat trickling off the side of his nose.

"Shit, man," he said, when Lucas was finished.

"Yeah. They're looking for you—you might be the only clue they've got," Lucas said.

"You know who they are?"

"Not specifically. Gar Poole knocked over a dope counting house in Biloxi, and the cartel wants its money back. We're thinking that Poole may have walked with several million. They want it back and they want to make a point about people who make the mistake of stealing from them."

Stiner said absently, "Bil-uck-see."

"What?"

"You said, 'Bi-locks-ee.' It's pronounced 'Bil-uck-see.'"

"I'll make a note," Lucas said.

"Goddamnit," Stiner said, sitting forward in the office chair. "What the hell am I supposed to do? I haven't seen Gar in years, and I don't know how to get in touch with him. If you bust me on those interstate warrants . . . well, you know who runs the prisons? It ain't the guards. If the right guy down in Mexico tells them to, they will chop me up into tuna chum."

"These guys are Honduran, not Mexican," Lucas said.

"Listen, if you had to get in touch with Poole, I mean, if somebody put a gun to your head . . . what would you do?"

Stiner thought for a bit, then said, "I know family people for a half dozen guys who are . . . connected. I guess I'd call up those family people, tell them to get in touch with their man, and tell their guy to have Gar call me. Somebody would probably be able to make a connection, or know how to get a connection made."

"Would one of those calls be going to Sturgill?"

Stiner's head came up. "Sturgill Darling? Is he in this?"

"Could be," Lucas said, keeping his face straight. Sturgill *Darling* . . . How many could there be?

Stiner looked away again, muttered something unintelligible, then said, "Well, that makes a little more sense, then."

"How?"

Stiner said, "Sturgill's mostly a setup man. Or used to be. He made his money spotting jobs. When Marilyn told me about Gar's drug job, I kinda wondered how he got onto them. Gar's not real big on spotting. He's bigger on the actual *doing*."

"Where would I find Sturgill?"

"Don't know. I've heard he's got a farm down in Alabama. He's like an actual tractor driver. Gar once told me that Sturgill's hometown is so small the Laundromat has a clothesline."

"How did you get in touch with him to get him to come to your party up in Nashville?"

"I'd see him around," Stiner said. "We all used to hang out on lower Broadway in Nashville, going to clubs. I ran into him and said, 'Come on over.' Marilyn tell you about that?"

"Marilyn told me almost nothing," Lucas said.

"Then how'd you track me?"

Lucas dug in his jacket pocket, produced his phone,

and held it up. "You know why they call them cell phones? 'Cause people who use them wind up in cells."

"I'll remember that," Stiner said. "What are you going to do with me?"

"Tell the FBI exactly where you are . . . but I'll wait a while. An hour, maybe. I'm going to give you my cell number. If those hitters, whoever they are, catch up with you, they'll skin you alive. That's the honest-to-God truth, John—that's what they'll do. The Tennessee cops are keeping an eye on your sister, but they can't do that forever—it's possible these people will be going back to her, if we don't take them out first. So, buy another burner phone, call up who you have to, figure out how you can get in touch with Gar. When you find out, don't call him. Call me. Gar will never know."

"What if he calls *me*, instead?"

"Then call and tell me about it. We can figure out where the call came from," Lucas said.

Stiner looked away: "I dunno, man."

"You told me what would happen if you go to jail . . ."

"Ah, shit. Gimme your number," Stiner said.

Lucas ripped a page out of his notebook, scribbled his cell phone number on it, and said, "Call me as soon as you get that burner. If I were you, I'd clear out of here. And right quick. I gotta tell the feds that I found you, but . . . I'll give you three steps. And, John? Don't make me find you again."

"Gimme three steps, like they say in the song." Stiner looked around the shop, the paint-shedding walls, the flaking acoustic tile on the ceiling, the plastic light fixture, the yellowing business cards and lost-cat notices on the bulletin board.

"Best goddamn job I ever had," he said. "I was, like, in management."

10

WHEN LUCAS left Stiner, he called Forte in Washington, arranged to get an airline ticket back to Nashville, and filled him in on Sturgill Darling.

"That's the guy I need," Lucas said. "There's a chance that he's the one who spotted the Biloxi counting house, and even if he didn't, there's still a chance he knows where Poole is hiding. He could be the planner, the spotter. You got the name, and it's unusual—get me an address."

Forte said he'd get that going, and added, "I got a call back from Louise on your travel. You've got a ticket back to Nashville, but you gotta hurry."

Lucas's next call was to the FBI. He told them that he'd spoken to Stiner, but hadn't had time for an arrest and the processing. "If you really want him, he's probably still around."

"We made some calls about him. We don't want him

all that much, but if we get a break, we'll go over and pick him up," the AIC said.

Lucas said good riddance to the Jeep at Hertz, checked his bag and the .45 with Southwest—he hadn't taken the training for *Law Enforcement Officers Flying Armed*, so couldn't carry aboard—and made it to the gate early enough to buy an *Esquire* Black Book magazine and a Snickers bar.

Two hours after he left Stiner, he was sweating at the back of the plane, holding tight to the armrests during takeoff. When they survived that, and got up in the air, he managed to relax enough to open the magazine. By the time he finished working through the men's fashion articles and discovered he'd need a new suite of neckties, they were descending into Nashville, and he was sweating again.

On the ground, he found an e-mail from Washington. They had a rural address for a Sturgill Darling, outside the small town of Elkmont, Alabama, not more than an hour and a half from where he was. The location was right, as Poole's pals seemed to come from the Greater Nashville area.

He could drive halfway there, bag out in the same motel where he'd been the night before, have a leisurely dinner and a nice breakfast, and still get to Elkmont before ten o'clock.

He also had a text message with a new phone number for Stiner. So far, so good.

WHEN LUCAS walked out the door at the Koffee Korner, Stiner, suffused with gloom, finished the Pabst and threw the bottle toward the trash can. He missed and it shattered on the concrete floor. He didn't bother to sweep up. He fished the last three bottles of PBR and two Cokes out of the refrigerator, looked around the office, got his baseball cap, and walked down the street to his apartment.

The apartment had come furnished, and while initially it had smelled strange, his own personal odors had taken over in the six months that he'd had the job and now it felt like home. No option, though. Maybe Davenport hadn't been telling the truth and the feds were on the way to pick him up, but maybe he *had* been telling the truth and Stiner had some time.

Over the next hour, he moved his personal possessions into the camper back of his aging Ford Ranger, said good-bye to the apartment, left a message for the owner, and took off. As he was passing a swamp, he threw his phone out the window. In the next hour and a half, he acquired two new prepaid phones, one from Walmart and the other from Best Buy.

A while later, as Lucas was bracing for the crash landing at Nashville, Stiner took out one of the new phones and punched in a number from memory. He didn't get a recorded message, just a beep. After the beep, he said, "A .270 is way better on deer. Call me on this number and soon. I'm serious, man."

Darling called back ten minutes later. He asked, "Better than what?"

"Better'n a .243."

"Long time, no hear," Darling said. "What's up?"

"You could be in deep shit. By the way, this is a brand-new prepaid phone I'm gonna throw away in the next five minutes, so you can't call me back. I was visited by a U.S. marshal and he was asking after you by name, in connection with a major job," Stiner said. "He knew you'd been at a party at my place, years ago. I told him I didn't know where you lived now, or what your phone number might be. I said I just knew you from hanging around lower Broadway."

"What exactly did he say?"

Stiner laid it out: about the murders of Poole's parents, about the two killers who'd started working over his sister. "Somehow they got you-know-who's name, and they're looking for him. They're going after anyone who knows about him. I told this fed I didn't know anything about it, that I hadn't seen any of you for years. Anyway, the marshal's looking for you. He really wants your friend, but he doesn't know how to get to him."

"Damn it. And you say these greasers are looking for my friend?"

"It's like a race. Your friend would do well to get far out of town, right away, and not tell anybody where he's going."

"But that wouldn't stop the greasers from looking, would it? If they get my name, they could be all over my family . . ."

"I hadn't worked it out that far," Stiner said. "I don't know your situation there. But they didn't stop at torturing anyone else's family. If they find somebody else who knows that you and your friend were tight . . . they could be coming."

Long silence, then, "Anything else?"

"No, except that I'm on the run myself," Stiner said. "I got nothing to do with any of this, but I don't want them coming for me. I'm crawling in a hole and pulling the dirt over my head."

"Tell you what, buddy," Darling said. "I owe you. When this all blows over, come and see me. I'll take good care of you."

"Yeah, well—thank you. I'll check in a year or so . . . if you're around."

They hung up simultaneously and Stiner waited until

there were no headlights on the back of his truck and dropped the phone onto the interstate, where it'd get run over nine hundred times before daylight.

That done, he called Lucas from the other phone, and when Lucas didn't answer, left a text message with his new phone number. Then he turned his truck around and headed south. His thinking was this: the cops would expect him to run, and since he came from the north, they might expect him to go back that way. If they checked the phone call he'd made to Davenport, they'd see it came from north of Orlando. He didn't have to run that far, though. Tampa would work. If the marshal ever called him back, he planned to string him along until he had a feel for what to do and then either run or hold tight.

The main thing was, he had to stay away from the two hired killers: the marshal wouldn't be sawing his leg off, whatever else he might do.

AS HE WAS DOING THAT, Kort and Soto were at work on the outskirts of Roswell, Georgia. Kort looked into the empty blood-clotted eye sockets of an elderly man named Henry Bedsow. Bedsow's eyeballs lay on the floor like a couple of bloody squashed grapes. She shouted, "That's all you got? Sturgill Darling? What kind of name is that? I don't believe that shit. You got ten seconds to tell me or I'm gonna rip your motherfuckin' tongue out by the roots, and then I'm gonna let you drown in your own blood. Who else? I don't believe this Darling bullshit. Who else, motherfucker?"

11

LUCAS GOT a later start than he'd expected the next morning; no problem, he'd just slept late, and the car clock said it was nearly eleven before he rolled down a narrow rural highway to the Darling farm.

The farm stretched across a natural bowl in the land, the bottomland along a river or creek; a twisting line of trees on the far side of the farm marked out the stream. The farm itself had a prosperous, well-groomed industrial air.

A neat white single-story house sat on the left, facing the road, a dozen trees spotted around the yard, throwing overlapping circles of shade. A broad, heavily graveled driveway separated the house from a six-slot white-metal garage, and at the back, ended at a white barn. As far as Lucas could see, there were no animals: the place was purely a grain operation, with soybean fields pressing at the sides and back of the two-acre-sized residential lot. A sliding door was open on the left side of the barn, and he could see the front end of a corn-green John Deere tractor.

Farms, in Lucas's experience, which wasn't extensive, usually showed bits of history around the edges: old chicken coops and machine sheds, maybe a neglected clothesline in the back, abandoned machinery parked in a woodlot.

The Darling farm had none of that. Everything looked new and well maintained, with rectangular beds of pastel petunias edging the driveway and sidewalks, while marigolds laid a circle of gold at the base of a flagpole in the center of the front yard. A silver propane tank squatted like a huge silver bullet on the far side of the house.

Lucas pulled into the driveway, saw a woman's face checking him from a side-door window. He touched the pistol under his jacket, climbed out, walked to the door, and rang the doorbell.

The woman opened the door, cocked her head: "You're not the propane guy," she said. She was tall, comfortably heavy, with neatly coiffed blond hair betrayed by dark eyebrows. She fit the farm.

"I'm a U.S. marshal," Lucas said. "I need to interview Sturgill Darling about an old friend of his. Is he around?"

The woman had been smiling politely, but now the smile faded: "It's that damn Gar Poole, isn't it?"

"Why would you say that?" Lucas asked.

"Because he's the only one I've heard of who'd have a marshal coming by. Sturgill hasn't talked to him for years, but I knew that sooner or later, somebody would be coming around looking for him." She hesitated, then unlocked the screen door between them and pushed it open. "You better come in if we're going to talk. Sturgill's gone off to Canada on a hunting trip, won't be back until week after next."

*   *   *

AS LUCAS STEPPED INSIDE, Darling watched from the garage. He'd heard Lucas's truck turn in from the road, and he'd called his wife to warn her that somebody was in the driveway and that it might be the law; or it might be the torture crew. If it was the cartel crew, he'd be outside the window with a tactical shotgun. He told her to leave her cell phone turned on and lying on the couch table so he could hear what was going on.

The night before, he'd checked the Internet for news stories on the Poole murders and the assault on Stiner's sister, and had gone into town to call Gar Poole from a pay phone to fill him in.

Poole had said, "There are only three people who know where I am and how to get in touch—I'll call the others and warn them. You probably ought to get lost for a while, get the old lady somewhere they can't find her. If we lay low long enough, they'll go away. They can't go running around the countryside cutting people up forever—they'll get caught."

"I'll do that—but I've still got some money here," Darling said. "It's hid, but I need to hide it better. If the cops came in and really tore the place apart and found it, I couldn't explain it. I got some farm work to do, too . . . but then I'll get out. I'll get back to you with a number on a new burner."

"You might want to skip the farm work and get out," Poole said. "That thing about sawing off my mom's leg—those are not people you want to fuck with."

Darling had almost two million dollars in cash at the farm. After getting off the phone, he'd bought a couple of sturdy, self-sealing plastic tubs, packed the money inside them, then after dark, carried them across the road to a brushy patch of ground and with his wife watching, buried them.

That done, he'd started cleaning up the barn. He'd been getting the equipment ready to bring in the beans, but now he'd have to put that off. He got the combine back together, called an outfitter he knew in Northwestern Ontario, and made arrangements to do some bear hunting.

In the morning, he finished cleaning up the barn and had been loading the truck with his hunting and traveling gear when Lucas turned up. He could watch the house from a corner window. Janice was a smart woman and would be okay with a lawman, he thought.

In case the very worst happened, and the big man in the suit wasn't the law at all, he waited with the shotgun in his hand.

THE WOMAN introduced herself to Lucas as Janice Darling, Sturgill's wife. She took Lucas to sit in the living room and offered him a glass of water or a Diet Coke, and he accepted the Coke.

After she'd settled into the chair opposite him, Lucas told her about the robbery in Biloxi, and the apparent response by the cartel, including the murder of the Pooles and the assault on Marilyn Campbell. Janice knew all of that, but pretended that she was hearing it for the first time.

"My God," she said. "They did that because they *thought maybe* these people knew where Gar Poole is? Are they coming for us? We've got four children, they're all grown up, but they could be found . . ."

"I don't know if they're coming for you or not, but it's not a risk you should take, especially with your husband gone," Lucas said. He'd been watching her closely as he told the story, and had seen her eyes glaze: she'd heard it before, he thought. She was lying: Sturgill Darling was probably somewhere close by. If he was gone hunting in Canada, he'd probably just left.

It might, he thought, be worth hanging around, somewhere out of sight, to see if Darling appeared . . .

If Janice Darling knew anything about Gar Poole or the Biloxi robbery, she was stonewalling.

"I can tell you that Sturgill has nothing to do with those people, at least their criminal activities, and never did. He did used to play some guitar up in Nashville, and hung out on Broadway, but that didn't go anywhere and he came back here. That's where he knew them from and that's the last he's seen of them. He's been farming for twenty years since then."

Lucas asked her to call her husband, but she said he didn't have a cell phone. He didn't believe that, either.

AS THEY WERE TALKING, Kort and Soto pulled to the shoulder on a hillside road a quarter mile away, looking down a bluff toward the farm in the green valley below. A creek meandered across the landscape, lined with trees. Soto didn't know shit about trees, and Kort was no better. Off in the distance, a couple of farms away, a train was rolling by, like a bunch of golden caterpillars racing to lunch.

The farm itself was a tidy rectangle, the row crops were dark green and low, with some of the leaves turning to gold as autumn crept into the South, and off to the right, at an adjacent farm, a couple of dozen rough acres were given over to pasturage, on which they could see two dark brown horses.

"That sorta looks like cotton down there, but I don't think it is," Kort muttered. "Don't know what it might be, though. Can't be corn. Corn's taller."

"It's wheat," Soto said of the soybeans.

"Yeah? Don't know about that. Never seen any wheat. Or oats."

Soto's head bobbed, and he said, "I can tell you one thing about Tennessee farmers for sure."

"We're in Alabama," Kort said.

"Same exact thing," Soto said irritably. "Anyway, one thing about Tennessee or Alabama farmers is, they'll have a gun handy in the stairwell. Somebody breaks into your house, won't be any cop close enough to save your ass. They got guns, like that kid in Franklin and old man Poole."

Kort shifted uncomfortably. She was sitting on a soft donut pillow intended for hemorrhoid sufferers, and while it helped, her ass still felt like she'd been hit with a baseball bat, and she was still seeping some blood into the Kotexes they were now using as bandages. "What are you sayin' here?"

Soto had a cinnamon-flavored toothpick rolling around in his mouth and stopped to pick out some obstruction in his lower jawline. "I'm not saying we can't do it, I'm just saying we got to be careful. We're not dealing with some street kids, here. These guys are hard-core criminals."

"Who must be doing well," Kort said. "That looks like a Benz sittin' in the driveway."

"Well, we know we're looking for a few suitcases full of hundred-dollar bills. A Benz is small change."

"Fuck it, then. Let's do it," Kort said.

Soto pulled on a pair of silvered sunglasses and put the car in gear.

LUCAS HAD GOTTEN one valuable thing from the interview with Janice Darling. The couch table had an array of family photographs on it, including several with a husky middle-aged man that Lucas thought must be Sturgill Darling: Darling with Janice Darling, the two of them posed with three girls of elementary, middle, and finally high school age, a photo of Janice and Sturgill on a big-game fishing boat with a boy who showed Sturgill's cheekbones and smile. If Lucas ran into Sturgill Darling, he'd recognize him.

A half hour after he'd arrived, Lucas picked up his legal pad and pen and was about to thank her for her time, when they both heard another car crunch up the gravel drive.

Darling frowned and asked, "Now who could that be? I'm not expecting anyone . . ."

She and Lucas both stood and looked out the living room window. A blue Toyota had pulled up behind Lucas's truck and a heavyset woman was climbing out. She looked around, then reached into the car to pick something up. When she turned, she had a clipboard in her hand.

Lucas turned to Darling and asked, "Do you have a gun in the house?"

"What?"

"A gun! Do you have a gun in the house?"

"A shotgun in the mudroom . . ." she said.

"Run and get it, then get in a bathroom, load it, and point the gun at the door and don't come out until you hear me yell for you."

Darling looked at the woman outside, who was headed toward the side door. "You think . . ."

"Almost for sure," Lucas said. "Now go! Go!"

She hurried off to the back of the house. Lucas pulled out his .45 and jacked a shell into the chamber and went to the door. He pulled it open as the woman was about to climb onto the bottom step. He couldn't see her right hand, which was under the clipboard. He pointed the .45 at her chest and said, "Get back! Get back! Get on the ground!"

She was surprised, but instead of protesting, she stepped backward and sideways, and Lucas followed her with his eyes and then snapped his head back toward the car, where he saw the far door opening, and a moment later a man stepped around the door and lifted a rifle over the hood of the car.

Lucas didn't quite think, *Rifle*, but the idea was there, and he threw himself back into the house, and a split-second later a burst of a half dozen slugs tore through the closing screen door as he dropped and rolled to his left and then scrambled to the living room window.

The walls of the house were almost no barrier to the bullets punching through the aluminum siding and interior drywall, but the shooter was making the mistake of sweeping the outside wall at waist level, while Lucas was rolling across the living room carpet to a window in the corner.

Another burst of bullets punched through the kitchen walls at the other end of the house, and Lucas risked standing up and then stepping in front of the window. He didn't bother breaking the glass but simply opened fire on the man behind the car, the window blowing out as he fired. To his left, the heavyset woman had gotten back to the car and was running around the back side.

Lucas had missed the man behind the car and the rifle turned toward him and he dropped again as a gust of slugs blew through the window. The guy behind the car had a fully automatic weapon, which was not surprising but created an awkward situation for a cop armed with a handgun.

Lucas rolled back toward the door and kicked it open and emptied the rest of the magazine at the car. The man popped up again, beside the driver's-side door, shooting over the roof now, and Lucas rolled the other direction this time, as more shots pounded through the door and the siding around the door, and crawled behind an antique Hammond organ that sat behind a side window.

He slammed a second magazine into the .45 and then peeked out the window. The woman was sitting in the driver's seat and the man had the rifle propped on the roof of the car, apparently waiting for any motion. Then the car was moving and the man jumped in the backseat and the car screeched in reverse out toward the road.

Lucas stepped to the door, and as the car made a clumsy backing turn onto the highway, he emptied the .45 into it, saw both the driver's side and back windows blow out; but the car accelerated away. The guy with the rifle fired a burst through the broken-out back window of the car and Lucas dodged back inside.

The car was three or four hundred yards away when Lucas ran out to the Benz and threw it in a circle out to the highway and followed. He didn't have to catch them, he only had to keep them in sight. Catching them, in fact, would be stupid; he had nothing that would contend with a machine gun.

He had two reserve magazines in the locked center console and he managed to unlock it as he rolled down the gravel driveway and fished the magazines out. The Toyota was perhaps a half mile ahead when he made it onto the highway and started after it.

He would sweat about it later but wasn't yet frightened. He was angry and excited, and focused on running down the Toyota. He needed to stay in touch, and he needed help.

Forte was at work in Washington. A secretary answered his phone, and Lucas screamed at her, and Forte came up, and Lucas sputtered, "I'm chasing the cartel guys. One male, one female. I'm a half minute behind them on a highway outside the town of Elkmont, Alabama. I need you to get onto the sheriff's office whatever it is here and have them call me and I'll vector them in . . ."

HE'D CLOSED the distance since he'd turned out of the driveway, and up ahead the Toyota braked and then made a hard right turn onto a dirt side road and started up a hill. Lucas would have the advantage there, with a hefty four-wheel drive, unless . . .

The "unless" happened. He was halfway up the hill, the Toyota having disappeared over the crest of the hill, when he saw the rim of blue off to one side. The Toyota had stopped and the rifleman was waiting, the gun again braced over the top of the car.

Lucas jabbed the brakes and dropped sideways onto the passenger seat when the windshield blew out, raining broken glass on his face, neck, and arms. He crawled over the center console as more rifle slugs pelted the front of the car, and pushed the passenger-side door, intending to drop onto the ground, where he'd be sheltered by the car's tires and could return fire. He'd gotten the door open when he realized that he hadn't shifted the car into "Park," and it was slowly rolling backward and around toward the roadside ditch.

"Shit! Shit!" He lifted his left leg and poked at the shift lever, which was mounted on the steering column, trying to shift the truck into "Park." He missed but managed to knock the lever upward, which shifted the truck into reverse and the slow roll accelerated and the truck backed itself into the roadside ditch, where it bounced and tilted and finally shuddered to a stop.

The gunfire had ended, but his phone was ringing.

Lucas risked a peek through the shattered windshield, saw nobody on the road, nobody in front of the truck. He sat up and pushed the "Park" button on the shift lever, and crawled out the passenger-side door and dropped into the ditch behind the truck.

He could neither see nor hear anyone moving along the road or through the roadside brush. He edged around to the back of the truck and looked up the road: the blue rim of the Toyota was gone.

His phone had stopped ringing, but then started again.

He answered, as he surveyed his own truck. He was deep enough in the ditch that he doubted he could get out without help. Into the phone he said, "Yeah? Davenport."

"This is Aaron Clark, I'm a deputy sheriff in Limestone County, Alabama. We got a call . . ."

Lucas broke in: "I've been in a gunfight at the Sturgill Darling farm off 132. The shooters went west on 132 maybe a half mile, then turned up a hill on a dirt road before they knocked me off the road into a ditch. I can't get out. They're driving a blue Toyota that's probably full of bullet holes. There're two of them and they've got at least one automatic weapon . . ."

Lucas described the woman and asked that the deputy send a wrecker to get him out of the ditch. The truck was leaning sideways, and he was afraid it would roll if he tried to move it himself.

"I'm going to run back to the Darling farm, make sure Mrs. Darling is okay . . ."

"We'll have somebody meet you there," Clark said, "and we'll get on that Toyota . . ."

WHEN HE was off the phone, Lucas moved back into the brush and snuck up the hill, looking for the blue car or any movement. He saw none: the car was gone. His face was burning: he'd been vaguely aware of it, but now blood ran down into one eye and when he wiped it away, his hand came back bloody from the heel to his fingertips, and he realized that he'd been cut up by shrapnel and glass, but hadn't felt it in the crush of the gunfight and chase.

He turned and started jogging back toward the Darling farm. Six or seven minutes later, he was on the porch and shouted, "Mrs. Darling? The marshal, I'm coming in . . ."

He heard a muffled call from the back and then Janice Darling appeared, holding the shotgun like she knew how to use it. She gaped at him: "Oh my God! What happened? You're bleeding, are you shot?"

"Cut up, I think. We should have some cops coming in . . . if I could use your bathroom?"

She led him to a small bathroom and he peered into the mirror. He was bleeding from a half dozen puncture wounds on his scalp, forehead, left ear, and the left side of his neck, and could feel more cuts down his back. He took off his jacket; there was blood, but not much, and several small bloody patches on the back of his shirt. One thing was for sure: his two-thousand-dollar suit was ruined.

"You need a hospital," Darling said.

"Yeah . . . but it looks worse than it is."

"You hope. Let me get a washcloth."

"Better not. I've probably got some glass in me, better let a doc take it out. If I rub on it, I might push it in further."

SHE PUT DOWN the shotgun, looked shocked, worried, and maybe softened up by the blood, so Lucas popped the question: "Is your husband really gone?"

"He was out of here at dawn," she said, with a blink of

an eye. "He's gonna be darn upset when he gets back and sees what happened to the house."

"Well, maybe he'll call from the highway somewhere and you can tell him about it," Lucas said.

She said, "Maybe." She didn't look even slightly embarrassed.

Lucas couldn't think of anything else to say, so while they waited for the local cops, he excused himself to call Forte in Washington and told him what had happened.

"How bad are you hurt?" Forte asked. "On a scale of one to ten?"

"No more than a one. Maybe less. I'll have to stop by an ER somewhere and get patched up, but not that bad."

"Okay, listen. I'm not gonna let you run around out there alone anymore. I've talked to SOG, we're sending a couple more deputies out there, Bob and Ray . . . Where do you want to meet?"

"I'll have to call you when I find out how bad my car's screwed up, but . . . I'm thinking Nashville, depending on what happens with running down these cartel people."

"Call me every five minutes and tell me what's happening," Forte said.

"Bob and Ray . . . wasn't that a comedy team or something, on the radio, back years ago?"

"Yeah, maybe—but these two aren't funny," Forte said. "Call me when you know where you'll be."

A SHERIFF'S CAR rolled up the driveway a minute later and Lucas and Janice Darling went out to meet the deputy, who introduced himself as Glen Long. When he was sure Lucas wasn't bleeding from any major wounds, Long said, "I'll ride you back into the hospital and get you fixed up. We haven't seen hide nor hair of that Toyota, though."

"We can't leave Mrs. Darling where these guys could find her if they come back . . ."

"I've got a sister with a different last name across the line in Tennessee," Darling said. "I'll pack up right now and stay with her until it blows over."

The deputy said they would put a car in her driveway until she was gone. And he asked, "Where's Sturgill?"

"Gone to Canada," she said. Her eyes flicked to Lucas: "We're hoping he'll think to call back before he gets there, but you know Sturgill. Once he starts rolling, he just keeps going. Probably won't stop before he gets to the border."

Lucas said, "Yeah, right."

ANOTHER SHERIFF'S CAR arrived, this one carrying the deputy, Aaron Clark, who'd called Lucas during the fight. "We've got the tow truck pulling your car out of the ditch. It's gonna take a while, they've got to edge it out sideways," Clark said. "If they try to pull it straight out, they think it'll roll. Not that I think it'll make much difference—I'd be surprised if it's not totaled. Every piece of sheet metal on the car has got at least one hole in it."

"You gotta tell everybody to take care if they spot that Toyota," Lucas said. "These people will kill you, cops or not."

"Everybody knows," Clark said. "I don't know exactly how they got past us, if they did—maybe they're hiding out in the woods somewhere. We had cars coming from all directions as soon as you called."

"Better start checking the local farms," Lucas said. "They could have pulled into one, hid the car in a barn . . . wouldn't be good for the farm people."

Clark looked at him, then said, "Oh . . . shit! Shit!" He turned and ran back to his car, got on the radio.

Darling asked, "You think . . . ?"

"I worry," Lucas said.

LUCAS WAS eventually hauled back to his truck by a sheriff's deputy. The Benz was sitting up on the road again, where the wrecker driver was getting ready to pull it up on the wrecker's flatbed. The deputy walked around the truck, shaking his head, and the driver said, "I gotta tell y'all, pulling it out of there sideways didn't do the truck any good. But there was no other way to do it. If I'd tried to pull it straight out, forward or backward, she was gonna roll, and then . . . well, it wouldn't have been good for nothin' but parts."

"My best guess, that's about all it is right now," the deputy said.

The driver nodded: "Probably right. All them bullet holes don't help."

Lucas removed everything removable from the truck and then was taken to a local hospital, where a nimble-fingered nurse pulled two tiny slivers of glass out of his neck and back. None of the wounds required stitches, but he would, the nurse said, itch for a few days: "I've been there," Lucas said.

While she worked on him, he called around, arranged for his truck to be hauled to a Mercedes dealer in Nashville, and called State Farm to report the accident. When the nurse was done, he got a change of clothes from his suitcase, went into the ER restroom, and put on the fresh clothes. He threw his cut and blood-soaked suit into the hospital trash.

The blue car wasn't found that afternoon or evening; nor did the sheriff's office find any dead farmers.

*　　*　　*

STURGILL DARLING had watched the gunfight from the barn. He'd been listening on the open phone as Lucas talked to Janice Darling and knew that Lucas was a federal marshal. When the cartel crew showed up, he'd watched, ready to intervene if the marshal had been shot down and the cartel people had gone after Janice.

When the marshal ran to his truck and went after the blue car, Janice had come out of the bathroom and asked, on the phone, "You still there?"

"Still here. They're all gone, but they'll be back. Probably the marshal with some deputy sheriffs. Are you okay?"

"I'm fine, but the house is a mess. What are you going to do?"

"I'm gonna hide right here in the barn. They've got no reason to search the place, and if they do look, I'll get up under the eaves where they won't find me. I'll get out of here after dark. You go on up to your sister's place."

"Okay. You be careful, Sturg."

"I will. Now you go on back to the bathroom, like the marshal told you. I'll watch everything from here."

WHEN LUCAS got out of the hospital, he spent a half hour typing up a report of the shoot-out at the sheriff's office and sent a copy of it by e-mail to Forte in Washington.

A sheriff's deputy drove him across the Tennessee line, where he was picked up by a Tennessee highway patrol car and driven into Nashville, to the Mercedes dealer, where he was told that a State Farm adjuster would be around the next day to assess the damage.

"He says he'll be here at noon," the service guy said. He was looking at Lucas's truck and shaking his head: "Seventy thousand miles and all those bullet holes, plus the interior damage and the mess under the hood . . . it's totaled, man. Might save the tires."

The amiable highway patrolman took him to the Hertz location at the airport. Lucas called Weather on the way to tell her what had happened. She was pissed, but didn't exactly say, "I told you so."

She said, "Be more careful. I keep telling you . . ."

"I'm trying and I got some help coming. They're sending down a couple heavies from the Special Operations Group. Sounds like the federal government's equivalent of Jenkins and Shrake."

"Good! That's good. You need the help, Lucas. For God's sakes, be careful."

Lucas got a Nissan Armada from Hertz and checked into an Embassy Suites hotel in downtown Nashville a few minutes after midnight and slept soundly, with the help of Tylenol with codeine, except for a few flashbacks to the gunfight, until ten o'clock the next morning.

At ten o'clock, he was awakened by a heavy-handed pounding on the hotel room door.

12

LUCAS PULLED on his pants and went to the door, left the guard latch attached, and peered out through the crack. A short but wide man stood outside, dressed in black high-rise jeans, a white dress shirt, and a black nylon jacket. He had buzz-cut hair and a flattened nose and muscles everywhere.

Behind him stood a much taller black woman, nearly as tall as Lucas, whose height was enhanced by an Afro of 1960s dimension. She had a sharply chiseled face, with a fingernail-sized scar on her left cheek. She was dressed in a blue shirt, tight black jeans, black suede ankle boots, and a black nylon jacket.

Lucas asked, "Who are you?"

The wide man said, "Bob and Rae. We were told you expected us."

Bob and *Rae*? He'd been expecting the Marshals Service equivalent of Jenkins and Shrake, the BCA's designated thugs. Bob fit, but Rae, not so much. "Ah . . . yeah. I'm not really quite up, but, uh . . . come on in, I guess." He unlatched the door and let them in.

"Late sleeper, huh?" Rae said, as she came through the door. "You know what they say about birds and worms."

"Most birds haven't had the shit shot out of them when they get up early," Lucas said.

"Heard it was mostly superficial," Bob said.

"Whoever told you that probably never had the shit shot out of them," Lucas said.

Rae was looking around the small suite and said, "How'd you get authorized for a palace like this one?"

"I didn't ask," Lucas said.

Bob shook his head: "There's a rookie mistake. If you've made any more, feel free to tell us about them, so we'll know what we're up against."

Lucas yawned and stretched, said, "Well, after two days in town, I've made more progress toward finding Garvin Poole than the whole fuckin' Marshals Service did when it had him on the Top Fifteen list for five years. That ought to be good for something."

Rae shrugged. "All we heard is that you broke your car and didn't catch the people who broke it."

Lucas: "Maybe you ought to wait in the lobby."

"That's no way to treat a brother marshal," Bob said. "Why don't you go brush your teeth? I'm getting some bad breath over here."

LUCAS WENT to the interior half of the suite, closed the door, shaved, showered, checked to make sure none of his cuts had started bleeding again, then put on a dark blue dress shirt, a medium blue Givenchy suit, and George Cleverley oxfords, which he buffed up. When he emerged from the back room, Rae checked him out and said, "I'm going back home. Can't compete with this shit."

"Bet he can't get his gun out as fast as we do," Bob said.

"That's why I hired you guys," Lucas said. "I'm basically the brains behind the operation. You're the muscle."

"Muscle, my ass," Rae said. "We're the Einsteins of the Marshals Service. Let's get some pancakes and figure out what we're doing today."

SHE KNEW NASHVILLE, and had a particular pancake house in mind, and Lucas followed them over in the Nissan. On the way, he called the Mercedes dealer in St. Paul and ordered a new SUV.

The salesman said, "I can get you a loaded GLS550 in two days in any color you want, as long as it's black. If you can wait a couple of weeks, I could get some other color."

"I'll take the black one—I'm out of town right now. Get the paper ready, I don't want to hang around there any longer than I have to."

"Got a bunch of new Porsches in, big guy," the sales guy said. "I could put you in a Cayenne Turbo S that would eat the 550 alive, any way you run it—straight line, curves, off the line . . ."

"Shut up, Dick. Get me the papers for the 550."

"The Porsche's in carmine red. Commit now and I'll give you five thousand off. No, wait—did I say five thousand? I meant seven thousand."

"Listen, Dick, I don't need some snowflake SUV with two inches of road clearance. Get me the goddamn 550. I'll see you in the next week or so."

"How many miles you got on the trade?" Dick asked.

"The trade expired yesterday," Lucas said. "State Farm is giving me cash, but not enough. There's no trade."

"Then . . . what are you driving?"

"A Nissan Armada."

"Oh my God, I wouldn't leave my driveway in one of those things."

"It seems . . . sturdy," Lucas said.

"Probably *is* sturdy. It's big enough you could land an F-16 on the roof," Dick said. "It's just that I'd die of embarrassment."

"I don't want to talk about it," Lucas said. "Get me the 550."

AT THE PANCAKE HOUSE, Lucas and Rae—Rae Givens—ordered blueberry pancakes, while Bob—Bob Matees, which he pronounced like the painter Matisse—ordered waffles because, he said, they were less fattening.

"Probably would be," Rae said, "if you didn't put an ice cream scoop full of butter on top of them."

"And then drowned them in fake maple syrup," Lucas added.

Bob said pleasantly, "Fuck you." He poured more syrup and said to Lucas, "As I understand it, you're an ex–state cop and you saved Michaela Bowden at the Iowa State Fair and she wired you up to get a special appointment to the service. Is that right? Can you introduce us to Bowden? I've got a few things I'd like to tell her."

"Like what?"

"Like she's gonna lose if she doesn't start hustling her ass around the Midwest."

Lucas pointed a fork at him: "Every poll in the country says you're full of shit."

"Not every poll. *L.A. Times* says she's gonna lose,"

Bob said. "They're right, unless she starts hustling her ass around the Midwest. Why the hell does she go to states that she's sure to lose, like Arizona and Texas, or that she's sure to win, like New York and California? What the hell is she doing in California?"

"There's gotta be a reason, they gotta know more than we do. They're political pros," Lucas said. He looked at Rae. "What do you think?"

"I *think* she's gonna win, but Bob's smarter than he looks. Actually, given the way he looks, he's way smarter. He's got me worried."

"So what about your appointment?" Bob asked. "What about Bowden?"

Lucas told them about his appointment, and Bob and Rae gave him some background on their own work. They were both career deputy marshals assigned to the Marshals Service's Special Operations Group, which tracked and busted federal fugitives. They were a cross between an investigative unit and a SWAT squad, and, as Bob said, "We got more guns and armor in our truck than a Humvee in Iraq."

Neither one of them was married, both had a divorce in the background, and Rae's ex-husband had custody of their two kids while she was out of town. She got them back when she was home.

"It works," she said. "My ex is a good guy, as guys go, so I don't have to worry."

"He *is* a good guy," Bob said. He tipped his head toward his partner. "They got a divorce because Rae . . . well, Rae isn't."

"Glad to hear it," Lucas said.

"NOW," said Bob, "tell me if this is right—you've never really had a clue about where Poole is, but you've been

interviewing his relatives, and some of them turned up dead, and one other lady got her leg sawn upon."

Lucas: "I also located the guy who might be the spotter who took Poole to the counting house . . ."

He told them about Sturgill Darling and the shoot-out at the Darling farm, Darling's alleged history with Poole, and how Darling's wife said he was on his way to Canada without a cell phone, to shoot a bear.

"Sounds like she was lying through her teeth," Rae said.

"With that kind of insight, you could become a St. Paul detective someday," Lucas said. "Here's the thing. It's possible that Darling has a burner phone. It's also possible that he doesn't. Most of these guys don't keep them after they use them. Which is the whole point of having a burner."

"We know that," Rae said.

Lucas continued, "While I'm over doing the paperwork on my truck, I'd like you guys to do two things—check with Verizon and AT&T and any other phone services that cover Darling's farm area and find out if he has a cell phone. If he does, we'll call it, see where he is. With any luck, he's planning to hook up with Poole. Or, maybe, he's just running. If he's just running, you guys can chase him down and squeeze him."

"What if he really doesn't have a phone?" Bob asked.

"He was already gone when I got to the farm. I suspect he got a call from John Stiner, my source down in Florida, and took off. But I don't think he'd do that and leave his wife behind. I think he probably fixed it with his wife to hide out herself, but she hadn't quite left yet. If Stiner is the one who tipped him, Darling probably took off the night before I got there, or maybe early yesterday morning. If that's what happened, then he may well have called Poole. He wouldn't have done that on his cell phone—he'd know that we could figure that out. If he had a burner, he could have called on that. But if he didn't have a burner already in his pocket . . . he might have gone into this small town where the farm is and made the call from a pay phone, if there is a pay phone."

"You want us to figure out if there's a pay phone and check the calls out of it in the last couple of days," Rae said.

"Exactly," Lucas said.

Bob looked at Rae and said, "All of that should take us, what, an hour? We could meet back here for lunch."

Lucas said, "I'm serious."

Bob said, "So am I. This is the kind of shit the FBI has down pat. I've got a line straight to the guy we need to talk to. We'll make a call and see you back here at noon."

Lucas looked down at his plate, still half full of soggy pancakes, and said, "Tell you what—find a decent restaurant and I'll pick up the check."

SOTO HAD HAD a brainstorm: he wanted to know about the cop who was tracking Poole, because they were running out of leads themselves, but maybe the cop wasn't. If they couldn't find Poole, maybe the cop could.

Where would they find the cop? At the Mercedes dealer, of course—the only one around.

Because the cop in the Benz would recognize Kort but might not recognize him, Soto left Kort in a shopping center and walked across a divided highway to the only Mercedes dealer in Nashville and cruised the parking lot as though looking at the cars. He spotted a black Mercedes-Benz SUV parked behind the building and wandered past it. He didn't have to get too close before he knew he had the right truck: there were no other SUVs that had been shot to pieces with a machine gun.

A thin, balding man in tan slacks and a blue sport coat was examining the truck and making notes on a clipboard. Soto walked past it, checked the license plate and the state. Minnesota? What was up with that? If the guy really was a cop, what was he doing in Tennessee?

His phone chirped and Soto answered and Kort said, "Get out of there. The cop just walked into the front of the store."

Soto hurried away, cut through a line of cars, and recrossed the street.

"I saw the car, got the tag," he told Kort. "Let's see what we've got."

THEY CALLED the College-Sounding Guy. Soto said, "I need a license tag run. From Minnesota. When we get a name, we need to check the name out, see who he is."

The College-Sounding Guy crunched on something that might have been a Cheeto and said, "Two hundred."

"Bill us, as usual."

"Call you back in fifteen minutes," the College-Sounding Guy said. Soto imagined he was tall, soft, wore glasses, and combed his heavily gelled hair straight back from his forehead. And he had pimples and was surrounded by sacks of Cheetos. How he got wired up with the people in Honduras would remain a mystery.

Kort and Soto sat and waited.

Kort said, "My buttocks . . ."

"I don't want to hear any more about your ass," Soto snarled. "It's *my ass, my ass, my ass,* all the time *my ass.* I know your ass hurts, now shut up."

"You're such a motherfucker," Kort said. "I'd like to get ten minutes with you and my Sawzall."

Soto looked at her with interest. This was something new: "Really? You really want to cut me up? I'll tell you what, bitch, you look at me sideways . . ." A switchblade appeared in one hand and the serrated blade flicked out. ". . . I cut your fuckin' nose off."

"Yeah, I . . . There's the cop."

Lucas walked out of the Mercedes dealership and around to the back where his car was, and out of sight. "Not gonna fix that wreck," Soto said. He sounded proud of himself.

"He's outa sight. I gotta get out of this car," Kort said. The pain wasn't so bad when she was standing up. She waited outside the car, partially concealed by a bush, and thought about Soto, and what a miserable jackass he was. Here she was, really hurt, because of his failing—his job had been to check the house, and instead he'd let a kid get the drop on them, like the worst fuckin' amateur in the world.

Jackass.

FIVE MINUTES after Kort got out of the car, Soto's phone rang, and the College-Sounding Guy said, "What you've got there is a federal marshal named Lucas Davenport. New on the federal job, but a longtime cop in Minnesota with a history of killing people. He is not somebody to toy with."

"To *what* with?"

"Toy with. Mess with," the College-Sounding Guy said.

"Can you look at airline tickets?"

"Sure, but if you want some ongoing monitoring for Lucas Davenport, it'll cost you a thousand a day. I'll have to check every fifteen minutes or so, if you want some warning on when he's flying, if he does. That's a full-time job, but if you want that, I can give you enough warning that you could get to the airport yourself. I could even make reservations for you."

"I don't care about that so much as where he's going,"

Soto said. "If he goes, I'd like to know what kind of car he rents when he gets there."

"In that case, I'll monitor flights for two hundred per day. That'll get you a check every couple of hours until he flies. Another two hundred for the car, make, model, and tag. I also got a special, today only, for our better customers. If he has a phone from AT&T or Verizon, I can hack into the company's GPS location server and tell you where his phone's at, at any given time."

Soto: "You can do that?"

"For a hundred dollars per check, as many checks as you want, but a hundred dollars each."

"Do that, and bill us," Soto said.

"You're on the clock, starting now," the College-Sounding Guy said, and he hung up.

When Kort got back in the car, Soto told her about the call. "That there's a guy worth knowing," he said.

"Sounds like a ratshit asshole frat boy to me," Kort said. She shifted uncomfortably in her seat. "I need to get a doctor to look at my buttocks. I think it hurts worse now than it did yesterday."

"I can make a call down South and maybe they have a guy, but it also might make them unhappy to know you've been shot."

Kort didn't say anything for a bit, then, "Let's see what it's like tomorrow."

THE THIN balding man from State Farm told Lucas that the Benz was totaled—"Seventy thousand miles and not a decent piece of metal on it—not even the roof," he said. "The interior's trashed, plus the engine compartment looks like somebody was pounding on it with a ball-peen hammer, and the mag wheels look like somebody used a chain saw on them."

"Just tell me how much," Lucas said.

The adjuster told him and the recommended payoff was far too low. Lucas threatened legal action and the adjuster couldn't quite hide a yawn. He refused to adjust his adjustment and told Lucas his insurance rates would probably be going up, given the nature of the claim, which involved all those bullet holes.

Lucas was still pissed when he walked into the restaurant where Bob and Rae had taken a booth; they were eating salads.

"Tell me something good," Lucas said, as he slid in next to Rae.

"There's one pay phone in Elkmont, and at six o'clock the day before yesterday, somebody made a call to Dallas. That was the only outgoing long-distance call from that phone, that day," Rae said.

"Poole's in Dallas," Lucas said. "That's about the time Stiner would have called Darling, and Darling went right into town and called Poole."

"Maybe," Rae said. "Darling does have a cell phone— Mrs. Darling was lying to you—but it's not up on any network right now. He pulled the battery and probably has a burner by now."

"So we don't know if he's running on his own, going to Canada to shoot a bear, or hooking up with Poole," Lucas said.

Bob said, "If he is in Dallas, we're taking all the credit for finding him. Me'n Rae."

"If you give me partial credit, I'll tell you what the next step is," Lucas said.

They watched him for a minute, then Rae asked, "What you got?"

*   *   *

"WHAT I HAVE is a name in Dallas—I pulled all the paper I could find on Poole, and there are two guys he worked with, seem to have been friends, who are not in prison or dead," Lucas said. "One is Derrick Donald Arnold and I have a Dallas address for him. The other is a guy named Rufus Carl Cake, who lives in New Orleans. We need to talk to Arnold, right away."

Arnold had a history of violence, according to Lucas's paper—brawling, when he was younger, jobs as a bouncer at a couple of strip clubs. He'd been busted twice and served time for strong-arm robbery and once was arrested but released without prosecution while working as a boat unloader for a marijuana ring in New Orleans. In his association with Poole, he'd apparently worked as an intimidator and the guy who carried heavy stuff.

"He a shooter?" Bob asked.

"On two of his arrests, they took shotguns out of his cars—not bird guns, but tactical pumps loaded with buckshot. No hard evidence that he ever used them."

"What's he doing now?" Rae asked.

"Don't know," Lucas said. "No law enforcement contacts for the last three years, except for a speeding ticket. The cop who stopped him ran him, and based on his record, asked to search his car. Arnold agreed, nothing was found. Doesn't look like he's ever spent much time in straight jobs, though. If we jack him up and find something—anything—we can use that as a hammer. Texas has a three-strikes law."

"I know a lot of people in the Dallas area," Bob said. "They could help if we need it."

"Good. Let's check him ourselves, before we do that," Lucas said. "I don't want to misfire on something and have Poole warned off."

"What about Cake?" Rae asked. "I know New Orleans."

"We'll check him for sure, if we don't get a hit with Arnold," Lucas said.

Bob: "What you've got is one name in Dallas?"

Lucas said, "No—I also know that before he disappeared, Poole was converting everything he had to gold coins. He supposedly was going to run to Central America or somewhere."

"Where does that get us?" Rae asked.

"If he didn't leave the country and if he hasn't been working, he's probably been cashing those coins to support himself. When we get to Dallas, first thing we do is check every gold-buying store in the area, see if they know his face."

"There're seven million people in the Dallas–Fort Worth metroplex," Rae said. "He'll be a needle in a haystack."

"But if he's there, at least we'll have the right haystack," Lucas said. "That's when we go after Arnold."

Lucas called Washington and talked to Forte, told him about the Dallas connection, and got tickets on a flight into Dallas that afternoon, with rental cars and reservations at another suites hotel.

They were still sitting in the restaurant and when he got off the phone, Bob asked, "How do you do that, man? We never stay in suites."

"Bowden connection," Lucas said. "Everybody's feeling their way along, trying to figure out how tight we are. In the meantime . . . I get perks. If they ever find out we're not that tight, it's back to the Holiday Inn."

"What time are we leaving?" Rae asked.

"Four."

"Probably ought to head out to the airport after we finish eating," Bob said. "Takes us a little extra time to get on the planes. We're flying with all that ordnance."

*   *   *

THEY PACKED UP and headed for the airport, Lucas with one bag, Bob and Rae with one bag each, plus a large wire-reinforced duffel full of guns and armor. They reconvened on the flight side of security at three o'clock. Rae said, "Our tickets are business class."

"Yeah?" Lucas shrugged.

Bob looked at Rae, then said to Lucas, "Boy, oh boy, you're my new hero, Davenport. Anytime you need help, call us. And if you only need one of us, call me—fuck Rae."

"Goddamn short people," Rae said.

13

LATE AFTERNOON, after a brief flight from Nashville: Dallas was hot, bright-sunny, vibrating with stress, cars in a hurry. Not a Southern city as much as a southwestern one. Lucas resisted the inclination to kiss the earth when he got off the plane, got another Jeep, but a bigger one this time; the truck seemed okay, though he got lost getting out of DFW.

When he finally got to the hotel, he found he'd arrived before the other two and checked in for all three of them, took his bag up to his room, and went down to the lobby to wait. Rae arrived ten minutes later, in a Camry, explained that Bob had gotten lost getting out of DFW and would be a few minutes behind her.

Rae hauled her bags up to her room and then Bob showed up in another Camry, shaking his head. "Tell me you didn't get lost at the airport."

"Can't tell you that," Lucas said, handing over the key card. "I'm in 505, let's meet there. I'll call Rae."

WHEN THEY were together again, in Lucas's room, Lucas showed them the list of gold buyers he'd downloaded from the 'net. They split the list three ways, and ten minutes later, were on their way out.

Rae had the closest one and called Lucas before he had the chance to get to his first stop. "We got a solid hit. They say he doesn't look exactly like the mug shot anymore, he's older and heavier, but it's him. He comes in once a month or so and cashes a coin, or sometimes two. He was last in a month ago."

"Excellent. Call Bob, tell him. Let's visit a couple more stores, but I think we got him."

Lucas stopped at a place called Arlington Precious Metal Exchange & Pawn, a storefront with dusty windows and a tangle of used power tools behind the glass. Inside, he walked past a lot of damaged musical instruments and obsolete film cameras to a guy who was leaning on a counter, smoking a cigarette and reading a free newspaper. The guy had looked up when the doorbell jangled, and when Lucas got to him, said, "You're a very well-dressed police officer."

"Thank you."

"Well-dressed police officers make me nervous," the man said. He was wearing cargo shorts with a weight in one leg pocket that Lucas suspected was a pistol, and a Tommy Bahama shirt with palm trees. "I haven't done anything, have I? I stay straight with the local cops. You're not local, are you?"

"No, I'm a U.S. marshal," Lucas said, the phrase still sounding odd to his ear. He took an eight-by-ten copy of

Poole's decade-old mug shot from his jacket pocket and asked, "Does this guy cash coins here?"

The man looked at the photo and said, "Yeah, he does. He looks a little older now—got a three-day beard most of the time, with some gray in it. Don't tell him I talked to you."

"Feels like a threat?"

"Yeah. First time he came in here, he had one coin with him," the man said. "I made him an offer. I didn't know him from Adam, so the offer was a little low. He said, 'Don't fuck with me, bro,' and I looked him in the eye and decided not to fuck with him. You meet a few guys like that, in this business."

"When was the last time he was in?"

The guy scratched his neck, then said, "Maybe . . . a month ago? Maybe more. He's about due. Usually comes in every month or six weeks. I make about twenty bucks a visit, so, you know, I don't mind seeing him, but I ain't holding my breath, either. He's not gonna make or break the monthly nut."

"Any idea where he lives?" Lucas said.

"Nope. I gotta tell you, sir, he didn't strike me as a person you want to be curious about. You notice I ain't asking what he's done. Don't bother to tell me."

Lucas took out a business card and handed it over. "Call me if he comes in. He'll never know."

"Sure," the man said, in a way that suggested he wouldn't be calling.

"You don't want to *not* call us," Lucas said. "You really don't want to be *any* kind of accessory. Not with this guy."

"Okay."

A little plastic stand sat next to the shop's cash register, with a deck of business cards on it. Lucas took one, read it, asked, "You're Deke?"

"That's me."

"Thanks for the help, Deke," Lucas said. "I'll call you every once in a while."

BOB FOUND the same thing that Lucas and Rae had: they checked nine stores between the three of them, and seven store operators remembered buying gold coins from Poole. Bob and Rae each found one store where the operators said they didn't remember Poole, but in both cases neither was the store owner/manager. Nobody knew where he lived.

Back at the hotel, they agreed that they'd found the city where Poole had been living, but he hadn't been to any of the stores less than a month earlier.

"Hasn't sold gold since the counting house was hit," Lucas said. "He's got cash and doesn't need to burn any more gold."

"What's next?" Rae asked.

"I've got to think about it. Go find Arnold first thing tomorrow."

"We could do some of that tonight," Rae said. "Look at his apartment, anyway. Maybe find out where he's working."

"We could." Lucas yawned. "This place has a gym, I'm going to work out first. We could get some dinner and talk about Arnold, whether to go tonight or tomorrow."

"I might look around for a playground," Rae said.

"A playground?"

Bob said to Lucas, "She travels with a basketball. She won't let me deflate it. It's the world's biggest pain in the ass."

Lucas looked at Rae for a minute, then asked, "Where'd you play?"

"UConn," Rae said.

"Starter?"

"Last two years, anyway," Rae said. Then, "You play?"

"I was hockey at the University of Minnesota," Lucas said. "When I was checking out the weight room here, I noticed that this place has a little basketball court."

Rae's eyebrows went up: "This place does?"

"Yes. I suspect a person of your academic caliber never played any street ball, though," Lucas said.

Rae said, "With that kind of insight, you could get a detective job in some broke-ass town in the Delta."

Lucas: "Does Bob play?"

Rae looked at Bob, then back to Lucas: "Stumps don't play basketball. Stumps wrestle."

"I play basketball," Lucas said. "Quite well, really."

Rae slapped her hands together and stood up, a predatory ivory-white grin slashing her face. "Fifteen minutes, on the court. One hundred American dollars."

FIFTEEN MINUTES LATER, on the court. Lucas was only a half inch taller than Rae, but he was sixty pounds heavier. Bob had found a chair somewhere and sat at the side of the court with a happy smile as he did a running commentary.

"These people don't like each other, I see the possibility for some really trashy action here, sports fans, it could get ugly . . ."

Lucas suspected Rae would be a better shooter than he was. Maybe a lot better: but he had the pounds and planned to use them.

"First rebound," he said. "Play to eleven, win by two, you put up the shot, gotta hit the rim."

"Brace yourself," she said.

Rae put up a shot from behind the three-point line, with the two of them side by side. If it went in, she'd shoot over until they got a fair rebound on the first shot.

The ball came off the right side of the hoop and they both went for it. Lucas gave Rae a hip to move her off the ball, took the rebound, dribbled out of the key, drove straight over her to the basket, scored.

With the ball again, he drove over her a second time. The third time she gave him a leg and he almost went down, lost the ball long. She brought it out and Lucas played too far off her, and she stepped behind the three-point line and stuffed it, tying at 2–2.

That set the game, Lucas playing rough and close, Rae struggling to get free. She had a beautiful stroke and, unless he kept her off balance, deadly.

Lucas, sweating heavily, took the lead at 8–7 and held it. At 11–10, he drove hard and with a last-second step to the left, made an over-the-head reverse layup and won, 12–10.

From the sidelines, Bob shouted, "Whoa! Whoa! The white boy rallies for the win! Ladies and gentlemen, this was totally unexpected . . ."

Rae scowled and said, "I got you figured out, white boy. One more game."

"We gotta talk about Arnold," Lucas said.

"Oh, *now* we gotta talk about Arnold."

From the sidelines, Bob called, "Ladies and gentlemen, is the white boy a pussy? Is he gonna pussy out of the rematch? Did our viewers know that *pussy* could be both a noun and a verb?"

One more game, Rae staying well back when she got the ball, running loose until she could shake free, slowing down, taking her time. She killed him, 11–7, and it wasn't that close.

"I got you figured now," Lucas said, wiping the sweat off his forehead with the bottom of his T-shirt. "I'll have a hand inside your nose every time you make a fuckin' move."

"Dream on . . ."

Bob called, "Dinnertime! No rubber match! Let's go eat."

LUCAS AND RAE took quick showers and they all went out to a nearby Italian place that the desk clerk said wasn't too bad, and it wasn't. They were all stinking of garlic bread when Rae said, "I'm bored. I say we go after Arnold tonight."

"I looked it up," Lucas said. "His place is over in northeast Dallas, Diceman Drive. Rear, about forty-five minutes from here."

"All together, or separate cars?" Bob asked.

"How about one of you ride with me and the other bring a backup car," Lucas said.

"Guy could be a problem, with those shotguns, and he might be more of a problem if he's still hanging with Poole, and is worried about it," Bob said. "How about if Rae rides with you, takes her M4 with her, and I bring my own. That way, we got some clout in both cars."

That was good with Lucas.

Rae got her gun and a vest and brought them over to Lucas's Jeep. As they were getting ready to move, Bob came over and said, "I talked to my guy at the Dallas cops, to tell them that we'll be around. They're cool with it."

Lucas said, "I haven't done much of this marshal stuff. What would be their options if they weren't cool with it?"

Rae said, "Well, somebody in the neighborhood could call them and tell them there's a tall black person with a machine gun and armor in their front yard, send help, and the cops could flood the place with fifteen or twenty squads and the SWAT team and kill everybody they don't recognize."

Lucas said, "The Dallas cops are supposed to be pretty good."

"They *are* pretty good," Bob said. "But you know, the way things are right now . . ."

"Good move, Bob," Lucas said. "Let's keep them informed."

THE NIGHT had come down hard by the time they found Diceman Drive. They were hooked up with Rae's cell phone on speaker and cruised the house twice. There were two structures on the lot, a small fifties-looking house with an aging gray Pontiac in the driveway, and what might once have been a garage or studio in back. Both places showed lights.

The front house had a metal stake in the side yard, with a circular path around it: a dog, and probably a protective one, though there was no dog in sight. "Gotta watch for the dog," Rae said into her phone.

"I saw that," Bob called back. "Probably ought to stop at the place in front, before we go around back."

THEY DID THAT—sitting in front of the target house for a few minutes, windows down, listening to an unidentifiable television drama leaking through the windows of the house in front. Crickets. After watching for a few minutes, Lucas called Bob and said, "Rae and I'll knock."

"Got you covered," Bob said. "If you start running, I'll be ready to hose the place down, so don't start running unless you're serious."

Lucas said, "I'll leave my phone on so you can hear it all . . ."

Lucas asked Rae, "You set?"

"Got my hand in my purse," she said. "I'll leave the

M4, for now." The purse was actually a holster purse and contained her Glock.

"Let's go."

THE DOOR at the front house was open, as were the windows, though all the openings were tightly screened. Lucas knocked, and a woman's voice said, "Somebody at the door. Mitch? Somebody at the door."

A moment later, a fat balding man in shorts, T-shirt, and bare feet peered through the screen at Lucas and Rae and asked, "Who the heck are you?"

Lucas held up his badge and said, "Federal marshals. We want to talk—"

The man said, "Bullshit! I'm calling the cops!" and slammed the inner door.

Through the screened windows, they heard a woman ask, "Mitch, who was it, Mitch?" and Mitch said, "Some fake cops. I'm calling nine-one-one."

Lucas had his cell phone on, turned to the speakerphone, and Bob said, "I heard that. I'll call nine-one-one and get back to you when it's straightened out."

Lucas stood on the porch and Rae stood back at an angle. A woman peered out of one of the screened windows and said, "If you're fake, you better go away, the cops are gonna be coming."

"We're federal marshals, so the cops are already here, as your husband will probably find out in a minute or so," Rae told her.

The woman said, "Oh," and looked back to where her husband was on the phone. "I think they might be real, Mitch."

Lucas's phone buzzed and Bob said, "We're clear with nine-one-one."

A minute later, Mitch came to the door, red-faced and

apologetic, and said, "Sorry about that. We've had some problems in the neighborhood. Got my mail stolen last month."

"By a tall white guy wearing a suit in the middle of the night?" Rae asked from behind Lucas's shoulder.

"It's okay," Lucas said, patching things over. "Sorry if we startled you. We need to ask about the man who lives in the back . . ."

"D.D.? What'd he do?"

His wife had moved up to his shoulder and muttered, "I told you he was trouble."

"He hasn't done anything as far as we know," Lucas said. "We're asking about an old friend of his."

Mitch said, "Well, he's back there. Feel free."

"Has he been in any trouble with the law, that you know of? Or any trouble at all?" Rae asked.

Mitch shook his head. "We don't see him that much. He works at a gentlemen's club during the day, sometimes he's got a girl who stays over. Most of the time he's back there alone with his bird."

"His bird?"

"Yeah, you know. He's got a bird. It's like a parrot, sort of," Mitch said.

"Cockatoo," the woman said. "Real pretty, all white. He calls it 'Angel.' It does look like an angel. A small one."

"Don't call him and tell him we're here," Lucas said.

"Sure won't," the man said.

THE HOUSE in back showed light at three windows; two of the windows were closed, and the third was occupied by a humming window air conditioner. Through the closed door, they could hear Florida Georgia Line's "Get Your Shine On," played loud. Lucas pushed the doorbell.

When there was no answer, he said, "Music's too loud," and banged on the door with his fist.

The music was turned down and a minute later a man in a sleeveless shirt, shorts, and flip-flops came to the door. His upper body was the size of a garbage can, and not all of it was fat, though some of it was. He squinted nearsightedly at Lucas, then at Rae. "Who are you?"

Lucas's badge again: "Federal marshals."

"Why? I haven't done nothin'," the large man said, though a thin trail of marijuana smoke had accompanied him to the door.

"We need to ask you about an old friend of yours," Rae said. "So we're coming in."

"You got a search warrant?"

Rae shook her head. "I hate to tell you this, D.D., but smoking weed is still a federal crime, and from where we're at, we can smell it."

"You gotta be kiddin' me."

"No, we're not," Lucas said. "We need to talk, so we're coming in. If you want to stand back?"

ARNOLD STEPPED BACK, and Lucas and Rae moved inside. The house was like a hunting shack, one big room with a bed in a corner, a dinette kitchen, and a clothes rack covering one end of the place. There were two enclosed spaces: a tiny bathroom and a floor-to-ceiling wire cage, in which a cockatoo sat on a tree branch.

The cockatoo peered at them and said, "Onk Gurty." The place smelled heavily of Campbell's Chunky Hearty Bean with Ham soup, a touch of the consequent flatulence, with a subtle overtone of newspaper-and-bird-shit. Two overstuffed chairs faced a TV, and an electric guitar was parked in a corner, with a bright orange lunch-box-sized amp. The guitar had a psychedelic twisted black-and-white checkerboard inlaid on the top.

Lucas pointed at one of the chairs and said, "Sit."

Arnold sat and asked, "What the heck is going on, man? I been clean forever."

"Except for the weed," Rae said.

"It's medicinal," Arnold said. "I'm in the compassionate use program."

"We're talking federal," Rae said. "We don't care what the law says in Baja Oklahoma."

"Everybody calm down," Lucas said. He took the chair next to Arnold, crossed his legs, and said, "We need some help. We didn't come to bust you on the weed."

"What kind of help?" Arnold asked.

"When was the last time you saw Garvin Poole?"

"Oh, shit," Arnold said. He looked at Angel, which clucked a couple of times and said, again, "Onk Gurty." Back to Lucas: "Man, I ain't seen Gar in six or seven years. I don't got any idea where he might be. He do something lately?"

"For one thing, he moved to Dallas," Lucas said. "Since you're right here . . ."

Arnold was shaking his head: "Man, if he's in Dallas, that's news to me. I don't want to have nothing to do with him. The last time I seen him, he didn't actually see me. I walked into this bar in Jackson, Mississippi, and Gar was sittin' in with the band. He had a beard, but I knew it was him. I snuck out the back door and took off. That was like I said, six or seven years ago."

"I'm not sure I one-hundred-percent believe you," Lucas said. "We've heard you two were tight."

"We were tight for a while—Gar and some other guys were providing protection for some dope dealers, and I was . . . well, I was working for them, and got busted for it. But anyway, that's when I got to know Gar. We both played a little guitar and we both like the music . . . we'd jam a little bit."

"Didn't know he was musical," Rae said.

"He can play country. You know he builds guitars? He built mine. They're called partscasters, because he makes them up from commercial parts, but then he decorates the body, you know, the soundboard and the headstock, he does some custom inlay on the fret board . . ."

Lucas: "He does it commercially? He has a website or something?"

Arnold shrugged. "Don't know, anymore. Back when I knew him, he used to do it like a hobby. He'd sell them, got some good money for them, too. But it was all word-of-mouth. You had to know him to get one."

"It's like a talent," Rae said. "Like his talent with guns."

"Yeah, like a talent," Arnold agreed. "I'll tell you, though, I never worked with him. He had this reputation—people who worked with him, they died. Got killed. He supposedly killed some of them, and some other ones, well, Gar would pull some crazy fuckin' stickup and wind up shooting it out with somebody. I didn't want anything to do with that shit. My idea of a perfect crime is getting a rub from one of the girls at the club."

"You had a reputation for carrying a shotgun," Lucas said.

The shrug again: "Listen, guys, when you did what I did, you were expected to carry a shotgun. It was like a lawyer with a briefcase . . . or a cop with a pistol. But I wasn't going to get in any big shoot-outs. If the cops showed up while I was working, my plan was to throw the shotgun in the ocean and give up. No fuckin' way I wanted to fight the DEA. Those guys got bazookas and damn little mercy."

Lucas's phone rang: Bob calling. "I think we're okay in here," Lucas said.

"Want me to come in?"

Lucas looked at Arnold: "Nah. We'll be out in five minutes. We got a possible felony here, but we're talking."

Lucas got off the phone and Arnold, sweating, said, "Man, it's not a felony. I don't even got an ounce."

"We need you to check with your friends, find out where Poole might be," Lucas said. "We need to hear from you."

"If I did that, somebody would come here and kill me," Arnold said.

"Not if Poole's in prison . . ."

"It's more than just Poole," Arnold said. "It's that whole gang he ran with."

"Like Sturgill Darling?"

Arnold's forehead wrinkled: "Who?"

They talked for another five minutes, and when they left, Lucas was fairly convinced that Arnold was a dry hole. As they were going out the door, Rae said, "If you told us one single lie, we'll be right back in your face."

"I believe you, baby girl," Arnold said.

Rae stopped: "Say what?"

"Ma'am," Arnold said.

ON THE WAY back to the hotel, Rae said, "I looked you up on the Internet after I beat you up this afternoon. I wanted to look up your hockey career. Couldn't find much about it."

"I was a defenseman back before the Internet. When I got ink, it was actually ink. You won't find it online," Lucas said. "If a guy from back then gets on the Internet, he's either a big-time shooter who went pro, or he's put it on himself."

"Anyway, I saw all that other stuff on you. Said you're rich," Rae said.

"I'm well-off," Lucas said.

"Internet said you were really, really rich," Rae said.

"I don't think of myself that way. I'm a middle-class cop who got lucky," Lucas said.

"This is like a sport for you? Chasing these people down?"

"No. It's what I do. Having the money is . . . really nice. If I didn't have any money, I'd still do this."

She nodded. "Okay."

AT THE HOTEL, Lucas said good night to the other two. "Think about it—how do we find our needle in the haystack?"

"I'll do that," Bob said. He laughed and said, "Never heard anything like that bird, I gotta tell you."

Rae and Lucas looked at each other, and Rae said, "Huh?"

Bob looked from one to the other and said, "You must've heard it."

"Heard it squawk," Lucas said.

"Wasn't squawking," Bob said. "Maybe you could hear it better over the phone—it was saying, 'Not Guilty.'"

Rae: "No."

"Yes."

Lucas shook his head: "Good night. Don't wake me up too early."

WHEN DERRICK ARNOLD was sure that Lucas and Rae were gone for good, he kissed his bird good-bye and walked out to the gentlemen's club where he worked his day job. The on-duty bartender asked, "What the hell you doing here this late?"

"Can't stay away, it's the tits," Arnold said. He walked around behind the bar, pulled a beer for himself, and then walked past the topless dancers in their half-glassed dancing booth, without giving them a glance—after you've seen the first ten or twenty thousand tits, you've seen them all—past the VIP areas where the chumps got lap dances, past the elevators to the Play Pens, where well-connected athletes and entertainers got more than their laps danced, past the restrooms to the kitchen. In the kitchen, he nodded to a waiter and dug around in the junk drawer, found the prepaid phone card, and carried it out in the hall to the emergency exit and the pay phone installed there, inside the door.

At the phone, he punched in the number for the pre-paid card, and then the number he had for Garvin Poole. The phone rang four times before a woman answered: "Yeah?" Cool voice, with a little whiskey in it.

"Is Gar there?"

A moment of silence, then, "Who's this?"

"A guy he gave this number to. I used to . . . unload. Don't want to say names."

"Wait one."

A moment later Poole came on and asked, "Unload where?"

"Galveston. One time we yanked about twenty pounds of weed out of a bundle and pushed it down our pants. My balls smelled like dope for a week."

"Gotcha," Poole said, laughing at the memory. "What's up, man?"

"A federal marshal came by my house tonight. He thinks you're in Dallas, but he doesn't know where. They came after me because I'm living in Dallas, too."

"I didn't know that," Poole said. "Where you at?"

"Got a place over in northeast Dallas," Arnold said. "Rather not say the address on the phone."

"You say anything to them?"

"Of course not. For one thing, I don't know anything but this phone number," Arnold said. "I don't even know that they're right, that you're here in Dallas. I thought you were still in Mississippi. I can't tell you much, except that they're here and they're looking hard. They think you were involved in some kind of dope robbery."

Another moment of silence. "You think they have any specific idea of where I'm at?"

"I'm pretty sure they don't. That's what they wanted from me. They didn't say why they were here, or why they thought you were here. They didn't give me much at all."

More silence: "Okay. Thanks, man, I owe you. I'll send a few bucks your way when I get a chance. How will I get in touch? Don't say your number on the phone . . ."

"My dad's got a number, if you remember him," Arnold said.

"I do. Still working oil?"

"Yup. Retires next year. Give him a call, if you need to get in touch," Arnold said.

"Thanks again," Poole said. He sounded like he meant it, and he was gone.

14

LUCAS WAS in a deep sleep when somebody began pounding on his door. He sat up, blinking, saw a street-light through a crack in the curtain. Still dark outside. He'd turned the overly bright clock away from him, and as the pounding started again, turned the clock and saw that it was 6:12.

"Coming," he called, thinking, *Fire?*

He looked through the peephole and saw Bob, and Bob did not look happy; he looked frantic. Lucas opened the door and asked, "What?"

. The words sputtered out: "Got a call from the Dallas cops. One minute ago. Somebody chopped Arnold up, he's like fish bait, and killed Mitch and his wife, whatever her name was."

"What!"

Bob started to repeat himself, but Lucas waved him off and said, "I got it. Let's get over there. You wake Rae up?"

"That's next."

"Meet you in the lobby in five," Lucas said.

"Make it ten. I wanna brush my teeth and I gotta get my gear out of here . . . I'll get Rae moving. She's pretty quick."

As Bob trotted off down the hallway, Lucas noticed that he seemed to be wearing nothing but a pair of thigh-length underpants and a T-shirt; no shoes. Lucas went back inside, cleaned up, and was out of the room twelve minutes after Bob trotted away.

Bob got to the lobby at the same time he did, carrying the oversized bag that he used for the ordnance, and Rae showed up two minutes later, trying to get on some lip-stick as she walked. "This is fuckin' crazy," she said. "We all going together? We need to figure this out before we talk to the cops."

"Your car's the biggest," Bob said to Lucas.

"The drug guys found Arnold," Lucas said, as they walked out to the parking lot. The day before had been hot, but the predawn air had a sharpness to it: autumn coming to Texas. "They've got to have a source some-where. It seems to me the only way they could go straight to Arnold is if they knew *we* were talking to him."

"Walk me through that," Rae said.

"If you work through the sheets on Garvin Poole, you'll come up with a lot of names of people who've been associated with him. Arnold is one of the more obscure—the only reason we went for him, the only reason we came here, is because Sturgill Darling made a phone call to Dallas. We weren't even sure that Poole was here until we went to the gold stores. That's when we decided to go to Arnold. How are a couple of thugs going to figure that out? Only one way—they have a source who told them what we're doing."

"Where's the source?" Rae asked. "In the Marshals

Service? How many people in the service knew we were going to see Arnold?"

"I didn't tell anyone," Lucas said. "I told my guy about the phone call by Darling, and he switched me over to a woman named Mary who takes care of travel."

"I told my chief at SOG and asked him if he knew Arnold. He didn't," Bob said. "I'd trust him with my life. Hell, me and Rae both *have*."

Rae: "Maybe . . . the Dallas cops?"

"Can't be the cops—I didn't talk to them until yesterday evening," Bob said. "If these two were up in Nashville—I mean, how'd they get here so fast? How would anyone in Dallas even know to tell them?"

Rae said, "It'd have to be somebody in the service who's not waiting for them to call. Somebody who's looking at the same reports Lucas has, who could call them directly. Might even be runnin' them."

"That sucks," Bob said.

THEY WERE DRIVING across town with the first dawn light, but the freeways were already getting stiff. The sun was up by the time they walked past the police lines around Arnold's place.

Dallas crime scene people were already working in the two houses and the yard, and a cop wearing corporal's stripes directed them toward a man in civilian clothes: "Lieutenant Hart, he's in charge."

Donald Hart was a tall, tough-looking black man who gave Rae a long look as they walked up. "You the feds?"

Lucas nodded. "Yeah. Anyone tell you what we're doing?"

"Not entirely. I got jerked out of bed an hour ago. We don't get that many triples, and when we do, they don't look like this one. What the hell are we into here?"

Hart leaned back against the fender of a squad car as Lucas introduced Bob and Rae and then briefed him. When Lucas finished, Hart said, "The killers are professionals. No tie to anything local."

"I don't believe so," Lucas said. "I can tell you for sure if I can take a look inside Arnold's place."

"That makes sense . . . that they're professionals. I thought they might be. I'll tell you about that in a minute. I'm not, uh, sure . . . how much do you guys deal with homicides?"

"I spent twenty-five years chasing homicides up in Minneapolis and all over Minnesota before I joined the Marshals Service," Lucas said. "Altogether, probably worked three hundred of them, either as the lead investigator or assisting."

Hart nodded. "Good. Sometimes we get federals down here who . . . get a little pukey when they see a dead one."

"People we deal with, we get a little pukey with the live ones," Bob said. "Dead ones don't bother us much."

"C'mon, then," Hart said.

HART SAID the couple in the front house were Mitch and Carla Bennett. They'd been made to lie down on the front room carpet, and each had been shot in the back of the head with a large-caliber weapon. Lucas told Hart that when they'd visited the night before, the windows had been open. They were closed now, and Lucas suggested that the crime scene crew print the window frames where somebody would have pushed them down.

"We'll do that. Most of the places around here would have had air-conditioning, so nobody heard any shots. Or any screaming, for that matter—they took their time with

Arnold," Hart said. "The thing that had us wondering about the head shots is that they didn't go through. Big hole in the back of their heads, but no exit wound. That said to me that they were using low-power cartridges, maybe .45s with very light loads. Not much noise."

Bob said, "Professionals. Rolling their own."

Hart nodded. "I thought that might be the situation, but didn't know who or why until you guys showed up."

ARNOLD WAS a mess. His legs were taped with gaffer's tape, tough fibrous stuff that he wouldn't have been able to rip off, even with all the power in his heavily muscled arms and legs. There was no tape around his mouth, but traces of tape adhesives. After they bound him, they gagged him and then began torturing him, with saws and what might have been a propane torch. Both of his legs had been partially severed below the knee, and his genitals had been burned off.

When they were done with him, they'd fired a single round through his forehead.

They hadn't touched the bird, which shuffled silently back and forth on its perch, Arnold's tiny Angel looking at a little piece of hell.

Lucas looked over the scene, turned to Bob and Rae: they both nodded, and Lucas said to Hart, "It's the same two. I can't tell you who the shooter is, but the Tennessee Bureau of Investigation has identikit pictures of the woman. Pretty good ones."

"Motherfuckers," Bob said. "Don't quote me, but they desperately need to be shot."

"Nobody gonna argue with that," Hart said.

Lucas asked, "Do you have a time on this?"

"The crew says probably about four in the morning,

give or take. The blood wasn't completely dry, and they can tell by . . . the stickiness, I guess . . . about how long it's been pooled there."

Rae said to Lucas, "If they knew we were flying down to Dallas, if they knew about the time the tickets were bought, they'd have time to drive here. I don't think they would have flown with specialty weapons like that .45, and you said they shot you up with an automatic weapon."

"Makes them harder to find, too," Bob said. "If they'd flown, we might be able to find a rental car."

Lucas said to Hart, "We'll leave this with you, Don. There's nothing here for us—we'll coordinate with you. The main thing we need to figure out is where the leak is. Somebody had to tell them exactly where we were going, tell them about Arnold and give them the address . . ."

Then Lucas stepped through the door, outside, cupped his mouth and nose in his hands, stood with his face looking down toward his shoes. He muttered, "Holy fuck."

Rae, behind him, asked, "What?"

Lucas walked a circle around the yard, head down, Bob, Rae, and Hart looking at him. When he got back, he said to Bob and Rae, "It's us. We told them. No, wait. *I* told them."

Bob: *"What?"*

Lucas looked up now: "Listen, we know they've got a line into law enforcement files. That's the only way they could have started tracking Poole. But an inside source wouldn't know what *we're* doing, not minute by minute. Bob told his SOG guy about Arnold, but says that guy wouldn't talk."

"He wouldn't," Bob said. "I've known him for fifteen years. He would not."

Lucas: "But if they have a hacker . . . if they have a

hacker, and he's a good one . . . I mean, I know a guy up in Minnesota who can pull files out of the NCIS all day long, who can look at Verizon computers anytime he wants. There might be a lot of guys who can do that. They've got one. Somewhere along the line, they identified me—maybe saw my license plate number. They've been following *my* phone, like I tracked Stiner down to Florida."

"Sonofabitch," Bob said.

"That sounds kinda far-fetched," Hart said.

"Doesn't to me," Rae said. "Think about all the files that have been hacked during the presidential campaign and how high up the hackers got. Seems like everybody can hack everybody . . . you just gotta know the right hacker. With the way things are now, a drug cartel is gonna have hackers. Maybe a lot of them."

"What are you going to do?" Hart asked Lucas. "If you're right, you gotta get rid of your phone, first thing."

Lucas's hands were still cupped across his mouth, still head down. "Can't help the Bennetts or Arnold," he said. "But I'm not getting rid of my phone. We can still use it."

Bob: "We're gonna suck them in."

"That's what we're gonna do," Lucas said, lifting his head. "I'm gonna kill the motherfuckers."

THEY FOUND a Best Buy off Highway 75. Lucas and Bob left their phones in the Jeep and Rae drove it away; a half hour later she was back for a flying pickup, and Lucas and Bob gave her a new burner phone, identical to the ones they'd bought. They thought the killers had probably tracked Lucas, but decided not to take a chance—maybe they'd tagged Bob or Rae.

"Now what?"

"Now we find a nice improbable and semi-trashy place

for us to go, not too far from the hotel, and we spend some time there, like we did with Arnold. Then one of us drives the Jeep back to the hotel with our regular phones inside, leaves the phones at the hotel, and drives back. We're gonna ambush their asses."

Rae said to Bob, "I do like the way he thinks."

RAE WAS still driving and Lucas used his iPad to look over the Dallas area, and decided to check the town of Addison, which appeared to be a highly mixed commercial-industrial town built around a general aviation airport, and not too far from the hotel.

Rae took the Jeep that way and they eventually spotted a town house complex surrounded by narrow lawns on all four sides, and a wraparound parking lot that was mostly empty. The front of the complex faced the concrete back side of a truck terminal. Two other concrete-faced commercial buildings stood at opposite ends of the street. If there should be any shooting, it would be as safe outside the complex as anywhere they'd seen. They cruised the neighborhood a couple of times, talking about possible setups, and then headed back to the hotel.

"One thing we've got to talk about . . . do we tell the Addison cops what we're doing?" Rae asked.

"If we're setting up to ambush a couple of killers, in their town, they might be a little nervous and maybe even a little pissed, if we had any other options," Bob said. "The usual unwarranted aversion to bullets flying around."

Lucas: "I know you federal guys—us federal guys— like to bring the locals in whenever possible. This might be an exception. We've got a safe spot to make a stop, and we're going to have to make a stop *somewhere* . . ."

"Your call," Rae said.

Lucas thought about it, then said, "Fuck it. Let's tell Addison we're doing surveillance down here and ask them not to cruise the area. If it all goes up in smoke, at least we'll have that for cover, you know—that we called them in advance."

"Sneaky," Bob said.

AT THE HOTEL, they moved some of Bob's armory around: Lucas got a heavy-duty vest, and Rae and Bob carried M4s, ammo, and vests to their separate cars. Lucas carried a battery-operated Altec miniature speaker out to his car. A quick stop at a Subway got them sandwiches and bottles of water, and Diet Coke for Lucas, and a second stop got them magazines and newspapers, and then they headed back to the town houses.

Once there, Lucas and Rae parked at opposite ends of the front parking lot, and Bob parked in back. Lucas hooked up the tiny Bluetooth speaker to the iPad, picked out a decent playlist, and settled in to wait.

Bob called his boss at SOG, told him what was happening, then called the Addison cops, got the chief, identified himself, told him about the surveillance, and asked that patrol cars not cruise the neighborhood too heavily. He gave his SOG boss as a reference. Lucas called Forte, his contact in Washington, told him the same thing. Then he called Rae, and Rae called Bob, to further establish their location if somebody was monitoring them.

Two hours after they made the parking lot, Lucas called Bob and said, "Come get the phones."

"On the way," Bob said.

Bob collected Lucas's and Rae's phones, drove them back to the hotel, then made calls on each of them—to Washington and back to the SOG headquarters. That done, he left the phones at the motel and drove back to the apartment and set up at his previous spot, and called Lucas and Rae on the burner phones.

"We're set," he told Lucas.

"Could be a long wait," Lucas said.

"Be worth it to take these sonsofbitches down," Bob said. "What they did to Arnold . . ."

15

THE COLLEGE-SOUNDING GUY had spotted Lucas flying out of Nashville for Dallas. As they were leaving to follow, by car, Kort stole a couple of pillows from a Holiday Inn linen closet left open by the cleaning crew. Her ass felt like it was on fire, and when she pressed on the wounds with toilet paper, she was getting some nasty-looking fluid.

"Might have an infection," Soto had said. He sounded like he didn't care, because he didn't.

"Hurts like hell," Kort had groaned. "I'm going to Dallas flat on my stomach. Ten fuckin' hours."

"Better get some pillows or something," Soto had said.

She'd done that and Soto had hauled their suitcases out to the latest rental, a Chevy Tahoe, from National. The thing should cost an arm and a leg, but since they were using a phony credit card and ID, and wouldn't be returning it, the cost didn't matter, and Kort could lie mostly flat in the back.

Soto made one last trip inside and came back carrying a bottle of gin, partially wrapped in a towel.

"What's that for?" Kort asked.

"Give me your hand," Soto said.

Without thinking, she stuck her hand out, and Soto grabbed it and pulled it toward him. At the same time he lifted the gin bottle, which she now saw had been broken off about halfway down, and jabbed the sharp broken edge into her forearm.

She managed to stifle a scream but threw herself away from him, farther into the folded-down backseat, looked down at her bleeding arm, and cried, "What the fuck?"

"Now you need to go to the emergency room and get sewed up," Soto said, and he climbed into the driver's seat. He handed her the towel and said, "Wrap this around it. Don't get blood all over the car, it'll start smelling bad."

"What the hell are you doing?"

"What happened was, you slammed a motel medicine cabinet door too hard and the mirror broke and cut your arm. Medicine cabinet looked dirty to you, you're afraid you're going to be infected . . . that's why I drove you to the emergency room."

"Emergency room?"

AT THE EMERGENCY ROOM, a nurse practitioner put a half dozen self-dissolving stitches in her arm, took the same credit card they'd used to rent the Tahoe, and sent them on their way with prescriptions for antiseptic cream, penicillin pills, and pain pills. They filled the prescriptions at a Walgreens and headed for Texas.

"Could have thought of a better way to do it," Kort grumbled from the backseat. The pain pills made her more comfortable and her arm had not hurt that bad to begin with. The penicillin pills, she thought, might even cure her aching ass.

"Don't bother to say thanks," Soto squeaked at her, and she didn't.

That night, as they crossed the Red River, the College-Sounding Guy called and said, "That Davenport dude spent an hour out in a Dallas neighborhood. He was at a house in northeast Dallas. Actually, there are two houses. I don't know this for sure, but I think he went into both of them."

"You got an address?" Soto asked.

"I not only got an address, I can get you a picture of the place. Give me a few hours, I might be able to get you names from the gas company, run them to see who they go to. Davenport's staying in a hotel over toward Fort Worth . . ."

Two hours later, he called again. "The people in the front house, the house closest to the street, are named Bennett, and I don't find any association with Poole, but they could *be* Poole and his girlfriend, since Poole's probably using a phony name. Now, the guy in the back, that's a different story. He was definitely involved with Poole in the past . . ."

"How do you know that?" Kort demanded.

"Everything is data now," the College-Sounding Guy said. "Give me your real names and I'll tell you your bank balance and what hour you were born."

"I don't need to know when I was born, because I already know that," Soto said. "What I need is another car when we get to Dallas. Find one for me . . ."

AS LUCAS, BOB, AND RAE were flying into Dallas, and Kort and Soto headed southwest toward Dallas, Sturgill Darling showed up at Poole's place. He, Poole, and Box sat in Poole's living room, talking.

"I'm not quitting the farm. That's my home and I'm not leaving," he told Poole. "When I get out of here, I'm going up to Canada. Shoot me a bear, build an alibi, and then head back home as innocent as one of the Lord's angels. I gotta believe they'll be all over me, though. It's gonna be a grind, getting through it."

"I'm not sure what you're doing here," Box said.

"We got two problems. The feds aren't going away, but they don't know about me—not really. Not the way they know about you guys." Darling nodded at Poole and Box. "If they put your faces on TV, I might be able to do things you can't. The other problem is these cartel killers. I don't know how they got onto us, but they are. We need to get them off our backs, and I know something that you don't."

"What's that?" Poole asked.

"I know where they come from. I know who they work for. I got a phone number. Knowing that, we might be able to figure out a way to set them up, wipe them out. I can't rest easy knowing that they're looking at my farm, at me and my wife."

"Wipe them out and they'll send two more," Poole said.

"Maybe, and maybe not. Maybe they'll cut their losses, especially if we tip the feds as to who's running them. We've got to get rid of these two, first thing. After that . . . well, you'll be hid again and I'll spend a hundred grand putting a security system around the farm—radar, the whole works. Best I can do."

Poole nodded. "I buy all that."

Box: "So do I. What they did to Gar's folks . . . they're nuts."

"How do we get this going?" Poole asked.

"Make a long-distance phone call to Honduras," Darling said.

"I'd have to think about that," Poole said. "They haven't gotten to anybody who knows where we're at—not yet. Dallas is a big place."

They talked about it during the evening and Box went out to a Whole Foods and got some ribs and organic sweet corn and they barbequed in the backyard, talking about everything, and nothing, and working through it.

Late that evening, Arnold called. Box answered, and then handed the phone to Poole. When Poole got off, he said, "The feds are here."

Darling: "Here in Dallas?"

"Yeah. You remember Derrick Arnold? D.D.?"

"Didn't know him, but heard the name."

"That was him on the phone. He's here in Dallas, too," Poole said. "I didn't know that, and he didn't know that I was, but the feds paid him a visit, names were Davenport . . . Givens, and something else. Federal marshals."

"Davenport's the guy who shot up the drug guys at the farm," Darling said. "I heard him introduce himself to Janice. She estimates that he's not somebody you want to fool with."

"Gotta get out," Box said. "Gar, we gotta go. Real soon."

"I think so," Poole said. "Tomorrow morning."

"How about calling Honduras?" Darling asked. "We could feed them Arnold, and when they show up at his place, take two assholes off the plate."

"Let's keep hold of the idea, but if we're getting out, and they don't know where we're going . . . then they're back to square one. And how can they know where we're going, if we don't?"

*　　*　　*

POOLE AND BOX got up early the next morning, both a little groggy, and found Darling sitting in a chair in the backyard, smoking a cigarette.

"Those will kill you faster than the feds," Box said. She and Poole came out and took chairs.

"Only smoke one a day," Darling said.

"That's okay then. Don't see how you do it, though," Box said. "If I smoked one, I'd smoke thirty-nine more."

They'd decided to move whatever they could, the really valuable stuff, to a secure storage unit.

"Can't do anything about the furniture," Box said. She was bummed by the evacuation of their house, the first house she'd lived in that she actually liked. She'd bought the furniture herself, with the help of an Ethan Allen design consultant, and still got a little thrill looking at it, like something from a Sunday newspaper magazine.

"Even if we had time, there'd be moving people who'd know where we put it, and people in the neighborhood who'd know what movers we used. We could get ambushed if we ever tried to pick it up," Poole said.

"Yeah, I know," she said. "But I love the stuff."

"We'll get more stuff when we get to wherever we're going," Poole said. "Better stuff."

THEY HAD four vehicles, an Audi A5 convertible for Box, a Mustang for Poole and a Ford F-150 pickup, plus Darling's pickup. Poole had shied away from the idea of a flashy car when they first got to Texas, but didn't take long to figure out that flashy cars in Dallas were like Kias in Jackson, and he *did* like fast cars.

This morning, though, he went back and forth to the pickup, loading up tools and guitars from the workshop, computers, televisions, stereo equipment, guns, silverware, dishes, all crammed into U-Haul boxes as fast as Box and Darling could do it.

Arnold had told Poole on the phone the night before that the feds didn't actually know their specific address, only that they were in Dallas. Arnold didn't know how they knew that: they must have some kind of source. Poole, Darling, and Box thought they had some time, though it was impossible to tell how much: it would be best to get out as soon as they could. They'd store the Mustang and the F-150, Poole decided, until they could come back and retrieve them. Box would take her convertible, because a single woman in a convertible looked harmless, and Poole would ride with Darling, because nobody was looking for Darling in Texas, as far as they knew.

They were done packing up the valuable stuff by mid-morning and still had more room in the storage unit, so Box got them to take over a dining-room table with chairs, the bed stand, a bureau and mirror, and two big chests of drawers. That was it, that was all the place would take. They moved the Mustang and the F-150 into separate units, and then Poole and Darling went into the management office and paid cash for two years' storage. While the owner was writing out a receipt—they got ten percent off for the cash, because the owner didn't plan to pay taxes on it, and everybody knew it—Darling was looking up at an overhead TV, and bumped Poole with his elbow.

Poole looked up at the TV screen, which showed a bunch of cops and lots of yellow crime scene tape around a house in Northeast Dallas. A female newscaster was saying, in a voice-over, "Unofficial police reports say that two people were executed in the Bennett house, and that the man in the rear house was tortured to death . . ."

The owner had finished with the receipt and looked

up and said, "You hear about that? Some guy got all chopped to pieces by some fruitcakes . . ."

OUTSIDE, Darling said to Poole, "I think that was Arnold. One of the cops on the TV looked like that Davenport guy who came to my place. I'm pretty sure it was him."

"If it's the cartel guys, and that's Arnold's place, and if Arnold gave them my phone number, and if they have a way to trace it . . ."

"Gotta move," Darling said.

They got back to the house fifteen minutes later and they were gone in thirty, with no solid plan. They headed north on I-35E, to Denton, and rendezvoused at the Golden Triangle Mall, at a free-standing Starbucks.

They got muffins and coffee. The place was crowded inside, but the outside tables were empty and they took one, in the sunshine. Box had brought her Mac Air from the car. "They got Wi-Fi here. Let me get online and see what I can find out about those killings down in Dallas," she said. A minute or so after she got online, she said, "Shit. Fox 4 is identifying the tortured man as Derrick Donald Arnold, says he works at the T-Bar—a gentlemen's club—and has an arrest record for assault and a variety of drug charges . . ."

"Now we know for sure," Darling said. "But we got a complication with that marshal being here."

"Not a complication anymore," Poole said. "Maybe they'll all find our house, but they won't find us."

Box sniffed. "I really liked that place. I was thinking we might get a cat."

The two men looked at her, and then Poole chuckled. "I guess we could. We could still do that. We need a place to settle in."

* * *

FORTY MILES to the south, Soto knocked on Kort's motel room door. They'd been up until five o'clock in the morning and had slept past noon. Kort let him in, and Soto asked, first thing, "How's your ass?"

"Some better," she said. She walked back and lay belly down on the bed, cranking her head up on a pillow so she could see him. "Still hurts, but I'm not getting any more of the juice out of the holes. I think the penicillin is working."

"Can you drive?"

"If I have to," she said. "Still got a dozen pain pills."

Soto nodded: "I'm gonna get the other car. You can wait here until I get back with it."

"What's going on?"

"The College-Sounding Guy has another place for us to check. A row of rental town houses," Soto said. "Forty of them. Davenport was there for almost two hours, up at the west end of the place, but we don't know exactly which one."

"We got a name?"

"We got a bunch of names. The College-Sounding Guy got them from the gas company. Two of the renters have drug busts, another guy's been up on assault. They might be guys we want to look at. But the main thing is, there's a live-in manager, and I'll bet Davenport talked to him. We get to that guy and we'll have some idea of what was going on."

"Think he'll talk?" Kort asked.

"I wasn't planning to ask him nice," Soto said.

"Sounds . . . funky."

"It is. But it's all I can think to do," Soto said. "You don't have to come in with me—I want the extra car there, in case of trouble."

"You're expecting trouble?"

"No, but . . . it's the same deal every time, dumbass. Two cars, if there's any way to do it. Already saved us once on this trip."

"What if Davenport found Poole and arrested him? If he was there for two hours . . . that's a long time."

Soto was shaking his head: "He went from the town houses straight back to his hotel. There wasn't any arrest. And he *was* there for a long time, which makes it more interesting. And then, the Boss is getting antsy."

Kort: "He called you?"

"Yeah. Wanted a full report. I had to tell him about your ass. He's really unhappy about that—says you probably left some DNA behind, so if you ever get looked at, they'll know you're the tool queen. Then they'll put some real pressure on you, and you'll spill your guts."

"Wouldn't do that," Kort said.

"Course you would. Never heard of anyone who wouldn't, if the choice was that or the needle," Soto said.

"Including you?" Kort asked.

"Fuck you," Soto said. And a moment later, "Yeah, including me. I met a guy in the joint down in Florida who was on death row for six years, and then they called it off and gave him life, instead. He said when he was on the row he'd sit there in his cell and imagine getting strapped into the chair—they still had the chair back then—knowing that it's coming. Day after day, thinking about it, dawn to dark, getting closer and closer. Says in the end, he would have said anything they wanted, to get out of it."

Kort thought about that for a moment, then pushed herself up off the bed and said, "Okay. Let's get it over with. We didn't get shit from Arnold. We gotta do something."

16

THE TOWN HOUSE COMPLEX was made up of forty-two separate houses in six brown-brick buildings, two ranks of three buildings each. The backs of the buildings faced each other across a rectangle of brown grass with three neglected swing sets and a large dirt square that might once have been a swimming pool.

Each building had a parking lot out front, and the lots were connected by driveways at the ends.

During the trap-baiting phase, Lucas, Bob, and Rae had sat with their working phones at the west end of the front lot, and hoped the killers, if they came, would have precise enough instructions that they would come to that corner.

Lucas was on the west end of the front lot and Rae was on the east end, eighty or ninety yards away. Bob was watching the back lots, in case the cartel people came in that way. The windows in the town houses were small.

Other than the small windows, they were essentially surrounded by the concrete walls of commercial buildings across the street and down the street in both directions. If it came to shooting, there shouldn't be any collateral damage.

They'd been waiting for an hour when Soto cruised by in the black Tahoe. Lucas couldn't make out the driver and the truck kept going, took a right at the corner, and disappeared. Four or five minutes later, another black Tahoe went by—but Tahoes were common in Texas, so it might have been a different one. The second time, he noted the tag, which was from North Carolina.

Between the two Tahoes, a half dozen other cars passed the front of the complex, and two turned in, and the drivers went into their homes. One of the cars that went by was a maroon Ford Fusion, driven by Kort, who was trying to stay as light on her butt as possible. A motel cushion helped, as did the pain pills, but she was still tender. Her .223 sat on the floor of the backseat, covered with a black blanket. She didn't see Lucas in the Jeep because he was lying well back, and he didn't recognize her in the Ford.

The maroon Ford went by a second time, and Rae called Lucas and Bob on their shared radios: "I'm interested in the maroon Ford," she said. "The woman inside seems to be looking at the town houses, even though she's not turning in. This is the second time she's done it."

"I can't see her face that well," Lucas said. "I'm getting some sun off the windshield where I'm at."

Bob said, "Well, I saw her turn at the corner up there, turn right and come down toward me, and then she turned right at my corner, and then turned right again at the end of the block, like she's going in circles. Want me to drop in behind her if she comes around again?"

"I'll do it," Lucas said. "I looked her right in the face

at Darling's farm. I'll recognize her if I see her again. That Ford's been moving fairly slow, I'll pass her and take a long look."

THE FORD didn't come back, not that they saw, until it was too late. The Tahoe came back, though, and turned into the front parking lot.

Lucas called Bob and Rae and said, "Rae, you see the black Tahoe?"

"Yeah."

"I think that's the third time that it's been around. It for sure has been around twice in the last fifteen minutes."

"All right. You gonna move on him?" she asked.

"Doing it now," Lucas said. "Bob, you want to come over to this side?"

"On my way. Thirty seconds."

Lucas would recognize either Soto or Kort, and they would recognize him, so he didn't try to get too close to the Tahoe. As the driver parked it, Lucas pulled into a space fifty or sixty feet away, behind another car and a pickup. The Tahoe's driver didn't get out right away.

Rae was looking at the driver from the other end of the block, through a pair of Canon image-stabilized binoculars. "He's just sitting there. All I can tell you is that he's a short guy. His head doesn't get to the top of the headrest. He has dark hair. Thin."

"That could be him," Lucas said. And, "I can't see him. Keep me up on what he's doing."

Bob called: "I'm setting up at the end of the parking lot. Right behind that rug company van. You see me, Rae?"

"Gotcha. If he gets out and walks to the town house he's in front of, you'll be shooting right at me," she said. "Don't do that."

"I will take care," Bob said.

"Okay, he's getting out," Rae called. "There's another car turning into the lot. I think he might have been waiting for it. Or maybe not."

"Maroon Ford?"

"No, it's one of those little cream-colored British Cooper things."

Lucas saw the Mini Cooper pulling slowly into the parking lot, driven by a heavyset, bushy-haired man wearing black plastic-rimmed celebrity glasses. He was talking on his cell phone. Lucas had never seen the man before, but he could see a short man walking on the other side of the car. The Mini paused in exactly the wrong place, from Lucas's point of view, and Rae called, "What do you think, Lucas?"

"I haven't gotten a clear look at him . . ."

The Mini Cooper driver finally picked out a parking space and pulled away. The short man climbed a stoop at the front of a town house, rang the doorbell, and took a furtive look around, peering directly at Lucas without seeing him in the Jeep. Lucas called, "That's him. That's the guy."

Bob called, "Coming in closer."

Lucas: "Good, but keep an eye on the guy in the Mini. Don't know what he's doing."

Rae: "I'm coming. Call it, Lucas."

Lucas was climbing out of the Jeep, keeping as much of the vehicle between him and the man on the step as he could. He said to the radio, "I'm going to call him down."

Bob: "The guy in the Mini has got keys out. I think he's going up to that town house . . ."

Soto pushed the doorbell again and Rae said, "Lucas, wait just one . . ."

Lucas didn't think he could and instead lifted his pistol and shouted "You! Stop! Federal marshals."

SOTO TURNED toward him and his right hand dropped diagonally to the left side of his belt line: a concealed weapon. Lucas could sense Rae running in from the east side and Bob was coming from farther west, staying close to the front of the town houses where Soto wouldn't be able to see him.

Lucas shouted: "Federal . . ."

And the town house door opened and a big man was standing there in a T-shirt and cargo shorts and Soto shoved him back and lurched inside.

Bob was still coming and Lucas screamed, "He's inside, might come out the back. Bob, cover the back!"

Bob pivoted and ran hard toward the end of the building and a second later was out of sight. Lucas ran toward the still-open door and Rae was coming up with her M4 and Lucas got to the door and saw the man in the cargo shorts pressed against a closet door and Lucas shouted, "U.S. marshals, where is he?"

The man called, "Out the back, he's got a gun . . ." and pointed, and Lucas and Rae went that way.

Lucas was at the back door and saw Soto a hundred feet away, angling toward one of the center buildings, and he shouted, "Stop! Stop!"

Soto kept going, then Rae leveled the M4 and Lucas said, "What?" and she fired a quick burst past Soto and into the brick side of the building behind him and Bob was coming and shouting, and Soto abruptly stopped and put his hands in the air. He had a pistol in one and hastily threw it on the ground.

Lucas called to the others, "Watch for another gun,"

and Bob shouted, "Into the dirt, facedown, into the dirt."

Soto, his hands above his head, knelt, then lowered himself facedown into the dirt. Rae had the rifle pointed at Soto's head, and Lucas came up from the side, and then Bob was there with handcuffs. "Bring your hands down behind you, one at a time . . ."

He did and Bob cuffed him. A minute later, they'd taken another pistol off the short man, from an ankle holster, and a heavy switchblade from a side pocket. Lucas pulled Soto's wallet out of a back pocket, took out a Florida driver's license that said "Stanley Evans."

Lucas looked at Soto and said, "Stanley Evans? Right."

"He'll be in the database," Rae said.

"Scared the shit out of me when you opened up," Lucas said to Rae. "I was afraid chunks of lead would be coming back at me."

She shook her head: "Low penetration rounds. They hit that brick wall and turn into dust. Certainly would have chewed up ol' Stanley, though."

She looked at Soto, who said his first words: "Fuck you."

Rae said to him, "Let's go for a ride, Stan."

KORT HAD TRAILED Soto to the town house complex, had checked the place out in two passes, finally agreed with Soto that he should go ahead and make the approach to the manager, whose apartment number they'd gotten from the town house complex's website, along with a map of the complex.

She was a block behind when Soto turned into the parking lot, and she stopped on the side of the street, watching. He sat in the car for a couple of minutes, doing

God knew what, then got out and walked toward an apartment door.

The rest of it happened like a bad dream: the cop from Darling's place popped out from behind a car, pointing a pistol at Soto, and then she saw a tall black woman running across the parking lot carrying a black rifle, and she grabbed her phone but it was way too late and the whole thing was going up in smoke . . .

She'd been thinking about what Soto had said about giving everything up to the cops, to avoid the needle, and she felt the panic clutching at her throat. She'd never been arrested. Soto would give her up . . .

The big cop, Davenport, ran across the lot and disappeared into the town house like an actor in a silent movie, and the black woman went in behind him. Then she heard the shots . . . a machine gun, not Soto's pistol. Was he dead? She put the car in gear and rolled toward the apartment complex . . .

THE MAN in the cargo shorts came out the back door and asked, "What happened?"

"Sorry about that," Lucas said. Bob had Soto by one arm, Rae had him by the other, Lucas was off to the side. "We had a complicated situation out front and he managed to get to your door. Didn't want to risk a shot with civilians around. Like you."

"He doesn't look all that tough," the man said. He was built like a construction worker, thick arms with a Statue of Liberty tattoo on the right bicep, a heavy gut. "I coulda kicked his ass."

"He is the worst man you'll ever see in person," Lucas said. "He might even be worse than anyone you'll ever see in the movies."

"No kiddin'?" The man was checking out Soto again. "No kiddin'."

Rae and Bob were walking Soto around the building, to the front parking lot, and Lucas hurried to catch up. Bob had his phone out and was talking to the Addison police, saying, "It would be helpful if we could have a crime scene person come by . . ." and a second later, with a hand covering the phone's microphone, he called to Lucas, "They'll have some cops here in five, crime scene guy in ten."

Lucas said, "Okay."

Rae was asking Soto, "Who were you trailing? We know you were trailing one of us, and thought it might be . . ."

They had come out from behind the building and were walking toward Lucas's Jeep. They would handcuff Soto to one of the steel seat supports and take him to the lockup at the federal building, until they could arrange something more permanent.

At that moment, the maroon Ford stopped on the street and a woman got out of the far side of the car and looked toward Lucas and the other three and Lucas saw the gun coming up and screamed, "Down, everybody, get down . . ." and his gun was coming up and as they all dropped to the ground, the woman swept them with a burst from an automatic rifle, and Lucas was banging away at the car with his .45 and Rae was struggling to get the M4 off her shoulder and then the woman was in the car and speeding away. Lucas's mag was empty and he dropped it and slammed in another and he turned and looked and Rae had her M4 up but wasn't firing, and Bob had his pistol up . . .

The Ford made a turn at the corner and was gone. Lucas ran halfway to the Jeep, realized that a chase would be hopeless—the Ford was out of sight for too long, he'd have no idea of where she went in the tangle of streets around the airport. He stopped, said, "Goddamnit," and turned and hurried back to the others to see if anyone had been hurt.

Bob was on the phone again, calling out a description, and said, "Then get me to nine-one-one . . . Wait a minute, I'll dial from here."

Soto lay flat on the ground, faceup, eyes open and fixed. Rae still had her gun up, looking out at the surrounding streets, shook her head as Lucas walked back, and then they both walked over and looked down at Soto. Rae said, "My God."

Soto's chest was soaked with blood. He'd been hit at least a half dozen times, Lucas thought. When he, Bob, and Rae had dropped to the ground, Soto had stayed upright, maybe thinking he could run out to the woman's car. Not a good idea.

Bob was talking to a 911 operator, giving a description of the fleeing car and where it was last seen. Rae was staring at the body. "What the hell? What the hell was that?"

Lucas said, "She wasn't shooting at us. She was taking out a guy who might talk."

Rae squatted next to Soto and shook her head. The man in the cargo shorts came out the front door, a beer in his hand, and looked at them and said, "Oh, boy. That's . . . Oh, boy."

AFTER THAT, it was paperwork and long conversations with bureaucrats at SOG and with Forte in Washington, and local cops coming and going, and the crime scene guy picking up the dropped revolver and brass and measuring distances. The medical examiner's van came and Soto's body went away, and a crew from the fire department washed away a six-foot-wide blood puddle on the tarmac.

The local police hadn't seen the shooter's car, except when they saw too many of them: the Addison police department stopped eight cars of the right description, but said they could've stopped a hundred, or a thousand, if they hadn't given up first.

By nightfall, they were mostly done with the routine, and Russell Forte called from Washington and said, "We got a quick hit on the fingerprints. His birth name was Marco Obregon, born in Miami, but he changed it to Marco De Soto, maybe to get out from under the other convictions. He's got a rap sheet about a mile long— convicted on attempted murder and aggravated assault and simple assault, acquitted on one charge of murder, nolo'd on another, convicted on possession of a firearm by a felon, acquitted on a couple of drug charges. He was like a walking monument to the credulity of parole boards. He's got an address in Coral Gables and an FBI is on the way there."

"We need the name of the woman he was working with," Lucas said.

"We're going for that," Forte said. "We haven't seen anything yet—maybe the FBI guys will turn something up."

BACK AT THE HOTEL, Lucas, Bob, and Rae changed clothes and then met in the bar and ate nachos and drank a few margaritas, and Rae said, "This has been an unusual day."

"Your people giving you a hard time?" Lucas asked.

"Nothing like that—they're more like excited. Wish-I'd-been-there stuff," Rae said.

Bob asked Lucas: "This happen to you much?"

"From time to time," Lucas said. "The weirdest thing

about today was, we might have saved Garvin Poole's life."

Bob popped a handful of salted peanuts and said, "Didn't think of that. But you're right. As long as that woman doesn't catch up to him. She's the one I wouldn't want to meet in the dark."

17

LUCAS WAS normally up late, but on this night, he'd turned the lights off at midnight, then lay awake in the dark thinking about the shooting, and about Poole. At two, he rolled over and looked at the clock: he needed some sleep, but he also wanted to get going early in the morning. Or get somebody else going. Rae had said she was an early bird. Two o'clock certainly qualified as early.

He turned on the bed light, crawled out of bed, picked up the phone, and called her room. She answered on the fifth or sixth ring and, sounding groggy, asked, "Who is this?"

"Lucas. You got a pen or pencil?"

"Uh, what happened?" she asked.

"I had a thought and I need you to do something tomorrow morning early," he said.

"Jesus, Lucas, you know what time it is?"

"Yeah. I'm looking at a clock. It's ten minutes after two. You got a pen?"

"Just a minute." A minute later she said, "Go ahead."

"I need you to go back to Arnold's house. Get an Addison cop to go with you if you need to. Look at his guitar. It's got a weird checkerboard top to it. I want you to see if there's a manufacturer's name on it. Arnold called it by some name . . . had something to do with parts . . ."

"Partscaster."

"Right. Like a Stratocaster. He said Poole built it out of parts. I want to know where he got the parts. When you find that out, I want you to track down the company and find out what Dallas addresses they've shipped parts to. Especially addresses that have ordered parts a number of times, to build entire guitars."

"I can do that, but you think this might have waited until the morning?" she asked.

"Nah. I get up late and wanted to get an early start on this. You get up early, so you can get started without me."

"Listen, waxworks . . ."

"I'm tired now, so I'm going to sleep. I'll call you when I wake up," Lucas said.

"Listen . . ."

Lucas hung up, turned out the lights. Grinned in the dark and fell asleep. He slept like a baby until twelve minutes after nine o'clock.

RAE STILL FELT groggy when her alarm went off at five forty-five. She'd usually do a half hour workout before cleaning up, but decided to skip it and get moving. Bob was also an early riser, so she called him, found him awake but not out of bed yet. "That fuckin' Davenport called me at two a.m. and gave me a job," she told Bob. "I figure if I have to start early, I might as well make you miserable, too."

"Did you take it lying down? Or did you show a little gumption?"

"Lying down. Besides, he had a good idea," she said. "I'll knock on your door in twenty minutes."

THE DALLAS MORNING was crisp and cool, with the nice smooth feeling that a hot place gets at night. Not quite real autumn in Texas, not yet. Rae drove, Bob yawning next to her, and they swung through a Starbucks for coffee.

"So what do you think of Lucas?" Rae asked when they were back in the car again. She'd told Bob about looking Lucas up on the Internet, and what she'd found.

"He's a smart guy," Bob said. "And he likes the pressure. You know that thing about getting too close to the fire and you'll get burnt? He's already been burnt a few times, and I believe deep down in his little black heart, he likes it. Likes the action. He's been chasing Poole for less than a full week and he's already been in two shoot-outs."

"Yeah. We gotta think about that," she said, sipping at her latte.

"I've already thought about it," Bob said.

"What'd you conclude?"

"He's like us," Bob said. "If he doesn't get killed, or get one of us killed, he could be somebody you could hang out with."

"A friend? You think?"

"Something like that. Maybe. At least you've got somebody to play basketball with."

"I'm interested in seeing how that's going to work out—is he gonna get tougher with me, like really rough, or is he gonna back off a bit? Not polite, exactly, but you know—try to finesse me."

"I don't know," Bob said. "What are you going to do?"

"I'm gonna try to cut his heart out," Rae said. "But I don't know if I'll get it done."

THE TRAFFIC wasn't bad going across town—they got behind a car with a bumper sticker that said "OLD AND RETIRED" and in smaller letters "Go Around Me."

They did. They were at Derrick Arnold's place by seven o'clock, met by an Addison cop who had a key.

They went inside, found that it had been thoroughly scrubbed and smelled of industrial-strength lemon-scented bleach. The bird was missing, and the cop said it had been picked up by the local humane society.

The guitar was where Rae had first seen it, sitting next to its amp. They examined it inch by inch and found several different brand names, on the bridge, the tuning machines, and pickups. All those looked specific to the parts, though; then Bob spotted the guitar case, which had been stuck in a closet, and inside, the papers for the guitar, including the guarantees for all the parts and also guarantees on the body parts from Poody Parts of India-napolis, Indiana.

"That's what we need," Bob said. He looked at his watch: "Too early, the place won't be open yet. How about some breakfast?"

ON THE RECOMMENDATION of the Addison cop, they drove out to the Ray O' Sun diner, ordered pancakes (Rae) and waffles (Bob), and eventually got a phone call through to a man named Cy Wynn, who said he was the owner and sole employee of Poody Parts; Poody himself was dead.

Rae told Wynn, "What we need is addresses for people from Dallas who bought parts from you."

"I'd be happy to give them to you, but my, uh, computer record system isn't exactly fast," Wynn said. "It could take a while to search through . . . a few hundred names, at least, in a place as big as Dallas."

They were on Rae's speakerphone and Bob said, "This would probably be a repeat customer, not a one-off. Might have bought a bunch of stuff from you. As we understand it, this guy built quite a few guitars."

"That'd narrow it down," Wynn said. "You know what brand name he sold them under?"

"There's really nothing on the guitar like a brand name. He supposedly hand-carved and hand-painted the tops and backs. The one we saw had this kind of distorted checkerboard on it, wrapping around the back, where it narrowed down and twisted into a painted hole . . ."

"Oh, sure, that's Chuck Wiggin," Wynn said. "Like Chuck Wagon, but W-I-G-G-I-N. He does good work, mostly on Les Paul, Tele, and Strat replicas. He's not in trouble, is he?"

"You got a name and address?" Rae asked.

"Yeah, sure, let me look in my Rolodex . . ."

While he was doing that, Rae muttered to Bob, "He doesn't have a computer."

Bob nodded: "Probably the last guy in the country with an actual Rolodex."

Wynn was back in thirty seconds and read off the address where he'd been shipping guitar parts. Easy as that.

LUCAS CAME to the door in his shorts and T-shirt, yawning, scratching his stomach; somebody had started banging on the door at 9:12. He peeked through the door crack, saw Rae, and said, "I probably ought to put on some pants."

"You ain't gonna impress me, one way or the other," Rae said.

"Okay, c'mon in. I'll go put on some pants anyway." He yawned again, leaving the door open behind him and asked as he walked away, "Find anything?"

"Yeah. We got Poole's address," Bob said.

Lucas turned and looked from one to the other. They weren't laughing, though they might have looked a little smug. "Now I really need my pants," he said.

LUCAS HEARD their story, then called Forte in Washington. "We've got an address for Poole. Haven't looked at it yet, but it apparently was good three months ago."

"Do not go there," Forte said. "I got SOG on speed dial."

"Got a couple of SOG guys with me now . . ."

"I know all about Bob and Rae—and I think three more deputies and a couple of technical people would be about right. Listen, this isn't about some dim-witted gun freak. This guy can shoot and has proven he's willing to do it. You sit there, I'll get a SOG team to you before noon."

Lucas told Bob and Rae about Forte's decision and they both nodded and Bob said, "He's right. Get a big enough team and it's a lot safer than some knock-on-the-door small-city detective shit."

"One thing we have to consider—Poole may know we're here," Lucas said. "His folks were tortured to death, and Darling might be down here after the dope guys tried to grab his wife, and TV's been all over the Arnold murder. He'll know it's the cartel. He'll know about me, too, from Darling. If Janice Darling was lying about him not having a phone, and I believe she was, he might have already run."

"I ought to cruise the place," Rae said. "Get an old car from some crappy rental place, colored girl with a do-rag, he'd see me as a maid."

"We'd piss off Forte," Lucas said. He thought about that for a moment, then said, "What the hell, he needs to get used to it. The sooner the better."

"Let's go," Bob said. "Hot damn, we're cookin' with gas."

"Another saying from 1945," Rae said to Lucas. "The Stump collects them."

THEY FOUND the right car near the airport, at Scratch'n Dent Rentals, and a half hour after they talked to Forte, Rae was squeezing herself into a Toyota Corolla with a hundred and ten thousand miles on the clock. The rental agent guaranteed that it would get through the day, at twenty dollars a day, not including gas.

Lucas and Bob trailed her toward the address they'd gotten from Wynn at Poody Parts, and a minute out of the target, found themselves driving through a low-income shopping area. Bob said, "I got a bad feeling about this."

Lucas said, "Uh-huh."

A minute later Rae called and said, "The address is a mail drop. U-Postem."

"We're coming in to talk," Lucas said.

They sat in the Jeep outside U-Postem, arguing about the next step. Eventually, Rae went inside to see if she could wheedle a legitimate address for Chuck Wiggin out of the clerk. The clerk was willing to cooperate, but didn't have the information.

Rae returned to the Jeep and told Lucas and Bob about her talk with the clerk. "He says if they made their customers give them an address and a phone number, they wouldn't have any customers. He looked at me like I was retarded for asking."

"No chance that he's an alarm? That he's calling Poole right now?"

"I don't think so," she said. "I believe him about not having the records, and if he doesn't have records, why should Poole give him one?"

Bob said, "Yeah."

Lucas called Forte: "That SOG thing? Never mind."

"What happened?"

"I decided Rae should cruise the place in a junker car. Turned out to be a mail drop."

"Damnit. I could taste the guy."

When Lucas was off the phone, Rae asked, "Now what?"

"We know he's around here," Lucas said. "We have to think. Is there any way we could get at a public record that would take us to him? Anything at all?"

THEY DROVE back to the hotel and sat around and thought, and called Forte and got him thinking about it: how they could possibly use a telephone, gas company, or power company bill to track down Poole's house.

"The problem being, he's not living there as Garvin Poole," Rae said. "He's got a lot of money and for a thousand dollars you can get a perfectly good Texas driver's license under any name you want, if you know the right guy."

"We know he probably came here about five years ago," Lucas said. "Wonder if he bought a house? Assuming he lives somewhere around his mail drop . . . wonder how many houses sold in this area five years ago?"

"Thousands," Bob said. "People were pouring in here like rats around a Pizza Hut dumpster. Besides, I don't think he bought a house. Ties up too much money and the realtors look at you too close. What I bet is, he found a house to rent and had a quiet talk with the owner. He says, 'No lease, we'll pay you three grand a month, and if the tax man asks us, we'll tell him we pay you fifteen hundred.' That's what he did."

"You may be right," Lucas said. "But that doesn't get us any closer to Poole . . ."

Rae started talking about checking Texas driver's licenses with a face-recognition computer at the FBI, but Lucas was skeptical: "He's got a beard and wears eyeglasses, and the pictures are probably pretty shitty. We'll get twenty thousand false positives."

Bob eventually was the one who had an idea that worked. He'd been in the bathroom taking a leak, came out and said, "That took some pressure off my brain. Look—we're thinking too much about *right now*. But if he's lived there for five years, I wouldn't be surprised if he had a hardwired phone at the beginning. Most people did. We ought to go back five years with everybody we know who knew him and look at their phone records. See who they called in Dallas."

"Can we do that?" Lucas asked. He really didn't know.

"Depends on the phone company. AT&T keeps the records for something like seven years. Verizon and Sprint don't keep them so long, but they keep them for a few years. What I'm thinking is, Box was close to her uncle. She even risked going to his funeral, when a lot of people there knew who she was and the fact that the cops wanted to talk to her. I say, let's look at the uncle's phone records . . ."

They called Washington, and Forte said, "Yeah, we can do that. You got a name for the uncle, address, whatever?"

They had some of it, and Forte said he could get the rest.

Nothing was going to happen for a while, and they eventually drove to a Half-Priced Books and browsed for an hour. Lucas bought a book that told him how to match his personal coloring to the colors of his menswear, Bob bought a book on Leica cameras, and Rae found one on Latin American art. "Now I feel like the dumbshit in the bunch, which definitely isn't the case," Lucas said as they checked out.

"You sure about that?" Rae asked.

"Who gets you business class airplane tickets?"

"You've got a point," Bob said. To Rae: "For God's sakes, don't piss him off."

ON THE WAY BACK to the hotel, Forte called. "Tell Bob he's a genius. We got an old number in Dallas, with Time Warner Cable, but it's still working. It goes back to a month after the Chattanooga armored car shootings. For a Marvin Toone."

"That's him," Lucas said, and, "You're a genius, Bob."

"I knew that," Bob said.

"I'll crank up the SOG team again," Forte said.

"Hold on until we cruise it. We've still got Rae's rent-a-wreck," Lucas said.

"Call me," Forte said.

Rae said, "Marvin Toone. Makes me laugh."

"They all do that, guys on the run," Lucas said. "Pick out a name that sounds sorta like their own. If he'd changed his name to Bob, and somebody called his name, he might not react like a normal Bob."

"No such thing as a normal Bob," Rae said.

"You got me there," Bob said.

"But we knew all that anyway," Rae told Lucas. "I was laughing because of the Toone thing. You know, a guitar maker, picking out a name like Toone."

"Didn't see that," Lucas admitted. "Maybe you *are* smarter than me. And we already know Bob's a genius."

"Could be onto something," Rae said.

THE TARGET HOUSE was in the neighborhood called Preston Hollow, homes ranging from nice to jaw-dropping, on quiet leafy streets north of Dallas's downtown. Bob rode with Lucas in the Jeep, while Rae put the do-rag back on her head and followed them in. When they were a block away, Lucas pulled to the side of the street and watched as Rae cruised the house. She had her telephone set on "speaker," and told them, "Nice house, but not one of the best. Two-car garage. Got a fence around the backyard, and I think I can see another small building back there. A studio or something. Nothing in the driveway. Nothing moving inside, that I can see. Gonna loop the block."

They watched as she did a U-turn two blocks away and came back toward them. "Can't see much . . . Old guy across the street came out for his mail . . . he's going back inside now."

They watched as she turned into a driveway across from the "Marvin Toone" house. Lucas asked, "What the hell are you doing?"

"Applying for a housekeeping job," Rae said, on the phone.

"She's being Rae," Bob said.

Lucas: "For Christ's sakes . . ."

Rae said, "Shut up now, I'm carrying the phone."

THEY HEARD her knocking on the door and then a man's rusty voice: "Yes? What can I do for you, missy?"

"Sir, I'm a U.S. marshal, and don't tell me I don't look

like one because I know that. We are doing research on the house across the street, a Mr. Marvin Toone . . ."

"Don't know him. Never heard of him," the man said.

"The man right across the street." She pointed.

"Name isn't Marvin anything. It's William Robb. Will. You got the wrong address."

"I have a photograph here . . ." Lucas and Bob couldn't see it, but envisioned Rae pulling out the most recent mug shot they had, printed on a piece of eight-by-ten paper.

The rusty voice said, "Well, that's Will, all right. He's older and he's been growing out a beard the last few weeks, but yeah, that's him. I can tell you that he and Lora had a friend come in yesterday, big kind of pickup with double tires on the back, whatever you call those . . ."

"Dually," Rae said.

"Yeah, and the friend stayed over, and this morning they were tearing around in their two pickups, and they had some furniture loaded in one, looked to me like they were moving out."

"Yes? Have they been back?" Rae asked.

"Not that I've seen. They have three cars, well, two cars and a pickup, and they left the pickup somewhere, and then they pulled out in two cars and the visitor's pickup. Exactly what did they do?"

"We're not sure he did anything . . . but if you have any way to reach them, don't do it," Rae said.

"I don't, except for walking across the street and knocking on the door. Are you sure you're a marshal?"

"Absolutely. I'm going to walk away, now, and across the street . . . Please don't come outside until I wave at you."

Lucas and Bob saw her walk to the driveway, get in her car, and then she told them, "I'm going to knock on Poole's door. I'm ninety-nine percent sure that they're gone."

"Don't do that," Lucas said. "We need to talk about it first."

"I'm gonna do what I'm gonna do," Rae said. "Might as well get used to it."

Bob looked at Lucas and said, "Really—get used to it."

Rae backed her car out of the driveway, backed far enough down the street that she could pull into the target house, got out, and said, "I'm doing it," and they heard her banging on the door. No answer. She said, "There's a slot in the front drapes."

She moved sideways and looked in a window and said, "Looks like a lot of furniture is missing. I'm coming out."

Lucas said, "Okay, we've got a reasonable ID from that old man, whoever he was, and a telephone number, that ought to be enough for a judge."

"Got a mass murderer and a baby killer and a cop killer, ought to be good enough for anybody," Bob said. "Call your man in Washington and see how fast he can get a warrant."

They had the warrant in an hour, delivered by two Texas Rangers who brought a crime scene team with them.

18

WHEN KORT fled from the town house shooting scene, she hadn't done anything clever, because she wasn't a clever woman. After turning a couple of corners, she ran straight south, as fast as she reasonably could, to I-695 and got lost in the traffic. She'd picked that up from Soto: getting out is almost always the best thing to do. There are more eyes around than you know and if you try to hide, somebody will see you.

She'd freaked herself out by shooting Soto, though she didn't regret it. She'd changed hotels, and that night she'd driven carefully out into the countryside and had thrown the black rifle in a roadside slough. She thought she'd done the right thing: the federal marshals would know that she and Soto had killed Poole's parents, the Bennetts, and Arnold, and Bedsow, the old guy in Roswell, Georgia.

And Soto had told her he'd give up anybody and everything to avoid the needle.

Would the Boss accept that? She didn't know.

She sweated it out for twenty hours, all the possibilities. Kort wasn't sophisticated in the ways of the world, but she'd seen Mafia and cartel movies, and accepted the movie premise that organized crime was like a huge FBI or CIA, that they would find you everywhere, that they had eyes on every street corner and every bar. She could imagine somebody dropping a quarter in a pay phone and saying, "I found that broad you been looking for."

Ridiculous, but she didn't know it.

Twenty hours after the shooting, she'd decided that honesty would be the best policy. She had a phone number that she'd written on a piece of cardboard that she kept in a wallet. It was fifteen digits long, all that would fit on the cardboard, to disguise the starting point. She'd never used the number herself, Soto had always done the calling, but now she lay on her stomach, on the hotel bed, and punched the number into her last burner.

And quickly hung up.

Lay with her eyes closed for ten minutes, choking with fear. No choice. She dialed it again, and a man answered on the second ring: *"Sí?"*

"Soto died."

"Is this the lady who travels with him?"

"Yes."

"I will pass the message. Is this phone good?"

"First-time burner," Kort said.

"We will call you back at this number in less than one hour."

In less than one hour, a different man called back, and she thought it was the Boss himself, the soft, remote voice, the electronic hum in the background.

"Tell me . . ."

"On the phone?" Kort asked.

"It's safe enough."

She told him all of it: she'd been wounded, that they had tracked the marshals, and therefore Poole, to Dallas. That they'd been sucked into a trap set by the marshals, that Soto had been caught. That Soto had told her that he would give up everything to avoid execution. That she thought it best that he not be given the chance. There was no possibility that she could take him away from marshals armed with machine guns, so she'd shot him. They'd been close to Poole, but now she didn't know what to do.

When she finished, the man asked, "Where are you now?"

"A Holiday Inn . . ." She found the address on a room card and gave it to him.

"You waited to call us."

"I was afraid . . . and running . . . and I had things to do. Things to get rid of," she said.

"Listen, lady, you have done very well. I am impressed. Stay where you are. Some more ladies will come to see you, today," the Boss said. "Throw the telephone away and get a new one. When you get one, call this number, let it ring once, and then hang up."

"I can do that . . ."

Before she finished, the connection went dead.

BOX, POOLE, AND DARLING were still in Denton, walking around the shopping center. Darling wanted to get out of Texas.

"If the marshals are looking for us, they'll have brought in the local cops and probably the state cops, too," he said. "But cops get screwed up when they have to cross state lines—bureaucratic bullshit gets them tangled up."

Poole asked, "What are you thinking?"

"We oughta run up to Oklahoma. We can be there in an hour. Maybe get a motel in Ardmore. We can sit around and think about it for a day or two."

Poole looked at Box, who nodded: "Makes sense to me," she said.

They left Denton, continuing straight north on I-35, a three-vehicle caravan, crossed the state line, and a little more than an hour later checked into three separate rooms at a Comfort Suites. Three separate rooms in case the cops found one of them, they'd have a fast temporary refuge in two others. They met in Poole's room, talked about the situation for a while, then Box said she wanted to get some decent food and went out to find a super-market.

As the door closed behind her, Poole asked Darling, "What are the chances of somebody randomly spotting us here? On our faces?"

Darling shrugged: "Slim to none. You've never had a beard, before now, that I've seen, and your ID is good. Nobody knows my face anyway. Nobody knows the tags on your vehicles, and they won't find them by looking up the name you used on the house. I've always had a couple spare sets of tags, and I put one on my truck as soon as I got out of Alabama."

Poole thought about that for a few seconds, then said, "I'm dry as hell. Let's take my car and find us a couple of beers."

"Saw an Applebee's coming in," Darling said.

THEY DROVE a couple of minutes to an Applebee's, got a booth in a corner away from other patrons, ordered a steak and beer for Poole and fish and chips and a beer for Darling, and Poole said, "Sturgill, I know you have fun with your shitkicker act, but you're the smartest guy

I know. I gotta run, I know that, but I don't know where to run to. Dora thinks Florida, but I got this feeling that Florida's one place the marshals might look. The cartel boys, too. What do you think? Someplace further on south? I don't speak Spanish and the cartels carry a lot of weight down there . . ."

The waitress brought their beers and they both took a swallow, and when she was gone, Darling put his elbows on the table, leaned forward, and said, "You want my opinion, and I don't think you'll like it, I'd say Edmonton or Calgary, up in Canada."

Poole opened his mouth to protest, but Darling put up a finger to slow him down, then said, "Listen. Those two places got more than a million people each. You can get lost in them. Edmonton has this shopping mall that's got something like a thousand stores in it—it's bigger than AT&T Stadium."

"Get outa here." Poole tried to catch a Cowboys game at least once a year—AT&T Stadium was the biggest building he'd ever seen, much less been in.

"I'm serious. Edmonton is an oil town. All kinds of people coming and going, all the time. Lots of Americans, all over the place, including oil workers from the South, Texas, Louisiana. Nobody will give your accent a second thought. It's actually kinda like Dallas, except for the winter."

"Freeze my fuckin' ass off," Poole said.

"You get used to it," Darling said. "You spend most of the winter indoors. And you're really only talking about a couple of years until things cool down here in the States."

"How would I get across the border?"

"I can fix that," Darling said. "I know a guy, honest to God, smuggles stolen heavy equipment across the Minnesota border into Ontario. Getting you across the border would be nothing—take your pickup, if you want."

"Canada." Poole rubbed the side of his face. "Jesus, I got to think about that."

"Think about speaking the language," Darling said. "That's a big deal. If you don't know the language, you've got to rely on somebody else for everything."

"How do you know so much about this?" Poole asked.

" 'Cause if I ever have to run, that's where I'm going," Darling said. "Canada. I worked through all of this, years ago, with Janice. We have money stashed up there and a couple of good IDs for each of us."

The food came, and when the waitress had gone again, Poole asked, "How about Phoenix or Vegas?"

"Mmm, if I had to choose, I'd say Phoenix. That's another place with a lot of tourists going through, people moving in and out all the time, and it doesn't have the surveillance that Vegas does. Vegas has a million cameras all over the place, and I gotta believe that the feds monitor the video feeds with their face-recognition technology. That place is like a sump hole for old Mafia guys."

"Okay. Not Vegas. How about California?"

"About a billion cops," Darling said. "You move there, you'll have fifty government workers looking at you, checking your tax records, asking where you moved there from, where you work now, how long you've been there. California is like a Nazi state with palm trees—'Papers, please.' Seriously, I've looked into all of this."

"Ah, shit."

"You got another problem," Darling said. "I don't want you to get pissed when I say it."

"Dora."

Darling twitched a finger at him. "You've been thinking about it."

"Yeah. If they're looking for faces, hers is . . . distinctive. She's pretty, and lots of guys look her over. Including cops. If I stay with her, spotting her could mean spotting me."

"I didn't want to mention it, when she's around."

Poole ate silently until his steak was nearly gone, then said, "You know, I'll take the chance with Dora. I'm not leaving her behind. People get to know me, they don't like me—I can feel it. Dora knows me and she still likes me."

"I like you," Darling said.

"And I like *you*," Poole said. "But we are rare people. I mean, what would you do without your wife and kids? Who would your friends be?"

Darling looked out the window at the parking lot, then shook his head. "I don't know, I'd be pretty god-damn lonely."

"So we're stuck with what we got, and who we are," Poole said. "That's what we got to work with."

Darling chewed on his lower lip for a few seconds, then looked across at Poole and said, "You can't walk away from Dora, but you could shoot that little girl."

Poole said, "Yeah, well . . . I don't know what that is. I guess it means that I'll take care of me and mine, but I don't so much give a shit about anyone else. *You* yell for help, I'll come, no questions. Some stranger catches on fire, I wouldn't walk across the street to piss on him."

THAT NIGHT they got together in Box's room and ate roast beef sandwiches she'd bought at a supermarket, and argued about their next move. Darling mentioned Edmonton, and when Box found out where it was, she shook her head. "No way in hell," she said. "My uncle was somewhere up there during the Cold War, at a radar station. He said it got dark in November and didn't get light until March. Even if I could handle the cold, which I couldn't, I couldn't handle all that dark. I'm a Southern girl."

They ran again through the other possibilities—Arizona, California, Florida. Darling even mentioned the possibility of simply moving thirty or forty miles over to Fort Worth, or down to Houston or San Antonio.

"You've already got a few good sets of Texas IDs, you wouldn't have to go through that routine again, getting new ones in Arizona, getting new tags and all that," Darling said.

"Wasn't that big a problem," Poole said. "You got these illegals coming across the border, there's a whole industry out there making good phony IDs. The guy I got my Texas IDs from could probably get us good Arizona IDs."

"Texas is too scary now. Especially since we've left the house. I think it's Arizona," Box said. "That's good with me."

Poole turned to Darling: "You think you're still okay in Alabama—and I know you're anxious to get going up to Canada."

"Got to go," Darling said. "I need the alibi if the feds come around again."

"Could you go with us to Arizona?" Poole asked. "You and me in your truck? I'm thinking you got that hideout spot in your camper back. I've got three million in cash and a million and a half in gold I got to hide. If the cops pull me over . . ."

"What is it? Two days' drive down there? I can do that," Darling said.

"What about me?" Box asked.

"I need you in a different car," Poole said. "I'm going to put some of the gold and cash under your spare tire. If something happens to me and Sturg, you'll still be outside with some resources."

LATER, in bed, Poole said, "We'll drive separate routes down to Arizona. You drive five miles over the speed limit all the way, don't attract any attention. Don't take a drink—not a single fuckin' cocktail. I don't want you blowin' a twelve and having the cops taking the car apart."

Box nodded and asked, "Where are we going, exactly?"

"Can't tell you that, yet. I gotta go on the Internet and do some research. After we get there, we'll get a decent motel and lay up for a while, check out the situation. Find someplace nice, quiet, white, maybe a little older. Rent a house, settle in."

"Sounds right," she said. "Could we get together at night, along the way?"

He shook his head. "I'll be driving a different route. I don't want them spotting you, tracking you, then spotting me. And vice versa. I think we're okay, but I don't want to take any chances. That's why we'll split up the money—if something happens to one of us, the other one's still outside and has some cash to maneuver with."

"Right now, we got one car too many," Box said.

"I'll drive it back to Dallas tomorrow, store it with the truck . . ."

"You know what?" Box asked. "I'd feel better driving the truck. Would you mind?"

"No, that'd be fine."

"Maybe I'll put a couple pieces of furniture in it," she said.

Poole laughed and then said, "That's not a bad idea,

actually. Antique lady, out scouting around. Cops won't give you a second look."

"When do we go?"

"Well, Sturgill's getting antsy about going up to Canada," Poole said. "I'd say tomorrow morning, early."

"I'm scared," she said.

"I'm a little tense, myself," Poole said. "But what it is, is what it is."

She looked at the clock and said, "I'm going to sleep with you overnight, but I'll go mess up the bed in my room before we leave. So it looks sleeped in."

"Why don't we make this one look fucked in?" Poole asked.

"Good with me," Box said.

AS POOLE, BOX, AND DARLING worked through their next move, Kort spent a lot of time pacing. Lying faceup on the motel bed was still painful. Facedown, she couldn't see the TV, which was rattling along endlessly about the upcoming election, and she was too cranked to watch it anyway. She still had a Ruger .357 with a belt clip, and she got it, loaded it, and clipped it to the back of her sweatpants and pulled her sweatshirt over it. The weight of the gun caused her pants to sag, but that was the least of her worries.

What to do when the other "ladies" showed up? If they came in with guns, Kort wouldn't go easy, but, she thought, she'd probably go.

Made her cry, thinking about it. Life so far had been one long roll in the shit. The only thing she really liked about it was using her tools. The surge of pleasure and power she got from torture was as addictive as methamphetamine.

She went out only once, bought a pay-as-you-go burner phone, made the one-ring call to the secret number, and stopped at a pancake house, where she bought a double stack of buttermilk pancakes with link sausages, ate until she felt nauseous.

The knock on the door came at mid-afternoon. She was lying facedown on the bed, listening to CNN, and the knock made her jump. She slid off the bed, pulled her sweatshirt down, smacked her lips a couple of times, pushed her hair back, went to the door, and said, "Yes?"

A woman's voice: "Open up. It's us."

"US" turned out to be two women, late thirties or early forties, thin and tough like beef jerky, short hair, one blond, one brunette, small gold earrings, and ink: tattoos running up and down their exposed lower arms and legs, peeking out of the V of their blouses. The taller of the two had a triangle of three crude ink dots on her right cheek next to her eye. Some kind of secret prison symbol, Kort thought.

The short one asked, "You got a gun?"

"Yeah."

"Well, don't shoot us," she said. "My name's Annie, my partner here is Rosalind—Rosie. We're not here to hurt you."

"Then what are you here for?" Kort asked.

"To help out," Rosie said. "We don't have all the details, but the Boss wants his money back. We understand that you've run into some feds along the way."

Kort backed away from the door, but kept her hand on her hip, close to the revolver, and the two women stepped inside. They looked around the room, then Rosie took the office chair at the small desk, and Annie settled into the one easy chair.

Kort said, "I can't sit so well. I got shot in the buttocks."

"So we heard," Annie said. "You never got it fixed?"

"We fixed it ourselves," Kort said. "Cut a bullet out with a razor blade, bled like crazy . . ." She told them the whole story of the wound, and when she was done, the two women looked at each other, some silent agreement between them, and Rosie said, "You got some major balls, honey. How's the penicillin working for you?"

"I still hurt, but I don't see any infection," Kort said.

Annie said, "We got some OxyContin out in the RV. I'll get you some."

Rosie: "Let's do that first. Then you tell us about these guys we're looking for. And the marshals."

19

LUCAS, BOB, AND RAE broke into the house through the front door, because that looked like the least used, and so the least likely to have fresh prints. The three of them walked through first, clearing the place, with a variety of Texas cops waiting outside, and as they worked through the house, Lucas realized that Poole was gone.

There was still furniture inside, but it seemed that several pieces were missing, leaving behind leg indentations on the carpets. While there was still some clothing in the closets, it seemed to him that the good stuff was gone: no new men's shoes, lots of old dusty-looking Nikes, and no women's shoes at all.

Lucas looked under the sink and found some garbage, topped by a banana peel and moist coffee grounds; he looked in the master bedroom suite, and the bathroom cabinets were mostly empty.

Bob and Rae had gone to check the garage and a backyard shed while Lucas was poking around the kitchen and bedroom. The garage was empty, except for a well-used lawn mower. So was the shed. Rae said, "It looked like he used to have a lot of tools and stuff, but they're all gone. There's a homemade workbench in there and a trash bin with a broken guitar neck in it. Gotta be the right guy."

"Didn't miss them by much," Lucas said. "A few hours at the most."

"How do you know?" Bob asked.

"Banana peel and coffee grounds," Lucas said.

"Huh?"

"There was a banana peel on top of the garbage. Looked good as new. How long does that last? Not even overnight, I don't think. I bet it was dropped in there this morning. The coffee grounds were still wet."

"Well, shit," Bob said.

"If you were *really* a genius, you'd have thought of that old telephone thing yesterday," Rae said to Bob.

One of the crime scene crew people came out and said, "They didn't wipe anything. There are fingerprints all over the place and hair and everything else, sexual residue on the sheets."

"Get the prints going," Rae said. "If you get good ones, we'll have confirmation in a couple of hours."

"We can get good ones."

THEY EVENTUALLY went out to the back of the house, to a gas barbeque and a wooden picnic table. They sat at the table and Bob said, "DNA will get us confirmations both on the murders in Biloxi and the armored car job."

"Take a few days on the DNA," Lucas said. "I'll be happy with a good set of prints, right now."

"So they're running and we've got at least three fake IDs," Rae said. "Let's see if Poole has a driver's license under any of those names, and if he does, see if we can link it up to some license tags."

Lucas nodded and took out his phone: "Gotta get Forte on the computer shit. And, Rae, grab one of those Rangers and see what they can get out of the Texas DMV."

Forte was pleased: "Man, you got them on the run. Get me those prints!"

ONE OF THE RANGERS ran down the property ownership—it wasn't Poole—and got in touch with the owner, who showed up two hours after they broke through the front door. He was a heavyset man, red-faced, with a belly that bulged over his turquoise-and-silver belt buckle. He parked his Lincoln on the street, then wandered over to a Ranger, who brought him to Lucas. "What the hell is going on here?" he asked. And, "You busted down my door?"

The Ranger said to Lucas, "This is Mr. Carlton, Davis Carlton—he's the homeowner."

"We're looking for a fugitive named Garvin Poole," Lucas said.

"This ain't no Garvin Poole," Carlton said. "This here is a man name of Will Robb . . ."

Lucas showed him the mug shot and he scratched his head and said, "Damn. That sure looks like Will."

He'd rented the house to a man he knew as William Robb, he said, and he didn't know why the phone would be in the name of a Marvin Toone. "I didn't pay for a phone, or have anything to do with it," he said.

He collected two thousand dollars a month from the man he called Robb, and said that Robb had told him that he was a disabled veteran who'd fought in Iraq and

Afghanistan, and was living on a government disability pension from having breathed in poisonous gas.

"Pretty nice house for two thousand," Rae remarked.

Carlton flushed and said, "He was a war hero, I gave him a break on the rent."

"That's real patriotic of you," Rae said.

Carlton had no idea what kind of vehicles Robb and his wife owned, except that one was a white pickup. "He'd drop the rent off at my office, that's the only time I ever saw the man. I came by every six months or so to check on the property and there was never a problem. They seemed like a real nice couple. The kind of renters you hope for."

WHEN CARLTON LEFT, everything slowed down: there was no record of a Marvin Toone or a Chuck/ Charles Wiggin with the DMV, although there were several William Robbs. Lucas called Forte to get him working on Dallas-area William Robbs, but told the others, "Won't be one of them. I can feel it."

"Fake names are cheap, like burner phones," Bob said. "They got a different one for everything. Phones and names."

"Goddamnit," Lucas said. "We need to get on these guys. In twelve hours of driving, Texas speeds, they could be a thousand miles from here. By tomorrow night, they could be in California or Florida and we'll be starting all over."

"Tell me what to do, and I'll do it," Rae said.

Lucas scratched his cheek, looked blankly at the back fence, then said, "Well, first, go change into some marshal clothes. Then, we all knock on doors. Talk to neighbors. We can at least find out what kind of vehicles they're driving, and what color they are."

"I got the old guy across the street," Rae said. "He seems like a curtain-peeker."

THERE WERE five properties that touched Poole's: one on each side, one directly behind, and two at the back corners; three more houses across the street had a straight look at the driveway going back to the garage. Nobody in any of the houses had useful information, including the old guy across the street.

Robb, they said, had a gray car—or maybe dark blue—his wife had a black convertible, and they also had a white pickup, a Ford. Then a teenager who'd heard the cops were looking for information about Robb's car came down and told them that it was a metallic gray five-liter Mustang, less than a year old. A beautiful car, he said, and Robb's pride and joy; and Robb was a cool guy, played a mean guitar.

All of which added up to slightly more than nothing.

Forte called: "You got him. The prints are a direct hit—Garvin Poole and Dora Box."

"We knew that, but good to know for sure," Lucas said. "Trouble is, by now they could be two hundred miles from here."

THE CRIME SCENE PEOPLE were still working the house, and Lucas, Bob, and Rae were standing in the driveway, comparing notes, when the old guy from across the street came ambling over. He had a furry white mustache and clear blue eyes. Rae said, "Mr. Case. How're you doing?"

"You said if I thought of anything, let you know. I thought of something," Case said.

"Yeah?"

He pointed across the street, to the house next to his: it was an imposing place, faux-Colonial with white pillars hovering over a circular front drive. "That's the Smith place . . ."

"Talked to them two hours ago," Bob said.

"They tell you about the wedding last year?"

Bob, Rae, and Lucas exchanged glances: hard to tell where this might be going. Rae asked, "The wedding?"

"Their daughter got married. About time, in my opinion, she was getting long in the tooth and had sort of passed herself around town. But that's neither here nor there. They got married down at St. John's and then they had a reception out to the country club and then they had an 'at-home' pool thing for members of the wedding party." He pointed again at the Smith house and the circular drive. "The wedding party was all in limos, maybe ten, twelve black limos, and they all came up that circular driveway, one at a time, two or three minutes part. All the people were getting out, kissing each other, going inside. A wedding photographer was out taking movies of them coming up and getting out of the cars."

Bob said, "Yeah?"

Lucas said, "The cameras were looking across the street to this driveway."

The old man jabbed a finger at Lucas: "Bingo. They didn't invite me to the wedding, but they invited me over to the at-home reception because they thought I was lonely, my wife being gone, and also because they planned to play loud rock music all night and they didn't want me complaining to the police. I was standing there on the porch watching them make the movies and I distinctly remember Will Robb coming and going in his truck."

Bob said, "I'll go get the movies," and headed across the street at a trot.

Rae said, "Mr. Case, you are a sweetheart."

*   *   *

BOB DID EVENTUALLY get the movies, but it wasn't all that simple. At first, the Smiths weren't at home anymore, but Case told them that Emily Smith was a realtor, and they managed to locate her. She came home and gave them a compact disc with the wedding movies on it, and watching on the Smiths' high-resolution television, they could see license plates on Poole's white pickup, but the movies were not quite steady enough to make out the numbers. The plates were white, so almost certainly from Texas.

Bob and Rae wanted to send the movies to the FBI's digital imaging experts in Washington, but Lucas suggested that they first try the wedding photographer.

The photographer wasn't working that day, but agreed to meet them at his studio. He turned out to be a short, stout, solemn-looking man who dressed all in black, including a black fedora and a black string tie with an onyx slide. He brought the movies up on a computer screen, grabbed several frames of each instance where the license tags appeared, and began enhancing them in Photoshop.

The numbers never did get particularly clear, but enough numbers were clear enough in the different frames that by putting several frames together, they pieced out a good tag number.

"If the FBI has the capabilities that they're rumored to have, they should be able to get them a lot clearer," the photographer told them. "But remember this—I hold the copyright on these photos, not the Smiths. You can use them, but you can't publish them. I don't want to see these on TV."

"You're being less generous than you might be," Rae observed.

"I gotta eat. If somebody's going to put them out to the TV stations, it's gonna be me and I'm gonna get paid."

"Don't do it without talking to us first," Lucas said. "If you put them out there, and the suspects see them, they'll ditch the plates and we'll come bust you for interfering with a federal investigation and maybe accessory after the fact."

"I'll talk to my attorney about that . . ."

"Sure, do that," Lucas said. "If he needs further clarification, tell him to call me."

BACK IN THE CAR, Lucas called the Rangers at the Poole/Robb house, gave them the tag number, and they promised to wallpaper the entire state with it, and all the adjacent states. Lucas warned the Rangers that the people in the truck were armed and willing to kill.

"So are we," the Ranger said.

"Before you do that—kill them—I'd like to talk to them," Lucas said.

"We'll do what we can," the Ranger said. "I'm making no promises."

WHEN LUCAS was off the phone, Bob asked, "What are the chances?"

"We're maybe fifty-fifty to get a hit," Lucas said. "How many white Ford trucks in Texas?"

"About a billion, give or take."

On their way back to the house, a crime scene cop called from the town houses where Soto had been shot. "We picked up a lot of brass from the .223 used to kill Soto. Most of it had been polished clean, but we found two almost identical thumbprints on two cartridges. We got back a solid hit for a Charlene Marie Kort. The feds have no other record of her, other than a couple of speeding tickets given to a woman with that name in Florida."

"If there was no other record, where did her prints come from?" Lucas asked.

"The feds had them, but they were submitted as part of a background check by a security guard company in Tallahassee, eight years ago. That's all we know."

"And we don't know whether this Kort actually was the shooter, or whether she just handled the ammo at some point," Lucas said.

"No, we don't. But the ammo with the prints is identical to the ammo that had been polished, and the prints look to us to be fresh. They're very clear, they're not interrupted by scratches or rubs that you'd expect if the shells had been handled a lot. If the shells are polished, we figure there can only be a bad reason for that—it's what you expect from a really careful holdup guy, or a professional shooter. Like this Soto guy. Somebody else might not be so careful, pressing a cartridge down into a magazine."

"Okay, I get that," Lucas said. "And since the other person is a woman, and Charlene Marie Kort certainly sounds like a woman . . ."

"Yes. We think you should look up Charlene Marie Kort."

Lucas called Forte and gave him the name.

"NOW WE WAIT," Lucas said. "Hope there's a lot of football on TV."

"Could be some intense hoops back at the hotel," Rae said.

"Could be," Lucas said.

Bob was shaking his head. "Something's going to happen," he said. "We got momentum. Either this Kort is going to turn up or we'll get a hit on the plates."

"From your mouth to God's ears," Rae said.

20

DORA BOX woke up at four o'clock in the morning, listened to Poole breathing beside her. They'd gone to bed early—Sturgill Darling always went to bed early, being a farmer—and now she was wide-awake, alert, ready to go. She lay as still as she could for five minutes, then crept out of bed in the dark, got dressed, went to the door, and peeked out. Nobody in the hall.

She scurried down to her own room, where her suitcases were, pulled the bedcovers around, tossed the pillow to the foot of the bed, so that it looked like the room's occupant had had a restless night, then headed for the bathroom to begin her morning rituals.

A lot of free-floating stress, she thought, as she washed her face. This would be a tough day and potentially a dangerous one. They didn't know anything about what the federal marshals or the drug killers were doing, so they'd be flying blind.

On the other hand, Poole was confident in their maze of phony IDs. "They might eventually break them down, but by that time, we'll have new ones in a new place."

Box believed him; or believed *in* him. He hadn't been wrong about much, in the time she'd been with him. Not until the Biloxi robbery, anyway. She thought, *If only he hadn't done Biloxi . . .*

The night before, they'd agreed to stop at the storage unit in Dallas, pull out the truck for Box, and help her load a few pieces of furniture in the back.

She'd finished her shower, got dressed, and headed back to Poole's room. As she opened the door, the alarm clock went off. Poole shut it down and a moment later was up and looking at her.

"Been up long?"

She shook her head: "Half an hour. I'm all packed. You hit the bathroom, I'll start putting your bag together."

"Don't forget to search the room," he said jokingly.

"Never." Wherever they went, whatever they were doing, Box always searched the motel rooms before they left. Once, years before, she'd discovered a partially read paperback that Poole would have left behind. On two other occasions, she'd found pornographic magazines under mattresses, and while interesting, they belonged to somebody else.

"Call Sturgill, make sure he's up," Poole said. He yawned, stretched, and touched his toes.

"Yes."

She called and Darling was ready to go. "You need help carrying stuff out to the cars?" he asked.

"If you want to, that'd help," she said. They'd divided the money and gold the night before, about two-thirds to go with Poole, the other third to be packed in her car, neatly layered in two carbon-fiber suitcases. Darling looked wide-awake when he knocked on the door. Between them, they got everything but Poole's duffel bag out to the cars and locked away.

"Still dark," she said, looking up at the bright overhead stars. "I'm hardly ever awake at this time of day, unless I've stayed up overnight."

"It's early for me, too," Darling agreed. "I usually get up around five-thirty. That's the prettiest time, especially in the summer. Dew on the grass, birds waking up, air smells clean."

"If we can get Gar moving, we can be in and out of Dallas before it gets light," Box said.

They were walking back across the parking lot when Poole came down the stairs, carrying his duffel bag. "Let's just go," he said. "We can eat on the road."

Box insisted on checking the motel room one last time, to make sure they weren't leaving anything; Poole and Darling waited impatiently until she got back. She said, "We're good," and they were on I-35 by four forty-five, traveling fast.

TWO HOURS LATER, they were at the storage units. Box traded her Audi for the pickup, backed down the narrow alley to another storage unit, and Poole and Darling helped her load a favorite table and chairs in the back and covered it all with a blue plastic tarp, tied tightly into the truck bed. Poole left his Mustang in another bay and loaded his share of the gold and money into Darling's truck.

Darling waited while Poole and Box said good-bye. "I'll see you in New Mexico," he said. "Once we're there, we'll be okay."

"Goddamnit, Gar, I wish we didn't have to split up," Box said, leaning into him.

"It's safest this way. We should be okay, we've still got a jump on them, but if one of us gets stopped . . ."

"I know, I know . . ." They spent a minute kissing good-bye, Box's arms wrapped around Poole's neck, until Darling called, "Sun's coming up." Poole pushed her away and said, "New Mexico."

"New Mexico," she said, and got in the truck.

ALTHOUGH their separate routes would be roughly parallel, Poole and Darling took the longer run. They planned to go south from Dallas on Highway 281 to Burnet, then west until they picked up I-10 into El Paso. Box would take I-30 through Fort Worth and then I-20 most of the way across west Texas until she also hooked into I-10 to El Paso. El Paso bordered New Mexico to the north and west, and Mexico to the south. They all had passports: if worse came to worst, they might be able to hide the money in the States and cross the border to Juárez, Mexico, at least long enough to slip the American law.

The sun wasn't quite up when Box left the storage units and had just peeked over the horizon when she got on I-30. From there it was smooth sailing out on I-30 and then I-20, heading southwest. She'd decided she'd stop for breakfast at Abilene, and then push on. The man-hunt would be in the Dallas area. The farther away she got, the better off she'd be.

Poole called at eight. "We're outa town. How're you doing?"

"Doing good. I'm on I-20. Thinking about breakfast at Abilene."

"See you tomorrow."

"Tomorrow, babe."

Then everything went to hell, and all at once.

She didn't see the highway patrolman until she was

right on top of him. She'd crossed a bridge, where low trees crowded right up to the highway, and there he stood, a radar gun in his hand. His car was parked behind him, off the side of the road.

Box tapped the brake, saw that she was no more than two or three miles an hour over the speed limit—she was in the slow lane, being passed regularly by most of the traffic—and her first thought was, *Okay*.

Then she looked in the rearview mirror and saw the highway patrolman running for his car. She was a quarter mile down the highway before he got to it, and another few hundred yards when the light bar came up and the patrol car hit the highway. She had no doubt in her mind, he was coming after her, and that was confirmed when he moved into the same lane.

She said, "Shit," and with panic tight around her heart, she floored the gas pedal. There was no way she'd outrun him, not on the highway—she could see him closing—and a few seconds later, saw an exit sign coming up. She took the exit, Highway 919 North, and a sign that said "Gordon."

There was no town at the end of the exit ramp and the cop was getting very close, hitting the end of the exit ramp as she made the turn onto 919. Still coming.

On 919, she pushed the truck as hard as she could, tried to get the phone up to call Poole, fumbled it, saw it drop into the passenger footwell: no way to get it.

"Oh my God," she cried. The cop was no more than a hundred yards behind her, and still closing. To her left, a dirt road cut off into the scrubby trees, and she said, again aloud, "Fuck it," and took the turn. By the time she got straight, the cop was right on her bumper, siren wailing into the morning. There'd been no rain for a while, and she started throwing a cloud of dust and could see the cop back a ways, and up ahead, an even narrower track. She took that one, deep into the woods, crashed across a dry creek bed, powered away, saw the cop hit the dry bed, get across it, still coming.

She had some hope, now. First chance, she left the track altogether, weaving through the trees. The truck bottomed once, twice, wheels grinding into the raw dirt, and then . . .

The cop was gone. She could still see the multicolored red-and-blue flashers back through the trees but she kept going, and when she couldn't see them anymore, stopped long enough to get the phone off the floor and call Poole, and started driving again.

When Poole answered, she cried, "They're all over me. The cops are all over me. I'm running through the trees . . ."

"What? What?"

"They must know the truck. I wasn't speeding, I was in the slow lane, and the cop saw me and he came right after me," she said. "I got off the highway into the woods, I'm running through the woods, I've lost them now, but I can't go back on the roads . . ."

"Listen," Poole said. "Now listen. How far away are they?"

"I don't know, I've lost them. I'm lost, I'm off-road, I'm back in all these trees."

"Keep going. See if you can spot a house, or anything that you'd recognize later. Anything. Then get the money and gold out and stick it under a tree or somewhere people can't see it. You gotta hide it. If you hide the money, they got nothing on you, babe. They got nothing."

The truck bounded over a hump of dirt and onto another dusty track. She wasn't sure, but she thought she was moving away from the cop car, the sun still at her back. Up ahead, she saw the corner of a metal building, and she said into the phone, "Okay, I see this building up ahead. Just the corner of the roof, it's silver. Okay, and off to the side, I can see the interstate through a hole in the trees. I must have come back to the interstate. I'm going to turn down that way."

She followed a line of dirt, not even quite a track, past the edge of a pond, and rolled up to a fence and said, "There's a fence, I can't get across it . . ."

Poole, calm: "Can you stop there?"

She couldn't see anything in the rearview mirror. "Maybe. I'll stop."

She stopped the truck, got out. She could still hear the cop's siren, but it must have been several hundred yards away. One of the low scrubby trees, ten yards inside the fence line, had branches that dropped all the way to the ground. She popped open the back doors on the truck, got the two black cases with the gold and the cash, hauled them over to the tree, and pushed them back through the knee-high weeds to the tree trunk. She stepped back, to check: the briefcases were invisible.

She walked back to the truck and said, "I put the gold and the money under a tree, in high grass. You can't see it, the branches come right down to the ground. I'm going to the tree . . ."

She went to the tree and paced off the distance to the fence.

". . . It's ten long steps from the fence. Probably ten yards, and I'm right across from the entrance to a road on the other side of the interstate. I'm only a little way west from the exit to Gordon, Texas. North side of the interstate, west of the exit. Gordon, Texas. G-O-R-D-O-N. From where I am, I'm looking right past the pond to the silver roof."

"Got it all," Poole said. "Get yourself out of there. Try staying on the back roads, see if you can find a place to hide until dark."

"I don't think that's going to work, babe," Box said.

"If it doesn't, don't say anything to the cops," Poole said. "Not a word, except 'I want a lawyer.' You've heard me talk about this. You want a lawyer."

"I've still got the gun."

Long silence, then, "You've never used one before. I don't think that's a good idea."

"I could ditch the truck and walk over to these buildings, see if I might catch somebody there."

"I don't think so. You don't have time to clean up the truck, get rid of prints and all that . . . You shoot somebody, kidnap somebody, then you're in the shit. I think you better throw the gun away. Sturgill is saying the same thing."

"Okay. I'll do that," Box said.

"Listen. Do you have that orange blouse with you? The one I bought in Dallas and you don't wear?"

"Yes, in my suitcase."

"If you have time, get it out of the suitcase and rip a piece out of it and tie it to the bottom of the fence like ten yards from the tree where the money is. Make it easier to find when we come back for it."

"If we come back."

"We will, babe. We will," Poole said.

"I'm hanging up now. Oh, God, Gar . . . I'm hanging up."

SHE FOUND the orange blouse, but instead of ripping it, simply bunched it up and tied it to the bottom of a fence post fifteen long steps west of the tree where the money was. She went back to the truck, got the pistol she'd kept for self-protection, and threw it under the tree with the money and gold. Then she got back in the truck, called Poole, and said, "Okay, baby, the orange blouse is on the bottom of the fence fifteen long steps west, that's WEST of the tree where the money is. You have to walk along the fence to see it. The gun's with the money."

"Move away from there, then. Take it slow. There's probably a road past those buildings, or a driveway, see if you can sneak out of there . . ."

"I'm gone again," she said. "I need both hands to steer, I'm back in this really rough place . . ."

She hung up, dropped the phone on the seat, and worked her way through the rough track to a smoother one, then down the track to the buildings. There was nobody around them, no vehicles, and she followed a driveway out to a dirt road and along the road for a few hundred yards parallel to the interstate.

The thought of surrendering to the police frightened her, more than she'd ever been frightened in her life. She cut across a hard-surfaced road, hesitated—it felt too exposed—then turned toward the interstate and drove past a restaurant and under the interstate and then south.

She might have gotten away, she thought later, if she'd only moved faster. Not a lot faster, if she'd just gotten under the interstate five minutes sooner. She'd crossed under it and was headed south, and she was thinking about the blue tarp on the back and how she ought to get rid of it because it was instantly identifying . . . when she felt the rhythmic beating on the windows.

She didn't know what it was, only that it was close, and a moment later, a helicopter passed overhead, and low, turning in front of her, the pilot looking straight down at her.

The jig, she thought, was up.

She kept going, a mile, a little more, then caught sight of the flashing light bar behind her, the helicopter still there in front of her. "Screwed," she said aloud. She picked up the phone, did a redial. Poole answered and she said, "They got me, I'm throwing the phone. Love you, Gar."

"Love you, babe," and he was gone.

She accelerated suddenly and the helicopter turned ahead of her, and she took the moment to throw the phone out the window. Another two hundred yards, the cop car closing from behind, and she pulled over, took a deep breath, got out of the truck, put her hands over her head.

The cop car stopped fifty yards away. The cop got out of the car, stayed behind his door, pointed a rifle at her; she thought it was a rifle. Maybe a shotgun. He shouted, "Everybody out of the truck."

"I'm all alone," she said.

The cop ducked back to the car, said something, and then shouted, "Walk toward me until I tell you to stop."

She did that, until he shouted, "Stop."

Another car was coming up from behind her, and she turned and saw another patrol car. The helicopter was higher now, but still overhead, still making noise. The two cops took a while to check out the truck, then patted her down and cuffed her.

One of the cops had curly blond hair and a name tag that said "Oaks," and he asked, "Where'd Poole bail out?"

"Who's Poole?" and then, "I want a lawyer," she said.

The other cop had dark hair with the shine of gel, and a name tag that said "Martinez," and he said, "Listen, honey, if Poole's back there in the trees and he shoots somebody to get a car, then you're going to the death house with him. You can't say, 'I want a lawyer,' and get out of this. You're still an accomplice."

She said, "I'm alone. I was always alone. I don't know any Poole. I bought this truck from a guy in Texas and when the police officer started chasing me, I panicked. I thought the price was too good, and I thought maybe the truck was stolen, so I panicked. I was always by myself."

Oaks said, "Nice try, Dora." He reached into his back

trouser pocket and took out a piece of paper and handed it to her. She remembered the photograph quite well: it had been taken at an office party when she was temporarily working at an auto parts place in Franklin before she went off with Poole. The likeness was excellent and her facial features had held up well over the seven or eight years since the photo was taken.

"I want a lawyer," she said.

"You'll get one," the cop said.

They took her keys and locked up the truck and left it where it was: U.S. marshals wanted to take a look at it, they'd been told. Box was transferred to the back of one of the patrol cars, and then Oaks made a call.

"Looking for a Marshal Davenport," he said.

"This is Davenport."

"We got your Dora Box for you," Oaks said. "You gonna pick her up or you want her delivered?"

"Tell me where you're at," Davenport said. And, "You're the best news I've had in a long time."

"I haven't ever been anybody's best news, not since my second wife went off with a tool pusher," Oaks said. "I truly appreciate you telling me that."

21

LUCAS, BOB, AND RAE were eating breakfast at Happy Frank's Barbeque and Flapjacks when the patrolman called Lucas.

"Got her, got Box," Lucas told Bob and Rae, when he was off the phone. "No sign of Poole, she was all alone. We gotta get out there."

"How far? This is a big state," Rae said. "We need a helicopter?"

Lucas ran out to the Jeep and got his iPad, brought it back to the table, and as he explained how Box had been spotted, he poked in Gordon, Texas, and found that it was a bit more than an hour away, by car, from Happy Frank's. He called Forte in Washington to tell him about Box, and Forte went away for five minutes and came back with the name and a direct phone number for the head of the Dallas Region of the Texas Highway Patrol, a Major Louis Highstreet.

Lucas explained the situation to Highstreet, the urgency of catching up with Poole. Highstreet was a slow-talking man with a dry Texas accent, but moved quickly enough.

"You just sit right where you're at and eat those flapjacks, Marshal, and I'll have a patrol car there in a few minutes. He'll run you back to your motel with his syreen, and then back through Fort Worth out toward Gordon. I'll have the boys in Gordon transport Miz Box to the city of Weatherford, which is the closest nearby jailhouse, if I am recollecting correctly. You can interview her there. If you get out of that motel right quick, you'll be talking to her in forty-five minutes. Then they can transport her to the federal facilities in Fort Worth or Dallas, at their leisure."

"Man, that would be great," Lucas said.

"And, Marshal Davenport?"

"Yes?"

"Say hello to Happy Frank for me, would you do that?"

Lucas got off the phone and said to Bob and Rae, "I love this fuckin' state."

LUCAS, BOB, AND RAE had come to Happy Frank's in a single vehicle, Lucas's Jeep, because they hadn't planned to do anything but eat and talk. Lucas didn't like to ride with other investigators when they were working a case, because much of the time they wound up having to do different things, in which separate cars were necessary. They needed to get back to the hotel to get cars and clothes for the chase, wherever it might take them.

"The problem is," Lucas said, as they hastily worked their way through the flapjacks and sausage, "Poole is getting further away every goddamn minute. We need to squeeze Dora, and we don't have much time to get it done."

"I've been reading your paper on her," Rae said. "She could be tough."

Bob said, "Yeah, I saw that thing about her cutting some guy's head off."

Rae: "I was thinking about her being a homecoming queen. Takes a mean, hard-eyed bitch to be homecoming queen. In my opinion."

"I haven't explored this area with you," Bob said. "I take it you weren't the queen?"

"Queen's court," she said. "This girl who beat me? If you'd told her that to be homecoming queen she had to kill her mom and grind her up to link sausage, her mom would have been a dead Little Sizzler the next day."

Lucas looked at the remnants of his sausage and said, "Thanks for that."

The highway patrolman arrived as they were waiting for the check: Lucas threw some bills at the table and they talked with the patrolman for a moment, got a cell phone number, then fell in behind him in the Jeep.

They were back at the hotel in ten minutes, out of it in five, and headed west for Weatherford, three vehicles tagging behind a cop with lights and a sy-reen, pushing aside the mostly incoming traffic until they were on the interstate, and after that, across suburban countryside mixed with small farms and blocks of dark green wood-lots at a steady ninety into Weatherford.

The Parker County jail in Weatherford was a low beige building that looked like it might be used for the storage of cardboard boxes, or something equally innocuous. The sheriff came out to see them and take them to the interview room where Box was being held.

Lot of cops were hanging around: this all felt like something large. Lucas, Bob, and Rae filed into the inter-view room. They'd taken the cuffs off Box, but she sat behind an interview table looking like an elf, a small slender woman with an oval face who'd been crying hard enough to mess up her eye makeup, giving her a raccoon-like appearance.

Lucas said, "I'm Lucas Davenport, I'm a federal marshal, and these are Bob and . . ."

Box interrupted: "I want a lawyer."

THE COLLEGE-SOUNDING GUY called Annie and said, "The highway patrol has arrested Dora Box."

"Damnit. Where are they?"

"They're at Gordon, Texas," the College-Sounding Guy said.

"Where's that?"

"West out I-20, an hour and a half from where you're at," he said. "Hang on a second. Something is happening."

He went away for much longer than a second, then came back and said, "They're moving her to the Parker County jail in Weatherford, for Marshal Davenport, who will interview her there. Davenport is on his way. Weatherford is about an hour from where you're at."

"Where did you get this from?"

"Monitoring the cop frequencies. Since Poole and Box started running, there wasn't anybody who was going to find them and move them other than the highway patrol, so I'm listening in," the College-Sounding Guy said. "Although nobody's calling it the highway patrol, they call it the DPS."

"That's short for Dipshits?"

"Could be, but it's actually the Department of Public Safety," the College-Sounding Guy said.

"Anything about Poole?"

"Nothing that I've heard. I think they only got her," the College-Sounding Guy said.

"Now what?" Annie asked.

"I don't have anything to do with that. You might want to talk to the Boss."

They called the Boss, got switched around from the original person who answered the phone to the man himself, and after some discussion, the Boss asked, "There is very much money involved here. Is there a chance to, ahm, to retrieve the Box lady?"

"Don't see how, right now. We could go take a look," Annie told him.

"If you try, we pay you two hundred thousand dollars. If you succeed, and get the money back, we pay you another two hundred and fifty thousand dollars."

"We will take a look," Annie said.

ANNIE HAD the phone on speaker and Rosie and Kort had been listening. When the Boss went away, Kort asked, "What do you mean, take a look? Are you crazy? Is he talking about shooting cops to get Box?"

"Not necessarily *shooting* cops," Rosie said.

"Listen, there's only one thing to do," Kort said. "We pretend to take a look, and call the Boss and tell him there's no way to get at her. Too many cops, all over the place. I mean, the Boss wouldn't want us shooting cops. Nobody cares about these criminals like Poole or Darling or even Darling's old lady, but they care about other cops. If we shoot cops, and they find out it goes back to the Boss, then the Boss is in big trouble. They'll go down there and kill him."

"You forget one thing," Annie said.

"What?"

Rosie: "There's four hundred and fifty thousand dollars on the table."

"Four hundred and fifty thousand, for shooting it out with the Texas cops?" Kort was incredulous. "You guys must be rich already. What's that money mean if you're dead?"

"You'd be surprised. They pay us okay, but we aren't getting rich. We drive from Galveston to Charleston dropping off the load, we get twenty thousand per run, two hundred thousand a year," Annie said. "Costs us a hundred thousand just to stay on the road. If we do it for too long, we'll get caught. We want to retire before that happens. Two hundred thousand . . . that's worth thinking about. Four hundred and fifty thousand if we get the money back . . . we won't be able to retire, but we'll be a lot closer to it."

"That would be excellent," Rosie said. "Move to Palm Springs, play some golf, take it easy."

"This is fuckin' nuts," Kort said.

Annie said, "Shut up. You don't know what you're talking about. It won't hurt to look, and if we can find some way to recover Box, that's all . . ." She groped for a word, and finally said, "Upside."

ONCE BOX spoke the "lawyer" word, the questioning had to stop. When he was sure there were no cameras or recording equipment running, Lucas tried non-subtle extortion: "I'm not going to ask any more questions until a lawyer talks to you, but I'll tell you, Dora. You're implicated in the murder of five people back in Biloxi. You were living with Poole, you knew he was a fugitive, even if we don't get him, we've got you. We'll take you back to Mississippi and let those people deal with you— and Mississippi can be pretty goddamn primitive when it wants to be, after a mass murder. You aren't walking on this one. Not without some help, and that's help we could give you."

Box looked at him, hate in her eyes, and Lucas began

to believe that she might once have cut somebody's head off. She said, "Lawyer."

LUCAS, BOB, RAE, and a highway patrol sergeant met outside the interview room and Rae asked the sergeant, "You got her purse?"

"We do. We've got both a purse and a travel bag."

Rae said, "Let's take a look."

The purse was a small Louis Vuitton leather satchel and contained a wallet with a driver's license in the name of Grace Pelham and another in the name of Sandra Duncan. Neither had an address that went back to the house in Dallas.

The travel bag contained two bottles of water, some tissue, a box of Tampax, some liquid hand cleanser, and in a small side pocket, a legitimate-looking American passport with a two-year-old photo of Box and the name Michelle Martin.

"These guys were psycho about security," Bob said, flipping through the passport. There were no visa stamps. "Wonder if they're running for the border?"

Lucas asked the patrolman to run the three separate names for connections to vehicle license tags. He nodded, said, "We can do that in a couple of minutes," and, "We haven't touched the truck in case you want it processed."

"I'm not sure what we'd be looking for, but I'd like to go through it," Lucas said. "How far is it from here?"

"Way we fly, another twenty minutes down the highway."

"Let's go take a look at it," Lucas said. "We're not going to get anything from Box right now. Major Highstreet said you could run her into Fort Worth for us. She might soften up once we've had her inside a federal lockup for a few days."

"We can do that. I'll lead you back to Gordon, I'll have one of the guys move Box into Fort Worth."

They left in a five-car caravan, two patrol cars with Lucas, Bob, and Rae bringing up the rear. As they were leaving, the patrol sergeant told them the two driver's licenses were legitimate, that there were no tickets issued to either one, and there were no vehicles associated with either name.

The jail was located in a residential neighborhood and Lucas paid no attention to the RV parked down the street, or to the small red car tucked in behind it. RVs and red cars were a dime a dozen.

THE FORD pickup truck was exactly where Box had left it, on the side of the road. A bored highway patrolman was keeping an eye on it.

When they arrived, he came over and introduced himself as Charles Townes, the cop who'd spotted Box's truck. "I chased her into the trees over on the other side of the interstate. Got hung up on a cut bank and by the time I got loose, I'd lost her. She might have got away if she'd been a little quicker, but we had a chopper out looking for some boy racers on the Fort Worth Highway. I called him in and he came right down and spotted her."

"Good work all the way around," Lucas said. "I'll drop a note to Major Highstreet, telling him that."

"Appreciate it."

Rae had a box of vinyl gloves in her gear bag, and they all pulled them on before they started digging through the truck. Bob found one thing of interest in the glove box: there were several insurance certificates made out to a Brian Dumble on the truck, dating back five or six years—and one certificate for a Lynn Marshall on an Audi convertible.

"They put the Audi certificate in the wrong vehicle," Bob said. "It's got the tag number on it."

"This is good. Have Townes check on Brian Dumble for a driver's license, and any cars connected to the name or to the Marshall name. Let's get that Audi tag number and the other stuff out to the patrol."

The truck had furniture in the back, and a suitcase full of women's clothing, but nothing that gave them anything useful. They were finishing the search when Rae said, "The most important thing is, we haven't found a single telephone."

"I was just thinking about that," Lucas said. "There's no way in hell that she didn't have a phone with her."

Townes was standing outside the truck and he said, "The helicopter pilot said she rolled down the window a ways back down the road and waved at him, like she was giving up. I wonder if she might have been throwing something out, instead of waving at him?"

"Good thought," Lucas said. "Can you call the guy?"

"Yup. I'll go do that," Townes said, and he went back to his car.

Lucas, Bob, and Rae had given up on the truck when Townes came back. He said, "I talked to the pilot, he said it wasn't too long before she pulled over. Probably less than a hundred yards."

"We need to look," Lucas said.

They had six people to walk the roadside ditch. Lucas wanted to start back farther than indicated by the pilot, so they wouldn't worry about whether they were cutting it too close. There was a dead tree on the far side of the ditch, halfway to their starting point, and the sergeant said, "Let me break some branches off that tree. Use them for pokers."

"Probably won't find it, if we have to poke around for it," Bob said.

"I'm not thinking about the phone, I'm thinking about snakes," the sergeant said, with a grin.

"Tell you what, I'll supervise the search from up here on the road," Rae said. "I don't do snakes."

The side of the road was a crush of dry yellow grass, some of it with nasty little yellow burrs; a perfect hiding place for snakes, in Lucas's opinion, though, being from Minnesota, he had no idea where a rattlesnake might hide in real life. In movies, they were usually coiled on a rock, where they were easy to spot; here, they'd come out of foot-high grass and nail your ankle. He worked his stick assiduously, and other than a bunch of grasshoppers, disturbed no wildlife.

They were sixty yards from Box's truck, snake-free, when the sergeant spotted the phone.

"A BURNER," Lucas said, as he squatted over it. "Cheapest one you can buy."

"Might as well pick it up—we know who had it, we're not losing anything by smudging up her prints," Rae said.

Lucas nodded, picked it up, turned it on. There was only one number in the file of recent calls. He looked up at Bob and Rae and said, *"Now* we're cooking with gas."

LUCAS CALLED Forte in Washington, gave him the number for the phone and the number that had been called on it. Forte said he'd track it and get back to them.

The truck, Lucas told the patrolman, should be taken to wherever the highway patrol took seized vehicles. "Somebody will get back to you about it, but I don't know who," he said. "There's gonna be a blizzard of paperwork starting about tomorrow."

"Where are we going?" Bob asked.

"Back to Fort Worth. They're running, and if they've gotten a long way down the road, we'll want to be close to an airplane."

"You want to go back in a hurry?" the sergeant asked.

"That'd be terrific," Lucas said.

Rae: "Should we stop in Weatherford, see if Box has changed her mind?"

Lucas asked the sergeant how long it would take to get from the jail to the airport: "Less than an hour," the sergeant said.

Lucas looked at the others, and Bob said, "I don't think we'll get anything more from her. Like you said, she might soften up if she's locked up for a couple of days. If you call Forte and tell him we need a chopper or a plane, it could be waiting for us when we get there . . ."

"Let's go to the airport," Lucas told the sergeant. "Lights and sirens."

LUCAS CALLED Forte and told him what they were doing; Forte said the phone search was under way. Forte called back a half hour later as they circled north of Fort Worth: "Okay, the target phone is down south of you, on Highway 84 near McGregor. You got a road map?"

"I got an iPad," Lucas said. "But I can't look at it right now . . . Just tell me."

"McGregor is well down south and it looks to me like they're headed for I-10, which will take them west into New Mexico, Arizona, and California. I-10 runs along the border with Mexico, so it could be they're planning on crossing."

"Box had a good-looking passport in her purse, under a different name," Lucas said.

"Okay, so there's that. Anyway, Box was on I-20, which also intersects with I-10 near El Paso," Forte said.

"Maybe they were planning to get together in El Paso—after that, it's a coin toss."

"They don't seem like people who'd be comfortable down in Mexico," Lucas said. "Though that's just a guess. Nothing in our paper suggests that either one of them speaks Spanish, or has ever been there."

"So what do you want to do?" Forte said. "I have a plane, if you want one. You could be in El Paso four hours before Poole gets there."

"Ah, Jesus," Lucas said. And, "All right. Let's do it. Tell us where to go."

THEY FLEW out of DFW an hour later, in an aging Learjet. Lucas knew it was aging because of the worn paint around the door and the worn seats in back. "How old is this thing?" he asked the copilot.

"Don't know exactly," said the copilot, who looked like he was twelve. "It's a good, reliable aircraft most of the time."

"Wait a minute . . ."

"Pilot joke," the copilot said. "But I really don't know how old it is."

"Were you born when it was made?"

The copilot said, "Better question would be . . . was my mom born? *Just kiddin'.* But really, I've flown this thing all over Texas and it's solid."

"If it starts to crash, I'm going to shoot you before we hit the ground," Lucas said. "Try to keep that in mind."

"You got guns?"

"Yeah, we got guns."

"That shooting thing . . . that was a marshal joke?"

Lucas gave him a hard look: "Maybe."

*   *   *

LUCAS STRAPPED himself into one of the worn seats and cursed himself once again for not going to Mass more often than Easter Sunday. He braced himself for the crash as they lifted off, and when there wasn't one, tried to sleep but failed. He wound up rereading the paper on Poole. Bob did sleep and Rae took a compact camera out of her gear bag and took some photos of the landscape below and one of Lucas reading the paper. "You are a picture of diligence," she said.

"I'm a picture of abject fear. If I had my choice between flying to El Paso or getting a colonoscopy, I'd have to think about it."

"Oh, my," she said.

They were on the ground, still alive, in El Paso at one o'clock on a hot October afternoon. Lucas had been there once before, when one of his men at the Minnesota Bureau of Criminal Apprehension, Del Capslock, had been shot by elderly gun smugglers.

Bad history.

Bad omen?

He wasn't sure.

None of them had looked at their phones while they were in the air. On the ground, Lucas looked at his and found a message from Highstreet, the highway patrol major, that said only "Call me immediately."

22

THE WOMEN were not getting along.

Annie and Rosie were not exactly fashionistas, but they had *style*. Tight black jeans and high-tech boots, silky-looking blouses, Rosie in pale blue and Annie in coral. They both wore expensive, masculine-but-feminine Aviators. Even the prison tats were keys to a hipness unachievable by the likes of Kort.

Kort, on the other hand, looked like she'd just been wheeled out of a Salvation Army store, after cutting her own hair with a jackknife. She could have spent three days in a beauty salon and it wouldn't have changed her face, her body, or the scowl she'd worn since birth—part of the burden she'd carried with her. The sadness and unfairness of her plight was somewhat understood by Rosie and Annie, who had had harsh upbringings of their own—Rosie had been turned out by her stepfather when she was fourteen, Annie had simply been kicked out by her parents when she was eighteen—but living with Kort's constant complaining, her fundamental evilness, her joy at seeing other people suffer, and her chain-saw voice, was becoming a trial.

The complaints never stopped: "What happened to the fuckin' air-conditioning? Must be a hundred degrees in here . . . The coffee really sucks, you think you might stop somewhere? I'm getting sick riding sideways . . . Can't believe you're doing this, you're dragging me into this . . ."

They'd driven from Dallas to Weatherford, where Box was supposedly being held in the county jail. They had towed Kort's rental car to Weatherford; it made them look even more harmless than the RV did, and they had the towing equipment to do it. At Weatherford, they'd looked at the situation, and then Annie and Rosie had cooked up what Kort called a harebrained scheme, and the other two women admitted that it might be.

On the other hand, it seemed like it might work.

They were watching the jail from the RV, and at that point, hadn't seen much except a lot of cops coming and going. Kort continued to bitch, and Rosie finally said, "You don't want to be part of it, we'll drop you off at a bus station. We do need your car. And if the Boss asks about you, we'll have to tell him that you split."

Kort thought about walking away, decided that as crazy as the rescue attempt might be, she'd rather not have the Boss on her neck, especially not if he had another Kort stashed away.

Still, it was worth arguing about, and Kort was still doing that when they saw Davenport leave the jail, trailed by two other plainclothes cops—"Those are the marshals from the parking lot where Soto got shot," Kort blurted.

"You mean, where you shot Soto?" Annie asked.

Kort didn't say anything and they watched the marshals and some highway patrolmen roll out of the parking lot in a convoy.

"Didn't have Box," Rosie said. She turned and looked at Annie. "Maybe you guys should unhook the car and stow the hitch."

"I can't believe this," Kort moaned.

She and Annie unhooked the rental car and stuck the hitch equipment back in the RV's cargo hold. When the car was free, Kort got behind the wheel while Annie rode shotgun. Not *literally* shotgun: *literally* fully automatic M16 with two thirty-round mags, purchased new from the Mexican Army and extensively tested in the swamps east of Houston.

When they were set, Rosie drove away and began rolling the RV slowly around the suburban roads on the east side of Weatherford, never straying too far from the cluster of roads that led from the jail to I-20.

LUCAS, BOB, AND RAE had just gotten up in the air when the College-Sounding Guy called Rosie and said, "They're checking her out. They're moving her."

The College-Sounding Guy was now an uninvited guest in the Parker County computer system, which, he said, was wide-open. "They made it easy to get into, because they got so many dumbasses who need to get into it. Their security stuff dates to about, oh, the moon landing."

Rosie called Annie, and Annie said to Kort, "You fuck this up, honest to God I'll shoot you in the back of the head. I got two felonies on my card, and if I get busted for this, I'm going away forever, so it won't make any difference if you're the third one."

Kort began to tear up: "You're so fuckin' crazy, you're both so fuckin' crazy . . ."

"Shut up and drive when I tell you."

KORT AND SOTO had had a good photo of Dora Box, so when Box was brought out of the jail, cuffed, and stuck in the back of a patrol car, they both recognized her.

"Okay, here's a problem," Annie said, looking at the highway patrol car. "That's a Dodge Charger, a totally hot vehicle. If he cranks it up, you're gonna have to jump all over the gas pedal. I don't think he'll do that, but he could."

"You fuckin' bitch, you fuckin' bitch . . ."

Annie popped the passenger door, went around and got in the backseat, got comfortable, took the M16 off the floor, and touched the back of Kort's head, just behind her right ear. "Get ready."

The patrol car rolled out of the parking lot, and Kort, staying well back, followed.

THEY DIDN'T HAVE the local knowledge to tell them how the highway patrolman would get to Fort Worth, but had guessed it would be one of three alternatives: straight south to I-20, diagonally east to I-20 on East Bankhead Highway, or diagonally east on Fort Worth Highway. They'd studied all three, working out possibilities, and guessed he'd most likely take Bankhead, with the Fort Worth Highway as the second choice. The south route probably the third choice.

They were hoping for Bankhead, and when the patrol car made the right turn onto it, Annie, in the backseat, said, "Yes!" and called Rosie and said, "Bankhead, be ready."

Rosie said, "Moving now."

*   *   *

ROSIE WAS on Allen Street, where she could get easily to either of the two most likely highways. When she got the call from Annie, she pulled the RV onto Bankhead, a block ahead of the highway patrol car, and accelerated away, six miles over the speed limit, headed for a street called Lake Forest Drive. Lake Forest had a big clump of trees north of Bankhead . . .

Annie saw the RV pull out ahead of them and ahead of the patrol car. They were a couple of hundred yards back, with one car between them and the cop. She said, "All right, pass now."

Kort had stopped complaining. She was hanging on the steering wheel with both hands, arms tense as ski-lift cables. She pulled up close to the car ahead of them, then swung out, across the double-yellow no-passing stripes, and back in behind the cop car.

"Faster now," Annie urged from the back. Kort heard her drop the window. "Faster now, faster, faster, faster . . ."

Kort was coming up fast, could sense the cop watching them in his rearview mirror. She couldn't see his eyes, but his head was turned toward it.

"Take him," Annie shouted. She'd pulled a blue cowboy bandanna up around her face, under her sunglasses. She was wearing a long-billed fishing hat to cover her hair. "Take him, goddamnit, take him . . ." and she touched the back of Kort's neck with the barrel of the gun.

Kort accelerated again, hard, pulling alongside the cop car. The cop was looking at them now, frowning, his face only six feet away, and Annie swung the machine gun out the window and blew his front tire, and as the cop car screeched off the road, she shot out the rear tire and simultaneously screamed, "Stop! Stop! Stop!"

Kort jammed on the brakes and Annie banged against

the front seat and swore, and then she popped the car door and she was out and running to the cop car, which had swung in an uncontrolled circle off the highway, and she was on it, the machine gun pointing through the driver's-side window at the cop, who was trapped in his seat, and she was screaming, "Let her out or I'll kill you. Let her out or I'll kill you . . ."

The cop's face was ashen with fear, looking down the barrel of the M16, two feet from his head. Annie heard the lock pop on the back door, and she yanked the handle, and she moved the gun toward Box and shouted, "Out. Out and get in the red car. Out and get in the red car. Get out or I'll kill you right here."

On the highway, a brown Porsche SUV had slowed, the driver watching the scene at the cop car. Box got out of the backseat of the cop car, hands still cuffed behind her, and jogged toward the red car. The Porsche had now stopped in the road, and Annie lifted the rifle and blew out its front tires, then fired another quick burst at the back fender of the cop car, rattling through the metal like a steel drum.

Box was in the backseat of the red car, and Annie piled in behind her and Kort took off.

She drove hard for two minutes, pulling fast away from the cars now piled up behind the Porsche. "Faster," Annie shouted. "Faster, goddamnit, or I'll kill you."

Kort had the gas pedal welded to the floor, then braked hard at Lake Forest Drive, took a left, accelerated past the trees, then off the road and into them. As she did it, Rosie was coming down the street in the RV. The three women in the red car, led by Kort, with Annie running hard, half-dragging Box, piled into the RV that was already rolling back to the corner.

Rosie took a right, back toward the place where the highway patrolman was now standing outside his car, talking into a radio. A half dozen cars, including the Porsche, were now off the road beside the cop car. Annie was kneeling next to the driver's seat and said, "Don't speed, but gotta hurry before they shut off traffic, gotta hurry . . ."

They went past the cluster of cars as two cop cars, light bars flashing into the afternoon, screeched around the corner off Fort Worth Highway. Rosie turned on Allen, drove out on the Fort Worth Highway, turned left. They passed the jail, and then Main Street, going straight west out of town.

Kort and Box were lying on the RV's floor, and now Box asked, "Who are you? Who are you?" though she was afraid she knew.

Kort said, "We want our money back."

Box said, "Oh . . . fuck . . . no."

A HALF HOUR LATER, as they pulled into the Walmart Supercenter in Mineral Wells, the College-Sounding Guy called to say, "The cops don't have any idea of what you might be driving. And don't tell me. You've stirred up a hornet's nest and I'd get as far away from there as you can, as quick as you can."

Annie, Rosie, and Kort gathered around Box, and Annie said, "You're going to have to tell us where the money is. 'Cause if you don't, this lady"—she tipped her head at Kort—"is going to go to work on you with some, you know . . ."

"Home improvement tools," Kort said, with a gleam in her eye. "You know—hammers, saws, drills, box cutters. That sort of thing."

Rosie said to Annie, "We might need some plastic sheets."

"We're at a Walmart, what better place to get them?"

Box, still cuffed, said, "I'll tell you where your money is, if you take the cuffs off. I'm not going to try to run, you're all meaner than I am. My arms and shoulders are killing me."

Rosie and Annie looked at each other, and then Annie said, "If you try to run, we'll kill you. We're not fooling about this, Dora."

"I believe you," Dora said.

"I'm okay with taking them off," Annie said to Rosie. To Box: "We've *got* some handcuff keys. I don't know why."

"Sure you do," Rosie said. "Because of April."

"Let's not talk about April," Annie said. "If I never see that chick again, it'll be way too soon."

"I don't know what you're talking about, but it sounds sorta hot," Box said.

Rosie and Annie looked at her, and Annie said, "Interesting."

WHEN THE CUFFS were off, and when Kort had stopped complaining about how that made everything harder, and working on Box with her tools would get some straight answers, Box rubbed her wrists and said, "It's this way. My boyfriend and I . . ."

"Gar Poole," Kort said.

". . . yeah, Gar. We split up and we are looking for a new place to hide, after Dallas came apart. Gar's got the money. We're supposed to meet in New Mexico, tomorrow or the next day. He thinks the cops have me now, but I have a phone number for him. We can call, you can listen in. He'll trade the money for me."

"You sure of that?" Annie asked.

"I'm sure."

Annie took out a cell phone, but Box shook her head.

"Not that phone." She pointed her finger in the general direction of Walmart. "They got all the cheap phones we need, right in there. We make one call, we throw it away."

Kort, for once, was on her side. "That's right," she said. "Everybody tracks phones."

"I knew that," Annie said. "Let's go get some phones."

23

LUCAS, astonished, got off the phone and turned to Bob and Rae and said, "Well, the dope gang showed up."

Bob: "Where?"

"The cop who was taking Box to Fort Worth—they shot up his car, grabbed Box, and took off. Nobody has any idea where they are."

Rae opened her mouth but nothing came out for a minute, then she sputtered, "You gotta be . . . How?"

"Pulled up beside the guy on the highway, blew his tires out with an automatic weapon, stuck the gun in his face, grabbed Box, and took off. Two women did it, one of them was probably this Kort, don't know the other woman, they were both wearing masks. Nobody got hurt, but the highway patrol's deeply pissed."

"There's one glass ceiling that's gone—now we got dope cartel gun-women," Bob said.

Rae said, "She's dead. Dora is."

Lucas ran both hands through his hair and said, "Losing my shit, here. Nothing we can do about it right now—let's move."

"Where?"

"Wherever he is. Poole. Gotta get the posse going," Lucas said.

They talked to Forte, who already had the posse moving.

"We've had a complication," Forte said. "That burner that Poole's carrying is T-Mobile and their coverage isn't so good in southwest Texas. He shows up, then he drops out. Still looks like he's heading toward I-10, he ought to be there soon, but right now, we can't see him."

"Can't sit on our ass, Russ. Goddamnit, we need to get on top of him. Help us out here."

"We're talking to the Texas Highway Patrol people about a roadblock on I-10, and they're willing to do it. Once he gets past a certain point, he won't be able to get off. The guy who's organizing things for the patrol is a Captain Tom Johnson. He wants to meet you at a Shell station out on the interstate . . ."

THEY RENTED two GMC Terrains, Bob and Rae in one, Lucas in the other. Once on the interstate, heading east and south, they passed a sprawling industrial complex on the south side of the highway, with distant hills that Lucas thought must have been in Mexico. A half an hour after they left the airport, Lucas led the other two off the highway at the Fabens exit and found Johnson inside, chatting with a cashier. Johnson was a tall man, with a wind- and sunburned face, and a brushy blond mustache. They took a table in the back and Johnson asked, "You heard about the problem in Weatherford?"

"We heard," Rae said. "I wouldn't exactly call it a problem, I'd call it a disaster. Anything new?"

If Johnson was offended, he didn't let on: "They found the car back in some woods, a red Camry. They must've had another vehicle hid out to pick them up."

"Of course they did," Lucas said. "It's Kort. Probably the same gun she used to shoot up Soto."

Johnson didn't know about that, so they told him about the murder at the town houses. "Sounds like cartel business," he said. "They're getting bolder all the time. A few years ago, they would have written the money off. Not now. Now they come and get it."

Lucas outlined Poole's probable route across Texas, and Johnson said, "We knew that much. What we thought was, we'd set up a checkpoint at the intersection of I-10 and I-20, which is down the road a way. Once they get that far, they're locked into the highway. We see anybody turning around, we'll run them down. I've got eight cars available, two men in each one, all of them with rifles."

"When are you setting up?" Lucas asked.

"Soon as you say, 'Go.'"

"Go. And we're going with you."

"After we get a couple of burritos," Rae said. "I haven't had anything to eat since that half-a-flapjack."

They ate burritos and Lucas bought a cooler, ice, and a six-pack each of Diet Coke and water, and some power bars, and they followed Johnson southeast across desert and then up into low yellow desert mountains, including one that looked like God hadn't actually so much made a mountain as He'd emptied out a giant sack of God-sized gravel, and then they crossed more desert toward the intersection of I-10 and I-20.

JOHNSON SETTLED into an easy hundred miles an hour, but the run out to the intersection took almost an hour and a half. They passed a few buildings on the way, and an occasional gas station, but only one substantial town at Van Horn, and that was it. I-10 and I-20 came together in a wide looping knot, and the patrol had already blocked off I-10's access farther west toward El Paso, and also the I-10 ramp to I-20.

Johnson led them to the easternmost checkpoint, where traffic, mostly eighteen-wheelers, was backed up a quarter mile. Lucas got out in the dirt, thought the temperature must be close to eighty-five or ninety degrees. He was still wearing a sport jacket, dress shirt, slacks, and loafers. As he stripped off the jacket, Bob came up and said, "At least it's a dry heat."

Forte called: "He's on I-10 now. We got another thing going—there was a call into his phone and he took it. The call came through a tower in Mineral Wells, which is west of Weatherford."

"That's Box, trying to negotiate, if the cartel's got her," Lucas said.

"That's what we think here. The phone's still there and we've got a half dozen patrol guys and some Rangers closing in."

"Bet it's a burner."

"No bet. But Jesus, Lucas, this is the most fun I've had in years. I'm talking to people everywhere. This is something else . . . I've got four or five guys here with me, watching the action. We got a guy putting pushpins in a map, for Christ's sakes. You need *anything* we can do, call."

"Yeah, well . . . I'm standing in the desert in a pair of Cleverley calfskin loafers that are slowly melting into the sand, so you know . . . cherish the air-conditioning."

"Ah, stop bitching, it's gonna be a great story," Forte said. "We've been looking for Poole since Bush 43. This is gonna be good. If you get him, of course. If you don't, you know, I never heard of you."

"Glad to know that somebody's got my back," Lucas said.

FORTE CALLED AGAIN twenty minutes later: "We spotted him again, but only briefly. He was in Fort Stockton. Now he's gone again, but he shouldn't be, unless he trashed the phone."

Lucas got his iPad and walked over to Bob and Rae's truck and got in the back, in the air-conditioning. "They lost him again, in Fort Stockton, but T-Mobile's supposed to have coverage along most of I-10, even if it doesn't on the back highways into Fort Stockton. Forte thinks he might have trashed the phone."

"Why would he do that?" Rae asked. "If he's negotiating for Box, he's gotta have a phone that they can call."

Lucas called up a map of Texas. The Verizon data came through grudgingly, but eventually he was looking at the road network between Fort Stockton and El Paso. There wasn't much of one. Lucas turned in his seat and said, "What if he's turned south? What if he's going down this way"—he drew his finger across the Google map—"and plans to cross into Mexico . . . here. I think that's a border crossing, it looks like the road goes across."

He spread the map, and called up a satellite view.

"Presidio. Never heard of it, but it's a crossing," he said, looking down at the satellite view. He traced a route, the only route, that would get Poole from Fort Stockton to Presidio. He touched the map again: "Whatever he does, he's got to go through this place."

Rae knelt on the front seat to look: "Marfa. I've heard of that. It's some kind of art town, I think."

"That can't be right," Lucas said. "It's pretty much no-where. Who'd go there to look at art? What kind of art?"

"I don't know," she said. "But I'm pretty sure I'm right."

"Too bad we don't have an easily accessed, widely distributed source of information so we could look it up," Bob said.

Lucas looked down at the iPad in his hands, said, "Fuck you," and brought up the Wiki for Marfa, Texas. "Says it's a major center for minimalist art," Lucas said. He looked at the landscape in the satellite photo of Marfa. "At least that seems right. They *got* minimalist."

"Make a call," Bob said.

"I don't want to miss this," Lucas said, looking out at the traffic jam.

"We're gonna miss it," Rae said. "We're sitting here on our asses, all those cute highway patrolmen are gonna make the bust when it happens. What we'll actually do is shake their hands and say, 'Good job.' "

"Screw that," said Lucas. "If we leave right now and if that asshole is headed to Marfa, we'll beat him."

"Gotta drive fast," Rae said.

"We can do that," Lucas said. "Give me a couple of minutes."

HE HOPPED OUT of the truck, walked over to John-son, who was drinking one of Lucas's Diet Cokes and sweating mightily, and asked, "You got this?"

"If he shows, we got it," Johnson said.

"His phone's off the grid. I'm worried that he's turned south, heading for this Presidio place, down on the border."

"Think he's got a passport?" Johnson asked. He rolled the cool Coke bottle across his forehead.

"His girlfriend did," Lucas said. "A good one, under a fake name. I'm thinking that me and Bob and Rae should head down to this town Marfa, take a look at cars coming through. If we go right now, we should beat him down there. Not by much, but by some."

"I'll send a car with you," Johnson said. "Give you an extra gun and some extra speed going down. I'll call around, see if I can shake loose some Border Patrol guys to help out at Marfa. If they've been planning to cross into Mexico, they might have been looking at Presidio the whole time. There are lots of people looking at faces in El Paso, on both sides of the border. And Juárez's got a bad rep, if that would work into their thinking."

"Then we're going," Lucas said. "Get him, though. If he comes through here, get him."

"We surely will," Johnson said. "And you take care of your own self."

THE HIGHWAY PATROLMAN who went with them was named Dallas Guiterrez, a big rangy guy who seemed happy to be moving. "There's some interesting road between here and Marfa," he told them. "I mean, the road surface is good, but there are some curves where you can get thrown. Don't push me too hard and I'll get you down there without breaking your necks."

"Lead on," Bob said.

Rae rode with Lucas, offered to drive in case he needed to talk on the phone or look at his iPad. He took her up on it, and she tucked in behind Guiterrez and Bob came up behind them.

The countryside was as barren as anything Lucas had ever experienced, hard desert outside the car windows, with low mountains that looked like they'd been worked over with God's own blowtorch, shimmering in the heat.

About a billion squashed rabbit corpses littered the shoulders of the road, tumbleweeds were jammed into ranch fences. Despite the heat and rock, the only comparable landscape Lucas had crossed, in terms of bleakness, was on a winter run to Canada through the lowlands of Northern Minnesota, which looked like a black-and-white photograph.

Guiterrez told them that the trip normally would take a little more than an hour and a half from where they were, but he expected to make it quicker than that. They did, but it was still an hour and fifteen minutes before they rolled into the northern outskirts of Marfa.

Halfway to Marfa, Rae said, "Big country, out here. When was the last time we saw a house?"

"I can't remember what a house looks like," Lucas said. And, "What do you have in your gear bag? More than two rifles?"

"Nope. Guns for Bob and me—two rifles, extra mags and ammo, boots, helmets, and vests. We threw in that extra vest for you, but no extra weapons. Boots won't help much out here, they're heavy and waterproof."

"If we find Poole, we gotta think he'll try to shoot his way through. He knows what's waiting for him if we take him."

"I got that. I'm working up a buzz."

Johnson called: "There's a Border Patrol station on the south side of Marfa, off the highway going down toward Presidio. The patrol guys are willing to set up a checkpoint if you want them to do that."

"I'll look it over when we get there," Lucas said. "Thanks for that."

MARFA ITSELF was a flat town, the high point probably the tip of a radio tower. Lucas had been in any number of flat towns on the northern plains, and Marfa would fit right in there: more pickups than sedans; a venerable county courthouse with a diminutive dome; a brick, concrete, and pole-building main street, no buildings higher than three or four stories; white houses made of concrete block with stucco, and wood-and-plaster; and vacant lots overgrown with weeds. The horizon was low, all around, with distant low mountains like camel humps. Big sky; big sun.

Unlike most flat high-plains towns, Marfa was also a major art destination, according to Wiki. An artist named Donald Judd had bought an old army fort and set it up as a museum. Lucas had never heard of him; but then, he'd never paid too much attention to painting or sculpture, though his wife was a patron of the Minneapolis Institute of Art and gave them enough money that she and the director were on a first-name basis.

They rolled through town from the north side to the south, past a water tower and then past a snazzy-looking hotel and out to the edge of town, where Guiterrez led them off the highway to a Border Patrol station.

They got out of their cars and a border patrolman behind a tall chain-link fence called out to Guiterrez, "Excuse me, sir, are you an American citizen?" and Guiterrez asked, "Have you been drinking, sir?" and the border patrolman said, "How ya doing, Dallas? You leading this shoot-out?"

"That would be the marshals here . . ." Guiterrez said, nodding at Lucas, Bob, and Rae. He introduced them to the border patrolman, who asked Rae, "Exactly how dangerous is this guy?"

"He's killed eight people we're fairly sure about, including a little girl and a highway patrolman. Who knows how many more?"

"Whoa. Shoot first and ask questions later, huh?"

"You mean us, or him?" Bob asked.

"Us, of course," the border patrolman said. "Come inside, our revered leader is gonna PowerPoint you or something."

THE REVERED LEADER was a tall, white-haired man name Travis O'Brien, who had colonel's eagles on his uniform, though nobody called him colonel. He shook all their hands and sat them down in his office and said, "This is an unusual situation. I'm not exactly sure where the Border Patrol gets involved in this, but I talked to people at our headquarters and they talked to some guy at your headquarters . . . a guy named Forte? . . . and the word came down that we should help any way we can."

"There is a Border Patrol element in this," Bob said. "This guy is going to try to cross the border with what will look like a good passport, but with an alias. He's set up a bunch of fake IDs, with backup documents."

Lucas, Bob, and Rae took turns filling in O'Brien, who finally asked, "When do you expect him to come through?"

"Probably in the next couple hours. If he's coming, he's well on his way."

"All right. Well, we'll get going, then. I've already talked to my folks and we're going to set up right down the road here, on a curve where the highway leaves town," O'Brien said. "He won't see us until he's right on top of us."

"Good enough," Lucas said. "We want to be on the line here, so . . . let's get set up."

THE BORDER PATROL knew all about highway checkpoints and had it set up in ten minutes. A double lane-change zigzagged through orange-and-white-striped plastic barrels, with green-and-white Border Patrol Chevy trucks at the ends of the lanes so that the lane shift couldn't be avoided. Cars coming from the south could be waved straight through, but cars from the north had to slow for the lane shift.

Armor-wearing border patrolmen carrying Colt M4s manned the end of the lane, checking drivers against the photos of Poole. Guiterrez, the state highway patrolman, parked at the south end of the lane where he could give pursuit if anybody did try to run the checkpoint.

Lucas walked through it and was satisfied that Poole wouldn't make it through, and with Bob and Rae, set up both of their vehicles pointed back toward town, in case Poole tried to do a U-turn away from the checkpoint.

Then they were ready.

Rae sat with Lucas, with Lucas in the driver's seat now, Rae ready with her rifle, already zipped into her vest. She borrowed Lucas's iPad to look at his selection of music, chose to shuffle a selection of Delbert McClinton songs, and they both sat back and waited, looking up the highway through their sunglasses.

Forte called a half hour later: "Poole's back on the grid, still on I-10. He's coming up to the roadblock. We ought to know something in half an hour. You want to stay there, or head back north?"

Lucas mulled it over and finally said, "Look, we'll wait here until they've got him. We wouldn't get there in time to help out anyway."

When he and Forte broke off, Lucas hopped out of the truck, walked over to the border patrolman who was in charge of the checkpoint, and said, "We got word that he's still on I-10. We're gonna wait until we hear something, but we might be able to tear it down in the next half hour or so."

Lucas walked back to his truck, stopping only to pass the word to Bob. Bob scanned the checkpoint and said, "Damn. I was kinda looking forward to this."

Lucas checked his face, decided that Bob was serious. "You ever been shot?"

"Been shot at, not hit," Bob said. "Not yet."

"It's not exactly the recreational moment you seem to think it is," Lucas said. "I got shot in the hip one time. Six inches over, would have hit me in the balls. Sort of clarified my thinking about shoot-outs."

"C'mon, don't spoil it for me," Bob said.

24

TWO HOURS EARLIER, Poole and Darling had stopped at a Burger King in Fort Stockton, and Poole said, "About goddamn time. I was getting tired of McDonald's."

Darling smiled, but it was only a reflex. He said, "I'm thinking on this, and the more I'm thinking, the more I believe that going into El Paso is a mistake. The cops must have been tracking Dora. I mean, how'd they know exactly where she'd be, so they could grab her off the highway? And then how did these lesbos get in a spot where they could take her away from the cops?"

"I figured they got her tags, somehow . . . neighbors or something," Poole said.

"That's a goddamn thin possibility," Darling said. "Who looks at tags? How would they have found that person? The Neighborhood Watch took your tags?"

He shut up as they got to the counter, where they ordered Whoppers and TenderGrill Chicken Sandwiches and fries and shakes, and carried them to a table away from other patrons. Darling took a bite from his chicken sandwich, chewed for a minute, then said, "Cell phones."

"How'd they get onto the cell phones?" Poole asked. "We've been buying burners every fifteen minutes."

Darling shook his head. "I don't know. But goddamn women, are we sure that Dora threw away her main phone, or left it behind? Sure she didn't call any relatives that the cops would know about?"

"She said she didn't."

"Yeah, but you know about women and cell phones," Darling said. He chewed for a while. "She probably had all kinds of information on her main phone—e-mails and shopping stuff and phone numbers. Websites. If she turned it off, figuring that it wouldn't hurt to take it with her . . ."

"I could call her back," Poole said.

Darling thought about that for a moment, then shook his head. "Suppose something else . . ."

"Go ahead."

"What if some federal agency figured out the burner she was using and started monitoring it . . ."

"Okay. I don't know how they'd do that, but okay," Poole said.

"She was talking to you about hiding the money and the cops were chasing her, and we figured they'd catch her. Then she said one was up ahead, on the road, and there was a helicopter overhead, and she threw the phone out the window. We know that much for sure. Now suppose one of the cops saw her do that. Or suppose they didn't see her, but when they found out she didn't have a phone, they figured she'd thrown it away, and they started calling that number until they heard it ringing. If they found that phone, it'd have the number of your burner on it. We've still got it and it's still turned on."

"Well . . . shit," Poole said, glancing around the

restaurant. There weren't many patrons, and none looked like cops. "If all that happened, then why haven't they grabbed us?"

"Because they wouldn't know exactly where we're at. We've been dropping service all the time. They might know more or less that we're on I-90, heading west. If that's what's going on, we'll run into a checkpoint that we can't get out of."

Poole rubbed his nose, picked up a french fry and shook it at Darling, and said, "All right. Goddamnit, I'm going to finish eating, I don't care what they know. Then I'm going to buy some water and some snacks and gas . . . and then I'll worry about it."

"And we might be worried about nothing," Darling said. "They might not have any idea of where we're at."

"Better safe," Poole said.

When they finished eating, Poole drove the truck to a gas station and when they'd finished gassing up, he looked across the lot at an RV, stuck his head in the truck door, and said to Darling, "Write down the phone number we got from the lesbos, then erase it from the burner and gimme the phone."

Darling did that, and passed the phone to Poole. "What are you going to do?"

"Watch." Poole ambled past the RV, where the owner was putting in diesel. "Nice vehicle," he said. "Heading for California?"

"Yeah, and maybe up through Phoenix to the Grand Canyon and so on." The RV had Michigan plates; the owner was a Midwesterner fleeing the oncoming winter, Poole thought.

"Good trip. Hotter than hell out here, though," Poole said.

"Not a place I wanted to stop," the man agreed.

"Well, take 'er easy," Poole said. He walked around the

back of the trailer, which had an exterior spare tire in a rack. He wedged the burner behind the tire and out of sight and then continued on into the store. He bought peanut butter crackers and water and orange soda, and a paper road map, carried them out to the truck.

"Saw that," Darling said. "I like it."

"They still got my picture, if we run into a checkpoint," Poole said. He unfolded the map and traced his finger down to the south. "We go this way. Away from El Paso. Cross the border, then go up to El Paso on the other side, cross back over."

"Oughta work, unless they've set up the checkpoint on the other side of town, right here."

Poole looked at the map. "You know, they could have done that." A young woman was gassing up a beige Nissan Cube at one of the other pumps, and Poole said, "Give me one more minute."

"What are you doing?"

"Girl's got Florida plates," he said.

He got out of the truck again, walked over to the woman, and said, "You're not heading eastbound on I-10, are you?"

She nodded, a little reserved talking to this man, and said, "Yes, me and my boyfriend. He's inside."

"We're heading west, but we heard part of the westbound highway was closed off because of a wreck. You see anything like that?" Poole asked.

She shook her head. "We came through there a few minutes ago. No sign of an accident, either side of the highway."

Poole nodded and said, "Well, thanks, ma'am. Didn't want to get stuck out in the desert."

Back in the truck, he said, "We're good. Let's go. Give me your burner, I'm gonna call the lesbos, tell them what we think."

He called, and Rosie answered. Poole asked, "This the lesbians?"

"Who wants to know?"

"Let me talk to the woman you picked up. This is her friend, but I don't want to say names."

After a few seconds of silence, Rosie said, "Wait one."

Another minute passed, then Box came on: "You okay?"

"We're worried. If they found that phone you threw out the window, they might be onto me and Sturg." He told her the rest of the theory and said, "We've turned south. We're going to cross the border at Presidio and come up the other side to El Paso. We don't think anyone's going to find the money at the border, and if they've tracked us down I-10, this would be our best shot at getting away from them."

"Oh my God, oh my God. The stories you hear about Mexico . . ."

"We'll be able to protect ourselves," Poole said drily. "We'll meet you in El Paso when we're sure the heat's off. Check into a Holiday Inn and we'll find you."

POOLE GOT OFF the phone and handed it back to Darling. They passed the RV on their way back out to the interstate. "Taking the phone to the Grand Canyon," Poole said, unscrewing the top on one of the orange sodas. And, "Wonder what Mexico is like?"

"Took my old lady to Cancún a couple of times," Darling said. "I liked it okay, but I don't think that's really Mexico. Cancún is to Mexico like Miami is to America. Hard to figure out."

As they took the turn south on Highway 67, Darling said, "Isn't this the goddamnedest country you've ever seen? Yellow and brown, except for those scrubby little trees. My part of the country is so green I get tired of looking at it, sometimes. But this . . . you gotta be a different kind of human being to live out here. Wonder if it ever burns? Looks like all that grass and shit would burn all the time."

"Cowboy country," Poole said.

"Haven't seen many fuckin' cows," Darling said. He was looking at the paper map and then out at the highway ahead. "You can pick up the speed a little. Won't see any cops out here, or damn few. I'd like to get to Presidio before dark."

EVEN EARLIER in the day, Annie, Rosie, Kort, and Box were cruising south on I-20 in the RV. They would get there after dark. Annie and Rosie had agreed that they shouldn't try to meet with Poole until the next day, when they had some light.

"He's not going to trade!" Kort shouted at Annie and Rosie. "He'll try to kill us. He's not going to give up millions of dollars for this . . . this . . ." She waved at Box.

"He'll trade," Box said. "We've been together a long time. He'll want to figure out something tricky, so you can't kill him. With all your guns and everything . . . I'll tell him about those . . . he won't take you on."

"Best he doesn't," Rosie said. "We'll kill his cracker ass."

Rosie and Annie told Box that she'd be sleeping on the couch in the sitting area, which was a pull-out affair, made for guests. "Seems mean, but we're gonna put the cuffs back on," Annie told her. "Getting this money back is a big deal for us. Big payday. You get loose and we got nothing."

"Where am I going to run to?" Box asked. "They're looking for me all over Texas."

That being the case, Rosie told her, if the cops stopped

them, there was a very cleverly built space between the cargo compartment and the floor of the bus where Box could hide if the cops stopped them. "It's where we put the cocaine when we're transporting," she said. "It's not real comfortable, but you can lie on your back and move around a little—we can give you a yoga mat to lie on."

Rosie showed Box how a tack-strip on one side of the carpet pulled free. The carpet, when rolled back, revealed nothing but a wooden floor. Annie pushed a concealed button under the dash, and a piece of the floor then slid smoothly aside, revealing the space below. "Custom work from this good ol' boy out in San Diego," Rosie said.

Box looked at the hideout and said, "My God, that's a lot of coke. How much can you get in there?"

"Five hundred kilos is the most we've ever done. Had to drive back roads everywhere, to dodge the scales," Annie said.

"Don't tell her all this shit," Kort wailed. "What're you doing? She'll tell the cops."

"If the cops get her, she goes to prison, or worse," Annie said. "No percentage in telling the cops anything."

AT MIDLAND, they stopped at a convenience store for snacks and then at a Buffalo Wild Wings for a meal before heading south. Kort argued that Box should be chained up and locked in the hidden compartment before they left the RV, but Box looked so defeated that Annie and Rosie made her promise not to run away, or cause a commotion, and Box said, "Like I keep saying, what am I gonna do, call the cops?"

So they all went inside for pulled pork sandwiches and wings and beer, and it turned out Box and Annie were both Cowboys fans, so they watched an NFL roundup channel about games from the Sunday before, until Rosie suddenly stopped eating and said, "Oh, shit. Look at that."

The other three women turned to a TV screen across the bar that was tuned to a news channel, on which they saw a thoroughly recognizable photograph of Kort.

Kort couldn't believe it: "How did they do that? How did they do that? Who told them?"

Box said, "Don't look at *me*, I don't even know what your last name is."

"Did Soto keep a motel key on him? If they ran down the motel room you guys were in . . ."

"We were in separate rooms . . ."

"But you were traveling together . . . Maybe you left a fingerprint somewhere."

Box, being practical, said to Kort, "Trade chairs with me."

"Why?"

"So you're facing away from the room."

THEY FINISHED the food in a hurry and as they did, Rosie said to Annie, "Now we've got two problems. Can we get them both under the floor?"

"Probably, but they might kill each other," Annie said.

"Which would solve our problem," Rosie said.

"Come on, guys," Box said. "I'm *not* a problem. I'm a *solution*."

"You're a dead woman, is what you are, if we don't get that money back," Kort said. She had orange Wild Wings sauce around her lips, which made her look as though she'd been bobbing for spare ribs.

Not a good look. Box said, "Wipe your face, for God's sakes. You look like a pig."

*   *   *

BACK IN THE RV, and on the highway, Rosie drove and Annie brought up a Verizon-linked hotspot, went online to the Dallas TV stations, and found photos of Kort, Box, and Poole, as well as a sensational story about Box's escape, aided by bandanna-wearing outlaws.

The story began: "In an escape reminiscent of the glory days of Butch Cassidy and the Sundance Kid, a beautiful young outlaw was forcibly taken away from a Texas Highway Patrol officer as she was being transported from Weatherford to Fort Worth . . ."

"Kind of like the 'beautiful young outlaw' thing," Box said.

"You are a little Southern rose," Annie said. "You ever think about switching sides?"

"Aw, for Christ's sakes," Kort said in disgust.

"Already played on both teams," Box said. "That's how I finally got together with Gar. I knew him in high school, but we never went out then, he was already an outlaw. Then me and a girlfriend picked him up in a Jackson bar, about ten years ago, took him back to his hotel room and flat wore him out."

"Really," Annie said. "I thought I picked up something like that." She turned to Rosie. "You pick that up?"

"I did," Rosie said. She asked Box, "Why're you with a man?"

"I like both, but men got that *thang,* you know? Women are good, but sometimes you just wanna have that *thang.* The muscles, too, and whiskers rubbing your legs."

"Stop that," Rosie said. "You're getting me all hot."

"Rosie sort of likes that *thang,* too," Annie said. "Every once in a while, anyway. I'm perfectly good without it."

"That's all so wrong," Kort said. "None of you ever read the Bible?"

They all looked at her, the torturer, and then at each other, and finally Rosie said, "Well, no."

*   *   *

TIME PASSED.

The RV's bathroom was tiny and Box had made no move to get away, had given no hint that she might be thinking about it, so they let her in there by herself. As she sat on the toilet, she pulled out four built-in drawers, quietly as she could, to see what she might find that would help in an escape\attempt, if she decided to make one. The first thing she found was a metal nail file, but it was so thin that she suspected it might break if she tried to stab someone with it.

The bottom drawer had a selection of simple household tools, including an eight-inch-long Sears Craftsman screwdriver, with a nice Phillips point on it. Box didn't think about it for long—she pushed it down into one of her socks, pulled up her pants, and flushed the toilet.

Annie was riding shotgun, with Rosie driving, and when Kort went back to the bathroom, Box eased the screwdriver out of her sock and shoved it beneath the bottom pillow of the pull-out couch.

With Kort in the bathroom, she asked quietly, "You girls know about what Charlene does to people?"

"We've heard some things," Rosie said.

"You're driving around with a complete monster," Box said. "She hacks up people while they're still alive. She likes it. That's what I've heard. She cut Gar's mother into little pieces with a power saw . . . and here she's talking about the Bible. She's nuts."

"Wouldn't be surprised," Annie said. "She shot her own partner to death. I can't even imagine that." She reached out and patted Rosie's thigh.

"Thanks, sweetie," Rosie said. "I agree that she's kinda mean . . ."

"Kinda mean? For God's sakes—" Box began.

Rosie interrupted: "If we get the money back, we'll drop her off somewhere. She can go be a monster on somebody else's bus."

Kort came out of the bathroom and said to Box, who was sitting in the middle of the small couch, "Get off, I want to sit there."

"Sit somewhere else," Box said. "I have—"

Kort hit Box with the flat of her hand, nearly knocking her off the couch, and Annie was up between them screaming, "Hey, hey, hey . . ."

Kort said, "She's a fuckin' prisoner, not a guest, and I want to sit there."

Box was covering her ear with one hand and looked up and said, "You *better* kill me, 'cause if you don't, I'm going to kill you."

Kort opened her mouth to reply, but when she met the icy snake-eyed stare from Box, she shut her mouth: she'd seen the same look in Soto's eyes.

Rosie said to Box, "You sit on one end, and, Charlene, you sit on the other, and knock this shit off. You're acting like children. We got enough trouble without you two adding to it."

The four women in the RV were south of Odessa when Poole called from Fort Stockton. He explained that he and Darling thought that Box's phone might have been used to track them, that the phone was now riding in the back of an RV, and that they were headed for Presidio. After some back-and-forth, they agreed to meet in El Paso if Poole and Darling made it back across the border.

Later, the women were rolling down I-20 when they saw the clutter of police light bars at the junction with I-10. They had no trouble merging west on I-10, and looking back, could see a traffic jam. I-10 had been closed off just before the merger.

"Gar was right," Box said. "They were tracking them

with the phone. If they'd kept going, the cops would have them trapped."

AT THAT MOMENT, Poole and Darling could see the first signs of Marfa, as a scrum of white dots on the horizon.

"Town's about the size of your dick," Poole said.

"That big? I thought you said it was nothing."

"Nothing we need to stop for, anyway," Poole said. "Couple more hours, and we're home free."

"I think we're pretty good already," Darling said. "That whole trip down here, didn't see a single cop."

25

LUCAS HAD taken three calls from Highway Patrol's Johnson over the past half an hour. The cell phone companies had spotted the burner approaching the checkpoint on I-10, then, not moving on I-10, at the checkpoint.

On the third call, Johnson said, "Goddamnit, Lucas, T-Mobile is saying Poole's phone is west of us now, heading into El Paso. I can positively tell you that Poole didn't come through here. We looked in every car and truck including the eighteen-wheelers, and we got six illegals and probably five pounds of marijuana, but no Poole."

"Could have gone back north, I suppose, if he's been talking to Box. Maybe figuring he can get Box back."

"Or he could be right on top of you, like we were saying—if that was him in Fort Stockton. Maybe he figured we were tracking him and he dropped the phone in one of the pickups or something."

"We'll give it until dark, anyway," Lucas said. "If he's

not coming this way, I don't know what our next move would be."

DARLING WAS at the wheel when they came around the curve at the south end of Marfa and saw the cars piling up and the roadblock, and Darling jabbed the brake and blurted, "Ah, shit!" and swerved hard right into the mouth of a dirt alley. Poole had been looking at the paper map and didn't see the checkpoint and grabbed the door handle to keep himself upright and said, "What? What happened?"

"Goddamn roadblock. See anybody coming after us, anybody?"

Poole looked in the wing mirror as they rattled down the alley and a dog on a chain lurched out at them, barking, and Darling hooked left into a clutch of trailer homes and Poole, looking left, saw flashes of red on the highway, which was parallel to them, and said, "Two trucks, silver SUVs, pulling out. Shit, they're coming fast as they can. Get us out of sight . . ."

"Lots of white pickups back here, that'll slow them down if we can get around another corner . . ."

They were on a dirt road that appeared to lead into the trailer park, and Poole shouted, "There!" and Darling took another right, weaving between closely parked mobile homes and cars and more pickups, including some that were white, and then Darling charged left through somebody's bone-dry yard and around behind a trailer and then back on a road . . .

Poole had both hands braced on the dashboard and was chanting, "Shit! Shit! Shit! Shit!"

He popped open the glove box and took out a .40mm Glock, shoved it into his belt, then popped his safety belt and knelt on the seat, pulled out a .223 rifle that they'd stuck in the back. "They don't know you, so you could still talk to them, maybe. I'm gonna bail," he said. "Find a place to park and play it cool."

"What? What?"

"I'm gonna bail." They were shouting at each other as Darling wheeled crazily between the mobile homes. He ran over a plastic Big Wheel that crunched like an egg, banged across an automobile bumper that was lying in a side yard. "Park the truck, find a place to hide. If it looks like they're about to get you, ditch the phone. If I make it out, I'll call your wife and we can hook up."

"Man, man, I dunno . . ."

LUCAS HAD passed the word to the border patrolmen, and to Bob and Rae, who were now sharing a truck, about the phone being west of the I-10 checkpoint. He was gnawing his way through a package of Snackimals animal crackers when he saw a white pickup truck hit the brakes two blocks up the highway to the north, then swerve, nearly out of control, into a side street to the west.

Bob rolled up next to him and shouted, "You see that?"

"We're going," Lucas shouted back. He had O'Brien, the Border Patrol boss, on speed dial and punched him up, and O'Brien picked up and said, "We saw it, we got guys who'll be coming up behind you. We'll get some more going around the south end of town so they can't get out that way. You think that's him?"

"Find out soon enough," Lucas shouted, and he dropped the phone on the passenger seat and focused on keeping the car under control. Bob had swung past him as he was talking to O'Brien and led the way to the point where the white pickup had turned off.

And found themselves in a short dirt alley, and at the

end of the alley, a T-intersection. A half dozen white pick-ups were scattered around a trailer park, on both sides of them, nothing moving.

Bob and Rae went right and Lucas went left, then took the next right deeper into the trailer park past a burned-out trailer and a loose dog. He bounced through a deep swale, his head banging off the roof of the truck, and he realized the beeping sound he kept ignoring was the safety-belt warning alarm, and then he was on a real blacktopped street . . . and nothing was moving.

He stopped, and looked out his passenger-side window, and saw Bob and Rae's truck a couple hundred yards away, also at a full stop.

Where had the pickup gone? Two Border Patrol trucks came up behind him, and Lucas got out and ran back to them and told the drivers, "Keep an eye on those white trucks, the parked ones, it might be one of them. Otherwise . . . I dunno. And keep your guns up. This guy is a killer, and I don't want him riding off in one of your trucks, and you dead."

Bob called: "There's a road going south and some dust in the air, I think he might have gone down there."

Lucas: "I can see it, I'm coming, I'm right behind you."

POOLE BAILED OUT of Darling's truck at a T-intersection. On the other side of a fence was a shed with a sign that said "Mañana." The ground was cut to stubble on the right side of the shed, but on the left there was enough grass to cover him. He took his rifle and said, "Be cool, buddy, and if I don't see you again, it's . . . been real."

"God bless you, man," Darling called back, and Poole slammed the door and Darling dropped the pedal to the floor and headed west; when the door had been open, and Poole was bailing, he thought he could hear every siren in the world, all coming for him.

He sped past a low white building that said something about the Border Patrol, and a bunch of Border Patrol trucks sat motionless behind a high chain-link fence. When he got to the end of the road, he could turn either north or south; north would take him back toward the sirens, so he turned south and sped down the narrow road, thinking a few seconds later that he may have made a mistake, because he was out in the open for what must have been a quarter mile; but at his speed, that was only fifteen seconds. *Corners,* he thought. He had to get around corners.

He took the first one he saw, another narrow street heading west, then another going south. At the next corner he stopped, for a few seconds, to assess his position. He was breathing hard, purely from the adrenaline. He had a choice of going farther west, but from where he was, it looked like a dead end. If he turned east, he might get closer to the sirens, but he was also closer to the highway to Presidio. If he could only get back to the highway, without the cops seeing him . . .

That was unlikely.

He had to think logically: the truck was probably done, the money under the floor was probably gone. He really had to get away from it. His main thought was: get away, at least until he could assess further.

He turned east. At the end of the road, he found himself looking down a long row of faded salmon-colored buildings, and off to his left, a parking area behind the buildings, with two white pickups parked in it.

He went that way, jammed the truck into a parking place between the two other trucks. What did he need? He needed his bag, he needed his gun, his phone, he needed to simply hide, to get out in one of the surrounding fields and lie down.

What if they brought dogs? Okay, he needed to get away from the sirens, find a car . . .

He got out of the truck, ran around to the back, grabbed a duffel bag, spilled the clothes out of it, got his rifle, a Bushmaster Minimalist-SD in .223, stuck two thirty-round magazines and four bottles of water in the bag, hesitated, said, "Goddamnit," jumped into the truck—only take a few seconds—pulled up the floor, grabbed a wad of cash, then another, stuffed it all in the bag, closed the floorboard, was out of the truck. He started toward the field behind him, stopped, swore again, went back to the truck and stuck the keys under the rubber mat on the driver's side. Then he turned and ran toward the field . . .

POOLE, out of the truck, on the ground, clambered over the fence on the left side of the Mañana shed and got down on his hands and knees and began pushing through the stiff yellow grass and weeds, moving as fast as he could while staying out of sight; it was like swimming, with thorns, and he was getting burs in his hands and could feel them clustering on his shirt and jeans, sharp little knobs, and fifty yards into the field the palms of his hands and fingers were burning with them, and when he looked at one hand there must have been twenty sandburs embedded in his flesh . . .

Up ahead, when he took a moment to peek, he could see a scattering of hippie-style brightly painted Airstream trailers, and some white teepees. Like Darling, he could hear what sounded like a million sirens.

He needed a car. He needed to find a single person in a car turning south. If he could get the person to stop, for an instant, he could kill him and take the car and get out into the countryside, where he'd have some options. He might have to kill his way west, but once he got to El Paso, he could find Box. She had hidden a million and a half in cash and gold, and if that didn't convince the lesbos . . . then he'd have to kill himself a few lesbians.

He moved on; couldn't see much, but he had to keep moving.

BOB WENT straight down the road where he'd seen the dust in the air, paused at an intersection to check for the fleeing truck, saw nothing, and Rae shouted, "Go," and he went straight past a sign that said "The Chinati Foundation" and into a gravel parking lot to a low salmon-colored building with a "Visitors" sign out front and three cars in the parking lot, but no white pickups.

Lucas went right, toward a narrow road out of the parking lot to the south—and saw Darling fifty yards away, running down the track, a canvas bag on his back. Lucas jammed on his brakes, got out, and shouted at Bob and Rae, "He's running, he's running."

Bob and Rae got out of their truck, both carrying their M4s, and Lucas was already running south after the fleeing man, and Bob and Rae, coming up behind him, saw the man go over a fence into the heavy weeds in an adjacent field. Lucas had his pistol out and fired two shots in that general direction, and Bob thought, *Not much chance at that distance . . .*

The man in the field went down, then popped up again, only six feet back in the weeds, and from the way he came up Lucas saw that he had a rifle and he screamed, "Gun," and went flat, got some dirt in his mouth and a sudden chill, on the ground, exposed. He began rolling, scrambling, left toward the buildings, looking for anything to get behind.

He heard a series of *bangs*, rapid rifle fire, and Rae

shouting, and when he looked back, Rae was on her back and Bob was climbing over her, covering her, and Lucas looked back down the road where the man had been and saw him jump back over the fence and run across the road into the cover of the salmon-colored buildings, which were adobe or brick or concrete, not something you could shoot through.

The man was moving fast, no longer carrying the bag, but still carrying the rifle. Lucas got off one shot, to no visible effect, and then he crawled backward, gun still pointing at the place where the man had disappeared, back toward Bob and Rae, where Rae was sputtering, "Get off me, get off me," and Bob said to Lucas, "She's bleeding . . ."

The shooter was nowhere in sight, and Lucas shoved Bob off Rae and found blood over Rae's shoulder and cuts on one hand. "Get the vest off her," Lucas said. The vest had side snaps, and they unsnapped it and peeled it back and Rae said, "Doesn't hurt . . . much . . . hand hurts the worst."

With the vest off, Lucas unbuttoned her blouse and pulled it aside and found a series of shallow cuts across the knob of her shoulder.

"Not bad, nothing penetrated," Lucas said. "Looks like somebody slashed you with a knife."

He looked around, picked up her M4. The gun had a gouge down what would have been the outside of the top-mounted Picatinny accessory rail. "Slug hit the gun," he said. "If it hadn't, you'd have a hole in your face."

She sat up. "That sonofabitch. I'm gonna pop his ass."

"You might need stitches," Bob said.

"I'll get them later," she said, rolling to her feet. She flexed her right hand. "When the gun came out, it yanked on my thumb. Gonna have a bruise, but I'll live. Where'd he go?"

"Ran behind one of the buildings," Lucas said. "I'm going around to the other side. Try to flush him out. Bob, call the Border Patrol guys, tell them what's going on, get them on the highway on the other side of that field, and get some more guys down here in armor."

"Careful," Bob said. "We'll push him from this side."

Rae picked up her rifle, pointed it at a phone pole, looking through the Aimpoint sight, and pulled the trigger once. A piece of reflective plastic the size of a quarter jumped off the pole.

"Sight's still good," she said. She asked Lucas, "You ever shoot one of these?"

"Yeah, but I don't want to take your gun," he said.

She handed it to him. "Take it. We'll need a rifle on both sides of the building, and I'm going with Bob down this side. We got the team thing worked out between us, and I've got my .40."

Lucas took the rifle and said, "Get the Border Patrol moving. We need Poole to know there's no way out. Maybe he'll quit."

"I don't think so," Bob said. "He thinks he's shot a cop. That's a no-no in Texas."

LUCAS JOGGED around the building and on the far side, peeked. He could see two large brick-and-glass buildings across the way, with domed roofs, like Quonset huts. He stepped out, slid down the face of the building, watching for anything, any sign of movement.

Somebody behind him shouted, "Hey!" and Lucas nearly jumped out of his skin. He brought the muzzle of the gun around and found himself looking at a thin, long-haired woman in a light blue T-shirt. She saw the gun and threw up her hands and screamed, "No!" and Lucas shouted at her, "U.S. marshal! There's a man with a gun out here! Get back inside and lock down! Tell everybody you know, lock down! Call everybody you know. Don't come outside!"

She ran away and Lucas brought the rifle back around, saw a twitch in a bush, nearly triggered off a shot before he realized it was a small gray bird flitting through the branches.

He was, he thought, in an odd place, and for a moment he thought it might be the remnants of an old college campus.

He was standing beside a double curving line of buildings that must have extended for the best part of a half mile to the south, and parallel to each other. To his right, as he looked south, the U-shaped buildings looked like they might once have been dormitories, with courtyards in the middle of each U.

The buildings faced a sidewalk that defined the curve, and were spaced maybe thirty-five or forty yards apart. On the other side of the curve was the second set of buildings, small rectangular structures that filled in the forty-yard gaps between the U-shaped buildings. Together, they made two C shapes, inscribed inside each other.

On the far side of the two lines of buildings, two large, domed brick-and-glass structures rose out of the prairie.

Taken together, the arrangement of buildings made it nearly impossible to clear out, without taking heavy risks. He got his phone out and called the Border Patrol's O'Brien.

"Got a problem. We need to surround these old buildings and then we need to clear them one at a time," Lucas said.

"It'll be getting dark soon," O'Brien said. "Once it's dark, it's gonna be tough. I need to bring some lights in here. We've got them, but it'll take a while. That old fort is a tangle—it'll be like trying to clear out a block of tenements in Brooklyn."

"It's a fort?"

"Used to be. Now it's an art place—Donald Judd and all that. Marfa's pride and joy."

"Well, whatever it is, we need to get him before dark," Lucas said. "We won't have to clear all the buildings, only the ones south of those two big buildings. We saw where he ran between them . . ."

"I'll get everything going," O'Brien said. "Give us ten minutes to get organized."

Lucas called Bob and told him that the Border Patrol was sending more people to help clear the buildings. "Get out wide of the buildings so you can see down the whole length of them. If he makes a break to the west, you'll see him. I'll get over here where I can see a break to the east."

DARLING WAS crouched behind one of the salmon-colored buildings. He called Poole: "I'm fucked, man. I shot a cop, and the place is gonna be swarming with more cops any second. Listen, there are three white trucks parked behind some of those pink buildings down south of you . . . southwest, I guess."

"I know where you're at. I heard the gun," Poole said.

"Okay. Anyway, our truck is in the middle, the keys are on the floorboard on the driver's side. Don't think I'm going to make it, and I'm going to call my old lady in a minute, to tell her."

"I'll head down your way. If I can help out, I will," Poole said. "I can't go out to the highway, the Border Patrol trucks are all over the place, guys with rifles. I could take a couple of them out, but that wouldn't get me anywhere."

"Okay. Do what you can," Darling said. Poole clicked off.

Darling called his wife. Before he could say anything, she asked, "Where are you?"

"Near El Paso, somewhere. I got cops all over me, I shot one of them. I'm not gonna make it back, sweetheart. They'll be tearing the farm apart . . ."

"Sturgill, Sturg . . ." Panic in her voice.

"I'm sorry, honey, but that's the way it is. Now listen, listen—when they identify me, they'll be all over you. Tell them the story we worked out. But the main thing is, stay cool. Don't mess with that money, it's safe right where it is."

"Sturgill, you gotta get away . . ."

"I'm trying, but it's not gonna work, I don't think. They'll be swarming me, any minute. I'm gonna make a run for it . . . but if I don't make it, you're the only woman I ever loved and I still love you, Janice. Take care of the girls . . . When things cool off, maybe move the money to Canada. You're smart, you'll figure it out."

"Sturgill . . ."

"Gotta go right now, sweetheart. Take care, forever."

"Sturg!"

He clicked off. After shooting the cop, he'd dodged behind one of the buildings, and when he came out the other side, had run as hard as he could, as long as he thought reasonable, and then one building more, expecting at any moment to be shot in the back.

He dodged behind one of the salmon-colored rectangular buildings, then took another chance and scrambled on hands and knees into the grassy field on the other side, and flopped on his belly.

Got a chance, he thought. *Got a chance*. The cops would think he'd be holed up inside one of the buildings and would take a while to figure out that he wasn't. From where he was, if he slowly and cautiously lifted his head, he could see men with guns on the highway, and then two Border Patrol trucks turned off the highway along a road or a track he couldn't see, started bumping through weeds, and turned toward him. Had to move: he went north, toward the two redbrick domed buildings. If he could just work his way past them, and into town . . . into a place with cars that the cops weren't watching . . .

POOLE HAD worked his way south, where he found that the weeds suddenly ended, giving away to closely trimmed ground. The highway was to his left, and he could see a Border Patrol truck a hundred yards down the way, with a border patrolman standing behind it, with a rifle pointed over the hood.

The hippie place, the trailers and teepees, were across a fence, and right there, ten feet away, was a hole in the fence. Had to take a chance, he thought, but first . . .

He lay on his back, loosened his belt, and used the leather to protect his fingers as he plucked two dozen sandburs from his hands and fingers. Hurt worse than when that dealer in Biloxi shot him. He had dozens more scratching at his legs, right through the denim.

When his hands were free of the burs, he crawled through the fence, out into the open. His belt was still loose, and he pushed the barrel of the rifle under the belt and down alongside his leg, then retightened the belt.

He crawled behind some trees, found that he could move in a curved path, not easily visible from the highway, toward the middle of the campground, or whatever it was, the place with teepees and trailers. He was doing that when Darling called, to say he was trapped. Poole didn't know what he could do about that, but if there *was* anything, he told Darling, he'd do it.

He would catch glimpses of the Border Patrol trucks down the highway as he walked along the line of trees, but nobody was looking at him: they were looking across the fields toward the low pink buildings. It occurred to Poole then that the cops might not know that there were two of them.

That they thought Darling was him.

There was a campground building off to the left of him, and if he could amble over there, find somebody getting into a car . . .

He started to make that move when he realized that there was no traffic on the highway. None at all. The Border Patrol had apparently plugged it at both ends, keeping traffic away from the ongoing shoot-out. Couldn't pull out on the highway if that were the case.

He turned away from the highway, saw a woman walking across the campground, a cell phone to her ear. What looked more innocent than somebody walking while talking on a cell phone? He dug his phone out and put it to his ear, and limped across an open area, the limp induced by the gun down his leg.

On the far side of the campground was a parking lot of some kind. Not until he got close did he realize he was looking at a big Border Patrol facility, behind a chain-link fence. He went to his left, and when he was past the Border Patrol fence, took a quick look around and slipped into the high grass in the field behind the Border Patrol lot.

He pulled the rifle out of his belt, crossed through a clump of trees, and found himself coming up behind some kind of concrete bunker. A military facility of some kind? There was a dirt path in front of the bunker, and he looked left and right, and found several more of the bunkers trailing away to his left.

Nobody around. He settled into one of the bunkers and a moment later, saw three Border Patrol vehicles coming down a road to the north, headed toward the two big domed buildings. Had somebody seen him? He didn't think so. Darling was down here. That's probably who they were looking for.

Poole thought about it, thought about Darling. Brought the rifle up, steadied it against the bunker wall, thought about it until he decided it was best not to think about it and fired a burst of a half dozen shots at the first two trucks. The trucks went sideways and he settled back down out of sight.

Heard people shouting . . .

LUCAS HEARD the gunfire, not from where he thought it should be. The shots came from behind the domed buildings and not down the line of smaller buildings. He called Bob: "Poole's moved. He's on the other side of those big brick buildings."

"We heard," Bob said. "What do you want to do?"

"I'll make a break for the first building. You and Rae set up where you are. If I'm wrong, and he pops up . . . take him out."

"Yes. Go anytime."

Lucas set himself to run, took a breath, got a tight grip on Rae's rifle, and sprinted across the open space to the first big building. The distance wasn't long, but he'd be exposed long enough that a good shooter might try to knock him down.

He nearly slammed into the glass wall of the building. No shots. He caught his breath, waved back at Bob and Rae. And his phone was ringing. O'Brien.

"We've had two trucks hit by gunfire, we got two guys hurt from glass splinters," O'Brien said. "We're not moving, because we can't see exactly where the gunfire's coming from, but we know he can see us. We've got to get our wounded guys out of there. We think the shooter's probably out in the field behind the old armory buildings . . . Anyway, we're stuck halfway down the street leading to Chinati, and one of the trucks will try to back out of there with our wounded guys. The other one has some guns pointing down into the field. If he gets up, we'll get him."

"Chinati? What's that?"

"The art place. That's where you're at. Look north. Can you see the trucks?"

Lucas looked north and on a road leading out of the parking lot he could see the front grille of one of the Border Patrol's Chevy trucks.

"Yeah, I see them. I'm behind one of the big domed buildings."

"Okay. We think the shooter's in the high weeds on the other side of where you are. Careful. He could be moving."

Lucas got off the phone, realized that the buildings had long glass walls on *both* sides, and that he could see clear through the building to the field on the other side. He couldn't see anything moving in the field. Took a moment to check the curved line of buildings behind him: didn't see anything there, either. Bob called: "Anything?"

"No."

"Then we're coming. We'll hit the other end of the building you're at," Bob said.

"Come ahead."

A minute later, Bob broke from the cover of the smaller buildings, ran heavily across the street, and set up at the far corner of the building. Rae followed him ten seconds later, and then all three of them were at the corners of the building, looking out toward the field.

Lucas said into the cell phone, "Okay, I'm going up to the front end, take a peek. See what I can see."

He was fifty feet down the length of the building and jogged toward the front: later, it occurred to him how stupid he'd been—if he could see through the building to the field, somebody in the field could see through the building to him.

He ran past the windows to the brick superstructure and peeked around the corner to the northeast, once, saw nothing, peeked again . . .

Bang!

He went straight down, his face burning, had the presence of mind to roll deeper behind the building. The shot, he thought, had come in from an angle, had to be from the northeast, and he shouted to Bob, "I've been hit. I can't see out of one eye, I'm down . . ."

Bob shouted, "I'm coming . . ."

Lucas pushed himself up and shouted in the direction where Bob had been, "He's got an angle on us, don't come any further than me."

Everything in his left eye was blurry and red and then Bob was kneeling next to him, and Rae came up, and Lucas said, "Don't poke your head around the building, for Christ sakes . . . How bad is it?"

Bob said, "You got the same thing as Rae. The slug missed your head by an inch, but must have hit the bricks. Your skin is full of brick splinters, on your forehead and in your hair. You're bleeding, but it's superficial, I think. You got a lot of blood rolling down into your eye, through your eyebrow."

"Probably why I can't see shit," Lucas said. His stomach was tight as a drum, from the stress. Blinded?

Rae said, "Hang on," and, a minute later, said, "Lay down in the dirt and turn your face up. I'm gonna wash your eye out. Bob, keep watch."

She had a bottle of Dasani water stuck under her vest and Lucas lay down, and she poured a stream of cool water into his eye and off his forehead. He blinked a few times and his vision began to clear.

She asked, "So you're wearing a really expensive shirt, right?"

"What?"

She asked again and he said, "It's a Façonnable . . . why?"

He felt a tug at his waist as his shirt was pulled free, and then a long ripping sound. "You may need a tailor," she said. "Sit up, I'm going to wrap this around your head to keep the blood out of your eye."

She tied the blue-and-white-checked material around his forehead and said, "There you go. You look like that picture of Geronimo."

Lucas got to his knees, his head aching, his scalp tightening, and said, "Okay, now we know where he's at. He's north of the building and east of it. He's stuck there, because the Border Patrol people are looking out at him. He might be able to crawl in the weeds, but he can't run."

"If I go around to the back end of the building, I can see out there," Bob said to both of them. And to Rae: "You sit here until you're sure Lucas is okay. We need to pin this guy."

"I'm okay," Lucas said.

"We'll see about that," Bob said. He jogged away with his rifle, paused at the far corner of the building, then turned it and was out of sight.

Lucas pushed himself up against the side of the building, his forehead burning from the impact of the brick dust. "When Bob's in position, we'll move some Border Patrol people down from the north and across from the highway. We'll start to squeeze him—it's just a matter of taking it slow, now. He'll break and run and then we've got him."

"Then we'll kill him," Rae said.

Lucas: "That's what I said."

Rae nodded. "What do you want me to do?"

"You go with Bob. If the guy tries to run, it'll be handy to have two guns down there." He handed her the rifle: "Take this back. I can't even stick my head around this corner. Better that you have it."

She took the gun. "What are you going to do?"

He pointed: "We've got these glass windows on both sides of the building. I can stand halfway down the building where I can see up and down that field on the other side. He'd have to be pretty lucky to both see me and be able to hit me through two big layers of glass—but I could see him, clear enough. If I do, I'll call you and Bob. You've got the rifles."

"That's a plan," she said. She peered through the glass. "Looks like the place is full of what?—washing machines or something? Look like expensive washer-dryers."

"It's supposed to be an art place," Lucas said. Inside the building, he could see aluminum boxes, probably waist-high, several feet wide, and deep. There were a lot of them, in three rows down the length of the building. "Maybe those are vaults, or something. Boxes that the art's in."

"Huh. Weird way to do it. Okay, I'm gone. Don't get yourself shot again."

26

WHEN THE SHOOTING began in Marfa, Dora Box, Kort, Rosie, and Annie were running west toward El Paso. They'd gone thirty-five miles from the intersection of I-20 and I-10, and the checkpoint, when Box's cell phone burped. She picked it up, looked at it, and with the other women looking at her, said, "Gar! Are you in Mexico?"

She listened for a moment, then said, "No! No! Oh, Jesus, Gar . . ." She looked up at the others and said, "The cops are on them. They're shooting it out. Gar said he doesn't think they're gonna . . ."

She went back to the phone. "Gar! You gotta get a car. Just run through those weeds as far as you can, down the highway . . . then crawl! Crawl! Screw Sturgill! He's the one who got you into this! You gotta . . ."

She listened again, said, "I don't want to hear that . . . I don't . . . Goddamnit, Gar," and she began to cry. Poole said something else, and, sobbing, handed the phone to Annie and dropped onto the couch and put her head down, in her hands.

Annie punched up the speaker so everybody could hear and said, "This is . . . one of her friends. What's up?"

"Dora will tell you, but basically, we're stuck here and there's a good chance the cops are going to take us down," Poole said, his voice as casual as if he were talking to a high school class about harmless germs. "We'll try to hold out until dark, but that's pretty . . . pretty . . . unlikely. Here's the thing. We were driving a white pickup truck—Dora knows it—with Arkansas plates, and Sturgill dropped it off behind some kind of art place. It's a place with big brick buildings with curved roofs. He parked it behind the buildings on the other side of the brick buildings. They're kinda pink-colored."

"I don't understand that. Give that to me again," Annie said.

Poole explained the arrangement of buildings, from what he could see from the bunker. "Okay, you got it? If you go around behind those pink buildings, the small ones, Sturgill said there were two pickups parked back there, both white, and he parked between them. If you can get in there, after dark . . . you might get to it. There's four million bucks, more or less, cash and gold, under the floor of the camper . . ."

He explained how the camper's floor worked, and Annie said, "Uh-huh. Got it. We can find that."

"That's your money back, or most of it," Poole said. "Dora's worth more than that, so it's a fair trade. If you wait too long, the cops are going to find it. But if you can get here tonight, we'll either be caught . . . or dead . . . or pulling them away from here. Then, maybe you could get at that truck."

"We'll take a look," Annie said. "We're going to throw this phone away, right now. If you got anything else to say, you better say it."

"One thing. If we do get loose, we'll leave a message at the Holiday Inn, in El Paso, about where we are."

"Got it."

"One more thing." There was a long moment of silence, then, "Tell Dora I love her, I guess. That's about it."

Box looked up and screamed, "No!" and Poole was gone. Box shouted, "Call him back! Call him back!"

Annie shook her head. "He's gone, Dora, and we've got to get rid of this phone. If the cops get his phone, they'll track us . . ."

She was pulling the phone apart as she spoke, ripped the battery out, tossed the pieces on the table. Rosie said, from the driver's seat, "I'm pretty sure we can get down there from Van Horn, which oughta be coming up quick. Somebody look at the maps . . ."

THEN KORT spoke up. "Wait a minute. You're not serious? You're not going to try to go down there."

"Not crazy, ugly girl," Box shouted at her. "We've got to get down there. Maybe there'll be some way we can help them . . ."

Rosie said quietly, "We won't be able to help them, Dora, because we won't know where they are, and we don't have any way to get in touch with them. We can go down there and look for the money, see if there's any way to get to it . . . but we won't find those men."

Box said, "Oh, Jesus, oh, Jesus . . ."

Rosie was shaking her head: "That's the fact of the matter."

"We know what his number is, we could call him, he'll keep the phone if he's on the run . . ."

Annie nodded this time: "If we can find a phone, we can do that. We're not going to use my phone or Rosie's, because that's the only way we have to stay in touch with the Boss. But we could call Gar if we find a pay phone."

"I'm laying down the law," Kort said. "We ain't going. We ain't going for Poole, we ain't going for that other guy, and we ain't going for the money. There'll be cops everywhere, and if anyone sees me, knows me from that TV show, they're gonna put me in a cage until they send me to the chair. Same for Box. We ain't going."

"I don't care if it harelips the Pope, we're going," Box said.

"Shut up and sit down, both of you," Rosie yelled over her shoulder. "If we see anything like a cop, we'll put you down below. You'll be safe enough. We've run fifty kilos of cocaine through a crowd of dope-sniffing dogs. But if there's any way to get our hands on that cash, we're gonna do it."

Annie said, "That's Van Horn up ahead. Look for 90 South. Looks like about an hour run down to Marfa, give or take."

Kort slumped back into the couch. "You motherfuckers. We're gonna die down there," she said.

27

LUCAS MOVED close to the windows, looking in at the storage area, or whatever it was—he had the feeling that he was missing something important about the building, but he didn't know what it might be. In any case, he could see past the aluminum boxes and out into the field where the gunfire had come from, north and east of the building.

O'Brien called: "We can't come in at you like we were trying, but we can come in from the back side of the place and that's what we're doing. We'll have a half dozen guys with you there in five minutes. They're bringing an extension ladder. We think we can get up on top of the artillery buildings with a sniper."

"Be good if we can do it . . ."

He was cut off by three quick shots from the side of the building and then Rae screaming, and Lucas shoved the phone in his pocket and ran down the length of the building where Rae was dragging Bob toward the back corner.

She saw Lucas and shouted: "He's hit! He's hit hard! We gotta get him outa here, we gotta get him to a medic . . ."

Lucas ran toward them and squatted over Bob, who looked up at him and said, "Hurts bad. Legs. He got me in the legs."

Rae took a folding knife from her pocket and began cutting his pants off, and Lucas saw Bob's rifle on the ground near the front corner of the building and asked, "Where was the shooter?"

"Down there." Rae waved south and east. "Never saw him. We were looking in the other direction, up north. We were sitting ducks."

"Poole's either got a way to get around without being seen, in which case we're in trouble right here, or there are two of them," Lucas said. "I bet that fuckin' Darling's down here with him."

"Then move me," Bob groaned, and he said, "Ah . . ."

"I'll carry him," Lucas said. "Try to help with his legs."

Lucas lifted Bob from under his arms and Rae lifted his thighs, and they trundled around to the back of the building and put him on the ground.

Bob groaned, "Ah, man," and Rae had the pants cut off, and they found two large and heavily bleeding through-and-through wounds, on both of Bob's thighs, eight inches above his knees, apparently from the same shot. He was bleeding steadily, rather than in pulses, so no major arteries had been taken out.

Lucas got on his phone and called O'Brien: "We need guys here right now," he said. "We got a guy hit bad in the legs. We need a chopper out of El Paso, I know they've got one . . ."

"Oh, gosh. Oh, gosh. I'll get it going," O'Brien said. "You should see our guys coming at any minute."

Bob was saying to Rae, "Not a tourniquet, not a tourniquet, plug the holes best you can, I don't want to lose a leg . . ."

Then they saw a half dozen Border Patrol guys running toward them, all carrying rifles. One of them knelt next to Lucas and Rae, and he said, "We've got an EMT on the way. Where's the shooter?"

"Could be two of them," Lucas said. "Both out in the field, one right, one left. Stay here behind the buildings. Let's move Bob to one of your trucks."

"Better to wait for the EMT, they'll bring a stretcher . . ."

Lucas nodded and said to Rae, "Stay with him until they take him . . ."

Rae's rifle was back where she'd dropped it while dragging Bob. Lucas scrambled on his hands and knees toward the gun, figuring if Rae hadn't been shot at, she'd probably been out of the shooter's sight when she dropped the rifle. He picked it up and scurried back behind the building with the others.

"What are we doing?" Rae asked.

"I'll talk to O'Brien and get something worked out." Lucas looked up at the sky. "It'll be dark in an hour or so and then we'll have a real problem."

"Couldn't be much worse than this," Rae said. She looked down at Bob, who was lying back, his eyes squeezed shut, his hands curling and uncurling with the stress and pain.

"Yeah, it will be. Those guys will sneak out of here, or try to. If they get out of that field, there's only one way they get completely away—find somebody with a car, kill 'em, and drive away. We either get them now or we could have some dead civilians on our hands. Maybe a lot of them."

Lucas took five minutes to place the border patrolmen

along the corners of the two domed buildings, plus one in the middle of each building, looking through the glass walls, trying to spot the shooters. The patrolmen included the sniper, who was carrying a bolt-action .308, but had no way up on the roof. "When we heard the shooting, we left the ladder with the trucks. Think we should get it?"

Lucas asked, "How many guys to carry it?"

"Two can carry it, but we can't go up the sides. The bottoms of those curved roofs are too steep. I'd have to get on at one of the ends."

Lucas looked at the buildings, shook his head: "Can't guarantee that he couldn't see you, if you went up at an end. If he can, you'd be a sitting duck on the ladder. Let's stay on the ground."

"Your call," the rifleman said.

TWO EMTS came sloping from behind the smaller salmon-colored buildings, carrying a stretcher. They bent over Bob and one said, "Not as bad as I was afraid of. Let's block up the holes and get him the hell out of here." And to Bob, he said, "You're gonna be all right, pal. We've seen worse than this at a Saturday night cockfight."

"Not that they're good," Bob said.

"No, no . . ."

"How about the helicopter?" Lucas asked.

"On the way, or will be in the next couple of minutes," one of the medics said. "Flying time is a little more than a half hour each way. They're putting a trauma doc on board."

Lucas said to Bob, "Take it easy," and to Rae, "Stay with him."

Bob tried to smile and grunted, "Yeah," and, "Shoot that motherfucker."

"Doing our best," Lucas said. He jogged away, on his phone to O'Brien as he ran. "We need to get together," he said.

"What do you have in mind?"

"How many trucks and guns do you have?"

LUCAS GOT the idea from pheasant drives: he wasn't much of a hunter, but he'd heard enough about the drives from people who were, like Virgil Flowers. O'Brien had a few ideas of his own, and a half hour before sunset, seven Border Patrol trucks bumped off the highway down into the dry field south of where the second shooter was.

"Don't have much time," Lucas shouted to the drivers. "We have to move right along. You shooters, you guys stay close to the trucks—don't stick anything out but one eyeball."

The trucks arrayed themselves across the field, spaced fifteen yards apart, giving them a sweep of more than a hundred yards. A border patrolman stood on the back left corner of each truck carrying a rifle, using the truck for cover.

The truck drivers sat in the passenger seats, low enough that nothing but their eyes were above the dashboard. Each of them had a traffic cone on the driver's side, the tip of the cone pressed against the gas pedal. It was ugly and awkward, but it worked. They had no way to brake, but wouldn't be traveling any faster than two or three miles an hour. Even at that slow pace, they'd cover a hundred yards in a bit more than a minute, and only had to cover a couple hundred yards to sweep the field.

The drivers were put in the passenger seat because everybody agreed that if the shooter opened up on the trucks, he was most likely to try to hit the driver . . . in the driver's seat. They used traffic cones to push on the pedals because it was what they had that would work.

When everybody was lined up, Lucas looked at the lowering sun and yelled, "Let's do it."

Lucas was behind the truck closest to the buildings, carrying Bob's rifle. The trucks began edging forward, Lucas and the border patrolmen walking behind, their rifles already at their shoulders, ready to fire.

DARLING HAD shot at the two cops, the short white guy and the tall black woman, hitting one, he thought, from the way the woman screamed and the guy went down. He hoped that the Border Patrol hadn't yet become fully involved with lots of personnel, that if he could rid himself of the cops from the silver SUVs, he might have a little more freedom of movement.

When the heavyset cop went down and was dragged out of sight, he began moving north, as quick as he could without giving away his position, snaking along in the grass. He stopped once, to call Poole and tell him what was going on.

"I don't know where you are," Poole said. "I think I might have hit one of the cops. I saw him peeking out from behind one of the buildings. If there were only two or three of them in those trucks, we might have knocked out two of them."

"I'm going to get as close as I can to those glass buildings," Darling replied. "If I get the chance, I'll rush them, see if I can take them out. It's about our only chance."

"All right. I'm in this concrete bunker. I can see the tops of both of the roofs. If they try to put a sniper up there, I'll clean him off for you. Let me know if you break through."

"Soon as it happens," Darling said. "We've only got maybe thirty or forty minutes until sundown."

Darling hung up, and still with a bit of hope in his heart, he continued crawling north, trying not to leave a rippling motion in the grass and weeds.

He was almost even with the back of the nearest building when he heard the trucks rushing down the highway. He risked a look over the weeds, saw the line of Border Patrol trucks heading south and then turning out onto the field. He said, "Goddamnit," aloud, crawled a few feet into a dense cluster of dead dark brown weeds, and used the cover to take a longer look.

The trucks were spreading out across the far end of the field, their headlights pointing toward him. They were going to try to flush him, he thought—and they'd do it, too, if he let them get close. The brown weeds were looser than the yellow grass, and after considering his dwindling options, he carefully moved into a prone shooting position, lined up on the driver's-side window of the middle truck, and fired a single shot.

He immediately heard men shouting. He lined up on another truck and squeezed the trigger again. The trucks stopped rolling.

Darling, satisfied for the moment, turned around to begin crawling north again. He'd moved fifty feet when he heard the truck engines working again, behind him. A few more feet and he came to a trampled area in the yellow grass. He'd have to cross it, and when he did . . .

He peeked again and saw people standing behind the glass in the nearest building—he wasn't sure if they were inside the building or on the far side. Whichever it was, they would be able to see him when he tried to cross the bald spot.

He got on the phone: "Hey, man, I'm trying to get up north. It'd help a whole lot if you could put a few shots through the windows of the second building. There are people either in there or on the other side, looking out here at these fields . . ."

"Give me fifteen seconds . . ."

Fifteen seconds later, he heard Poole open up and the glass shattering in the domed building, and he low-crawled across the bald spot, just as he'd been taught in the Corps. On the far side, he disappeared back into the weeds, now aiming at the space between the two big buildings, the place where the two cops had been when he shot at them.

If he could get into the gap, and if there weren't many cops, he might be able to break back through.

O'BRIEN WAS on the phone to Lucas, after checking by radio with the truck drivers: "Nobody hurt, we're all okay. Keep moving, I think this is gonna work."

The trucks began moving again, still at the slow walking pace, and Lucas kept the rifle up. Then a patrolman, two or three trucks over, shouted, "I think I saw him. I think he's angling toward the space between the buildings. He's maybe twenty-five yards into the field."

Lucas shouted back, "If you got a clear line, if you're not going to hit anything else, put a couple shots in there, see if he breaks out."

The patrolman did that: *Bap! Bap! Bap!*

Lucas, who was looking toward the area, thought he saw a wavelike motion in the weeds, somebody moving on his knees and elbows. He aimed Bob's M4 at the area and fired four more shots: *Bap! Bap! Bap! Bap!*

A half second later, the trucks took ten or twelve incoming shots from a different angle, from the northeast. "Everybody okay? Everybody okay?" Lucas shouted. Everybody was unharmed except for one truck driver, who'd taken some windshield glass in his shoulder above his vest but said he was okay.

O'Brien, who was with the trucks north of the big buildings, called: "Did you get a fix on those shots?"

"Came down from the northeast . . . but can't say exactly where from. There's a whole bunch of concrete bunkers over there, must be part of the old fort. I think he could be in one of the northern ones."

O'Brien said, "Those aren't bunkers. They're artworks."

"What?"

"Artworks. But they're perfectly fine bunkers, if you think of them that way."

Lucas was looking back at the area next to the building, and again, thought he saw movement. He shoved the phone in his pocket and brought his rifle up, and at the same instant two other border patrolmen fired from behind the trucks . . .

Lucas added two shots . . .

THE FIRST SEQUENCE of three shots whistled over Darling's head, and he thought, then, of throwing up his hands and quitting. If Poole was killed, there'd be no witnesses to the shootings in Biloxi, and if he hadn't killed either of the cops he'd shot at . . . He'd be looking at years in prison, but maybe not the needle. With his wife on the outside, with a ton of cash, he'd have at least a possibility of busting out of prison. A corrupt guard, a prison gang with connections . . .

Then the second deck of four shots came in, three narrowly missing. The fourth hit him right in the asshole, he thought, knifing up into his guts and then out, around his navel. The pain was blinding, and he curled up against it and cried out once, "Ahhhh . . ."

He kicked, once, twice, against the pain, and two more shots came in, one hitting him in the leg, the other knocking the heel off his boot and twisting his ankle.

He couldn't crawl anymore. He heard the trucks coming, the relentless sound of their engines. He touched his stomach and his hand came away soaked with blood. He got the phone out, called Poole, said, "I'm done for. I'm hit bad, my guts are all over the place. If you need to make a move, I'm gonna sit up and hose down everything I can see. Ten seconds and that's probably all I got."

Poole, after two seconds of silence, said, "See you in hell, man."

Darling choked back a laugh, because laughing would hurt too badly. "See you in hell."

The line of trucks was only fifty yards away; some of the Border Patrol shooters knew about where he was, Darling thought. He got a grip on his rifle, which was greasy with his blood, pointed it in the general direction of the trucks, and began firing, emptying the rest of a thirty-shot magazine toward them. He hurt so bad that he didn't think he could go on, but managed to pull out the other thirty-round magazine, dropped the first one, got the second one seated, and he rolled over toward the glass buildings and dumped the entire magazine into them . . .

He was hit in the head by a shot from behind one of the trucks, and was killed instantly.

LUCAS WAS shouting at the patrolmen, "Easy now, easy, I think we got him . . . Easy now, watch for that guy out front, in case he tries something crazy . . . watch him."

Another ten seconds and Lucas saw Darling's body in the weeds to his left, and when they'd pulled even with the body he shouted, "Stop! Trucks, all stop."

Without real brakes, the trucks rolled to a ragged stop

in the yellow weeds, with Darling off to their left. Lucas called, "I'm going to step over to the left. I think I'm covered by the trucks, but you guys, give me more cover. If you see motion over there, kill him . . ."

When it seemed that everybody was ready, Lucas risked five fast steps over to the body. He recognized Darling from the photo back at the farm—the one with the girls on his lap.

He didn't look at all peaceful in death; he looked like he'd fallen in a meat grinder, his shirt and pants soaked with blood, with a gaping exit wound over one eye.

Lucas turned: "We got one."

A minute later, he was back behind the trucks and they were rolling toward the area where he thought the second shooter was hiding. Lucas was sweating heavily and smelled of sweat and blood, both his and Bob's, and probably some of Rae's. He wiped his face with a shirt-sleeve and brought the rifle back up.

"Let's finish it. Drivers, let's go."

WHEN DARLING opened up on the trucks and then the buildings, Poole crawled out of his concrete bunker, flat on the ground, and around to the other side of it. From behind it, he couldn't see either of the two domed buildings, but they couldn't see him, either—and he was visually protected from the highway by the line of trees that ran parallel both to the line of bunkers and to the highway.

He could hear the trucks pushing closer up the open field toward his position. He didn't think the cops knew exactly where he was, but he had no margin for error. He had to move. He stayed flat, pushing mostly with his toes, for a hundred yards, his rifle in front of him, toward the trees.

Tough going: more sandburs, other thorns and insults. He took a few seconds to wonder if the snakes had already gone underground. He hadn't seen any, up to this point, but he didn't want to run into a rattler in the weeds. He didn't. When he'd gotten into the trees, he carefully moved into a clump of heavy brush where he could stand up to see what was going on.

Behind him, the trucks were coming on, and in front of him, he could see three Border Patrol trucks parked on the highway, with a patrolman standing behind the hood of each one, looking out over the field. Each one with a rifle. He could easily shoot one of them, but then he'd be dead.

Between himself and the highway, down to his right, he could see two long cigar-shaped white tanks that probably held propane. Off to his left he could see a white house, two stories high with a red roof, and behind it, a water tower.

The thing that most interested him, though, was what looked like a border fence and trees by the house to his left. The trees led all the way from the line of trees that he was in, to the highway. There were possibilities that way, but none the other. He went left—he couldn't stand, the trees weren't thick enough, but he could duckwalk, which was a lot better than crawling, and it was only forty or fifty yards.

Again, his hands and arms were burning with burs and thorns, and he could feel them poking through his sweat-soaked shirt into his chest. He tried to ignore them but couldn't, not the ones in his hands, and he stopped long enough to pull them out.

A minute later, he was at the intersection of his line of trees, with the trees and fence going out to the highway. He made the turn and, moving with glacial slowness, crossed over the wire fence and let himself down into the yard of the red-roofed house. Anyone looking out a window could see him; he hoped they wouldn't do that. He moved forward along the fence line, and a few minutes later, he was at the highway.

He couldn't cross it: too many people could see him, and there was no cover whatever on the far side. But the house had a white stucco wall along the front of the lot. If he crawled north along it, he would be looking into a parking lot with a half dozen cars right across the fence.

LUCAS HAD reoriented the line of trucks to move diagonally northeast through the field. When Lucas had nearly gotten himself shot, the shooter must have been at the northeast side of the big field. They were moving straight toward it, on a hundred-yard front, as they'd done with Darling, but nothing was moving.

They were approaching the line of artworks/bunkers. Whatever else they might be, they were also perfect firing platforms. When they'd gotten to them, with no sign of life, Lucas got the sniper to climb atop one of them, where he could see down the arc of bunkers that extended to the south.

"If anything moves, nail it," he told the patrolman.

On the far side of the bunker, he could see a fairly substantial line of trees a hundred yards away.

To the patrolman coordinating the trucks, he said, "I'll bet he's in the trees. I'm going to take a couple of guys and go over and work through there. You finish sweeping the field, and if you don't flush him, turn around and back us up."

"You take care," the patrolman said.

"Yeah, and you, too," Lucas said.

Lucas got two volunteers and as the trucks spread out for another sweep, Lucas and the other two men stayed behind them until they could step into the trees. The trees thinned to the south and were more widely spaced, so they turned north.

"Like this," Lucas said to the other two. "Always keep a tree directly in front of you. When you get to it, stop moving, keep your rifle up, check out the area in front of you, looking around from behind the tree. When you think it's safe, say so, and the next guy will move past you. Don't ever go more than ten or fifteen feet at a time, so if the shooter pops up, the guy in back will take him out. Got it?"

They got it, and they began working their way north. They'd gone only a short distance when they came to a fence and a thinner line of trees, leading out to the highway, past a red-roofed house.

"What do you think?" Lucas asked, his voice quiet. "Go north, or out to the highway?"

One of the patrolmen said, "The trees look like they're getting thicker the further north they go. If he sticks inside of them, he'll eventually get back to town."

"He'll have to cross a street to do that," the other one said.

"Yeah, but the sun will be down in fifteen minutes and it'll get dark quick. Once it's dark, he could get lost in town," the first one said.

"The thing is, he probably doesn't know where the trees lead," Lucas said. Then he said, "Look, you two go on, in the trees. Really careful. I'm going to take a quick jog out to the highway. If there's nothing out there, I'll be right back. Don't shoot me when I come back."

"Let me call everybody and tell them what you're doing," one of the patrolmen said. He took a radio out of a vest pocket, made the call, describing Lucas: "Doesn't have a hat, he's in a light-colored shirt, and he's wearing a vest."

When he'd finished the call, they all agreed that they'd all be careful. Lucas climbed the wire fence and began moving out to the highway, while the two patrolmen pushed farther north in the trees.

POOLE HAD crossed the fence on the north side of the red-roofed house's front yard, and sat only partially con-cealed by a clump of weeds. He'd been moving for a long time, and now, sitting still, his major sensory input was himself: he stank.

Ahead of him, not more than ten or twelve yards away, several cars were parked outside a low building with a sign that said "El Cósmico." He realized that he'd man-aged to run in a circle, that he was back to the hippie place with the teepees and weird trailers.

There was no traffic on the highway, which had appar-ently been blocked at both ends of the gunfight. He needed one of those cars and he needed the driver, be-cause he needed the driver's keys. If he could grab a driver, he could force him into his car, hit him on the head with his .40, shove him onto the floor. The cops would have to open the highway when it got dark, they couldn't keep it closed forever.

If he could hold out until then.

And he saw a single driver come out of the El Cósmico place, walking toward the cars in front of him. He set his rifle aside, slipped out the .40, waited. She was walking to a car almost directly in front of him. Perfect. The nearest Border Patrol car was a hundred yards away, and if he did it quickly and quietly . . .

She came around the back of the car, a tall, thin, red-headed woman, a Texas-looking woman with freckles, her keys in one hand, stepping toward the car. She couldn't go out on the highway, she must've checked into one of the teepees or whatever . . .

Poole stood up and lunged toward her. She didn't see

him coming until he was ten feet away and he said, fairly loudly, because there was nobody else close enough to hear him, "I've got a gun and if you make any noise or scream, I will shoot you."

She dropped the keys and said, "Oh, no . . . are you . . ."

"Yeah, the cops are going to kill me if they catch me, so I don't really give a shit at this point." He was right on top of her, took her elbow, said, "Get into the back-seat . . . We're gonna hide out for a while. Keep quiet and you won't get hurt."

When she sat down, he thought, one fast hard blow to the head would take her out, maybe permanently. *What it was, was what it was.*

She was scared, but not quite frozen with fear, said, "My keys . . ."

He stooped quickly, picked them up, pushed the button that unlocked the car: "Get in."

LUCAS HAD moved slowly down the fence line. Near the end, he saw a border patrolman, one of the ones standing behind a truck, watching him. He stood, waved the rifle over his head, patted his armor; the border patrolman was talking into a radio, and a few seconds later, waved him on.

Lucas moved on up the fence, hurrying now. He could see nothing along it, wanted a quick look along the front of the house and then he'd get back to the trees. When he'd turned the corner in the front yard, he looked down to his left and saw Poole talking to a redheaded woman beside a gray foreign car. He couldn't see a gun, but Poole was talking rapidly and the way the woman was standing, Lucas thought he probably had a gun in the hand Lucas couldn't see.

He brought the rifle up and walked across the yard, moving as noiselessly as he could. He was completely out in the open but Poole was talking to the woman, and then bent over, and Lucas thought for a second that he'd been seen or heard, but then Poole stood and handed something to the woman—keys?—and Poole said something that Lucas couldn't make out, and Lucas was close enough and shouted, "Poole, if you move, I'll kill you."

But then the woman, who'd been standing beside Poole from Lucas's perspective, lurched between them. Poole, reacting almost instantly, swung his gun hand up around her neck and shouted, "I want a car!"

Lucas, looking at him through Bob's red-dot sight, saw Poole's head looming behind the woman's, big as a gourd. He didn't listen to what Poole was saying, but concentrated on the red dot and his trigger squeeze, and shot Poole through the nose. Poole went down as though somebody had hit him in the face with a fastball, but with his arm still crooked around the woman's neck, and she went down on top of him.

The woman started screaming and rolled off the body, and as Lucas walked toward the fence, his gun still up in a shooting position, she got up and ran frantically back toward the El Cósmico building.

Lucas crossed the fence, while behind him a couple of Border Patrol trucks revved up.

Poole was dead on the ground.

The sun had just hit the horizon, scarlet rays playing across the gravel parking lot and over the supine body, which was leaking blood into the parking lot. The El Cósmico door slammed as the woman lurched inside, and Lucas looked down at Poole and said, "Gotcha."

28

THE FOUR WOMEN had seen any number of unusual things on their way south to Marfa, including a huge white blimp called a radar aerostat, according to the sign outside the launch site. When Rosie looked it up on her smartphone, it turned out it was a radar platform used to search for low-flying drug planes coming across from Mexico.

"Wonder if they've got one for low-flying drug RVs," Annie joked; only Rosie chuckled. Annie was driving now, Rosie was putting together cheeseburgers in the RV's tiny kitchen and the vehicle was suffused with the smell of cooking meat.

The countryside was new to Box, who hadn't been much west or south of Dallas, even though she and Gar had lived in Texas for five years. The Marfa area had low funky-looking mountains, lots of yellow grass and weeds, and alien-looking roadside plants with nine-foot-tall stems that stuck up out of palms, or maybe cactuses, or possibly aliens.

They'd finished eating the cheeseburgers when the lights of Marfa came up in the gathering dusk. Then, not far ahead, they could see the red blinking lights of a checkpoint and only three vehicles waiting to go through. Annie said, "Uh-oh. Rosie, get those two out of sight. Now! Hurry! I don't want to slow down."

Rosie pulled the floor up, and Box and Kort stuffed themselves into the hole, lying side by side. There was space above their heads and below their feet, but not more than six inches above their noses. When Rosie slammed the door back into place, everything went pitch-black.

"You crazy fuckin' bitch, you got us into this," Kort growled at Box.

"Shut the fuck up, I'm really fucking tired of your whining all the time," Box snarled back.

"Shit . . ." Kort threw an elbow into Box's ribs, hard enough to hurt.

There wasn't enough height to swing, but Box reached over with one hand and grabbed Kort by the lips and twisted. Kort let go with a muffled scream and beat awkwardly at Box with one fist and then Rosie started stomping on the floor and shouted, "Shut up, shut up, we're coming to it."

Box let go of Kort's lips and Kort said, "When I get out of here, I'm gonna beat the shit out of you."

"Fuck you some more," Box said.

They felt the RV braking to a stop.

UP ABOVE, Annie opened the RV's front door and a border patrolman asked, "Evening, ladies. Do you have any other passengers?"

"No," Annie said. "What's going on? Is there trouble?"

"We've had a problem with some men trying to get down to the border at Presidio. Are you on your way to Presidio?"

Annie shook her head. "No, sir, we're going to Marfa to see the Donald Judd exhibits. Is there trouble in Marfa?"

"You should be okay in Marfa. Do you mind if I take a peek inside?" He lowered his voice. "We want to make sure that you don't have a gun pointed at you or anything . . ."

"Sure, come on in," Annie said.

The officer climbed the first step, looked down the length of the RV, and said, "If you're gonna make a break from a kidnapper, now's the time."

"There's nobody else here," Rosie said.

The officer backed down the steps and smiled and said, "You're fine. Have a good time in Marfa. It's a great little place. Go see the Marfa lights."

"We will," Annie said, and rolled them through the checkpoint.

When they were well away, Rosie wondered, "If our maps are right, this museum place is all the way down to the end of town. Wonder why they're checking vehicles coming *into* town?"

"I suppose, looking for what we're doing—maybe a rescue attempt by another person. Like Dora, or Kort," Annie said.

Rosie glanced back at the neat blue carpet that concealed the smuggling space. "I'm tempted to leave them in there. Of course, maybe they're already dead."

"That'd solve a lot of problems . . . but I suppose you ought to let them out."

*   *   *

WHEN ROSIE opened the floor hatch, Box, the smaller and more lithe of the two women—Kort was to *lithe* as a packing crate is to *agile*—virtually sprang out of the enclosure and said, "Everything's okay?"

"We're fine, the cop said so himself," Rosie replied.

Kort was struggling to get out of the smuggling space, the bottom half of her face as red as a Coke can where Box had twisted it. Rosie finally reached down, took her hand, and helped pull her up.

"I ought to kill you right now," Kort said to Box. Box sat on the couch, looked at Annie and then Rosie, ignoring Kort, and asked, "What's the plan now?"

"We're gonna get as far south as we can and see what's going on. We're gonna want you two sitting down, so nobody can see you from the outside. If we need to get you back in the hold, you gotta go quick, we'll leave the door open," Rosie said. "Nobody knows about me and Annie, but everybody's looking for you two. We think that checkpoint was for somebody looking to rescue Poole, or kill him. Which would be you, Dora, or you, Charlene."

"Shouldn't be doing this at all," Kort said.

"Yeah, well, we are," Rosie said.

They took it slow going through town, a somewhat scruffy-looking place with lots of vacant lots and tumble-down houses, but some nice downtown buildings as well. They took the turn onto Highway 67, south toward the border.

They'd only gone a few blocks before they saw what looked like a law enforcement convention on the right side of the highway, cop cars and Border Patrol vehicles with flashing lights, and cops walking around unhurriedly.

"Okay, that's bad," Rosie said. "The cops aren't worried."

Box: "Are you saying . . ."

"That's what I'm saying, honey. I'm sorry. You knew it was likely," Rosie said.

Up ahead, a cop was directing cars off the highway, onto a detour to the east. They took the detour, realized that it would take them all the way out of town, and followed some other cars on a loop back into town.

Across the highway, they could see bright lights in the parking lot of a place called El Cósmico, and a circle of cops, like a football huddle, looking at something on the ground.

Box said, "Oh, God, oh my God . . ."

"Easy, honey," Rosie said.

After a minute, Annie said, "That's not where Poole said the truck was—it could still be out there. Think we can find it? I'm kinda lost here."

"Glad you asked," Rosie said. She went back to one of the storage closets, got out her laptop and the Verizon hotspot, plugged in the hotspot, and brought up the laptop. With a few keystrokes she was on Google Maps, and then the satellite view.

"Here's where we are," she said, tapping the screen. "From what Poole told us, the truck has got to be right . . . here."

She touched the screen. "If we go over here to Waco Street, and then west, all the way, and then down to here, and back east on Katherine Street, we ought to be able to look right at the trucks. If there are three white pickups and nobody around them . . ."

"Gonna have to hurry, the cops will be looking for it," Annie said.

"Then let's go," Rosie said.

They followed the line that Rosie had laid out on the map and Kort kept her mouth shut for once. Coming back on Katherine, they could look right into the parking area where the three trucks were . . . The trucks were still there, all three of them, and so was a big light generator and a dozen cops around the middle truck.

The back of the truck was open, and Kort, peeking out through a side window, said, "Shit. It's that guy. The Davenport guy, the cop we were tracking. They got the truck."

"So we're done with it. Now we get out of here," Rosie said. "You guys get back, we're coming up to a cop . . . back in the floor."

Box and Kort scuttled back to the hidden hold and dropped inside, lying side by side again. Up above, a cop was waving Annie around the corner and away from the cops in the parking area. Annie took it slow and they left the lights behind. Rosie opened the lid on the hold. "We're going. You're both still alive?"

Box and Kort climbed out of the hold, and Kort turned on Box and said, "Now it's you and me."

Rosie tried to intervene, but Kort, who was strong, shoved her in the chest, nearly knocking her on her butt, and a second later Kort swung at Box, hitting her in the eye. Box fell back on the couch and Kort put one knee up on the seat cushion, getting ready for a couple more punches, but Box was groping under the cushion, came up with the Phillips screwdriver, and as Kort's eyes widened for a fraction of a second, Box drove the screwdriver right through Kort's frontal bone, two inches above her eyeline.

Kort staggered backward and then fell on her ass, propped up against the pots-and-pans drawer.

Rosie was back and she stared down at Kort. The red-striped plastic handle of a Craftsman screwdriver was snug against the skin of Kort's forehead, the shaft of the screwdriver deep in her brain. Rosie said, "Oh. My. God."

Annie picked up the tone and glancing back over her shoulder, asked, "What?"

"Dora stuck a screwdriver in Charlene's brain."

"What?"

Rosie bent lower and said, "She's not dead."

"Let me stir it around a little bit and she'll be dead," Box said. "I had enough of her shit."

"No kiddin'," Rosie said. "Remind me not to piss you off."

"Now what?" Annie called.

"You ought to find a place to pull over and come and look at this," Rosie said.

Annie pulled into a dark side street, pushed herself out of the driver's seat, and came to look. A thin stream of blood, but not really much, trickled out of the screwdriver hole and down the center of Kort's nose.

"She was a monster," Box said. She was standing back a bit, her arms crossed defensively, as if anticipating criticism. "She deserved what she got."

"Still not dead," Rosie said.

"Hasn't even closed her eyes," Annie said. She tapped Kort on the shoulder, then gave her a little push. Nothing on Kort's face changed and she made no noise at all. She didn't blink.

"*Still* not dead," Rosie said. "She's breathing. She's got a screwdriver in her brain, a steel rod, how come she's not dead?"

"Don't know," Annie said. Kort blinked.

"Now what?" Box asked.

Annie shook her head. "I'll tell you what, Dora, this really isn't good. I'm not really up for finishing her off." She scratched the side of her face, peering at Kort, who still hadn't moved, except to blink.

"What are we going to do?" Rosie asked Annie.

"Well . . . I guess we could drop her off somewhere," Annie said. "Wouldn't make much difference to her, wherever we left her. Wouldn't want anybody to see us doing it."

"She could identify us," Box said.

"If she could find us—but we're not from around here, and she doesn't know our last names or anything," Annie said.

"I say we stir that screwdriver handle around a little," Box said. Kort blinked. "We won't have to worry about her identifying anything."

"I got a feeling she won't be doing that anyway," Annie said.

Rosie stood up. "Okay. Let's go."

THEY WENT looking for a place, and as they did, Box cleaned her fingerprints off the screwdriver handle with a hand wipe. They eventually found a closed Stripes convenience store and dropped Kort off between a couple of gas pumps. Kort sat between the pumps like an oversized lump of modeling clay, still staring straight ahead, blinked once. As they pulled away, Rosie asked the other two, "Think she'll be all right there?"

Annie shook her head and said, "No, I don't think so."

TEN MINUTES behind them, a tourist pulled into the Stripes, hoping that it might still be open. It wasn't, but he saw the figure sitting between the gas pumps, and though he didn't want to, stepped over and took a look.

His wife called from the car, "Larry—come back. Leave her to sleep it off."

Larry walked around the car and said, "I think we should call the police."

"She's probably a drug addict."

"She could be," Larry said. "Her bigger problem seems to be that she's got a screwdriver stuck into her brain."

*   *   *

ANNIE, ROSIE, AND BOX drove north out of Marfa. They'd grown silent after the Kort incident and were thirty miles up the road before Rosie asked Annie, "What do we do about the Dora problem?"

Box spoke up before Annie could answer. "Listen, the three of us could get along. Now, I need to tell you something and I need to ask you something. You talk about this Boss, and how he sort of cheapskates you on the money."

"Yeah, but we don't mention it to his face," Rosie said.

"Well, the Boss is going to find out that the money is gone, right? That the feds got it," Box said. "It'll be in the newspapers. The cops will be showing off. Nothing you could do about that. You did your best."

"He won't be happy, but he won't take it out on us," Rosie said. "He's pretty rational."

Box nodded. "Okay. Good. He's rational. Now, what if I told you I know where there's almost a million and a half dollars, more or less, in cash and gold, a few hours from here. Nobody knows about it but me. *Nobody knows.*"

Rosie and Annie glanced at each other, and then Annie asked Rosie, "What's that movie line you like? From the famous movie?"

"I think this is the beginning of a beautiful friendship," Rosie said.

Annie pointed a finger at her: "That's the one."

29

A DEEP AND SULLEN SILENCE seemed to drape the town of Marfa after the firefight in the fields beside the highway. The Border Patrol kept people away from the buildings where the shooting took place, except for a couple of employees of the Chinati Foundation, which ran the place.

The state cops were called in to process the shooting scenes, but wouldn't get there until the next day. The bodies were left where they fell, covered with black plastic tarps, and watched by border patrolmen, as much to keep the coyotes away as to protect the scenes.

Shortly after the last fight, a helicopter roared in from El Paso and took Bob away. Lucas met Rae wandering around by the foundation headquarters, put an arm around her shoulders: "How is he?"

"Aw, he'll be okay. Take some time, some rehab. The

medics slowed down the blood loss. He was still okay when they loaded him into the chopper."

"You talk to your SOG people yet?"

"No, I haven't gotten around to it. I'm sort of stunned," she said.

"So's everybody. Let's find a place to sit, you can call your guys, I'll call Forte and fill him in."

They did that. Everybody was unhappy about Bob, everybody was happy that Poole and Darling were dead. "Five people murdered at one spot, including that kid," Forte said. "We needed to take them off the board, any way we could. Not to go all bureaucratic on you, I'd like the names of all the Border Patrol and Highway Patrol people who cooperated with you—when we put out the press release, we'll go big-time on the help they gave us. This will be a nice story tomorrow, give us a chance to put some serious grease in the wheels. And . . . say, did you find any cash? Or gold? That could be big."

"Tell you about that in an hour or so," Lucas said. "I think I know where their vehicle is."

AFTER HE got off the phone, Lucas told Rae about the grease comment, and she said, "I don't know about you former small-time cops, but grease is close to the top consideration with the federal government. Might even be *the top*. Don't care who got killed, how many got killed, but they do care about the grease."

"You okay?" Lucas asked.

"Shoulder hurts. Medic looked at it, said it's a bunch of cuts, he gave me some antibiotic cream for it, told me to see a doc as soon as I can. How about you? You look a lot worse than me, that bloody rag around your head."

"Got a little headache, that's about it," Lucas said. "Scared the hell out of me when I couldn't see at first."

"How's your eye now?" Rae asked.

"I can see fine, but my eye is watering a lot."

"Let's go find one of those medics . . . take a quick look."

THEY FOUND a medic, who looked at Lucas's eye with a magnifier, said he couldn't see much, but that Lucas's eye was bloodshot. He irrigated the eye, which made it feel worse than it had before the irrigation. The medic said that was normal.

He then washed off Lucas's forehead, said there was a lot of brick dust embedded in the skin above his eye. He suggested that Lucas have a doctor check it. "If you get an infection, it could leave some scarring. Go see a doc."

RAE TOLD HIM the SOG people were mostly concerned about Bob and would fly a couple of supervisors into El Paso to talk with him. "Gonna ask him if you fucked up, is what they're going to do," Rae said. "I already told them you didn't, that we were all great, but there's gonna have to be an after-action report. Hope you're ready for a blizzard of paper."

"Want to see an even greater blizzard?" Lucas asked. "Follow me and listen carefully."

He led Rae around the buildings, to the place where he'd first seen Darling crossing a fence, into the field. "He was carrying a bag. He lost it somewhere along the way . . . and I gotta believe he'd dumped the truck right where he was crossing into that field. There are three white trucks parked by the buildings."

Rae said, "Money. Let's get some lights and more witnesses."

They rounded up O'Brien, the Border Patrol boss, and Guiterrez, the highway patrolman who'd led them down from I-10, and a couple of other guys, everybody armed with heavy-duty flashlights. They located the place where Darling had crossed the fence by the crushed-down weeds on the other side, and six feet into the field, found a light brown canvas duffel bag.

Lucas pulled it open. Inside was some paper, two passports, and enough cash, as Guiterrez put it, "to choke a Texas hog."

O'Brien said, "We know about cash seizures. Bring that bag outa here, and I'll have a couple of our guys count it, with witnesses."

Rae said, "That might not be all of it. Lucas thinks he knows where Darling ditched his truck."

Lucas swiveled his flashlight across the dark field to the buildings, to a line of white pickups parked behind it. "Let's get that museum lady out here. She should know who belongs to which trucks."

The museum lady did know: the two trucks on the ends were a museum truck and a truck that belonged to a museum worker. The one in the middle—the one with the Arkansas plates—she didn't know.

But she didn't want to talk about that—she wanted somebody to take her down to the two dome-topped buildings that were at the center of the fight. "Why won't you let me down there? Why—"

"Crime scene," O'Brien muttered, and then they ignored her.

LUCAS TRIED the truck's driver-side door and it popped open. He shone his flash around the inside, spotted the keys on the floor. Two border patrolmen took a long look at the truck's interior, then they all went around to the back and popped the hatch on the camper top.

There were some bags inside, full of clothing and paper, but no money. Then one patrolman said to another, "Carlos . . . does that floor look right?"

Carlos squatted by the back of the truck, squinted at the floor, then looked beneath it, and then at the floor again, and finally said, "It's a few inches high. Not much, but a few."

The first patrolman crawled into the truck and with the rest of them watching, began pulling and tugging and prying at pieces of the interior, and finally popped up a hidden hatch. "That's good work, right there," he said, of the hatch. "Somebody give me a flashlight."

He shone the flashlight into the hatch, then got his head down closer to the floor: *"Madre de Dios."*

Rae: "Mom sees money?"

The patrolman looked up: "Mom sees a buttload of cash and what looks like a pile of gold coins in a plastic box."

Lucas said to O'Brien, "Gonna need more counters, more witnesses."

Rae said, "Hot damn."

Nobody noticed the RV crawl past them, a couple hundred yards away.

BECAUSE OF all the accounting rigmarole, they didn't know until ten o'clock that they'd found three-point-two million in currency and about six hundred thousand in gold coins, the amount of gold value dependent on the market.

O'Brien pronounced himself pleased. He linked his fingers across his ample belly and said, "I'm pleased."

Rae said, "Fuckin' A."

Lucas called Forte at home with the count. Forte said, "I'm far too suave to say it gives me a hard-on, but right now I definitely got a party in my pants."

LUCAS PAID no attention to O'Brien when he finally told the persistent museum lady that he'd have a patrolman escort her to the domed buildings. She and a patrolman disappeared a moment later.

Bob called from El Paso. "They didn't want to let me talk, but I am anyway. They're telling me I'll be down for a couple of months, including rehab. They're gonna take me into the operating room as soon as this nurse stops washing off my dick . . . yes, you are, you're washing my dick, don't try to sneak around it . . . and it'll be a while before I come out. I'll call as soon as I wake up tomorrow. You find any money?"

They were telling him about the money when a woman started screaming. Lucas said, "Oh, shit," and picked up his armor and Bob's rifle and followed Rae at a dead run around the buildings and then around the second set of buildings . . .

And saw the museum lady shrieking while a patrolman tried to placate her.

Lucas and Rae stopped running and took it slower and when they came up with their guns, the wild-eyed woman looked at them and screamed, "You killed my Judds. You killed my Judds."

The milled aluminum boxes they'd seen behind the glass were neither kitchen appliances (Rae) nor boxes for holding the art (Lucas) but were, in fact, the art itself. Of the hundred boxes in two buildings, twelve had either through-and-through bullet holes or bullet gashes. All the windows in the first building had been shattered or cracked, but the woman wasn't worried about the windows.

Rae asked her the wrong question: "You're sure this happened tonight?"

The woman began screaming incomprehensibly, literally tearing at her hair, dashing from one aluminum box to the next, looking for more damage.

When she'd finished her survey, only slightly calmed down, she said to O'Brien, the senior officer in uniform, "You don't know what you've done."

"We were fighting it out with crazy killers," he said.

"You managed to destroy millions and millions of dollars' worth of irreplaceable art."

A patrolman in the back muttered, loud enough for everyone to hear, "Shit, I could get a load of those up at the Home Depot."

They all turned to look at him. Not at all embarrassed, he added, "In a variety of decorator colors."

Somebody laughed, which made the woman cry again, and then everybody felt bad, for a while.

THEY WERE still milling around, checking periodically with the Highway Patrol for possible sightings of Dora Box, when O'Brien hurried out of the foundation office and said to Lucas and Rae, "We need to get over to the Stripes station."

"What for?"

"A woman's been stabbed, in the head. A sheriff's deputy thinks she might be this Kort woman you're looking for."

They made it to the Stripes station in five minutes, where the two overworked EMTs were staring at a woman who was seated on the concrete next to a gas pump. They walked past a cop who was keeping rubberneckers away, and one of the EMTs said, "We called for the chopper again . . . I don't know what we can do here."

Lucas took a look. The woman was Kort, all right, sitting straight up, her eyes fixed and peering straight ahead, with a screwdriver handle sticking out from her forehead. Lucas asked, "Is she alive?"

"Yeah, she blinks every twenty seconds," the EMT said. "We've tried to communicate with her, but nothing happens. We ask her to blink or move a finger if she hears us, but she doesn't respond, she doesn't blink on command. When we try to pick her up, her legs don't work. We need the chopper and a neurosurgeon. This is not something you throw a bandage on."

"Anybody know how she got here?" Rae asked.

The EMTs shrugged, and a sheriff's deputy, who'd come over to listen in, said, "A tourist found her. He thought the station was open and pulled in, and saw her sitting by the pump. He thought she was a drug addict, until he saw the screwdriver handle. Nobody knows how long she was sitting here, or who dropped her off."

O'Brien leaned down and waved his hands in front of Kort's eyes. She didn't blink. He took his hand away, and a few seconds later, she did blink. "Every twenty seconds," the EMT said. "You could set your watch by it."

An hour later, she was flown out of Marfa for El Paso, still blinking every twenty seconds.

THE NEXT MORNING, Lucas spoke to a doc in El Paso, who said that Kort had died an hour earlier during an operation to remove the screwdriver. "She had some brain function and the neuro guy had her coked to the gills with antiseizure medicine, but as soon as they removed the screwdriver, she had a massive seizure and died. She also has a recent bullet wound in her butt, and apparently self-treated that. Anyway, she's gone."

Lucas hung up and as he punched in Forte's phone

number to report Kort's death, he thought, *Coked to the gills?*

When he told Rae about it, she said, "Ah, that's just Texas."

Later that day, Lucas and Rae went to El Paso to see Bob, who was looking good, given the fact that he'd been shot through both legs. "Biggest question now is whether I have vascular damage," he said. "I can wiggle all my toes, and if somebody pinches my knees, it hurts, so no major nerves were killed off, as far as anyone can tell. Take a while to find all that out, but I won't lose any legs. I could be back in a couple of months."

"That's good, because our boy Davenport wants us to work with him on his next big one," Rae said.

"Business class, suites hotels?" Bob asked.

"Count on it," Lucas said.

When they left Bob, they both went to the emergency room, where a nurse practitioner rewashed their not-very-bad wounds and pronounced them okay, although they should have gotten more comprehensive treatment about fifteen hours earlier. On the way back to Marfa, Lucas said to Rae, "Bob's hurt worse than he lets on. He'll be doing good if he's back by next summer. He might even be able to cash his chips on a disability, if he wants that."

"He won't, he'll be back." Rae teared up. "I wish I could shoot that motherfucker Darling again."

THAT SAME DAY, Rosie pulled the RV off the road near Gordon, Texas. There wasn't anyone around, and they carefully and watchfully walked the interstate fence until they spotted the orange blouse. The three of them, Rosie and Annie and Dora, hauled the two black cases out of the weeds under the pine tree. Dora popped them open, and Annie said, "Ohhhh . . ." in what was nothing less than an orgasmic groan.

"Let's get them back to the RV," Dora said. "And let me get my blouse."

She unknotted her blouse from the fence pole, and Annie came up from behind her, put one hand on the pole and the other on Box's ass, and asked, "Little kiss?"

A guy going by in an eighteen-wheeler looked up and saw them and said to himself, "Ooo, no, no, no, no way. Oh, man, don't do that to me, not ten days from home . . ."

LUCAS AND RAE were back in Marfa, in quite a nice hotel, for the next three days, in the predicted blizzard of paperwork. The hotel people wanted them out of their rooms as soon as possible, because of an enormous influx of art lovers, there to inspect the damage.

A good-looking young woman called Lucas, who had been identified to her as one of the lead cops, a fascist. Rae asked, "Me, too?"

The young woman looked at the tall black woman and seemed to struggle for a moment with all the possible politically correct replies, and got off the elevator without attempting one.

WITH THE PAPERWORK done, the crime scene measured and discussed, sworn statements given, Lucas kissed Rae on the forehead at the El Paso airport and said, "Rubber match, next time we hook up. Work on your game."

"Like I need it," she said. And, "You take care, big guy."

She took her business-class tickets and walked down the Jetway and out of sight.

*　　*　　*

THAT SAME DAY, John Stiner was hired to be an assistant manager at a new Starbucks in Tampa, Florida. The Starbucks regional man said, "We're quite impressed with your qualifications. Year or two, you could be running your own store."

"I'm looking forward to it, sir," Stiner said, and thought, privately, *How in the fuck do you look at yourself in the morning, you boring, paper-pushing cocksucker?* "I'm really anxious to make Starbucks my future." *And maybe getting in the shorts of one of your tight little baristas . . . or maybe more than one.*

ON THE VERY SAME DAY, a team of marshals swarmed Darling's Alabama farm. They found nothing, but one agent spotted a heap of raw dirt across the road from the house, in some brush. He brought Janice Darling across the road to look at it. "It's a gopher, you dummy," she told him. He was from New York City and didn't know gophers from wolverines, and so accepted her answer.

She'd dug up and moved the money the day before. In a year, she thought, she'd be in Toronto under a new name and still desperately missing Sturgill.

ON A BRIGHT TUESDAY a couple of days after he got back, Lucas and Weather drove to their polling place, where they voted for Mrs. Bowden for President. That night they went to a Bowden victory party, which didn't work out all that well: by ten o'clock, people were slinking out of the place.

"Wolf Blitzer can kiss my ass," one of the partiers told Lucas, as they shuffled down the sidewalk.

*   *   *

VIRGIL FLOWERS, a BCA agent and old friend, was in town the next day, and stopped by to check on him. He cut through the post-election gloom: "Hey, man. The world goes on, you know what I mean? Go out in the backyard, burn some steaks, fire up a doobie, relax. Oh— and tell me about Marfa . . ."

There were no doobies to be had, but they burned some steaks and with the cold weather moving in, ate at the dining table, drank some Leinies, and Lucas told them all about it.

He said, "I'll tell you, Virgil, things are getting strange out there. This whole case was pinned on . . . guess what?"

"Uh, let me see. Couldn't be intelligent investigation, we can rule that out . . ."

"Telephones. Everybody was leaning on telephones." Lucas took a phone from his pocket and held it up, then looked at it, at the shiny black glass. "They're so great, these little machines are, that we all agree to be spied on for the privilege of carrying them. The phones know where we've been, when we were there, and lots of times what we were doing there—what we were buying, who we were talking to, and where *those* people were. They can even tell how fast you were moving, in case somebody wants to prove you were speeding. They know who you talk to, who your contacts are, what credit cards you have, where you bank. We all know that, but we can't get away from them. Even crooks know it, and even *they* can't get away from them."

"All you'd have to do is not have one," Flowers said.

"You can't do that—listen to me, *you can't do that anymore*," Lucas said. "What if you left your phone at home and had a heart attack or rolled your car over on a back road? How would you call nine-one-one to ask for help? And if you're a crook and leave your phone at home while you're sticking up a bank, but you carry it all the rest of the time . . . you automatically look suspicious. You *always* carry the phone, and this one time, during the bank robbery, you *left it at home*? I don't think so. Sooner or later some prosecutor will convict somebody of something because he *didn't* have a phone in his pocket."

"You need another drink," Flowers said. And, "Say, how's Letty doing? Is she coming home for Christmas? Maybe I'll call her up."

"Only at the risk of your life," Lucas said.

"What? You'd shoot me for calling up Letty?"

"Oh, no, I'd just tell Frankie," Lucas said. Frankie was Virgil's girlfriend, and not a stranger to violence. "I'd say, Frankie? Guess what . . ."

Flowers held up his hands: "All right, all right. Joking there about Letty . . ."

ON THE MONDAY after the election, Lucas, still with a bandage on his forehead, went into the marshals' offices in Minneapolis carrying his briefcase, which contained nothing but the paper from the Poole case.

Hal Oder, the U.S. marshal for the District of Minnesota, saw Lucas in the hallway, unlocking his office door, and called, "Davenport—my office."

Lucas finished unlocking his door and dropped his briefcase next to his desk, hearing the footfalls clacking down the hall, then Oder shoved his head in the doorway and snapped, "Don't tell me you didn't hear me."

"I heard you, but I ignored you," Lucas said.

"Things are gonna change around here," Oder said. "You don't have Bowden watching your back anymore. If you expect to stay here, you're going on the duty roster.

You're going to be pulling regular shifts and that includes prisoner transfer. I'm going to . . ."

Lucas put a finger to his lips and when Oder stopped talking, said, "Hal. You really shouldn't say anything more until tomorrow afternoon. After your appointment."

Lucas saw the fear suddenly flare in Oder's eyes: "What appointment?"

"You have an appointment. You just don't know it yet. Now get the fuck out of my office."

THE FOLLOWING AFTERNOON, Oder had begun to relax. He'd checked with his secretary every fifteen minutes about unexpected appointments and there hadn't been any. Davenport had been bullshitting him, for reasons Oder couldn't figure out. Then, at one forty-five, a message popped up on the corner of his computer. It said "Your appointments are here."

Oder went to the door, where he saw the Democratic governor of Minnesota—the man who, until the week before, had been expected to become Mrs. Bowden's vice president—walking down the hall toward him.

He was trailed by another man, a short man carrying a shovel. Oder didn't recognize the short man for a moment, then realized that he was Porter Smalls, the once and future Republican U.S. senator from Minnesota.

The governor smiled and thrust out a hand, said, "Hal, I think we've met a couple of times. How are you?"

"Uh, is this about Davenport?" Oder asked, as he shook the governor's hand.

The future Senator Smalls said, "Yes, yes, it is. Let's go in your office and talk about it." His shovel still had the sales stickers on the face of the blade. Oder didn't ask about it.

When they were settled into the office, Smalls said, "I will now tell you a short story. Two years ago, Senator Taryn Grant, the bitch from hell, had some child porn put on my campaign computer, then murdered her way through the election and into the U.S. Senate. Into my seat. This is not a secret. Tell your children about it, if you wish. The governor here is an old friend, and though we're in opposing political parties, he knew that I was innocent. He assigned Lucas to find out what happened. Lucas did. I was cleared of the child-porn stories too late to keep me from losing my Senate seat, but at least I didn't go to prison. When it's all said and done, though, Minnesotans remember. If you watched the elections last week . . . Did you watch the elections?"

"Yes, I did," Oder said.

"Good. Then you'll know that I'm going back to the Senate. In a landslide. I wouldn't be doing that if it weren't for Marshal Davenport. Of *all* the law enforcement officials I've met in my life, *of all of them*, and there have been *many*, he is far and away my favorite. Am I making myself clear?"

"Yes, you are," Oder said.

"Good." Smalls turned to Henderson and said, "Anything you want to say, Elmer?"

"Nothing, except that there's an excellent chance I'll be running for Taryn Grant's Senate seat, in the primary, the next time it comes up. I believe I can beat her. Lucas is also *my* favorite law enforcement officer, though he can be a pain in the ass at times. In any case, both Senator Smalls and I expect that he will spend many happy years working here as a deputy marshal. Without interference, from anyone, including politically appointed personnel."

Oder didn't say anything, but looked from the governor to the senator, his face going red.

The two politicians stood and smiled, and Smalls said,

"I bought this shovel for you. You can leave it in a corner to remind yourself."

Oder managed, "Of what?"

"Of the fact that if you mess with Lucas, you'll probably never again have a white-collar job. Certainly not with the federal or state governments. So you might need a shovel and you'll have one right handy."

Henderson, a tall man, leaned forward, put his fists on the edge of Oder's desk: "I'm a very polite upper-class Anglo-Saxon male and I only rarely stoop to use unpleasant language. There are some exceptions. This is one of them. I'm telling you, Hal—don't *fuck* with him. *Don't . . . fuck . . . with . . . him.*"

Oder nodded.

Smalls looked around the office and asked, "Where do you want me to stick the shovel?"

TURN THE PAGE FOR AN EXCERPT

Lucas Davenport has crossed paths with her before—a rich
psychopath who ran successfully for the U.S. Senate, where
Lucas predicted she'd fit right in. He is also convinced that she is
responsible for three murders, though he's never been able to
prove it. He's heard rumors that she found her seat on the Senate
intelligence committee, and the contacts she's made from
it, to be very . . . useful. Pinning those rumors down is likely
to be just as difficult as before, and considerably more dangerous.
But they have unfinished business and, one way or the other,
Davenport is going to see it through to the end.

1

"TIRED?"

Porter Smalls looked across the front seat at the driver. The summer foliage was dark around the Cadillac as they rolled up the dirt lane. The south branch of the Potomac River snaked along below them; the windows were down and the muddy, fishy odor of the river filled the car.

"A little—in a good way," Cecily Whitehead said.

Whitehead had taken a cold shower in the cabin's well water shortly before they left, and dabbed on a touch of Chanel No. 5 as she dressed. The combined odor of the two scents was more than pleasant, it was positively erotic.

"I'll drive if you want," Smalls offered. He was a small man, like his name, thin and tough-looking, as though he'd spent time on a mountain bike. He had white hair that curled down over the collar of his golf shirt, flashing too-white teeth, and rimless made-for-television glasses over pale blue eyes.

"No, I'm fine," Whitehead said. She buckled her seat-belt over her shimmery slip dress, which in earlier days might have gotten her arrested if she'd worn it out of her bedroom. "You finished the wine—if we got stopped for some reason . . ."

"Smart," Smalls said.

He kicked the seat back another couple of inches, crossed his hands across his stomach, and closed his eyes.

ABOVE THEM, in the trees, a man had been watching with binoculars. When the silver Cadillac rolled down the driveway, past the mailbox, and made the left turn onto the narrow lane, he lifted a walkie-talkie to his face and said, "I'll be home for dinner."

A walkie-talkie, because if nobody within three miles was on exactly the same channel at exactly the right time, there'd be no trace of the call; nothing for even the NSA to latch onto. Nor would there be any trace of the five rapid clicks he got back, acknowledging the message.

He was on foot, with his pick-up spot a half mile away. He'd walked in on a game trail and he walked out the same way, moving slowly, stopping every hundred feet to watch and listen. He'd never sat down while on watch, but had remained standing next to the gnarly gray bark of an aging ash: there'd be no observation post for any-one to find, no discarded cigarette butts or candy wrap-pers with DNA on them. He'd worn smooth-soled boots: no tread marks in the soft earth.

He was a pro.

U.S. SENATOR PORTER SMALLS owned a cabin in the hills of West Virginia, two and a half hours from Washington, D.C.—close enough to be an easy drive, far enough to obscure activities that might need to be obscured.

He and Whitehead, one of his wife's best friends—his wife was back in Minnesota—had locked up the place and headed back to D.C. as the sun wedged itself below the horizon on a hot Sunday afternoon. The timing was deliberate: they would enjoy the cover of darkness when she dropped him off at his Watergate condo.

Smalls and Whitehead had spent an invigorating two days talking about political philosophy, history, horses, money, life, and mutual friends, while they worked their way through Smalls' battered '80s paperback copy of *The Joy of Sex.*

Smalls was married, Whitehead not, but she drove the car because of a kind of Washington logic concerning sex and alcohol. A little light adultery, while not considered a necessarily positive thing in Washington, was certainly not to be compared with a DWI as a criminal offense. Banging an adult male or live woman might—*maybe*— get you a paragraph on a *Washington Post* blog. But God help you if Mothers Against Drunk Driving jumped your elective ass.

So Whitehead drove.

Whitehead was a fifty-year-old political junkie and Republican Party moneywoman. She was tall and thin and tanned and freckled, with short dark hair so expertly colored you couldn't tell that it had been—the occasional strands of gray gave it an expensive verisimilitude. She had a square chin and looked a little like Amelia Earhart. Like Earhart, she flew her own plane; in Whitehead's case, a twin-engine Beechcraft King Air. She owned a mansion on one of Minneapolis's lakes, and a two-thousand-acre farm south of the Twin Cities, on which she raised horses.

Smalls' wife didn't know for sure that Whitehead was sleeping with her husband, and the topic had never been mentioned. For the past four years Smalls' wife had been living with her Lithuanian lover in a loft in downtown Minneapolis, a topic that had come up between them any number of times.

Lithuanians had long been known as the sexual athletes of Northern Europe. Smalls was aware of that fact, but no longer cared what his wife did, as long as she didn't do it in the streets. Actually, he hoped she was happy, because he was still fond of the mother of his children. He made a mental note to take her to dinner the next time he was in the Twin Cities.

"BE THERE BY TEN," Whitehead said.

"I've got that dimwit Clancy at noon," Smalls said, not opening his eyes.

"Dim, but persistent," Whitehead said. "He told Perez that if Medtronic gets the VA deal, Abbott will have to cut jobs in his district. Perez believes him. It might even be true."

"Tough shit," Smalls said. "If Abbott gets it, Medtronic might have to cut people. That ain't gonna happen. Not as long as Porter Smalls knows that our beloved majority leader has that backdoor job at Rio Javelena."

"If you ever mention that to him, he'll find some way to stick something sharp and nasty up your rectum."

Smalls smiled: "Why, Ceecee . . . you don't really think I'd ever actually *mention* it to him, do you?"

Whitehead glanced at him. "I hope to hell not. No, I don't think you'd do that. How are you gonna let him know that you know?"

"Kitten will think of something," Smalls said.

Whitehead smiled into the growing darkness, their headlights ricocheting through the roadside trees. Kitten Carter, Smalls' chief of staff, *would* think of something.

She and Whitehead talked a couple of times a week, plotting together the great glory of the U.S.A. in general and Porter Smalls in particular.

Although tall and thin, Whitehead was a lifelong yoga enthusiast and show horse competitor. She had a strong body, strong legs and arms, and for a woman, large strong hands. She wheeled the Escalade along the track faster than most people might have, staining the evening air with dust and gravel. She'd spent much of her life on farms, shoveling horse shit with the best of them, driving trucks and tractors, and knew what she was doing, keeping the twenty-two-inch wheels solidly in the twin tracks.

A half mile down the river, the track crossed a state-maintained gravel road, and with a bare glance to her left, she hooked the truck to the right and leaned on the gas pedal.

TEN MINUTES LATER, they came over a high hill and in the distance Whitehead could see a string of lights on a highway that would take them to the Interstate that would take them into Washington. The river still unwound below them, down a long hill, the last fifty feet or so sharpening into a bluff.

A minute later, Whitehead said, "What an asshole. This jerk is all over me."

"What?" Smalls had almost dozed off. Now he pushed himself up, aware that the truck's cabin was flooded with light. He turned in his seat. A pickup—he thought it was a pickup, given the height of the headlights—wasn't more than fifteen or twenty feet behind them, as they rolled along the gravel at fifty miles an hour.

He said, "I don't like this."

Still at the crest of the hill, the truck swung out into the left lane and accelerated, and Smalls said, "Hey, hey!"

Whitehead floored the gas pedal, but too late. *Too late.* The truck swung into them, smashed the side of the Escalade, which went off the road, through roadside brush and trees, across a ditch and down the precipitous hillside. Instead of trying to pull the truck back up the hillside, which would have caused it to roll sideways, Whitehead turned downhill for a second, then said, her voice sharp, "Hold on, Porter, I'm gonna try to hit a tree. Keep your arms up in case the airbag blows . . ."

Smalls lifted his arms and the car bounced and bucked across the hill, still heading sharply down toward the bluff below as Whitehead pumped the brakes. He didn't actually think it, but Smalls knew in his gut that they only had a few seconds to live.

Then they hit a line of saplings, plowed through them, hit a tree that must have been six inches in diameter, breaking it cleanly off. The impact caused the truck to skew sideways while still plowing forward, and now Smalls felt Whitehead hit the accelerator and the engine screamed as the oversized tires tried to dig into the hillside, and realized that she was essentially *barking* with each impact: "*Ay, ay, ay, ay . . .*"

They were still angling downhill, but much less steeply now. They hit another small tree, and the vehicle snapped around, and then hit a bigger tree. The airbag blew and hit Smalls in the face and he was aware that the truck was beginning to tilt downhill, toward the bluff, and that the driver's-side window suddenly blew in. They'd almost stopped, not thirty feet from the edge of the bluff, but were not quite settled, and the car blundered another few lengths backward and smashed into a final tree, which pushed up the passenger's side of the truck. The Escalade slowly, almost majestically, rolled over on its roof and came to a stop.

Smalls said, "I smell gas. We better get out of here."

He looked sideways at Whitehead, who was hanging upside down from her safety belt. The overhead light had come on when the door opened. Her eyes were open, but blank, and blood was running from the corner of her mouth.

He called "Ceecee, Ceecee," but got no response. Blood was pouring down his face and into his eyes as he freed his safety belt and dropped onto the inside of the roof. He unlocked the door and pushed it open a few inches, where it stuck on a sapling. He kicked the door a half dozen times until it opened far enough that he could crawl out.

As soon as he was free, he wiped the blood from his eyes, realized that it had been coming from his nose, as he was hanging upside down. As he cleared his eyes, he stumbled around to the back of the truck, popped the lid, found his canvas overnight bag, and took out the chrome .357 Magnum he kept there. He tucked the gun in his belt and looked uphill: no sign of anyone. No headlights, no brake lights, nothing but the gathering dust, the knee-high weeds and the broken trees.

He hurried to the driver's side of the truck, wedged the door open as far as he could, unhooked Whitehead's safety belt and let her drop into his arms. He had to struggle to get her out of the truck, but the odor of gas gave him the strength of desperation. When she was out, he picked her up and carried her fifty feet across the hill-side, then lowered her into the weeds, knelt beside her and listened for a moment, the scent of her, Chanel No. 5 and well water, now mixed with the coppery, meaty odor of fresh blood.

But he heard and saw nothing: nobody on the hillside. He whispered, "Ceecee. Ceecee, can you hear me?"

One headlight was still glowing from the SUV and he dug out his cell phone and called the local sheriff's department—he had them on his contact list. He identified himself, told the dispatcher what had happened, and that the incident might well have been a deliberate attack.

The dispatcher said deputies would be there in five minutes. "Be sure the emergency flashers are on," Smalls told the dispatcher. "I'm not coming out of the weeds until I'm sure I'm talking to the right guys. We'll need an ambulance; my friend's hurt bad."

When he got off the phone, he cradled Whitehead on his lap. The ambulance, he thought, wouldn't be in time: it was, in fact, already too late for Cecily Whitehead.

THE COPS CAME, and an ambulance, and when Smalls was sure of who he was dealing with, he called them over. They told him what he already knew: Whitehead was dead, had sustained a killing blow to the left side of her head, probably when a tree branch came through the driver's-side window.

Smalls retrieved his government paper from the Cadillac as the cops and the EMTs took Whitehead up the hill in a black plastic body bag. She was put in the ambulance, but Smalls said he didn't need one: "A bloody nose, nothing worse. Give me something to wash my face."

The lead deputy asked who'd been driving, and Smalls said, "Ceecee was."

"We need to give you a quick Breathalyzer," the deputy said.

"Yes, fine," Smalls said. "I had a glass of wine before we left my cabin, Ceecee didn't have anything at all."

The test took two minutes. Smalls blew a 0.04, well below the drunk-driving limit of 0.08, although Smalls was an older man, and older men were hit harder by alcohol than younger men.

"Be sure that's all recorded," Smalls told the cop. "I want this nailed down."

"Don't need to worry," the deputy said. "We'll get it right for you, Senator. Now . . . did you see the truck?"

Smalls shook his head: "He had his high beams on and they were burning right through the back window of my Caddy. It was like getting caught in a searchlight, or something. I couldn't see anything . . . and then he hit us."

The deputy looked down the hill. "She did a heck of a piece of driving. Another twenty, thirty feet and you'd have gone over the edge and hit that gravel bar like you'd jumped out of a five-story building. Makes me kind of nervous even standing here."

THE AMBULANCE LEFT for the Winchester Medical Center, Smalls following in a state police car. Whitehead's death was confirmed and Smalls was treated for the impact on his nose. It had continued to bleed, but a doc used what he called a "chemical cautery" on it, which stopped the bleeding immediately, and gave him some pain pills. Smalls said, "I don't think I need the pills."

"Not yet," the doc said. "You will."

When he was released, the deputies took him aside for an extended statement, and told him that the Cadillac would be left where it had landed until a state accident investigator could get to the scene.

When he was done with the interview, Smalls called Kitten Carter, his chief of staff, and arranged to have her drive to the hospital and pick him up. She said she would notify Whitehead's mother and father of her death.

When there was nothing left to do, he asked to be taken to the hospital's chapel. The police left him there, and Smalls, a lifelong Episcopalian, knelt and prayed for Cecily Whitehead's soul. Less charitably, he had a word with the Lord about finding the people who'd murdered her. Then he cried for a while, and finally pulled himself together and began thinking seriously about the accident.

That had been no accident.

It had been an assassination attempt, he believed, and he thought he knew who was behind it. Justice, if not exactly a court judgment, would come.

He said it aloud, to Whitehead: "I swear to you, Cee-cee, I will get them. I'll get every one of the motherfuckers involved."

Whitehead hadn't been particularly delicate, nor particularly forgiving: if she were already experiencing the afterlife, he had no doubt that she would cherish the revenge.

KITTEN CARTER ARRIVED at the hospital. She'd been on her cell phone for three hours by the time she got there. The first news of the accident would be leaked to reporters who owed her favors and who would put the most sympathetic interpretation to the night's events.

". . . lifelong friends and political allies who'd gone to the cabin to plot strategy for the summer clashes over the health-care proposals . . ."

THE LOCAL DEPUTIES turned the crash investigation over to the West Virginia State Police. The second day after the accident, an investigator interviewed Smalls in his Senate office, with Carter sitting in. Smalls, with two black eyes and a broad white bandage over his nose, and dressed in a blue-striped seersucker suit with a navy blue knit tie, immediately understood that something was wrong.

The investigator's name was Carl Armstrong and when

he'd finished with his questions, Smalls said, "Don't bull-shit me, Carl. Something's not right. You think I'm lying about something. What is it?"

The investigator had been taking notes on a white legal pad inside a leather portfolio. He sighed, closed the portfolio and said, "Our lab has been over your vehicle inch-by-inch, sir. There's no sign that it was ever hit by another truck."

Carter was sitting in an easy chair, illegally smoking a small brown cigarillo. She looked at Smalls, then frowned at Armstrong and said, "That's crazy. The other guys took them right off the road—smashed them off. What do you mean there's no sign?"

Smalls jumped in: "That's exactly right. The impact caved the door in . . . there's gotta be some sign of that. I mean, I was in a fairly bad accident once, years ago, and both vehicles had extensive damage. This one was worse. The hit was worse. What do you mean, no sign?"

"No metal scrapes, no paint, no long glancing blow . . . the only thing we've found are signs that you hit several trees, on both sides of the truck and the front grille and hood," Armstrong said.

"Then you're not looking hard enough," Smalls snapped. "That guy crashed right into us, and killed Cee-cee and damn near killed me."

Armstrong looked away and shrugged. "Uh, well, I wonder if he actually hit you, or maybe just caused Ms. Whitehead to lose control?"

"She hadn't been drinking—"

Armstrong held up a hand: "We know that. She had zero alcohol in her blood and we know she was driving because of blood on the inside of the cab. We don't doubt anything you've told us, except the impact itself."

Carter: "Senator Smalls has provided a written statement in which he relates the force of the impact."

"There's a low gravel berm where they went over the side, we're wondering if Miz Whitehead might have hit that hard, and the Senator might be mistaking that for the impact of the truck."

Smalls was already shaking his head: "No. I heard the truck hit. I saw it hit—I was looking out the driver's-side window when it hit . . ."

"There's no paint from another car, no metal, no glass on the road . . . no nothing," Armstrong said.

Carter said to Smalls, "Senator, maybe we need to get some FBI crime-scene people up there—"

Smalls put a finger on his lips, to shut her up. He stood and said, "Carl, I'm going to ask another guy to talk to you about the evidence, if you don't mind. Kitten and I really don't know about such things, but I think it'd be a good idea if we put a second pair of eyes on this whole deal."

Armstrong had dealt with politicians a number of times and Smalls seemed to him to be one of the more reasonable members of the species. No shouting, no accusations. He flushed with relief, and said, "Senator . . . anything we can do, we'll be happy to do. We'd like to understand exactly what happened here. Send your guy around anytime. We'll probably give him more cooperation than he'll even want."

"That's great," Smalls said, suddenly congenial. "I'll drop a note to your superintendent, thanking him for your work."

"Appreciate that," Armstrong said. "I really do, sir."

WHEN ARMSTRONG HAD GONE, Carter asked, "Why were you pouring butter on him? He didn't believe you. I mean, Jesus. Somebody killed Ceecee and almost killed you. If you let this stand, the whole thing is gonna get buried . . ."

"No, no, no . . ." Smalls was on his feet. He wandered over to his trophy wall, filled with plaques and keys to Minnesota cities and photos of himself with presidents, governors, other senators, assorted rich people, including Whitehead, and politically conservative movie stars.

Musing.

Carter kept her mouth shut and after a couple of minutes, Smalls, playing with an earlobe and gazing at his pictures, turned and said, "I'm surprised by . . . what Armstrong said. No evidence. But I'm not astonished. Remember when I told you the first thing I did was get my gun, because I thought the guys who hit us might be paid killers? Assassins? Professionals?"

"Yeah, but I don't—"

"I was right. They were," Smalls said. "I don't know how exactly they did this, but I'm sure that if the right investigator looked under the right rock, he could find someone who could explain it. We need to get that done, because—"

"They could be coming back for another shot at you."

"Yeah. Probably not right away, but sooner or later." Smalls left the trophy wall, walked to his oversized desk, pushed a button on an intercom. "Sally . . . get Lucas Davenport on the line. His number's on your contact list."

"That's the guy—" Carter began.

"Yeah," Smalls said. "That's the guy."

JOHN SANDFORD

"If you haven't read Sandford yet, you
have been missing one of the great
summer-read novelists of all time."
—Stephen King

For a complete list of titles and to sign up for our
newsletter, please visit prh.com/JohnSandford